Weekend

Weekend

TANIA GROSSINGER
and
ANDREW NEIDERMAN

ST. MARTIN'S PRESS
NEW YORK

Copyright © 1980 by Tania Grossinger and Andrew Neiderman
All rights reserved. For information write:
St. Martin's Press, Inc. 175 Fifth Ave., New York, N.Y. 10010
Manufactured in the United States of America

Library of Congress Cataloging in Publication Data
Grossinger, Tania and Andrew Neiderman
   Weekend.

  I. Neiderman, Andrew. II. Title.
PZ4.G8779We   [PS3557.R663]   813'.54   79-26808
ISBN 0-312-86006-4

DEDICATIONS

To a very special friend, with love.
Tania Grossinger

To my parents, who taught me that good and evil
are things of the heart.
Andrew Neiderman

And for each other.

ACKNOWLEDGMENTS

The writing of WEEKEND would not have been possible without the very real support and encouragement of our agents and editors. To Anita Diamant, Humphrey Evans III, Tom Dunne, and Bob Miller, our heartfelt thanks.

prologue

Dr. Sid Bronstein stood up straight and backed gravely away from his dark field microscope. His eyes blinked as though he had just emerged from a total blackout. His bushy eyebrows nearly touched when he frowned and shook his head.

"Can't be," he muttered and leaned over the eyepiece again. Against the pitch-black background, the pulsating stream of rod-like bacteria looked like a speeded-up old-time movie of flashing neon lights.

He shut off the microscope and turned slowly toward the doorway that led back to his examination room. His patient, a diminutive Chinese man brought in from the Congress hotel, lay uncomfortably on the examination table. He grimaced and pressed his hands tightly against his abdomen. When Bronstein approached, he turned to him expectantly, hope for relief evident in his eyes.

"How long have you been sick?"

The ailing janitor had been brought in unable to control his digestive function or bowels. He was so weak he had to be guided by Bronstein's nurse. "His name's Tony Wong," she said before depositing him at the table.

Tony lifted his hand, demonstrating four fingers.

"Four days?"

The janitor nodded.

"Christ. If it's what it looks like," Bronstein said, mostly for his own benefit, "it's a wonder you're still alive. When did you urinate last?"

It was obvious from the confusion on Wong's face that he didn't understand a word the doctor was saying. Bronstein tried again, this time first pointing to his groin and then to the toilet.

"When you pee last?"

"No pee," Tony managed to whisper. "Too much hurt. Just shit all time. Thirsty too."

Sid reached over and took an oral thermometer out of the glass container. He placed it under Tony's tongue. Then he felt for pulse. While he checked his watch, he remembered that Sylvia was probably waiting impatiently at home. They were due at his in-laws for dinner in half an hour. Now it was unlikely he'd make it at all, an act guaranteed to displease her. She had little compassion for his patients when they threatened to interfere with her social schedule.

Tony Wong's pulse was thready. That, along with his pinched facial expressions, scaphoid abdomen and abnormally swollen body corroborated Bronstein's preliminary suspicion. He took the thermometer from Tony's mouth. The janitor worked at one of the largest resorts in the Catskills. They would probably have over a thousand people there this weekend. He shuddered to think of the consequences if what he thought was true.

Tony's temperature had dropped dangerously, indicating severe electrolyte imbalance.

"Let's see how much you weigh," Bronstein said. He lifted the Chinaman's arms and was distressed by the fragility of his frame as it leaned against him for balance. He registered ninety-five pounds, easily twenty pounds underweight even for a man of his height.

Tony rubbed his hands against the skeleton of his ass.

"Gotta go, doc," he said, pointing anxiously toward the bathroom. "Fast!"

The doctor put his arm around him for support. "Anyone else at the hotel sick like you?"

"Don't know." Tony's voice, already thin and high pitched, was strained. "No talk much. No got any friends." He closed the bathroom door. Bronstein stood nearby for a moment thinking. Then he went to his library.

Amazing how the mind works, he reflected. From the bookshelves he took down his anthology of world diseases—their descriptions and symptoms, causes and treatments. As soon as he had set eyes on this Oriental, something had been triggered in his memory, some past image of disease resurrected from his days as a medic in the Philippines. He quickly found the pages he was looking for, then picked up *Merck's Manual* to double-check. The description on page 114 was precise:

> An acute specific infection involving primarily the ileum and manifested by profuse diarrhea, vomiting, muscle cramps, dehydration and collapse. Also intense thirst, sunken eyes, wrinkled skin. Fatality rate, 50 percent in untreated cases.

He closed the book thoughtfully as the ringing of the phone jarred him back to reality.

... 2

"Where the hell are you, Sidney?" His wife always called him Sidney when she was angry.

"I have an emergency."

"How come you always have emergencies when we have to go to my parents for dinner?"

"Believe me, Sylvia, I don't plan it that way."

"Well, how much longer are you going to be?"

"I don't know. It could be a while. Something very serious just came up, something . . ."

"That's just great," she interrupted. "The Bentley's on the fritz and I was counting on you to . . ."

"Take a cab, Sylvia." He drummed his fingers impatiently on the desk. "This is not the time for one of your scenes. I'll get there as soon as I can."

He said good-bye without waiting for a response, clicked the phone and dialed the hospital.

"Admissions," he said when the thin, mechanical voice answered. It was then, and only then, that he realized what he was about to do. For a brief moment he hesitated, ignoring the insistent "Hello? Hello?"

What if he confided to his colleagues what he really suspected and then, by some fluke, he was wrong?

"Rita, Dr. Bronstein. I'm sorry. Listen, I'm sending over an admission from the Congress and I want him kept in Isolation. The name's Tony Wong."

"Preliminary diagnosis?" There was an unusual pause. "Doctor?"

"Suspected gastrointestinal infection," he said hesitantly, "possibly contagious. Call downstairs and have them send over an ambulance to my office immediately and give me the fourth floor nurses' station please."

"But you said Isolation, doctor. That's the fifth floor."

"Right," he said. "Sorry." God, he thought, what's happening to me today?

"And doctor, while I have you on the phone, are you aware that Mrs. Kresky has used up all her Blue Cross days? Mr. Deckelman said . . ."

"Rita, I'll look into it later. Really, this is an emergency. Just connect me with the fifth floor."

"Yes, doctor."

"Fifth floor, Sue Cohen."

"Sue, hi. Sid Bronstein. I'm sending you a patient for Isolation. He's suffering from severe dehydration, possibly uremia. Set up IV five g's sodium chloride, four g's sodium bicarbonate and one g potassium chloride to one liter of pyrogen-free distilled water. Infuse at fifty mils per minute. Also I want a stool specimen and five hundred mgs of oral tetracycline every six hours."

"Food poisoning?"

"I think so," Bronstein said, crossing his fingers superstitiously. It suddenly occurred to him that the driver of the hotel's house car was still waiting outside. He hung up, buzzed the receptionist and asked her to send him in.

"You might as well go back to the hotel, Gary. I've sent for an ambulance."

"That bad, huh?"

"I don't know how this man could have been left so sick for so many days."

The driver shrugged.

"They thought he had some kind of virus. He just came over, you know. Fresh off the boat. The first two days, Halloran thought he was drunk."

"What about his roommates?"

"They ain't been around for nearly a week. Lots of guys take off for a few days before the Fourth. Last time to have a fling before the season begins." He winked at the doctor. "Know what I mean?"

"Yeah, yeah," Bronstein said, still deeply in thought. "Okay. I've got to go back to Mr. Wong."

As soon as the driver left, Bronstein dialed the Congress.

"Give me Jonathan Lawrence, the general manager, please. This is Dr. Bronstein."

"Hi doc, Rosie. He's in a meeting, his secretary stepped away and he asked me to hold all his calls. It should break any minute."

"Get him to call me immediately. It's important."

He put the receiver down and looked through the door at his microscope. To confirm his suspicions, he'd have to test with antiserum, a diagnostic substance used so rarely it was never stocked in hospitals in the Catskills.

He suddenly realized that Tony had been in the bathroom longer than he should have. He went to the door and knocked. "Tony, are you all right?" He waited. No response. He turned the knob and pulled back, surprised at the pressure from within. Tony's body, collapsed against the door, fell forward at his feet.

...4

one

Sandi Golden moved slowly around the corner of the stucco white building that served as housing for the chambermaids and stopped just in front of a lighted window. Once before, walking around the great lawn between the main building of the Congress and the "old farmhouse" where she lived, she had accidentally looked through the window and spotted the naked buttocks of a man. At first she was stunned, then she found the sight exciting.

Growing up on the grounds of one of the Catskill's largest resorts, she had come to realize at a very early age that pleasure of any sort was a commodity, whether it be food, entertainment or sex. Her parents had made valiant efforts to shield her from the all-pervasive hedonism but it was almost impossible, especially during the hot summer months when it seemed almost everything was permissible.

She leaned over until she was just able to look past the sill. Not more than ten minutes before, she had seen Caesar Jiminez, a plumber, escort Margret Thomas, a chambermaid, through the shadows between the laundry and the staff dormitory. It was his naked buttocks she had seen the first time and ever since that night she had made it her business to listen in to whatever chambermaids' gossip she could. They called him "Superman" after a well-known stud in Havana, bragged about his staying power, and compared the length of his "thing" to that of a baseball bat. One maid even boasted that he did it to her twenty times in a row without ever getting soft, whatever that meant.

For all her so-called sophistication, living in an atmosphere where people used four-letter words as casually as "please" and "thank you," she actually knew very little about the mechanics of sex. She knew, of course, there was something called "the missionary position," and something else people referred to as "69," but just how it all worked, she wasn't sure.

She had never really been able to talk to her father about adult man-woman relationships. It was a topic he continually put off, calling her his "Little Princess" and promising there would be time enough when she was older. But now he was gone and if his death had done anything, it had forced her mother to work so hard there was hardly any time left for them to talk about anything.

Actually, they rarely even saw much of each other these days. Ellen Golden was so preoccupied with learning to run the hotel that her customary conversations with Sandi usually consisted of one word, "later." Not that she ever doubted her mother loved her . . . through the years they had usually had a good, albeit lately awkward, relationship, and Sandi supposed that throwing herself into work was her mother's way of getting over Phil's death. But at the same time, it was a hell of a spot for a thirteen-year-old kid to be in.

At first, Sandi stood on her tiptoes but could see no one in the room. Then she heard the bedsprings. She pulled herself back as Margret walked to the dresser and looked into the mirror. She wore only a half slip and bra. For a few moments, she stood there combing out her hair. She had gigantic breasts that sagged against the cups of her undergarment and strained the straps so forcefully they pressed into her skin and formed ridges alongside.

Sandi estimated Margret to be a woman in her forties. She was a big-boned Scandinavian with wide hips and heavy upper legs. A line of dark blond hair ran down her spine, disappearing into nothingness at the base. There were many small red blotches, mainly from the heat, along her back and shoulders. Her belly was slightly puffed out and clearly visible. She took a deep breath and pulled it in.

"Getting pretty for me, eh?" Caesar said. Margret pretended not to hear as she continued to comb her hair.

"Damn dust. You'd think by now they'd have all the rooms airconditioned so we could keep the windows closed. It gets so dirty I have to wash my hair every day."

Sandi wanted to lean further over and look for Caesar, but was afraid of being spotted. Suddenly he appeared, naked from the waist down. She caught just a slight glimpse of his erection peeking up and out from between his legs. He pressed himself against Margret, moving his waist in a rhythmic circle.

"You'll poke a hole right through my slip with that drill of yours."

He laughed, then backed up to unfasten her bra. She kept on playing with her hair as if none of what he was doing really affected her. The moment the hook unfastened, the front of the bra gave way, her breasts heaving forward to her obvious relief. Caesar reached around and cupped them, their nipples protruding between his fingers.

"Feels good, eh?"

. . . 6

Her moan was barely audible. Sandi felt her own breasts tingle as she imagined a man's hairy hands sliding over them.

"How do you want it? Like the last time?"

"Only one way?" She pretended great disappointment and he laughed. He stepped back and released her, swirling her roughly toward the bed. As he spun around and faced the window, his swollen member was clearly visible. It came as quite a shock to Sandi. She had never seen an erect penis before and suddenly there it was, only a few feet away, like an overblown giant purple sausage standing up and waving back and forth, almost as if in greeting. Funny, she always thought when there was an erection it was supposed to go out, not up.

Caesar went back to the bed as Margret slipped out of her slip and did a pirouette, holding it up much like a bullfighter holds his cape. Caesar growled, took the hem between his teeth, and pulled it away. Suddenly Margret disappeared from view.

Damn! Kneeling down, Sandi crawled to the other side. When she peered in this time, she was looking directly at the bed.

Another surprise. Instead of Caesar lying on top of her, which is how Sandi thought people did "it," Margret was straddling Caesar's legs, almost sitting against them. She leaned back and braced herself with her hands on the bed as he reached up and massaged her breasts, first with his hands, then with his tongue, first one, then the other. Quickly Margret began to move, up and down, to the left and to the right. Caesar's hand went between her legs, rubbing in rhythm with her movements. She began to moan her appreciation.

Sandi felt her mouth water and her heartbeat increase rapidly. There was a warmth in her crotch, followed quickly by a wetness. She backed away from the sight, frightened by the effect it was having on her body. Her breathing had become even more labored. Margret's voice grew louder but Sandi was afraid to look back. She took a step away, then another and another. Soon she was running across the grass, forcing herself to move quickly because the effort helped subdue the sensations screaming for attention in every nerve.

Finally, she stopped at a bench near the rock garden and tried to catch her breath. The images of what she had just seen continued to flash through her mind. The bright lights of a car coming through the main gate washed over and startled her for a moment. It was as if she feared being caught alone in the dark, standing there reliving all of those forbidden acts. She looked at her watch. It was 11:15.

There didn't seem to be much point in going home. Chances

were her mother was still at work. The sound of voices in the dark drove her back to the main building where, still shaking, she snuck into the rear of the Flamingo Room. Cloaked in the dimness of the intimate night club, she looked up at the stage where Bobby Grant was crooning a love ballad. The flickering multi-colored spotlights distorted the shadows around the tables. Everywhere there seemed to be tapered fingers—reaching, touching, groping for each other. The young singer moved his body rhythmically to the beat of the drum. Sandi studied his hips and fantasized what it would be like to straddle him the way Margret Thomas had straddled Caesar. Looking around to make sure she was unseen, she let her legs part a tiny bit and moved her fingers along her thighs. Touching herself tenderly, she finally gave in to the uncontrollable ecstasy as Bobby Grant continued to croon, completely unaware of what was happening in the dark.

"Dr. Bronstein, can you hold please. I have Mr. Lawrence on the line."

"It's about time," he said, immediately regretting his tone. He was standing in the corridor near the emergency room of the Community General Hospital. Some interns and nurses were carrying on a conversation at the nurses' station and the emergency room doctor stood by a patient strapped down to a rolling bed. Bronstein looked behind himself instinctively. No one appeared to be paying him the slightest attention. Even so, he huddled closer to the phone.

"Doc? Sorry it took so long for me to return your call. It's been a bitch of a day."

"For all of us." Bronstein gazed up at the IBM wall clock and noted he was an hour late for dinner. "Look, Jonathan, I can't talk to you from here. We've got a major problem. Can you meet me at my office in fifteen minutes?"

"It's going to be hard. You won't believe what's going on up here. I've got a million things to do before the weekend. Can you come over to the hotel instead?"

"Impossible," the doctor said. "My office, fifteen minutes." He hung up abruptly and started down the hall.

The general manager was waiting in front of the doctor's office when he arrived a quarter of an hour later. "I only have a short time so you better make it fast," he said. "It's like a madhouse up there, trying to get everything ready for tomorrow's mass incursion."

Jonathan stood a good inch and a half shorter than the M.D. but his stiff appearance made him seem almost taller and stronger. The wind wouldn't dare muss a hair of his prematurely gray trim. The knot in his tie was always just right, the crease in his pants too perfect. He never removed his jacket, indoors or out. It was rumored he ironed his shorts.

He was a muscular well-proportioned man with hard sharp features that all too well reflected his abrupt personality. In dealing with people he maintained an arrogant coolness that usually annoyed subordinates and increasingly bothered guests, especially the old-timers used to the warm familylike atmosphere the Goldens had established at the Congress over the past fifty years. It was difficult to pry personal facts from him, not that many were tempted to try. His tight-lipped businesslike approach was ascribed by some as a side effect of a proper New England upbringing. Others considered his snobbishness downright anti-Semitic, an irony not lost on his colleagues at one of the Catskills' largest "Borscht Belt" hotels.

"Are you aware that your personnel director sent a man named Tony Wong down here an hour ago and I've had to have him hospitalized?" Bronstein walked into his office and offered Jonathan a seat.

"Tony who?"

"Wong. One of your custodial people. He works in the kitchen."

"Is that what you brought me down here to . . ."

Sid had wanted to build up to it dramatically, to explain his theory step by step, but it was obvious the general manager was in no mood to mince words.

"I'm almost certain Wong has cholera," he blurted out. For a moment he felt relieved. He wouldn't have to carry the burden alone. He looked expectantly at the manager, hoping for a reaction that indicated he might be as horrified as the doctor.

Jonathan sat like a sphinx. It was as if he had just heard that a file clerk had stubbed her toe. "You're crazy," he said evenly. "Cholera went out with the Middle Ages . . . or at least it doesn't happen here. It's not an American disease."

"That doesn't mean it can't be brought in," Bronstein explained. "You know as well as I that a lot of summer transients hired for menial labor come from employment agencies in Chinatown that send up illegal aliens. Usually they've been smuggled in from the

Far East on cargo ships where the living conditions are anything but sanitary. Any one of them can be a carrier. We really have no time to waste."

"What makes you so sure that's what it is?"

"I'm almost positive that what I saw under the dark field microscope were cholera vibrios. I've seen them before when I was stationed in the Philippines. He also has all the superficial symptoms, intense diarrhea, dehydration, vomiting, pain and thirst."

"Go on."

"What complicates the matter in Tony's case is that sunken eyes, wrinkled skin and certain other facial characteristics symptomatic of the disease are also common among elderly Asiatics. It's possible, but doubtful, he just might have severe food poisoning or bacillary dysentery. I can't make a positive diagnosis without a specific antiserum."

"What's that?"

"A drop of serum from a rabbit that has been immunized specifically against cholera. If he were in better shape, I'd rush him to a New York hospital by ambulance, but as things stand now, I'm afraid to risk it. And it'll be a couple of days at least before I can get the necessary diagnostic material delivered."

"I presume you didn't discuss this with anyone at the hospital."

"No. I had him admitted with a preliminary diagnosis of intestinal infection. I didn't see any point in creating a turmoil until something was actually confirmed."

"Which it may never be."

"Which I hope it will never be," Sid said. "But it's vital you understand the significance of what I'm saying. Cholera is dangerous. It kills. And because of this there are certain precautions that should be taken. If it's what Tony really has, an epidemic could break out at any time and God only knows how many people could be affected."

Jonathan calmly took out his pipe and scooped some tobacco from his leather pouch. "You're dealing in 'ifs' and 'maybes.' I'm trained to deal in facts, the bottom line. Why don't we wait until we have a definite diagnosis?"

"I'm not sure we can afford to be so casual. By rights, I should have already reported my suspicions to the health authorities, but because I'm the hotel physician I thought I'd give you the courtesy of—"

Jonathan interrupted him angrily "Let me tell you how I see it, Bronstein. We're booked solid, capacity, the first time this year. You know how many weeks we had less than two hundred people in that place. I don't have to describe the ugly financial situation the Congress is in. You're not an outsider." His face reddened as he became more excited.

"A rumor about something like cholera could not only destroy our season, but possibly our entire future. Can you imagine anyone wanting to come up to the Congress if they heard that someone on the staff came down with a deadly communicable disease . . . even if it wasn't true?"

"It might not be a rumor."

"And it might not be a fact." He shook his head. "Listen," he continued, "you admit it could be something else. There is that possibility."

"Yes," Sid said, "I think it's remote, but there is that possibility."

"Then let's take it one step at a time. There's no point in going to the authorities until you know for sure. There're two things you've got to remember. First, if you told them you thought one of our janitors had cholera and you were wrong, you'd be the laughing stock of the profession up here. Second, forget about the Congress for a moment. Look at the bigger picture. If word of a public health investigation got out before it was really necessary, you'd devastate the reputation of the whole resort area for years to come. Do you realize that just about every person living in Sullivan County, including yourself, is in some way dependent on the hotel industry? Organized labor, other employees, the suppliers, supportive services, the professions, banks, the construction industry? Look at the mortgage note your father-in-law holds on the Congress. What do you think would happen to his investment if the place went under?" Jonathan paused to let his words sink in. At the same time a picture of Sylvia's angry face flashed through the doctor's mind. "It was as if you were putting a gun to these people's heads and pulling the trigger."

"Look, Jonathan, I understand what you're saying and I'm trying not to go off half-cocked. I just want to do what's right for all of us." He stood and walked across to the window. How ideal, he remembered thinking in medical school, to be able to work in a vacuum. And how impossible, he realized, once he had set up practice and started a family. There were always political, economic and personal situations to consider. He turned back to the general manager.

"As a physician, I've got to be sure that this thing hasn't spread. If we can determine that even if it is cholera it's an isolated case . . ."

"If it wasn't, someone else would have come down with it by now, wouldn't they?"

"Not necessarily. There's an incubation period. Tony was sick for four days. That gives us two or more to be concerned with." A thought suddenly occurred to him. "I have a suggestion. Let me call my cousin, Bruce Solomon. He's a researcher at Mt. Sinai and he's had experience with tropical and exotic diseases. I'll see if I can get him to come up for a couple of days until we get a definitive diagnosis. He can trace Tony's steps, do a little detective work, find out who he's been in touch with and who else, if God forbid I'm right, might be a carrier. We'll fix it up so no one on your staff will have to know."

"Sounds good to me," Jonathan agreed.

"But if he finds any evidence of—"

"One step at a time doc, okay? Incidentally," he said, refilling his pipe, "you didn't call Ellen Golden about this, did you?"

Bronstein stared at him for a moment without speaking. "No," he said softly. "No. I didn't have the heart. With Phil's recent death and her having to kick off the summer season without him, she's under so much pressure I didn't want to add to it. But you're right. She's going to have to know."

"I'll take care of it as soon as I get back. You've got enough to worry about."

"Make sure she understands exactly what we're doing and why. No matter what the final decision is, we both know the ultimate responsibility is on her head, so it's important. And if she wants to call me," he continued quietly, "tell her . . . anytime."

Jonathan caught the sad look on Bronstein's face. "Still blaming yourself, huh, doc?"

"Not blaming, exactly. I just keep wondering if there was something I should have caught. Phil had a complete physical here the month before. I'd hate to think I might have overlooked . . ." He shook his head. "Just proves how important it is not to take things for granted."

"We're not taking anything for granted, Sid. We're just not getting hysterical when there may not be a reason." He took the pipe from his mouth and tapped the ashes out in the bowl as he stood up. "I'll stay in touch." Almost on cue, the phone rang.

"We're up to dessert, Sidney. I thought you'd like to know."

"Believe me, Sylvia, I just got back to the office. I was up at the hospital. There was this janitor from the Congress—"

"A janitor? she shrieked. "A lousy janitor? Couldn't you have gotten Julius to take the case for you? He appreciates any nibble you send his way."

"It wasn't quite that simple."

"With you nothing is simple. Anyway, are you coming over here or not?"

"I'll be there as soon as I can," he said, wishing somehow that everything could be different.

He remembered the look on Tony Wong's face and went back to his private desk to look up his cousin's New York number, frightened in the deepest recesses of his soul that he had only postponed, not eliminated, disaster.

two

It was a glorious Friday morning, one that made Magda, the forty-seven-year-old Hungarian beauty who served as hostess for the Congress, thank God she was alive to enjoy it. If she were superstitious, she might have considered it an omen, that such a dazzling day could only be a forecast of a magnificent weekend and season to come.

Taking the scenic route from her cottage to the old farmhouse a half mile away, she walked past the first tee of the newly designed golf course, so expertly manicured and nurtured that it looked like something created artificially in the hotel's stagecraft basement. Surely the technicians came out at night while the guests slept and rearranged those little divots and sand traps. She chuckled at the thought and took in a few deep breaths of the crisp fresh country air, made even sweeter by the hundreds of colorful dahlias, marigolds, daisies and peonies that dotted the flagstone pathway. She marveled at the beauty of the monarch and tiger-tailed butterflies that fluttered above and smiled as she passed the sign Sandi had put up near one of the gardens when she was eight years old. "Please do not pick us. We bloom for your pleasure. Thank you. The flowers." Even though it wasn't yet nine o'clock, the sun felt as if it was at full strength and she welcomed the shade the tall oaks and elms provided as she continued on her way.

Arriving at the farmhouse a few minutes later, she tapped lightly on the outer screen door. "Good morning. Anybody up?" Ellen Golden leaned out of the window directly above. The two-story residence still bore the same wooden shingles and black shutters Pop Golden had hammered on forty years ago.

"I thought we were going to meet in the coffee shop."

"It was such a nice day, I thought I'd get some fresh air before the crowd arrives. I offer myself as your personal escort," Magda said, bowing with a flourish from the waist.

The farmhouse was characteristic of so many of the old buildings constructed in the Catskills at the turn of the century—two-level, multi-roomed wooden structures with numerous architectural afterthoughts added on as the original farmers started to take in boarders. This one still had the cast iron grillwork that took hours to clean properly.

Ellen opened the screen door and pushed back a few strands of her light brunette hair. Even though it was outdated by over a decade, she still wore it in the same pageboy style Lauren Bacall had popularized in the forties. Phil had liked it that way. "You've got her sexy voice and the body that goes with it. Bogart is one celebrity I'll make sure we don't invite up here." Right now, even though she was only thirty-eight years old, she sure as hell didn't feel sexy. She looked wistfully back into the house.

"Maybe I should wake Sandi and say good-bye before I leave."

"Maybe you shouldn't. She'll know where you are. Besides, she was up pretty late last night. I saw her in the Flamingo Room close to midnight last night ogling Bobby Grant."

"I'm afraid I'm leaving her alone more than I should."

"She probably loves it," Magda said, taking her friend by the arm. "When I was her age, I loved to feel independent. So did you."

"Girls her age need guidance, especially when they've just lost their father."

"I'll keep an eye on her for the next couple of days."

Ellen nodded and then closed the door silently behind them. They started slowly down the stairs, each wooden step reacting with a familiar squeak.

For Ellen, stepping off that porch was like descending into another world. A city block ahead of her stood the grand main building, towering and impressive in its architectural simplicity, baked in a reddish pink stucco that reminded travelers of Marrakech at sunset. In contrast, ribbons of iron fire escapes criss-crossed the sides, black dull metal that seemed reluctantly slapped on to satisfy various safety codes.

It was a tall building, seventeen floors high, one of the largest in the rural Catskill world where even a twelve-story skyscraper looked gigantic. The view from the penthouse was breathtaking. On a clear evening, one could easily see sixty miles around. One guest even swore he saw the Empire State Building from his terrace, a claim Ellen and Phil laughingly chalked up to a full moon and the effects of an equally full bottle of Scotch.

There, to the left, were the half dozen clay tennis courts, already in use by the early risers. The quick snap of a serve, the sound of the ball slapping across the court, the squeak of sneakers turning and twisting, all of it was audible as the two women made their way from the farmhouse.

As they continued on the central pathway to the main building, watching the grounds keepers and gardeners already at work mowing and scything the lawns and hedges, Ellen nudged Magda and pointed to the clusters of small cottages on their right. They were primarily private bungalows, each with its own patch of grass and flowers, mostly sought after by honeymooners and illicit lovers.

It was strange to have to admit, but after nearly fifteen years, the hotel, all 650 rolling acres of it, still had the power to hypnotize her. Phil used to say it was the world's most demanding mistress. It had a presence and personality of its own; it often took more than it gave but in the long run was worth it and it would probably still be there long after they were gone. Today, unfortunately, as she looked around at the land she loved so dearly, Ellen wasn't quite as sure.

Despite the fact that they were one of the Catskills' few year-round resorts, they were still heavily dependent on a strong summer season. The ten weeks between July 4th and Labor Day were crucial because winter facilities notwithstanding, there were still weeks during the spring and fall when they were lucky to break even. On top of that, in the midst of her untimely transition into power, she was confronted by the phenomenon of a changing vacation world; a world, in 1958, of jet airplanes, prepackaged tours, and the lure of Miami and the Caribbean. And then there was Jonathan.

"I dread going in there with Jonathan and the accountants next week," she said, as they continued across the lawn. "Phil mentioned a few months back that we could be headed for serious trouble, but he was always too busy to get into specifics. I just hope I'll be able to understand what they're talking about."

"You'll learn," Magda reassured her. "You may not know all the answers but then again," she asked with a shrug of her shoulders, "who does? All you have to remember is that you've had fifteen years of live-in experience and in many areas, probably have a better idea of how things should run than they do."

"I hope I can convince them of that."

"Convince yourself. Once you do that, you can convince anybody."

Ellen gave her friend a smile that did more than express her thanks. "I don't know what I'd do without you."

"And I don't know what I'm going to do if I don't get some

breakfast." She held her hands to her stomach in mock agony. "Are you ready to hear about our plans for the weekend?"

"Ready as I'll ever be," Ellen said, feeling a surge of excitement. Magda built her confidence. "Let's get started."

Without further conversation, they quickened their pace toward the main building, drawn to it like a magnet by its problems, challenges and demands.

Melinda Kaplan was dragging her son up to the Catskills for the second time in three years, carting him along on a journey his father laughingly referred to as her "Sexual Transfusion."

"It's Operation New Man," he said, "and believe me, your mother plots it out like a military strategist. I feel sorry for the first soldier she captures. He doesn't stand a chance. I should know."

He laughed again and went back to his drawing board. It was always like that when Grant made his weekly visits. His father would take off on some topic, his favorite being "your mother, Melinda," then return his attention to the work at hand, causing Grant to feel more like a piece of the furniture.

"You're fifteen years old, son," he had recently told him. "By now you must be learning enough about women to understand what hell I went through living with your mother."

Then, when he got home, Melinda would begin. "What wonderful things did he have to say about me this time? Were any of his sluts over there, because if they were. . . What did you talk about? Did he tell you what a horrible woman I am again because if he did . . ."

Usually it got so bad he would run up to his room and turn on his Chubby Checker records so loud it hurt even his own ears.

"Turn that damn shit down," his mother would scream but he didn't care. He'd do anything he could to torment her, the same way she and his father tormented him, always using him as the pawn.

He started setting the fires with the same kind of apathy and nonchalance that characterized most of the other things he did. In fact, that was the biggest and most frequent criticism in all the letters and conferences relating to his school work.

"Grant Kaplan is totally indifferent to his work, completely unconcerned about his productivity."

"Kaplan doesn't appear interested in anything, including himself."

"Grant has little enthusiasm. He pretends to listen but doesn't hear a thing. He just doesn't seem to care."

"I'll talk to him about it," Melinda would always say.

He remembered the first morning she had come to his high school. He was thoroughly embarrassed by the way she had sauntered into the building in her low-cut dress and flirted so outrageously in front of everybody with the young dean of students. Christ, did she have to be on the make everywhere, even in his school?

"It's been so hard for us these past three years," she told the dean. "I get absolutely no help from his biological father." She loved to refer to her "ex" now as "biological." Grant understood the emotional implication, but it still made him feel like the result of some sort of laboratory experiment.

And that's exactly how he was beginning to feel. Even now, at this crucial meeting, he really didn't have any feeling. If the dean was having a problem hiding his hard-on, that was his problem, not Grant's. As usual, the discussion ended with both sides promising to try harder to motivate Grant, neither one knowing or caring that his mind was millions of miles away.

The first fire was so small and insignificant, he actually left right after it was set. It was a shed behind Gerson's Luncheonette, a few blocks from where he lived in Teaneck, New Jersey. He found the can of gas behind the '58 Ford in the driveway. He was just wandering home from school, taking a longer route than usual, when he saw the can, the empty shed, and made the connection. For the first time in a long time, he had come up with an idea that interested him.

He had been smoking since he was eleven, not bothering to sneak most of the time because his parents were too busy arguing to take notice, so he already had a spare pack of matches in his pocket.

He lifted the can with the gas in it so casually that even if someone was watching, it would never occur to him that Grant was doing something wrong. Then he went to the back of the shed, found a place where the boards were loose, and stuffed in the soaked rags. A minute later he looked behind him, reassured himself there was no one around, and threw the rest of the gasoline over the area.

He tossed in a lighted match and was just able to get back fast enough to see it go up in a whoosh without singeing his hands and face. The colors were interesting enough, but the heat was more than he bargained for. He watched for a moment, then moved on as if nothing had happened.

By the time he reached the corner of his block, he heard the sirens. He waited for the fire trucks to pass, then went home as usual. His mother didn't ask why he was late. Most of the time she wasn't even there, preferring to spend her afternoons drinking late lunches with the girls, going to the hairdresser or shopping for the latest fashions. He didn't even look for news of the fire in the local papers the next day. In fact, for a few days afterward, he nearly forgot about it altogether. That was before the supermarket.

"You're going to have a great time at the Congress this weekend," Melinda was saying. "I hear they have a new teen room filled with all sorts of pinball machines, ping-pong tables and . . ."

"Ginger peachy."

"Well, Christ," she said, taking her eyes off the road. "If you don't give anything a chance, what the hell do you expect?" She had to swerve back as the car behind began to pass and the driver honked his horn. "Drop dead!" she screamed. "Son of a bitch has to ride right on top of you. Look at all those idiots crowding up."

"You did cut him off, mom."

"That's right, Grant. Be critical. Ever since the last visit to that father of yours, you've been critical of everything I do. Look," she added. "any other fifteen-year-old would be jumping for joy about going to a resort hotel for the July Fourth weekend."

He started to jump up and down on the seat.

"Cut it out. I said, CUT IT OUT! I'm warning you, Grant, if you ruin this holiday for me. . . ."

He stopped jumping for joy on the front seat and looked out the window at the monotonous scenery off Route 17. The speed of the car tended to liquefy it and make it all a blur.

His thoughts began to wander. The supermarket. He remembered it with unabashed glee. Now that was a blaze! He had noticed the loading door in the back was opened one evening and thought . . . It was easy enough to pull off and the idea seemed amusing at the time, although the next day he was disillusioned with the dirty remains, the charred frame, the debris. He had started the incandescence at night, which was at least visually exciting. What made it most interesting was the incredible number of people the fire attracted. All those men, women and children out there, watching, talking, their eyes widened with amazement and all because of him, Grant because of what he had done. And to think the dean of students thought he lacked imagination!

"We're getting close," his mother announced, suddenly excited at the thought of all the sexual possibilities the next four days held in store. There was a lightness in her voice, a happy note Grant vaguely recalled from days of pre-adolescence when they were all together, when the world had a semblance, a logic, a pattern. "See that sign."

He gazed at the billboard that read,

THE CONGRESS HOTEL
ONLY THE BEST FOR OUR GUESTS
FIVE MILES TO YOUR LEFT

"I can hardly wait."

She looked at him crossly, then stopped for a light.

The Congress hotel, Grant thought. The first time he had been there, right after the divorce, he had hated it: all those organized teen activities, the dumb children's dining room with murals of Snow White and the Seven Dwarfs on the walls, and going to sleep alone in the room every night because his mother was down at the bar planning to do who knew what with who knew whom. Everyone always on his back to participate, join in, be part of the group. Up there it was a sin to be a loner even if you were just a kid. And then, when he finally got up the courage to start up a conversation with a pretty girl the same age, she ignored him.

He didn't want to think about that any more. They were approaching the entrance to the hotel and he concentrated on the tall, modern main building. He closed his eyes for a long moment and, as the car wheels droned on, he imagined the large edifice reflected against the night sky. It was all lit up, but not with candles and decorations. Coming out of the top was this giant flame, the tips of it licking at the stars. What a sight, he thought, and with all those people looking up... Some of them would probably think it was an extra thrown in as part of the July 4th entertainment. Unless they were stuck inside. He smiled at the thought.

"What's so funny, Grant?"

"Huh?"

"You're sitting there with an absolutely idiotic smile on your face."

"Oh, that. I just remembered a joke someone told at school."

"I'd like to hear it. I need some good ones for the dinner table. Nothing like a good joke to make a first impression."

Her son thought fast. "How do you get a Jewish girl to stop fucking?"

...20

"What kind of language is that?" Melinda asked, but she had to admit it was an interesting question. Something she hoped she'd never have to find the answer to. "I don't know. I give up. How?"

"Marry her!"

"Grant, that's disgusting. It sounds like something your father must have told you." It was kind of funny though, she thought, especially since so many people came to the Congress especially for one or the other.

Grant didn't bother to respond. He was looking down the highway and thinking about the hotel again, imagining the bright red and yellow flames reaching up as if to embrace the moon. It was really something to think about, In fact, he was almost looking forward to getting there.

"Good morning, ladies," Moe Sandman said as he came out from behind the horseshoe-shaped counter at the center of the coffee shop. The clean white apron was tied snugly around his flabby widespread hips.

"How was it last night?" Ellen said.

"Fourteen dozen bagels, seven pounds of cream cheese, over ten pounds of lox," he said, rubbing his bloodshot eyes.

"You'd think we didn't feed them enough at dinner," Magda chuckled.

"You worked the nightshift, Moe?" He nodded. "Since when are you doing double shift?"

"Since Jonathan Lawrence made me cut back. According to your general manager, we're overstaffed down here. According to my feet, he should have his head examined."

"It's the first I've heard of it," Ellen said.

"I don't like to complain, but . . ."

"Let me look into it."

They gave him their orders.

"What are you going to do about it?" Magda asked after he had left.

"I'm not sure. I suppose a general manager should be able to hire and fire but—I just wish I knew how much leeway Phil gave him."

"It shouldn't matter what Phil gave him. You're going to have to establish your own relationship with Jonathan now and decide how much leeway you want to give him." Ellen nodded, but not convincingly. "Whatever made Phil hire a man like that anyway?"

"He believed the hotel industry was going to go through major changes after the next two years when the sixties roll around and he wanted to be prepared. He felt the Congress would benefit from someone trained at the Cornell School of Hotel Administration, someone who understood things like computerized reservations, convention sales, open bid purchasing."

"But to choose such a cold fish."

"He didn't worry about that. He figured there'd always be someone from the family to supply the warmth. Besides," she added, "deep down I think he really believed he'd live to be the proverbial hundred and twenty. But let's put that aside. Tell me the problems you see coming up this weekend. I don't want to sound like a total idiot when I talk to people around here."

"For starters," the hostess began, "we have almost three single women for every single man. You know what that means?"

"Phil would say the guys are going to get screwed to death," she said with a laugh, "and there'll be a lot of bitchy broads at checkout time." Then she turned serious. "I wonder why the ratio is so off-balance."

"To be honest, darling, I think it's because other hotels offer more facilities that appeal to the male sex."

"Phil used to say there's only one facility that interests the male sex." She caught herself. "Oh, God, I've done it again."

"Done what?"

"Said 'Phil used to say.' I've got to stop thinking only in terms of what Phil would say."

"You will," Magda said gently. "In time."

Ellen shrugged. "Under the circumstances, how is Mr. Pat going to handle the seating in the dining room?"

"With great care. And he'll probably suggest that his single busboys and maybe even his not-so-single ones go down to the Flamingo Room after work and use whatever strength they have left to push some of the lonely ladies around the dance floor."

"I never liked that suggestion coming from management," Ellen mused, "but I guess it's just one of those necessary evils. As Phil would say, it goes with the territory."

They both ignored the repeated reference to her late husband, and Magda continued to give Ellen the rundown on the number of families, new guests, out-of-towners coming up, when she suddenly remembered. "Incidentally, Bob Halloran tells me one of the custodial people was checked into the hospital last night. I didn't get any of the details."

"One of our regulars?"

"No. Someone new."

"I'll check with him when I get back to the office," she said. "I hope it's nothing serious."

She was so grateful that, knock wood, she, Sandi, Magda, the people she loved and trusted, were in good health. Severe illness, especially so close to Phil's death, was the last thing in the world she'd want to cope with now.

"They must be doing something right," Bruce Solomon said, looking at the long line of cars backed up waiting to get through the main gate. Sid Bronstein just grunted. He had seen it all before.

"What the hell are they doing anyway?"

"Checking names. Making sure no one gets on the grounds without a reservation. It serves two purposes, actually. It eases the mob scene in the lobby when so many people arrive at the same time, and it caters to a certain sense of snobbishness, a confirmation that no outsider can get for free what they are paying for so dearly."

"Good thinking." Bruce ran his stubby fingers along the sides of his face, checking the closeness of his shave. He hadn't had much time to pull himself together once he got Dr. Bronstein's call early that morning. Twenty-eight and single, he had what many women tended to describe as a disarming sweetness, a camouflage if ever there was one for in action, he was neither sweet nor disarming. His eyes moved constantly with a penetrating gaze, scrutinizing, observing, analyzing, always questioning.

"Actually," Sid said, staring at the fins of the Cadillac in front, "scenes like this are rare up here these days. Business has been dropping off radically. In fact, many of the smaller resorts have been forced to close down."

"It's hard to believe," Bruce said, remembering all he had heard and read about the fabulous Congress.

"You can't imagine the overhead in running a place like this. The Goldens are reputation rich and dollar poor."

"Meaning?"

"Meaning they're mortgaged to the hilt. Unions have thrown

...23

payroll expenses sky high. The property taxes are unbelievable. And to keep up with competition like Grossinger's and the Concord, they've had to expand, refurbish, redecorate and make plans to do even more. The joke around here is that some day they'll have to build an indoor mountain if they want to meet the competition. The problem is that every capital expenditure results in another mortgage. Some of the notes are owned by the banks, some by the builders themselves, and others by creditors. My father-in-law's even involved. When they say everyone in the county's wrapped up in the hotel industry in some way, they're not kidding."

"I don't know much about it, I suppose," Bruce answered, trying to suppress the wry smile on his face. "I'm probably the only Jewish boy from the Bronx who has never been to the Catskills, not even as a busboy. And just think, the first time I arrive, I'm a guest of the house!"

"Don't kid yourself, buddy. You're going to earn this stay, I promise."

Bruce could see his cousin was anxious to get down to business. "Okay, Sid, tell me specifically what it is we're up against."

"As of now, I've got one man in the hospital who I'm almost positive has cholera. And I'm not sure, if that's what he has, that it hasn't spread."

"Shit. How long do you think he might have had it before he came to you?"

"It's hard to tell. First his boss thought he was drunk and that's why he had the stomach pains. The guy himself speaks very little English and by the time someone felt it was serious enough to get him to me, the poor bastard was about to collapse. I'm going to park in the VIP lot around the corner," he added, turning off the main drive.

"Considering that the incubation period for cholera is anywhere between a few hours and six days," Bruce interrupted, "we should be able to zero in on this thing rather quickly, don't you think? How much do you know about the guy?"

"Not much, though I suspect he snuck into the States on a cargo ship from the Far East. It could very well be a freak thing, an isolated case, but that's one of the reasons I want you here."

"Let's keep our fingers crossed."

Sid agreed, concentrating on getting his car into the reserved space.

"Can you carry your bags in?"

"No problem."

"We'll meet with Jonathan Lawrence right away. He's the general manager."

"What's he like?"

"Fiercely ambitious, more interested in the hotel as a financial institution and his position in it than how his decisions affect its people."

There was something about the way Sid said it that made Bruce feel uncomfortable.

"We'll go through that door there," Bronstein said. "It bypasses the front lobby which is a madhouse right now."

"Who knows about this thing . . . and my role in it?"

"Jonathan, me and by now the owner, Ellen Golden. She's a good lady, recently widowed, with a hell of a load on her shoulders right now. I just hope she can stand up to the pressure."

"I can't say I envy her."

They walked through the side entrance. Even though it was thirty yards from the lobby, they could still hear the din of the crowd. Bruce was curious so he peered around a corner. The scene of bedlam amazed and amused him at the same time. How in the hell could they get anything done in all that confusion? Everybody seemed to be screaming at everybody else but nobody seemed to be moving. The crowd had bunched up in front of the main desk and despite the pleas of bellhops, desk attendants and security people, they refused to form any sensible lines. Suitcases were everywhere—piled on carts, stacked near couches and chairs, in the hands of guests. Bellhops weaved in and out of people, pushing whatever luggage they could.

The main check-in area was surprisingly small for a hotel of such repute and the abundance of furniture only added to the closeness. Many of the guests were collapsed on the cheap vinyl love seats and easy chairs, their clothing bags dragging on the floor beside them. A few young women seated themselves on the worn nylon rug near the newspaper counter, content to bury themselves in the *Daily News* until the pandemonium diminished.

"What are you doing?" Sid asked, peering over his shoulder.

"I don't believe this. How does anyone keep track of what's going on?"

Despite the efforts at the security gate to slow things down, it appeared as though the crowd was increasing geometrically. The receptionists at the check-in counter were swamped and Bruce felt they would all throw up their hands at any moment and desert, leaving the guests in a state of uncontrollable frenzy. Through the picture windows he could see the cars lined up in rows outside the front entrance. Carhops were literally jumping into the driver's seats and pulling away with doors swung open and passengers half out. Bellhops stacked what they could on luggage carriers and fought their way into the backup in the lobby. Bruce shook his head incredulously.

He could hear the refrains being barked out in the lobby by the reservations people: "Just a minute sir. I'll be right with you, miss. He's first, ma'am." Intermingled were the sounds of people recognizing one another, people laughing, children crying, bellhops begging guests to move out of their way.

And there, in the middle of it all, stood Magda, greeting oldtimers with the love and affection they had come to expect and newcomers with the sense of warmth and friendliness that personified the Congress.

"Quite a place," Bruce said as the two of them walked down the corridor to the executive offices. The secretary looked up quickly and smiled when she saw the doctor.

"He's expecting you, Dr. Bronstein. Go right in."

"Thanks, Suzy. This is my cousin, Bruce Solomon. You'll probably be seeing a lot of him. In addition to being our guest, he's going to be doing a little work for us on the side."

"How nice." The twenty-year-old redhead smiled and crossed her legs to advantage. Bruce merely nodded, digesting, at the same time, the way she looked at him. Hopefully, he thought, he'd be able to find a few moments to mix business with pleasure.

Jonathan's office was done in a most tasteful manner. There was an antique desk, a long table covered with file folders and memo pads, a couch, and three Louis XIV chairs to its left. The walls were ascetically bare. Nor were there any personal mementoes on his desk. All in all, the office was perfectly organized, its personality characterized by its absence. Jonathan stood when they entered.

"Our medical detective," he said without further ado, extending his hand in automatic greeting. Bruce took a dislike to him instantly.

"Bruce Solomon," Sid Bronstein said.

"Sit down please." Jonathan pointed to the chairs furthest from the desk. "I suppose the good doctor's already filled you in."

"I think I have a pretty good idea of what we might be up against, yes."

"I don't want to get into the medical situation with you guys," Jonathan continued. "God knows, I know very little about cholera. But it's imperative I talk about the Congress's situation for a moment."

"Sure, I—"

"We're walking a tightrope here and I'm not just talking about a potential epidemic or whatever you want to call it. Though it may seem difficult for outsiders to understand, this place is almost tottering on bankruptcy and has been for the last couple of years. Sid knows all about this, as do others in the community, so I'm not revealing anything terribly secret. We need a good season to keep our heads above water. If it gets around that we have a medical researcher checking out a potential cholera outbreak, it could cause problems from which we may never recover."

"Bruce is fully aware of that," Sid interrupted, "and he's a professional. He knows how to go about his work. I don't think you have to worry on that count."

"Fine. For a cover, I suggest you pretend to be an insurance investigator. We continually have them around here reevaluating our policies. That is, if you know anything about insurance."

"About as much as you know about cholera," Bruce countered.

"Well, there shouldn't be a problem. If anyone bothers you, just tell them you're under direct orders from me. That should take care of anything."

"Sounds like you have them terrified."

"I try to. If you give people the proverbial inch . . . especially now with the boss gone—"

"Incidentally," Sid interrupted, "speaking of the boss, how's Ellen taking all this?"

Jonathan winced at the reference to Ellen as his superior. "Better than you'd expect," he lied. "She feels she can stand up to anything as long as I'm in control. She's agreed to let me handle the entire matter anyway I choose, so I suggest rather emphatically that you make sure not to bother her with any of the details and work directly through me."

They agreed.

"What exactly do you do, Mr. Solomon?"

"I do diagnostic lab work at Mt. Sinai, concentrating on rare diseases."

"He's modest," Sid said. "He just published an outstanding paper on diseases indigenous to the Far East."

"Anyway," Bruce continued, "when Sid called, I had some vacation time coming so I thought it might be a good time to—"

"So you're not overly concerned then with the situation here?"

"Concerned? Of course I'm concerned. From a medical standpoint, it's obviously dangerous. Frankly, I'm terrified of the possibilities. What is your population now, guests and all?"

"With staff, almost 1200."

Bruce glanced at Sid who looked down.

"Are you sure you really understand what this could mean?"

"He told me enough," Jonathan said, nodding toward Sid. "He told me the symptoms can be confused with severe food poisoning or bacillic dysentery."

"One of the ways in which the disease is spread is through food that could be infected, so if someone who works in the kitchen is a carrier..." Sid interjected softly.

"I understand. Everyone here would become a potential victim. *If—*"

"The danger now, as I see it," Bruce said, pulling his chair closer to the desk, "is that the incubation period ends in six days and if we find evidence of a potential epidemic condition, you're going to have to quarantine the entire place for that whole time. That means nobody in or out." Jonathan glared at him in semi-shock, the reality hitting him for the first time.

"At our expense? Do you realize what that would do to us financially, not to mention to our reputation?"

"Running the hotel is your problem, Mr. Lawrence. Mine is finding out whether we might have an epidemic situation on our hands."

"What do you plan to do first?" Jonathan asked. It made more sense to him to pretend to cooperate than to argue at the moment.

"I'll get as much information as I can on the infected custodian. Has he been off the grounds the last few days as far as you know?"

"I have no idea. You'll have to ask Bob Halloran, my personnel director."

"Okay, I'll do that first. I also would like to have the water and milk supplies analyzed," Bruce said. Sid agreed and they made a note to do that.

"Again," Jonathan emphasized, reverting to his old self, "please be careful when you talk to people. Rumors start flying at a hotel like this even when there is no foundation. I'll call Halloran and let him know you're coming. He'll cooperate, but it's only to be expected that he'll be curious about what you're up to."

Bruce agreed to be tactful and he and Sid Bronstein stood up. Before they could leave, Jonathan's intercom buzzed.

"It's for you, doc," he said, handing Bronstein the receiver.

"Dr. Bronstein here. Yes, when? Dammit! I'll be right over. Don't call the coroner until I get there." He stared as he handed the phone back to Jonathan.

"Tony Wong just died."

"Well," Bruce muttered, "as of now, if it's cholera, you have a one hundred percent mortality rate."

three

Jonathan Lawrence sat back in his chair dejectedly. Why now? Why, just as he was on the verge at age thirty-four of achieving the two things he wanted most in his life, money and power, did things have to get so screwed up?

Ever since legalized gambling had been introduced in Las Vegas, there was speculation it would some day also be approved in New York State. As early as January of '58, rumors were rampant that the proposition would be passed by the legislature and put to the voters in the form of a referendum in the next election.

From Jonathan's point of view, if the referendum were approved it would be the best thing that could ever happen to the Catskills. It would perform miracles for the economy, creating the much needed excitement they required to compete with resort areas all over the world. It was important to him that the Congress be the first to get into the action; the first resort to open a casino, the first to cater to an international crowd, and the first to invest in building convention centers that would attract large groups of businessmen and organizations with money to spend.

Jonathan was not the only one interested in gambling coming to the mountains. Five years ago, unbeknownst to Ellen, when money was especially tight, he had met with some syndicate people at Phil's behest and negotiated a loan at outrageous interest for $250,000. The interest had been repaid, but not the principal itself.

Not uncoincidentally, the week Phil died the man he had dealt with contacted him by phone. He wanted to know if Jonathan thought that under the circumstances Ellen might be interested in selling or, at the very least, see her way clear to having a silent 51 percent partner, a partner who would erase the loan and make extra money available for whatever expansion was necessary to make the Congress the showcase of the Catskills. It was also made clear that if the answer was no, the loan would have to be repaid immediately, even if it mean bankruptcy for the Congress.

These people wanted to get in—fast—before other organizations did. And they held a carrot out to Jonathan. If he could make the arrangements, he would be given a substantial raise and the position of president of the new corporation.

At the time, with Ellen so deep in grief, he didn't think there would be a problem but now, with her getting more active in the day to day affairs of management, he had a sinking feeling it wasn't going to be quite that easy. On the other hand, he knew she was concerned about having to bring Sandi up at the hotel by herself and once she started to discover how complicated the job actually was, she'd probably welcome anyone who could relieve some of the pressures.

A few days ago, his contact informed him they were sending a representative, a Nick Martin, up for the Fourth to look the place over, check out its operation and come back with a decision. If the place looked good and Jonathan made the arrangements with Ellen, they were ready to make a deal immediately. If not . . .

And now this. Jonathan began to sweat. To think a potential multi-million dollar operation, which he was going to head, could be in danger because some Chink died of probably nothing more serious than food poisoning.

He slammed his fist on his desk. Cholera, his ass. If Nick Martin got wind of what was happening, that there was the possibility of an epidemic and what it would do to the hotel's reputation, they'd pull out as fast as a guy hearing his girl had V.D.

The medical investigation had to be contained. He was sorry he had given his approval in the first place but it was too late now to turn back. He was playing a dangerous game with dangerous men on both sides. The most important thing now was to know exactly what was happening every step of the way so he would know precisely what measures he'd have to take, if and when he needed to.

Bob Halloran, a tall sinewy young man with legs so long a friend once said his upper body must have been placed there as an afterthought, walked quickly across the back lot to get to the "dungeon," as the lower level staff's dorm was often called. They had called him at his basement office. Some sort of commotion going on down there was threatening to get out of hand. That was just what he needed now, with one of the silver sterilizing machines on the blink, trouble with a front elevator and an outbreak of cockroaches in one of the cottages . . . more problems.

He could already hear the yelling as he turned down the small knoll. Two of the Puerto Rican dishwashers and Margret Thomas, the chambermaid, were going at it in the entranceway, egged on by friends of both sides.

"What the hell's going on?" he asked Domingo, the laborer who had called him earlier.

"Those two, José Lorca and Pablo Gomez, have been shacking up with some of the whores down at the bowery building." Halloran looked at him incredulously. For that he had been called away from his desk?

The bowery building had never been his favorite place. It was a seedy apartment house a half mile down the highway from the Congress, an eyesore if ever there was one. The Goldens had tried for years to buy up the property but for some reason, the owners refused to sell.

"They said they had to go there because Tony the Chinaman, their roommate, was so sick they couldn't stand to be in the same room with him."

"Well, Tony's in the hospital now and they can go back. What's the problem?"

"They asked Margret to clean up their room and she refuses. Says she's only paid to clean the dungeon once a week, she did it five days ago, and they can go fuck themselves."

"And the President of the United States thinks he has problems."

"The guys say they'll quit if she doesn't and I figured you didn't want to have to go looking for more dishwashers on the July fourth weekend."

"You're right, Domingo. Good thinking." He turned his attention to the fracas.

"All right, hey Margret, HEY!"

She turned away from the dishwashers as soon as she saw who it was, but the Puerto Ricans continued to argue as though she were still there.

"Let them clean their own mess," she said to Halloran.

"It's not really their mess," Domingo interceded. "That's their complaint."

"What kind of mess are we talking about?"

"You heard how sick Tony was . . . throwing up and shitting all over the place."

"Yeah, so?"

"So the place stinks. They say there's filthy stuff and crap all over. I don't want to go in there."

Halloran stepped back and wiped the sweat off his forehead. It was beginning to get hot. He took Margret's arm and pulled her a few feet away.

"Where are you taking me? I ain't done nothing wrong."

"Relax," he said. "I'm not taking you anywhere. I'll tell you what I'll do."

She put her hands on her hips defiantly as she shifted her weight from one hip to the other. Her gargantuan breasts that had so amazed Sandi jiggled suggestively and for a moment Halloran lost his train of thought.

"Put your eyes back in," she said directly to his face. Margret Thomas was not one to be put out by authority.

He turned red. "Look," he said quickly. "I don't need more aggravation today. Clean their fuckin' room and I'll put you in for a whole day of overtime."

"A whole day?" She relaxed her stance. "You ain't shittin' me now, are you?"

"Would I shit you?" He laughed, knowing full well what he'd really like to do to her. "A whole day. But keep it to yourself. It's nobody's business but ours."

"One day's pay. That's a deal." She turned and walked quickly back to the dungeon. The Puerto Ricans quieted down and things appeared to get back to normal.

Halloran walked over to Domingo. "I think everything's under control now. Thanks for letting me know."

"Hear anything about Tony?"

"Who's had a chance to check? I'll try to find something out when I get back to the office." With that he turned and walked away.

Once inside the dungeon, Margret Thomas filled a pail of water and shook in a generous portion of cleanser. She was happy with herself. Usually she hated to work in the help's quarters . . . no tips or extra-friendly guests . . . but to earn an entire day's pay for cleaning just one room . . .

Tony's rommates stood in the hall watching as she kicked the bent-in aluminum pail set on small wooden rollers. They squeaked over the rough cement floor. Everything about the interior of the dungeon was ugly. The hall walls consisted of naked sheet rock spotted with graffitti in foreign languages, blotchy streaks of dirt, stains from spoiled food and wine, even heel stains resulting from kicks of anger and frustration. Margret turned back and gave Tony's jeering roommates the finger. Then she pushed open the door of their room. The stench drove her back against the wall.

Never in all her twenty years as a chambermaid had she seen anything like it. Towels, spotted with vomit and excrement, the linen and blankets overflowing with it, and smelly crumpled drippings along the walls. Her stomach turned and she thought she, herself, would heave. When she looked back inside, she saw roaches crawling across the floor, feeding off the blotched linoleum.

She considered forgetting the whole thing. Then she thought about the money. She could do it quickly. She would do it quickly. Pushing the pail further inside, she hurried through the door and began to gather up the soiled towels, holding her breath and cursing as she worked.

"Son of a bitch," Manny Goldberg said, pounding on the top of his steering wheel. "I gotta drive outta New York, fight the fucking traffic all the way, just to get to the front of this hotel and wait bumper to bumper to get in." He rolled his window further down and stuck out his head. "Move your ass," he screamed.

"Manny, for godsakes, calm down," his wife said, poking him in the ribs for emphasis.

"For the prices they charge around here, the least they can do is give some service."

"Which doesn't mean you have to act like an idiot." Flo turned the rear view mirror toward her face to check out her new permanent wave. The ride up had been hard on everything, her hair, her makeup and especially their tempers.

"Will you please leave that mirror alone? I've told you a million times not to twist it like that. Whenever I have to check out the rear, you have it so out of place I can't see a damn thing behind me."

"It's your own fault. I've asked you a hundred times to put a vanity mirror behind the sun visor."

"This is a car, dammit, not a ladies' room." He sat back and manipulated a thick Monte Cristo from his shirt pocket. Though not exactly a short man, he was a good twenty-five pounds overweight, far from the sex symbol he imagined himself to be. His cheeks were bloated and the sweat had already accumulated under his armpits and around the confines of his collar. He stuck the cigar lasciviously in his mouth, chomping off the end in the process. Flo turned away in revulsion.

They were not unlike many other couples who frequented the Catskills, each indulging in extramarital affairs and pretending the other didn't know. He had married into her father's garment business and, along with his brother-in-law, had eventually taken over. Now he was trying to explain to Flo that it might soon be all his.

"Why," she asked," "would Mike want to sell out his share, especially now when the business is doing so well?"

"I told you. He's heavily in debt and he needs money fast. He's desperate for someone to bail him out so, if in return for his stock I can get him the cash he needs by Tuesday morning. . . ."

He exhaled a mouthful of smoke in her direction. It amazed her to realize how much she had once been attracted to him. He was a raw animal in those days, an animal she could never get enough of. But lately, the base sensuality was beginning to border on brutality. Both in and out of bed, she found herself growing more and more afraid of him.

She sorely needed a respite from their day-to-day life together. Thank God for places like the Congress!

"I don't understand," Manny said, finally pulling up to the security booth, "why you shmucks can't figure out another system. It's like the Long Island Expressway here on a Friday afternoon."

"I need your name, sir," the guard said, impervious to the insult.

"Shit! No, I mean Goldberg. Like in Manny Goldberg."

The guard checked his list. "Of course, Mr. Goldberg. We've been expecting you. Just follow those cars to your right." He pointed as he spoke.

"You think this is my first time here? Save your breath for the suckers behind me."

"Can't you be a little more gracious?" Flo suggested. "The man's only doing his job. Someday you might appreciate their security system."

"The only thing I'll appreciate now is a cool Tom Collins."

"You're not going straight to the bar, are you?"

"Look," Manny said, pulling up to the front entrance, "this is a vacation, remember? We're supposed to have a good time and right now, for me a good time means getting a drink."

"The luggage's in the trunk," he said, handing the keys to the carhop. "I'll be back before you get your room key." He left her steaming and went on his way.

Flo slipped out of her seat carefully and pressed down the sides of her dress. Then she began to look over the young bellhops.

"Right this way, ma'am," the kid with her luggage said. She followed him through the main entrance. Manny was already out of sight. "I'll just leave your stuff here on the side until you get your room assignment. My name's Jack and I'll be here whenever you need me."

. . . 35

That's good to know, she thought. It may be sooner than he thinks. "Oh," she said, spotting the hotel's security chief near the reservations desk. "There's Rafferty. Rafferty," she shouted above the crowd, "It's me, Flo Goldberg."

Vince Rafferty excused himself and started across the lobby. The tall ex-New York City cop had recognized her immediately. He couldn't help remembering the last time in the Robin's Nest cottage three years ago.

"You're my first Irishman," she had told him. "And to think I thought the Irish only had freckles on their face." She had done things to him he thought Jewish women never did and he'd looked forward to an encore the next time she came up, but that time she chose a Greek bartender instead. Well, maybe this year, he thought, though he had also heard last time around that she had taken a shine to Billy Marcus, the young bellhop from Penn State. He wondered. Was he getting too old?

"Hi, Flo," he said, giving her a peck on the cheek. "Where's your number one?"

"In the bar as usual, fortifying himself. Raff, I think I'm going to need your service." She looked at him in such a way he wasn't sure whether there was a double entendre in her choice of words or not.

"I brought a lot of jewelry up this time. We made a killing on the stock market." Rafferty nodded, saddened that there was no entendre at all.

"You want a safe deposit box, then?"

"I think it's a good idea, don't you? I know you've never had trouble here with stealing, but I guess one can never be too careful."

"And you probably brought up more than you can wear."

"You've been around here too long. You're beginning to sound more and more like my husband. Tell me," her voice softened, "how've you been, really?"

"No complaints. Getting older day by day but so far no ladies have checked out on my account." The buttons of his shirt strained as his shoulders stretched the garment. Flo let her eyes fall quickly, then slowly rise again.

"I'll bet."

"Why bet? Find out for yourself?"

"I just might do that. Take care of my valuables for me?"

"Anytime," he said. "C'mon, I'll get you on the express line."

* * *

...36

"The first thing I've got to do once we get to the room is shower. I'm all icky from the trip. Look how my clothes are sticking to me." Melinda practically stepped on the bellhop's foot as she pulled the V-neck portion of her blouse further out and blew air down her cleavage. Grant lingered behind until they got to the elevator, at which point he caught up quickly and sulked in the far corner. He had his hands in his pockets and glared angrily at the floor. He knew exactly what the bellhop was thinking. From now on, whenever they'd walk through the lobby, there'd be looks and remarks and his mother would smile stupidly and wiggle her ass.

"Yeah, it's a hot Fourth," the bellhop said, as she rubbed against him not altogether ingenuously in the crowded elevator. Grant squeezed his fingers tight against his palms. The elevator ride was gratefully short and they followed the boy to their suite.

"Just put those suitcases on the rack, sweetie," she told him, pointing toward the open double closet to her left. It was a gigantic walk-in model, almost as large as the bedrooms in some of the newer high-rise luxury apartments in Manhattan. The bellhop moved slowly, enjoying the way she moved around to open the drapes and inspect the furnishings in her room and Grant's. Her tight red skirt clearly outlined the well-shaped behind and the way she wiggled it left little to the imagination. Nonchalantly, she unbuttoned a button on her blouse.

"Don't you just feel like walking barefoot on these rugs?" she said as she shook off her heels. The thick brown nylon pile carpet would be good for more than wading in without shoes, it occurred to her. Her eyes moved critically over the large antique end tables and dressers covered with Carrara marble. Whoever had decorated the room had exquisite taste, she was glad to see. The powers that be at the Plaza and Waldorf could certainly learn something from the Congress.

She walked around to the queen-size bed, wondering if she could possibly get away with stealing the elegant comforter for her bedroom at home. Her hands rubbed sensually over the rich brass headboard. Without giving it a thought, and much to Grant's embarrassment, she began to bounce up and down on the mattress, letting her skirt rise well above her knees. "Not like those roadside motel numbers," she said, giving it the Melinda Kaplan seal of approval. "Not that I really know," she giggled. She fluttered her eyes coyly at the bellhop who she knew was enjoying every minute.

Her jumping had caused another button to become undone on

her purple shantung blouse. With her bra nearly exposed, she went for her purse. She hesitated a moment, catching her own image in the wide mirror above the small vanity table to her right. "God, I really do need a shower!"

"Here you go," she said, holding two dollars out with her hand while the other brushed imaginary lint from his shoulder.

If only they were alone. "Thank you," he said, pocketing the bills, at which point she turned, unbuttoned what was left of her blouse, and headed for the bathroom. Before she could close the door, he saw the remaining clothes peel off her body and drop to the floor. When he stepped out in the hall, he leaned against the corridor and prayed his hard-on would disappear as fast as it came. Room 1465. He made a mental note. He'd have to figure out a way to get back at some point when that gawky kid was out of the way.

Grant didn't move from the couch the whole time she showered. He stared up at the pale white ceiling and tried to understand why it annoyed him so that she was so damned attractive. Sometimes he wished she'd cut her face with glass and get a terrible scar. Even his father admitted she was still beautiful. "One thing I've got to say for her, Grant, is that she keeps her figure 100 percent. She's some piece of ass, your mother is."

How he hated that expression and how many times he had heard it . . . especially from the fellows at school when they thought he couldn't hear. "Boy, is Grant's mother a piece of ass. What I wouldn't do to get into that!" What was he supposed to do? Donate her to the charity auction they held every year? It was his mother they were talking about, for Christ's sake, his mother. Didn't anybody understand?

It never occurred to him he might be jealous.

"Are you still on that couch, Grant?" She stepped out of the bathroom, an oversized terry cloth towel wrapped around her body and a smaller one around her head.

"What else is there to do?"

"Oh, God, don't start that the moment we arrive. Put on your bathing suit and go down to the pool. Maybe you'll meet some kids your own age. There's got to be lots of teenage girls up here this weekend."

"I don't feel like swimming."

"Look Grant," now she was getting serious, "all I'm asking you to do is to give it a chance. Get involved in something. You don't have to fall in love with the place, but there has to be something, someone you'd like. And you'll never find out if you just mope around the room." Besides, she thought to herself, I'll never have any privacy if you're always hanging around.

He got up and walked to the window. They were very high up so the view was encompassing. He could see the main highways in the distance, heavy with traffic now. The cars moved like insects. He wished he had the power to step on them and squash them into the macadam. And the people walking around the grounds below, they looked more like mechanical wind-up robots than human beings to him.

As he stood gazing down, he was struck by the sheer immensity, of the place. To think that he, Grant Kaplan, would be able to do anything significant to damage it was ridiculous. He was outnumbered, outsized and outclassed. It depressed him to have his fantasy deflated.

Melinda was still chattering away, repeating her now too familiar speech about his not being a loner, mixing with others, developing relationships, etc. He imagined a small long-playing record in her head. She just pressed the button and on it went. She could do lots of other things at the same time because the record ran itself. He was sure, for instance, that even now while she was talking to him, her mind was on other things. He was afraid to think about what.

When he turned from the window, he looked into her bedroom where she was standing in front of a vanity mirror, clad only in the bikini panties she had newly purchased last week. They had a hole where the crotch would normally be. As she brushed out her hair, her firm breasts vibrated. He found it embarrassing to admit, but his mother's body really appealed to him and he could understand why strangers enjoyed looking at her the way they did. As for her, in some strange, peculiar way, she enjoyed showing off to him too.

What if he had an erection, he thought, staring at her with fascination. No, that would be sick. After all, she was his . . .

Most of his friends got erections constantly, at least they said they did, but Grant had always had difficulty. He was as turned on, at least in his head, by pictures of foldouts from *Playboy* as they were and even one night at a dance he had gotten his hands on a girl's tits but . . . nothing. Of course, Melinda never knew.

"All I can tell you," (she started another record in her head), "is to be very careful when you're with a girl up here. I trust you know enough not to get a girl pregnant." Wonderful, he thought, just picturing himself going to the canteen and asking for a box of rubbers. Not that it would ever come to that, but . . .

"I don't make mistakes with girls," he said.

"Well, there's always a first time and I'm just trying to give you some motherly advice."

"Did you ever make a sexual mistake?" he asked, suddenly very curious.

"Grant, for God's sake. That's something I don't plan to discuss with my fifteen-year-old son. Now, are you going downstairs and make some friends or not?"

"I'm not sure. Maybe I'll wait and go down with you."

That was obviously the last thing she wanted. "For God's sake, you're not a baby. Can't you do anything on your own?" She gave up in frustration and slammed the bedroom door in his face.

four

"I'll shoot over to the hospital now," Sid said after they had left Jonathan's office. The bellhop had taken Bruce's bags and was waiting to show him to his room. "I've got to make rounds and then get back to my office. Why don't you get started with what you have to do and I'll check with you later in the afternoon."

"Sounds good." They started down the corridor as the bellhop led the way. "I've got to tell you I have the distinct impression the general manager is not exactly thrilled to have me around."

"Don't jump to conclusions. The toughness is just Jonathan's manner. He doesn't like having people he can't control hanging around his turf. But he keeps his promises. If he says he'll cooperate, he will."

They stopped by the side door that led to the parking lot. "Good luck." His cousin waved.

Bruce followed the bellhop to his room. When the door was opened, he hesitated. What a disappointment! Some free ride—it never occurred to him that a hotel of this size could have such tiny rooms. The bellhop seemed to sense his letdown because he dropped the suitcase as quickly as he could and turned to leave. Bruce put a dollar in his palm and contemplated the scene—an ordinary single bed with a thick plywood headboard, two rather worn dressers, one with deep scratches on the drawers, and a small closet to his right with only a few hangers in it. The rug was worn through to the seams and what once had probably been a bright yellow color had now faded into a piss lemon hue. The pale white cotton curtain on the small window on the fire escape looked so thin it was practically transparent.

He shook his head and walked into the bathroom, half expecting to find the trappings of a cheap motel—drinking glasses in cellophane paper and a ribbon of crepe with the hotel's name draped tightly across the toilet seat.

There was no pretense . . . this was the cheapest room in the hotel, probably used for latecomers desperate to get anything they could, or guests the management wanted to make sure never came back. Thanks, Jonathan, he thought. I know you went out of your way to make me feel at home.

Without bothering to unpack, he quickly changed his shirt and got down to the business of tracking Tony Wong's activities over the last few days.

Jonathan had given him a diagram of the hotel so he could get around without difficulty. The first man to see was that personnel director, Bob Halloran. He checked the map, noting where the man's office was located in the basement, and took the elevator down. When the door opened, he stepped out into a relatively dark corridor. Dim bulbs spaced out along the way threw heavy shadows over the concrete floor and walls. Sounds from above traveled down through the pipes in a symphony of vibrations and knocks. A nasal hum emanated from the electric generators halfway down the corridor. At its end was the hotel laundry, where Bruce could hear the subdued voices of custodial personnel sorting linens and putting them in the huge washing and drying machines. The dampness made him shiver and reminded him of the pathology lab where he trained.

Halloran's office was just to the right. When he got there, he found it empty but the door was open so he walked in.

It was a small windowless office, overcrowded with one desk and chair, certainly not a pleasant place to work. A folding chair was placed against the right wall, giving the impression there were never more than two people in the office at one time. On the wall immediately behind the desk were series of charts depicting employees schedules, shifts, rotations, etc. He was about to leave when he heard footsteps.

"Can I help you?" Bob Halloran asked as he walked into his office.

"I'm Bruce Solomon and—"

"Yes. Mr. Lawrence told me you'd be around. Something about insurance. Last inspection we had a couple of weeks ago, everything checked out okay. What's the problem now?"

"I'm involved with health, not property insurance," Bruce said quickly. "I understand you had a worker here get sick, Tony Wong?"

"Yeah, Tony the Chinaman. He's in the hospital. What about him?"

"I just need a few facts, actually." He eyed the folding chair and when Halloran took his seat, Bruce sat down too. "Do you know if he was off the grounds at any time immediately before he took sick?"

"I doubt it. He just came over from Hong Kong and I don't think he really knows anyone away from the hotel. He's only been here a week. But if anyone would know it would be his roommates."

"Roommates?"

"Yeah. Two of them. In fact, I just left them. They've been shacking up down the road because Tony was sick and when they came back and saw the condition of the room, the way Tony left it full of shit and everything, they wouldn't move back until I got it cleaned up. Had a helluva time getting a chambermaid to do it, too."

"Someone cleaned it? When?" He was starting to pick up a clue that pleased him not at all.

"She started when I was leaving . . . might even be finished by now."

"Who is she?"

"Who's who?"

"The chambermaid. I've got to see her right away."

"Margret Thomas? I don't see what . . ."

Bruce stood up. "Is she still in Tony's room?"

"Hold on. I'll call over and see." He lifted the phone and dialed an extension. "I still don't understand what this has to do with insurance. "Hey," he said into the receiver. "This is Mr. Halloran. Is Margret Thomas still there? She's cleaning Tony the Chinaman's room." He put his hand over the mouthpiece. "You wouldn't believe some of the weirdos we wind up hiring over the summer." Okay, thanks," he said. He turned to Bruce. "Nope, she already left. And to think I'm paying her a whole day's overtime. She must have done some job."

"Where do you think she would be now?"

"Maybe back in her room, that is if she's not already out celebrating her extra pay."

"Can you call there? Please," he added, sitting back down on the chair.

"Sure." Jonathan had instructed him to cooperate, but this wasn't making any sense. What could Margret have to do with—"It's ringing. How is Tony, anyway?"

"I don't know," Bruce lied. "Those roommates of Tony. What do they do?"

"Dishwashers." He held up his hand. "Hello, who's this? Graciela, this is Mr. Halloran. Would you do me a favor, please, and see if Margret Thomas is in her room?" He waited for an answer, then hung up. "No go. She's not there either."

"If she was the last person to touch any of Tony's things, it's imperative I find her immediately."

Halloran tried to get a grasp on the situation. He was smart

. . . *43*

enough to know that something was going on that had nothing whatever to do with health insurance, but just exactly what it was—

Bruce plunged ahead. "And Tony's roommates. Are they in the kitchen now?"

"They aren't due for a couple of hours."

"Let me use the phone," he said, not waiting for a reply. He dialed the switchboard and asked for the general manager. Jonathan's secretary picked up immediately. "Hello, Suzy, this is Mr. Solomon. I have to speak to him right away."

There was a slight pause, then Jonathan's cool hello.

"I need three of your people rounded up right away and a private place to interrogate them."

"You're not panicking already, are you?"

"No, Mr. Lawrence, just doing my job. Bob Halloran will give you their names." He handed Halloran the phone. He listened for a moment, then gave Jonathan the requested information.

"You can meet with them in a storeroom down the hall."

"How long will it take to round them up?"

"Security should find the Puerto Ricans within a matter of minutes. There's not many places they hang out around the hotel. With Margret, it might prove more difficult. She tends to get involved with lots of people," he said with a wink.

Each minute seemed like an hour. For Christ's sake, Bruce thought, I hope they hurry up. We could be playing with fire and it might already be too late.

"Thar she blows," Charlotte Fein said, pointing to the Congress hotel a few miles away. The slim brunette stood up from her seat near the front of the bus and raised both hands toward the ceiling. Then she bent forward in a "Praise be to Allah" fashion and there was a roar of laughter from the crowd on the Shortline's Catskill Express. Her girlfriend, Fern Rosen, tugged on her skirt.

"Sit down, you idiot."

"Idiot? Have you no respect for the temple of love? If Mohammed could have his mountain, there's no reason we can't have ours too!"

Fern shook her head incredulously and looked out the window, still not believing she had let her mother talk her into this *mishigas* in the first place. Less confident and shyer than most girls who came to the Congress, it was not an experience she particularly looked forward to.

"Why not just relax and enjoy yourself," Charlotte said. "Don't be so nervous all the time. Remember our mission," she whispered, loud enough so that everyone within twelve rows could hear, "We're under orders. We're to find two nice Jewish boys, fall in love and get engaged before the end of the weekend."

"Or else they won't let us back across the George Washington Bridge," Fern added, surprised at her own contribution to this inane conversation.

"Ah," Charlotte said, "you had the same lecture before you left, too, I see."

"What do you think? Here I am, twenty-three years old, a bookkeeper at Mutual Life and date an average of once a month. In my mother's and her neighbor's eyes, that makes me a social retard."

"It's the same with me," Charlotte volunteered. "The whole time at dinner, every night, I sit and listen to what my mother was doing by the time she was my age. There she was, twenty-five years old, raising three kids, slaving like a *shvartsa* to keep a clean house, and sacrificing her life so her husband could get ahead with his. Why is it, do you think, that according to Jewish wives, no Jewish husbands ever made it on their own?"

"At the rate I'm going," Fern said, "I doubt I'll ever find out."

"Well," Charlotte went on philosophically. "I don't think we can lose anything by trying. I've been here a couple of times before but never came away with anything worthwhile. But that was when I lived in the Bronx and was considered GU—Geographically Undesirable. Who knows, now that I'm in Manhattan . . ."

"Yet so many marriages and romances are supposed to get started in the mountains. I just read about it in *Coronet*. *Time* had a story on it, too."

"I read an article also," Charlotte laughed. "It was in *Ripley's Believe It or Not*. With me it always ends up Not." She gestured toward the bus driver with her eyes. "Who knows, we may have to settle for him on the way back."

Fern hid her smile in her copy of the *Post*.

"How come you're still reading? We're almost there. Aren't you even a little bit excited? After all, it's your first time."

"I'm excited, I'm excited," Fern pretended, actually not the least bit excited at the prospect of being typed as just another of a number of women that her friends at work liked to call "on the make." Being aggressive was foreign to her personality and it certainly didn't help when a girl at the next desk told her the day before, "The Congress is such a meat market. Everyone out to try before they buy, looking for the best piece." It was definitely not Fern's style. The not unattractive, but certainly not striking, blond preferred dealing with men on a one to one basis. To be just a face in a crowd, to have to be so competitive . . .

Charlotte pulled out her compact and took one last look before the bus pulled in. Not bad, she thought, not bad at all. A little more tan would have helped, but a few hours at the pool would rectify that in no time. She tipped the mirror slightly so her bosom was reflected. Her breasts protruded evenly, the Bali's wireframe making her look bigger than she was. That's fair play up here, she thought. She'd take all the help she could get.

Fern watched her girl friend inspect herself. Despite the act Charlotte put on, always the girl with the quip, a laugh a minute, Fern knew she was deadly serious about finding a man. It was the most important thing in her life.

"Watch your step, everybody, watch your step," the driver sing-songed as he opened the exit door. "The bellhops will take your tagged luggage to the lobby so you can go directly to the registration desk and get your room assignments."

Charlotte followed Fern down the steps. "I don't see him," she said.

"Who?"

"My Don Juan. I thought I'd step off the bus and fall right into his arms. My mother promised it would happen like that this time."

"So much for mother always being right," Fern said, feeling not a bit unlike Daniel getting ready to enter the lion's den. "Well, here goes nothing!"

They headed through the main door and for a few minutes, simply stood in the lobby taking in the scene. At the top of the stairway to the right, large billboards featuring the faces of enter-tainers were hung just above the round double doors that led toward the nightclub. From their perspective, Charlotte and Fern could make out that Buddy Hackett and Alan King would be featured Saturday and Sunday nights.

Things had quieted down quite a bit at the reservations counter. What an hour ago had seemed an impossibility, that the right people would get their right keys and right luggage to their right room, had actually come to pass.

Early check-ins had already changed into their resort outfits— women dressed in colorful cotton blouses and pedal pushers and men strutting around in brightly designed shirts to match their plaid or striped bermuda shorts. Some of their kids ran around wearing polo shirts with the name "Congress" emblazoned across the chest.

A gust of cool air swept across their faces. Fern brushed back her bangs and looked around for the source. Air-conditioning came out through vents carefully hidden in the wall paneling. It was part of the hotel's unique heating system that permitted cool air to circulate through the ducts in the summer and hot air in the winter. They were about to move forward when a bellhop turned his cart too sharply and spilled half a dozen pieces of luggage on the floor. A number of people began clapping and shouting *Mazel Tov,* all to the extreme embarrassment of the bellhop who worked frantically to right the cart and restack the luggage.

"Let's get going," Fern said, "before we get run down. It would be a heck of a way to start a holiday."

"You're right. We'll check in, change and go straight to the pool. And don't forget, if any strange men approach you, be grateful."

"I'm a strange man," Manny Goldberg said, overhearing her last words. He had just come out of the Flamingo Room and was headed for some fresh air. The ever present cigar twirled in his mouth as he rolled the end of it with his tongue. Saliva formed disgustingly at the corners of his lips. Charlotte moved away as he put his arm around her shoulder.

"Honey," she said, "that strange we don't want." She took Fern's elbow quickly and moved closer to the reservation desk.

"Independent bitch," Manny mumbled. He knew the type. They're all alike, he thought, play hard to get and then, when you spend some money on them, they spread their legs so fast you could fall right in. He looked about for a moment as if he had lost his way. Then he remembered he needed air and headed for the exit.

"What's going on?" Jonathan asked. Bruce got up quickly and followed him into the basement corridor. "Why this panic over a chambermaid?"

"She hasn't been located yet."

"So?"

"Look," Bruce said, lowering his voice some, "here's what I've come up with so far. Tony's only been on staff a week. If he did have cholera, he probably picked it up on the ship."

"Then he didn't get it here at the hotel?"

"It doesn't look that way."

"Well then," he said, obviously starting to relax, "that pretty much lets us off the hook, doesn't it?"

"Not exactly."

"What do you mean?"

"I gather that when Tony got really sick the second night, his two roommates moved out. But the first night, when he might have been contagious, it's possible they contracted a mild case and are carrying it themselves. More important, when they returned, the place was so filthy they refused to clean it up themselves."

"And Margret Thomas was the one who cleaned it," Jonathan said quietly.

"That's right, probably handling all sorts of contaminated material in the process. We've got to be sure we know exactly where all the linen went and where she's been with those soiled hands. If she touched any food—"

"Hey," Halloran stuck his head out of his office. "I got Margret on the phone. We finally found her."

"Is she on her way down?"

"Yeah, and she's plenty pissed. Says we're screwing up her whole day."

"What exactly have you told the dishwashers?" Jonathan asked, turning back to Bruce.

"Nothing yet. Look, here's what's got to be done. They've got to get to a hospital for tests and observation. From what I've determined so far, they're the only ones who might have picked it up. It's a standard procedure to isolate possible carriers."

"What hospital?" Jonathan's eyes narrowed.

"Well, as Sid would be the first to admit, the hospital in town isn't at all equipped to handle this. We need a place where cholera antisera are available. I would have brought some with me but we didn't have any in the lab. I immediately put it on order."

"In other words, you want to send them to Mt. Sinai."

"I see no reason why not."

"There's a damn good reason why not. We need a place where we can control, as much as possible, anyone talking about it." He scribbled something on his memo pad. "I'll take care of it. I'll call Ellen Golden's New York physician and have him put them in University Hospital. I'm sure if they don't have antisera, they can get it. We've called on this doctor for favors before. I trust him and he knows when to keep his mouth shut."

"All right," Bruce said reluctantly, "but if we had them in Mt. Sinai, I could ride closer herd on things." Jonathan was not about to budge. "Okay, do it your way. You should also know, incidentally, that Sid sent one of Tony's specimens to my lab for diagnosis last night."

"So quickly?"

"There was no point in wasting time. We should get some results in a day or so and at least have his case diagnosed one way or the other. Now I'd like to be sure of the whereabouts of this Margret Thomas every minute since she left Tony's room."

"I'm sure security will get her here soon enough," Jonathan said. "Once she gets here, why don't you keep all three of them down here and I'll get hold of my driver. He'll bring the hotel car up to the basement entrance and will be ready to drive them to the city as soon as you're through asking questions. Don't bother explaining why you're asking. I'll take care of that."

"They're probably not going to like being whisked away like that."

"Don't worry, that's my problem. I'll make it worth their while. Just give me a few minutes alone with them before they leave. I'll also take care of Halloran."

Bruce nodded. For reasons he couldn't quite put his finger on, he was suspicious of all this cooperation. Then he went back into the room with the Puerto Ricans. Jonathan remained in the hall. He took out a cigarette and lit it, exhaling the smoke slowly.

Just lucky, he thought, that he had come down to Halloran's office when he did. This medical hustler might've really fucked things up by making his own arrangements. New York hospitals, isolation, specimens, all this noise over nothing. No one else in the whole hotel was complaining of stomach ailments and here this Solomon was, panicking over a chambermaid and two Puerto Rican dishwashers. Even if the Chinaman did have cholera, and he strongly doubted it now, it was obviously a one-shot.

He'd send Margret and the two spics to New York, all right, but it sure as hell wasn't going to be to any hospital. "I'll give them each a hundred bucks," he mumbled to himself, "and tell them to take a few days off . . . at least until after the weekend. By then this imaginary crisis will have ended and it won't have made a damn difference. It's the only way to handle it."

He hurried on to speak to Halloran and give instructions to his driver.

He was proud of the way he took control of the situation. He could imagine what Ellen Golden might have done; probably burst into hysterics and then close the place for a week "just to be sure," cost and reputation be damned. He smiled smugly, feeling quite justified in his drive to wrest control from her.

five

Nick Martin took a copy of the *Congressional Record,* the hotel's daily gossip sheet, from the pile on the reservation desk and waited for the receptionist to get off the phone. Though he had checked in just after the crowd had peaked, he was impressed with how professional and efficient the office staff was. It came as a surprise because when his associates had investigated the business practices of other Catskill resorts, they discovered that the various pressures associated with the summer season resulted in a great deal of inefficiency and waste. Management overbooked, overserved, overspent and simply accepted the losses as an inevitable part of their overhead, practices his backers wouldn't tolerate for a moment once they were in control.

"I'm sorry," the receptionist said, "but Mr. Lawrence isn't in his office right now. I left your name."

"Thank you." The receptionist smiled and eyed the diamond pinky ring on his right hand. He put the copy of the newsletter back neatly. She was fascinated by the deportment of this man. Missing was the frenzied, nervous anxiety that most guests projected when they first checked in. Despite the heat and humidity, he stood smooth and unruffled, looking for all intents and purposes as if he had just stepped out of the pages of a fashion magazine. Light blue was an excellent color for him, contrasting as it did with his dark, Mediterranean features. He was obviously not a run-of-the-mill guest.

"Is that the bar over there?" he asked, gesturing toward the Pelican Lounge. Soft piano music drifted out from the long room with its subdued lighting.

"Yes, sir, the Pelican Lounge."

"What's the owner, a bird lover or something? I see in the newsletter they call two of the buildings the Robin's Nest and the Cardinal Cottage."

"I don't know, sir," she said, obviously considering the question for the first time. Nick smiled at her expression and walked across the lobby to the lounge. He hesitated in the doorway. Multicolored Japanese lanterns were spaced along the ceiling, casting a rainbow of colors and shadows over the long bar to the right. Much of the light was caught up in mirrors and reflected over the walls and small tables surrounding it. At the end of the room was a small tier with white railings where the tables were cloaked in even more shadows. Just off the end of the bar, a black piano player ran his fingers gently over the ivory keys, providing soft background music. There was a small platform beside him used later in the day when the room featured a three-man combo.

The bartenders worked quickly to satisfy the demands of the small group congregated at the bar while two bar waitresses, dressed in red and white form-fitting uniforms, moved cautiously about the small tables. An occasional peel of raucous laughter broke the mood.

What a great place to locate a line of slot machines, Nick thought as he walked to the bar. He ordered a Dewar's, neat, and took out a Gauloise from his case. No sooner had he snapped his lighter than he felt a tap on his shoulder and turned to look into the face of Melinda Kaplan.

"May I borrow some of your fire?" she asked softly. His right hand, holding the lighter, remained frozen in the air.

"Excuse me?"

"A light," she said, sliding onto the stool beside him. "for my cigarette."

"Oh, yeah, sure. Sorry." He reached over, snapped the 24-karat gold lever, and touched the end of her cigarette with the tip of the small flame. Its glow danced in her eyes. He looked her over expeditiously. Though obviously a bit older, she could certainly give the chorus girls in Vegas a run for their money.

"Just got here, huh?" she said, blowing the smoke up toward the ceiling.

"How can you tell?"

"You haven't changed into your tourist costume. You're still wearing a tie."

He laughed. "Can I get you a drink?"

"I thought you'd never ask." He gestured toward the bartender nearest them. "Vodka and soda with a twist," she said.

"Actually, you're right. I just did check in. Haven't had time to learn the rituals."

"There are only two of any consequence. The first one is to eat until you're stuffed."

"And the second?"

"Use your imagination."

... 52

He laughed. "I'm Nick Martin."

"I'm thirsty," she said. Nick watched her sip her drink, her lips sucking suggestively on the straw.

"I was under the impression most women in the Catskills were shy and withdrawn."

"Most are. See those four girls sitting by themselves at those tables?" She pointed to the far end of the bar. "They'll be sitting like that all weekend."

"But not you."

"Especially not me. It would be such a waste, don't you think?" She turned so her breast brushed briefly against his arm.

"I'll drink to that." They lifted their glasses in a toast. "But that doesn't tell me your name. How should I go about calling you?"

"Very softly." She brought her face closer to his. He stared into her flashing green eyes.

"All right, Very Softly, you've figured out this is my first trip here. It obviously isn't yours. So tell me, what's good and what's bad?"

"I'm good and everything else is bad," she said. "Why not let me prove it?"

"How do you know I'm alone?"

"You've got a certain air that says 'I'm available.'"

"Could be." She ran her eyes slowly up and down his body.

"My name's Melinda Kaplan." She extended her hand.

"Hi, Melinda." He enveloped it in his.

"Well, now that we've gotten that over with, when do we make love?"

He signed the tab and they walked out in the direction of the elevators.

"Oh, excuse me," Jonathan said. He had just opened the door to Ellen's office. A tall dark man was lounging on the couch. Seated beside him, her fingers intertwined with his, was the most breathtaking young woman Jonathan had ever seen. She was dressed in a simple, but obviously expensive, yellow-striped shirtwaist. A thin gold chain, stunning in its understatement, dangled from her neck. A five-year-old boy sat quietly on the carpet in front of them while his older sister, her hair as golden as her mother's, stood examining the plaques and pictures on the wall. The man rose to his feet immediately.

"That's all right. We were just about to leave."

"Come in, Jonathan," Ellen said. "This is Jack Feigen and his wife, Toby. Toby, Jack, Jonathan Lawrence our general manager."

"It's a pleasure," Toby said. Jonathan tried to remember the last time he had met such an exquisite female. There was something absolutely magnificent about her expression . . . so open, so honest. He was almost sure he had seen that face somewhere before. It was only a few seconds later that he realized she hardly looked Jewish at all.

"Jack and Toby are old friends of Phil's . . . and of mine," she added quickly.

Feigen extended his hand as Jonathan approached. "How do you do?"

"Get up, Larry," Toby said, kneeling down to pick up her son. "Say hello to Mr. Lawrence."

"Hello there," Jonathan said. Usually he despised inane introductions to little children but in this case . . .

"And this is Barbara."

"Hi," she mumbled, looking over her shoulder but obviously more impressed with the photos of the celebrities.

"We didn't get up until today," Toby said.

"Well," Jack said, filling the silence quickly, "we'd better leave these executives alone. Ellen's been telling us about some of your problems and I must say, the hotel business is much more complicated than I ever imagined."

"Most things are," Toby added, taking her little boy by the hand. "It was nice meeting you, Mr. Lawrence. I hope we'll see you again before the weekend's over."

"I'll make it a point," he said. It was the first time he had ever said that to a guest and meant it.

"See you later," Ellen waved.

"Jack was an old friend of Phil's," she explained to Jonathan as he pulled a chair over to her desk. "They went to college together. For years he was trying to get them to come up and then when they finally decide to. . ." She stared sadly at the closed door.

Jonathan cleared his throat. He hated sentimentality. "I was on my way down to tell you about the Foxes."

"The Foxes?" She snapped back to reality. "What happened?"

"They canceled. The whole party, in-laws, children, grandchildren, the works."

"Why?"

. . . 54

"They asked if we had built the indoor tennis courts we promised last year. Seems the entire family wants to be able to play at any time. They also complained about the dietary laws, said they were under the impression we were going to relax them somewhat and serve bacon and shellfish like some of the other hotels have been doing."

"I see," she said thoughtfully, "but I don't think Phil ever meant to give anyone that impression. If he was going to do something as drastic as that, I'm sure he would have discussed it with me first."

"Maybe he just didn't get around to it. You know how busy he was the last couple of months. But during that time, Ellen, he and I had a number of discussions about changes that are going to have to be made. It's not just the Foxes," he went on, "it's a lot of people. We've got to expand our athletic facilities, add nine more holes to the golf course, build some more tennis courts, if we want to attract more men, and there's been a lot of grumbling, especially during the past year, about the strictness of our kitchen. The whole world doesn't keep kosher, for one thing, and not everyone who goes on vacation is Jewish. If we're going to survive—"

"You may be right," Ellen said, "but now's not the time to talk about it. Maybe next week."

"You can't keep putting it off," he said. "There are certain financial commitments."

"Not today. Please. And that wasn't my reason for asking you to drop by. What I want now is an explanation for what's been happening with the coffee shop."

"Happening?"

"Moe Sandman tells me you forced some cuts in the staff. Isn't that a bit unusual right before a major weekend?"

"Oh, that. Not really. The receipts just didn't warrant the number of people we have on salary there. The motel chains have done a detailed study of the employee requirements for their coffee shops. It's a scientific analysis based on a year's research and they've come up with an excellent formula for staff/customer ratios."

"But the Congress is not a motel," Ellen interrupted.

"No matter. The same considerations are involved."

"I don't think so, Jonathan." She was beginning to feel confident in what she was saying. "Our clientele is accustomed to warm, personalized, individual attention. They want to be pampered and made to feel special. That's why they come here and don't go to a motel in the first place. Ask Magda. She'd be the first to tell you."

"But Magda isn't working with our assets and liabilities on a day-to-day basis."

"Nevertheless, our service is one of our biggest selling points. I must insist you build up the coffee shop staff again. Besides, it's too much for Moe and . . ."

He nodded. Give in on this, he told himself. Pick your battles carefully. Let her think she's boss.

"Okay, Ellen. It's no big deal. If you feel we should, we will." Ellen relaxed.

"She's a very beautiful girl, isn't she?"

"She?"

"Toby Feigen."

"Oh yes, yes." He had not meant his interest to be that obvious.

"She used to be a model. Did the Noxema commercial on television."

"So that's where I saw her. I thought she looked familiar."

"She gave it all up for marriage and a family. They're one of the most devoted couples I know." Jonathan didn't have to look at her to know she was thinking of Phil again.

"I've got to get back to the accountant," he said. "Some figures I have to go over."

"Sure. I'll talk to you later on."

He nodded and started out of the office. God, she could be so depressing. It was like dealing with a child. How much longer would he have to put up with her?

"Mr. Lawrence," the receptionist called as he stepped out to the lobby. "Your secretary just called. There's a Nick Martin asking to see you. He just checked into the hotel."

"Fine. Have him paged and sent to my office." Perfect timing, he thought.

Sandi Golden put her hands gently under her barely visible breasts in the hope of creating the suggestion of a cleavage. It didn't work to her satisfaction and she flopped back over the bed in frustration. It seemed so unfair. I bet Margret Thomas wasn't this flat chested when she was my age, she thought, recalling the love scene she had witnessed with the maid the night before.

She turned over and looked at one of the photos of Bobby Grant taped over her dressing table mirror. The band singer had scribbled his autograph too widely, the "Y" covering a part of his beautiful right cheek, a cheek she'd give anything to kiss just once.

If only mom was a bigger-breasted woman, she thought. I'd probably develop faster. She had heard that was the way it worked—it was in the genes. Sammy, a busboy from Queens College, once told her Jewish girls have bigger breasts because of all the heavy kosher food they eat. "It's a biological fact," he said. That was the week she ate ten knishes at once and got sick. It was all bullshit, she thought. The only way Jewish food would help her figure was for her to stuff matzo balls in her bra.

She reached back under the pillow and took out her copy of the year's bestseller, *Lady Chatterley's Lover*. She had finished it weeks ago, something her mother didn't know, but kept it around to reread certain pages. She was especially excited by the descriptions on pages 195 through 197. Each time she read them, she tried picturing herself in similar situations with Bobby. If only she had breasts that swung like that, she thought. One time she actually took a position on the bed to simulate the action in the book . . . but nothing happened.

Reading the pages made her flush, almost as much as she had when she'd seen the real thing. She felt a warmth come into her vagina, making the insides of her thighs tingle with goose bumps. Her nipples got so hard she was afraid they might get stuck that way for good and everyone would know exactly what she was thinking. Changes had come over her body so quickly the past year. Sometimes they made her ache so badly she'd sit on the couch and hug a pillow to herself, pressing it hard against her body in an attempt to satisfy those urgent needs she didn't quite fully understand.

She had just finished the last paragraph when the telephone rang. It was her best friend, Alison Samuelson, who had come up with her family for the holiday.

"Hi there," Alison said, "we just got settled and I can't wait to see you. Can we meet at the pool in a half hour? That way we can catch up and grab some lunch at the same time."

"Sounds good," Sandi said, wondering if Alison, who was a year older, knew anything more about sex than she did. "See you soon, and listen, I've got some terrific things for us to do this weekend." She smiled at the thought of showing Alison what really went on at the maid's quarters. Maybe they'd even meet some boys and try some stuff out themselves. She hung up and went in to brush her teeth.

* * *

The head salad chef and half a dozen members of the dining-room staff worked frantically around the long tables set up at the head of the pool. Busboys, in single file, carried out trays of meats and large bowls of salads, assorted fruits and Jell-Os. At the end of the long tables, they set up platters of small pastries and urns of coffee. The chef snapped orders at the busboys and waved a long wooden spoon in their direction. Guests in bathing suits hovered nearby, eyeing the delicacies.

Off to the right the two bartenders at the small cocktail bar moved at a leisurely pace, one mixing drinks for the cocktail waiters who brought orders from the guests on the lounges, the other filling orders for the half dozen guests who milled around the bar. The four-piece band on the immediate left played lively dance music that kept a number of couples, mostly women, busy doing the cha-cha and mambo on the tiled area by the showers.

The music, the conversation, the sounds of preparation, all combined with the squeals of laughter from the children in the kiddy pool to create a soundtrack of summer delight. The air was permeated with the odor of coconut oil, baby oil, and assorted suntan creams, creating a sweetness that lingered about bare backs, and red legs and arms. Everywhere there was an abundance of naked flesh. Men with soft stomachs sucked in and held their breaths as they paraded past women in sunglasses with inscrutable eyes. Young women postured on the lounges, unfastening the tops of their bathing suits, but just so far. Dangling straps tempted the imaginations of men who stared through the glare.

The water in the Olympic-size pool was a cool aqua blue. It jetted in through the mouths of two stone lion faces, creating a refreshingly clear white foam. The lifeguard sat on his high chair looking important, but stoic, as he observed the action from his seemingly aloof position. He was statuesque, the "god of sunfun," with his bleached blond hair and enviable tan. His muscles glistened when he occasionally blew his whistle and gestured at teenagers who were getting too wild in the pool.

Sandi and Alison paraded between the rows of chaise lounges as they approached the main section. Sandi wore a long terrycloth robe and wide sunglasses. Her thongs slapped the tile as she sauntered along. Alison trailed behind her, wearing a conservative one-piece that pulled her bosom so tightly against her it diminished the size of her breasts but exaggerated the plumpness in her rear end. She carried her beach towel over her shoulder and, without the benefit of sunglasses, squinted her eyes practically closed. Suddenly Sandi stopped and turned slowly to the left, gazing out over the crowd.

"I don't see him, damn it."

"Who?"

"Bobby Grant. He usually sits in the section closest to the band. Sometimes they ask him to sing. I wanted you to see how gorgeous he is in a bathing suit."

"I guess I'll have to wait. We might as well take those lounges in the second row, there," Alison pointed. "It's really getting crowded."

"Um." Sandi started again and accidentally kicked a sandal that had gotten in her way. It rolled over the tiles and plopped into the pool.

"HEY!" Grant Kaplan shot up from his lounge and went after his shoe. He had to jump into the pool and dunk himself to get it, for it was already sinking to the bottom.

"Oh my God," Alison said.

"It's not my fault. He left it out in the middle of the path."

Grant pulled himself over the side of the pool. "Thanks a lot."

"You should have kept it under the chair where it belongs."

He let the sandal drip into the pool. Sandi watched him for a moment. He wasn't bad looking, she thought, kinda cute the way his ears stuck out from his head.

"Just leave them in the sun a few minutes."

"They're sensitive," he said, coming back to his chaise. "They might burn."

"Very funny. I'm Sandi Golden and this is my friend Alison."

"Hi," Alison said. Grant remained mum. The man and woman on the lounges to his left took one look at them, gathered their things, and walked away.

"Might as well sit here," Sandi said. "You don't mind, do you?"

"Long as you don't kick anything else of mine into the pool."

Sandi threw her beach towel on the lounge beside his and Alison sat down on the other one. She pulled down the bottom of her suit to relieve her hips of the tension. Sandi looked around again and then, in a very dramatic gesture, dropped her robe to her feet. Alison gasped.

The bikini pants cut just above the seam of her rear end, dipped at the sides, and crossed about an inch under her belly button. The bra uplifted her small breasts, but the sides of it were so abbreviated that what was revealed seemed more than there actually was. The suit was black with thin gold stripes. Heads turned. There were a few whistles. Men standing nearby stopped in mid-conversation and stared in silence.

"Where did you ever get a bathing suit like that?" Alison asked.

"Like it?" Sandi turned to show it completely. "It's French. The newest style. The boutique just got them in."

"Your mother actually let you wear it?"

"Well, not exactly," Sandi said, knowing full well what her mother's reaction would be. "She hasn't seen it yet, but I think I'm safe for a while. She's so busy she'll never get anywhere near the pool." She picked up her robe and took the suntan lotion out of her pocket. "Could I ask you for a favor?"

"What is it?" Grant said. He had been lying back, trying hard not to be impressed with this girl. God, she was pretty. But she was probably too old for him anyway.

"Just rub some of this lotion over my back and shoulders." She turned and handed it to him without waiting for his reply. "Thanks," she said when he hesitated. He pressed the tube and a blob of orange gel popped onto her skin. "Don't you want to tell us your name?"

"Grant."

"Grant. That's one of my favorite names, isn't it, Alison?"

"Oh yeah, sure." Alison was still getting over the shock of what Sandi looked like in that bikini. Nobody would ever believe that she was just a thirteen-year-old kid.

"Are you here with your parents?"

"Just my mother," Grant said, rubbing out the gel into small gooey circles. When he came near the strap of her top, he stopped. "My parents are divorced."

"Really?" She turned around. "How come?"

"I don't want to talk about it."

"That's too bad. I thought maybe you could tell me something about living with a single parent." She took back the suntan cream, then turned and lay on her stomach, staring at him. "I bet you're having a lousy time so far, huh?"

"That's for damn sure."

"If I came here as a guest, I think I'd have a lousy time too."

"What do you come here as?"

"The owner's daughter," she said, trying not to make a big deal of it. Grant didn't change expression. She liked that. "Going to the Champagne Hour tonight?"

"Not if I can help it."

. . . 60

"Neither are we."

"But I thought . . ." Alison began. Sandi kicked her with her right foot. "I'm going in the water," Alison said. "It's too hot around here."

"You wanna do something different tonight, Grant?"

"What's different?" The idea of something different turned him on.

"You'll see. Meet us in the Teen Room at nine."

"I'll have to check my appointment book," he said. She laughed. Then without warning, she scooped up his sandal.

"C'mon," she said, tapping him gently with it. "Let's play dive for the footwear."

"Hey!" He sat up but she was already at the edge of the pool. "Bring that back." It was too late. She was already in the water. He looked for a moment, then finally made a move to get up. She was laughing hysterically and holding the sandal above her head. Despite his reluctance, he ran and jumped in after her.

Jonathan got up quickly as Nick Martin came through the door. He extended his hand.

"How was your check-in?"

"Smooth, but I understand I missed the big rush."

"Sit down," Jonathan said, gesturing toward the couch. He walked around the desk and took his seat. "You're going to see this place at its best. We're booked to capacity."

"The grounds are beautiful. I can just imagine how it'll be when slot machines, blackjack, baccarat and craps are added to your other attractions."

"It'll be fantastic," Jonathan said, his face lighting up with anticipation. There was no way in the world he was going to let this possibility get fouled up.

"For the life of me," Nick said, "I can't understand why this place is such a marginal operation."

"It's simple," Jonathan said, "we're running behind the times. It's 1958 and they're still running this place like a turn-of-the-century borscht belt boarding house. You wouldn't believe the inefficient operation and maintenance procedures they tolerate."

"But you're the general manager," Nick said. He eyed Jonathan cooly. There was no humor in his expression. Jonathan squirmed in his seat.

"I'm questioned at every turn. Just today Ellen Golden made

. . . *61*

me put staff back in an area where I showed her in black and white they were unnecessary. She just doesn't understand it's not a mom-and-pop candy store operation any more; it's big business. She has no concept of financial feasibility."

"What's she like?"

"A naive woman with no business perspective, no vision regarding the future. Her husband kept her at the social end of things but now she's got it in her head she wants to take over the business operation as well. One season with her at the helm and we'll sink faster than the *Titanic*."

"Suppose we decide we like this place. Will she go for a silent partnership?"

"I thought so in the beginning but now I'm not so sure. In addition to everything else, she has a thing about gambling and how it would destroy everything the Congress stands for."

"You surprise me, Mr. Lawrence," Nick said quietly. "I understood, from our previous conversation, that you could almost guarantee her interest. Now what you're saying is quite different. Am I to understand you haven't been altogether honest with us the past few weeks?"

Jonathan was momentarily stunned. "Of course not. I'll be able to deliver her exactly as I promised. It just might take a little longer, that's all. Believe me, I want this deal to come through as badly as you."

"I'm sure you do. But, as the saying goes, time is money. If you don't deliver, we'll go somewhere else, after calling in our loan and possibly bankrupting you, of course. Actually, it's not such a bad idea. One hotel less to compete with."

"Please, Mr. Martin, there's no reason to do anything rash. I just need some time to talk to her, that's all. I'm sure that once she's aware of just how bad the situation is, I'll be able to get her to see things my way."

"All right. I'll give you until tomorrow. If not, I'll speak to her myself and, I might add, find my own president of the corporation if she agrees to see things my way without your help."

Jonathan sat up sharply. "I'm sure that won't be necessary, Mr. Martin."

"Fine," Nick said and he stood up to leave. "Oh, one more thing, Mr. Lawrence," he said as he reached the door, "I trust that from now on you will be totally on the up and up with us regarding what's happening here, that you won't be holding anything back. If there's anything my people in New York like less than surprises, I can't think of it."

For a split second Jonathan flinched as he thought about the cholera possibility. If Nick ever found out he was keeping that from him—but how could he? Only he, Sid Bronstein and Bruce Solomon knew about it and there was hardly any way their paths would cross.

"No surprises. I promise."

"Good. Then I'll be in touch."

As Nick closed the door, Jonathan sat back and took a deep breath. Somehow everything seemed to be going wrong. It wasn't fair. But then again, it never was. And it never had stopped him before.

six

The tension, the electricity, the anticipation. It was everywhere, and Bruce Solomon couldn't help being caught up in it. He was genuinely looking forward to the evening ahead but at the same time felt a nagging guilt that perhaps there was still something more he should be doing to track down the possible carriers. After all, he wasn't at the Congress to have a good time. Then again, there was really nothing more he could do until he got the results of the lab tests from New York. Besides, he rationalized, the better he understood what went on at the hotel, the more effective and less likely he would be to overlook anything of importance. At any rate, there was nothing to be gained from sitting alone in his room and brooding.

Feeling almost justified, he let himself luxuriate in the pulsating waters of the sunken marble tub. The hotel did so many things to make a guest feel rich and pampered, even when stuck in a modest room like his. The bathrooms were filled with dispensers of various shaving lotions, shampoo and French colognes. The beds had built-in vibrators. By merely dialing a specified number one could order a masseur or masseuse to the room, get the latest weather forecast, set up tennis, golf or dancing lessons, reserve a table in the night club or order gourmet specialties and drinks from the kitchen or bar. It was, for most, a fantasy come true.

The gala "Welcome Cocktail Party" was due to begin in fifteen minutes. His cousin Sid had mentioned that men often dressed for it in formal attire and Bruce hoped that his blazer, gray slacks and ascot combination, the best he could come up with with two hours notice, wouldn't make him look too much like the hick he was beginning to feel he was.

He rubbed a dab of hair tonic into his curly black hair, giving it a sheen many women would envy. He began to feel better about himself. Twirling a short strand that fell haphazardly on his forehead, he looked at his image roguishly in the mirror. It could be worse. "Go get 'em, killer," he chuckled. He took off.

It was a sight to behold. The sweep of pale chiffon dresses, the sharply pressed tuxedos, the dazzle of pearls and diamonds, the peals of laughter and loud, exuberant conversation, all dominated the corridors and lobbies with rich vibrant images—a montage of people caught up in a swell of abandon and gaiety. On this lovely Friday evening, the hotel had turned into a luxury liner on a voyage of unadulterated pleasure.

Every word, every gesture, seemed exaggerated and everywhere there were groups of people looking, staring, taking things in. The happy couples prouder of each other than ever, the singles more aggressive than usual, their eyes darting about to see whose attention had already been caught and who still looked good enough to latch on to.

It's a long way from the Bronx, Bruce thought to himself as he began his hegira to the cavernous Gold Room.

To the right of the entrance were a series of tables set up with an elegant buffet—Nova Scotia smoked salmon, fresh-water sturgeon, caviar, both red and black, smoked whitefish and lox, Swedish sweet and sour meatballs, chopped chicken liver castles, barbecued beef ribs with special sauce, thinly sliced prime rib and filet mignon, sweet and sour chicken wings, mini egg rolls, cocktail franks in a blanket, Hungarian stuffed eggplant and cabbage, watermelon and fresh pineapple sculptures, mouthwatering petit fours, a kosher cacophony of gourmet specialties. The chefs and bakers outdid themselves each Fourth in trying to tempt, torment and tear away even the most resistant dieter from the mast of his restraint. "Well . . . maybe . . . just this once. . ." All slogans of surrender. "After all, we're paying for it!"

Bar waiters, balancing their trays of Dom Perignon like amateur Nijinskys, maneuvered themselves deftly through the crowd, offering refills before one had to ask. In the back, a five-piece combo played for those who wanted to dance, though eating and drinking were by far the most popular activities.

Magda the hostess, striking as ever in a shimmering violet shantung, moved purposefully among the celebrants, affectionately greeting people she knew and bringing special friends over to Ellen who stood by herself a few yards away from the entrance. Even guests who hardly knew her made their way over to Mrs. Golden, touching her hand, kissing her cheek, and offering subtle gestures of condolence. She bore it all stoically, her lips locked into a smile as if in a freeze frame photo, seemingly the epitome of control and dignity.

Occasionally she would pause from her small talk, turn and take a sip of champagne. Only then, her shoulders hunched, did she give the slightest hint at the turmoil raging within. It was her first major holiday without Phil and she missed him terribly. Try as she did to get caught up in the tumult and excitement, the pressures of the past six weeks were beginning to take their toll. How she wished she could see an end in sight!

Bruce, of course, had no way of knowing this. The only face familiar to him was that of Jonathan Lawrence, who seemed to go out of his way to avoid him. The hotel manager, coming into the room via the service area, moved about like an insurance adjustor, his greetings perfunctory, his charm, what little of it there was, artificial. Warmth and hospitality, the cornerstones on which the Congress had established its reputation, had no place in his personal or professional life. As far as he was concerned guests were commodities, bodies to be checked in and out with machine-like regularity. They were to be housed, fed and entertained—en masse. Personal attention, catering to individual needs, was a waste of time.

People didn't return to the Congress out of some romantic concept of loyalty, he had recently concluded. That was an outmoded and outdated fantasy, something Ellen Golden would have to get through her head. Guests came back for one reason and one reason only. They couldn't get the same value for the price anyplace else. It was as simple as that. Anything else was a figment of an old-timer's imagination.

He stopped short as he saw the expression on Bruce's face as, champagne in hand, he stood in front of one of the tables of hors d'oeuvres. He had obviously never seen so much food, so elegantly prepared and displayed. Perhaps, thought Jonathan, he might use this observation to advantage. Maybe, if he played his cards right, he could get this medical detective to get so wrapped up in the special delights of the hotel he would forget about quarantines, cholera, and epidemics altogether. It wouldn't be the first time somebody had succumbed.

"Okay," Charlotte said, pausing for effect in the doorway of the now very crowded Gold room. "Pick a winner!"

"Will you please stop it?" Fern blurted out, embarrassed to even make an entrance at this point with her friend. Charlotte had been much, much too loud on their way down to the cocktail party. Fern was positive the woman in the elevator with her six-foot-tall husband despised her for the obvious way she was flirting with him.

... 66

Then, to make matters worse, she had practically propositioned the attendant at the information counter in the lobby.

"Listen, honey, contrary to what you may have heard, good things don't happen to those who wait. You have to make them happen—especially if you're looking for action!"

"I never said I was looking for what you call 'action.'"

Charlotte turned and looked at her again, very unhappy with the way things were turning out. They had had their first argument in the room about clothes. Fern was wearing a high-neck, long-sleeved, three-quarter-length *shmatta* that even Klein's basement would have rejected. Her hair, tied back in a bun so tightly it pulled the edges of her forehead up on her scalp, made her look twenty years older than she was. Her makeup, what little of it there was, added nothing.

"You've got to be kidding," Charlotte told her. She had just zipped up a copy of a bright red strapless featured recently on the cover of *Vogue*. Her cleavage was magnified by a padded bra purchased specially for the occasion. Her auburn hair, recently styled by Mr. Albert of 58th St., fell neatly around the nape of her neck and she had spent nearly an hour painting her face with what seemed to be a pound of mascara, eye liner, shadow, and lipstick. "This is a hunt we're on, not a retreat."

"I'm not comfortable pretending to be something I'm not."

"Who's telling you to be something you're not? You're a woman, aren't you? You're entitled to some fun in your life. Virginity doesn't guarantee a long and happy life, my friend. It doesn't guarantee a thing."

"It's not just a question of virginity," Fern said, a deep blush accomplishing naturally what all the cosmetics on Charlotte's counter could never hope to do.

"Then what is it a question of?"

"There's got to be more in the world than just sex. What about love, for instance?"

"What about it?"

"To be with a man just because he's got a you-know-what between his legs is ridiculous," Fern went on. "I'd rather be by myself. Then, at least, I know I'm not being used."

Charlotte quickly dropped the conversation, but was not at all pleased at having burdened herself with a dud. "As if I don't have enough difficulty meeting someone as it is," she mused.

"We might as well get something to eat," she suggested as she made her way through the crowd to the serving tables. Fern followed reluctantly just as Bruce, trying to balance two plates and a drink, turned around awkwardly and nearly knocked Charlotte off her feet.

"Oh, I'm so sorry. Excuse me," he said, his face almost as red as the nearby tablecloths.

"No harm done," Charlotte said, holding on to his shoulder for support. "How's the food?"

"The best I ever tasted. Those little liver things, I think they're called knishes, are delicious."

"How marvelous," she said, lifting two from his plate and popping them simultaneously into her mouth. "I just love little liver things."

He was about to respond when his eyes were drawn to Fern standing uncomfortably at her side. "I think someone's trying to get through."

"Oh, that's just Fern. Fern," she said, grabbing her roommate brusquely by the arm, "I want you to meet—"

"Bruce. Bruce Solomon."

"Hi," Fern said, barely lifting her head. He felt a surge of pity for the obviously unhappy young lady.

"And you must be the hotel's hostess, huh?" he asked, turning his attention back to Charlotte.

"Me? Goodness no," she said. "I'm just a virgin in distress."

"In distress? Why?"

"Because I'm a virgin."

Fat chance, Bruce thought.

"For Godsakes, Charlotte," Fern said.

"So your name's Charlotte."

"Charlotte's the name and fun's the game," she said, assuming a dramatic pose, "but first things first. Are you up here by yourself or is there a wife in the background shooting evil darts at me for talking to you?"

"No wife, not even a girlfriend. I'm afraid I'm as stag as I'll ever be."

"Isn't that a coincidence," she said, taking him possessively by the arm, "so are we."

Flo Goldberg excused herself from the group of chattering women and walked to the oak bar where Manny was gathered with his cronies. He was talking with a cigar in his mouth again, rolling it around lasciviously with his teeth while spots of brown saliva drooled over the top of his lower lip. It was thoroughly disgusting and for a moment she had to swallow hard to keep down the little cocktail franks. Finally she took a deep breath and pulled him away.

"What is it, for crissakes? Everything's got to be a mystery, a secret?"

"Relax, will you. I'm not going to keep you from your dirty stories. I'm just going up to fix my makeup. If I'm not back before the party ends, I'll meet you in the dining room."

"Your makeup looks good enough to me."

"Shows how much you know."

"Yeah, yeah. Okay, I'll meet you in the dining room." Suddenly he remembered something. "Listen, I left a package of cigars in the little suitcase. Bring 'em back with you when you come down."

"You know you can't smoke in the dining room on Friday, Manny. They keep *Shabbes* up here."

"Don't worry about it, huh? Just bring 'em."

He turned back to the group of men, said something quickly with a gesture toward her and joined them in a raucous laugh. She paid no attention, by now she was used to him, and hurried out of the room. When she stepped into the lobby she checked to see there was no one there she knew and, satisfied, walked in the direction of the service desk. Billy Marcus came out from the little office behind, buttoning his three-quarter blue bellhop's jacket from bottom to top. Having caught her attention, he looked around nervously, then came out from behind the counter.

"Good evening," Flo said smiling.

"Mrs. Goldberg. What can I do for you?"

"Do you think," she said, taking her room key out of her purse, "you could go up to my room and get a package of cigars from the small suitcase under the bed?"

"Sure thing."

"Many thanks," she said, handing him the key. As he walked to the elevator, she went over to the information desk, pretending to check for messages. Then she quickly followed him to her room. She had only to knock once.

"Hello again, Mrs. Goldberg," Billy grinned.

"We've got about fifteen minutes," she replied tersely, throwing her pocketbook on the nearest chaise. In a matter of seconds she had unzipped her cocktail dress, the underside of her upper arms jiggling unceremoniously as she pushed it down over her hips and clumsily wriggled out.

"Congress quickie, eh?" Billy said.

Flo didn't bother to reply. She was all business. Instead of working her girdle off, she unsnapped her stockings and folded the elastic material up over her abdomen so she could remove it at the same time she did her panties.

He just stood and watched. A curiously built twenty-two-year-old with a football player's shoulders and a matador's hips and ass, Marcus was a good six inches taller than Flo. His shiny blond hair had a thickly rich texture that gave testimony to his good health and virility. His tanned freckled face reminded her of a young Van Johnson.

Women had no difficulty molding Billy into their fantasies and Flo was certainly no different. Her favorite was to run her fingers up and down his erect prick, imagining at the same time that she was being seen on the new cinemascopic screens, so flesh-toned and life-like in 3-D that men in the audience had orgasms in their seats just at the sight of her.

It was time for Billy to get started. Methodically, he proceeded to kneel so he could play with her nipples. He closed his eyes, trying to lose himself in his own fantasy. Often while making love to one woman, he thought of making love to another. And then there were the times when he had to force himself to think about other things, just so he'd have the lasting power. Like last week when he made love to that pimply faced twenty-year-old daughter of a VIP. The whole time he replayed the last game of the 1956 World Series. But Flo was having none of it. She rushed him along.

"Christ, is this safe? I mean—"

"It's safe. Of course it's safe." She was tugging at his belt. "Manny's at the bar and he's going to meet me in the dining room in fifteen minutes."

"Hold on," he said. He had at least wanted to take off his uniform and get his pants neatly folded. But it was obviously too late. Dropping to her knees, she clawed down his jockey shorts and embraced his legs so savagely he nearly toppled backward on the bed.

"Hey, take it—"

"God yes," she moaned, mistaking the words for a request. She nearly choked on her enthusiasm. As her lips tightened, she thought she could feel the movement of blood through the tiny veins in the stem of his penis. It had hardened against her tongue. The realization made her dizzy. She released him and pressed her cheeks against his balls, inhaling the musty odor. Then she reacted to the vaginal wetness soaking through the crotch of her panties.

Impatiently, she pulled them off, dropping them like a flag of surrender.

"Quickly," she begged. "I can't wait."

Billy straightened up and then fell on top of her body. Her legs dangled clumsily over the edge of the bed. He set out to tease her, threatening entrance, then pulling away pretending disinterest. She was having none of it. She wanted him NOW, completely, totally, fully.

"Hurry up," she cried, "this is no time for games. I've got to be there before they serve the soup."

"Yes ma'am," he replied as if on cue. "At your service."

He entered her quickly, her arms pounding him lightly on the shoulder at first, then somewhat harder with a rhythm akin to the cha-cha—in, out, cha, cha, cha. One, two, one–two–three.

"Careful," he said between grunts. "Don't mess up my jacket. I just had it cleaned and pressed."

Afterward she tried to work the flush out of her face with cold water and fresh makeup. He was gone when she came back from the bathroom. She checked herself in the mirror, straightened up the bed, and left. When she reached the lobby, she saw people still going into the dining room. "Good," she thought, "I'm not late."

Suddenly she heard her name. She turned with a shock as Billy Marcus strode toward her, clutching something awkwardly in his fist.

"What is it?" she said breathlessly, her hands pressed tightly, almost protectively, against her hips. "What's wrong?"

"Your husband's cigars," he said, holding out the package. He leaned forward. "I thought you might have been joking but I decided to check the suitcase anyway."

"Thank God," she said with a sigh of relief. "It's a good thing you did. Thank you," she went on, loud enough for the elderly couple on the sofa to hear. "And this is for you."

She pressed something deep into his hand. Her fingers squeezed his for a moment, then, suddenly ravenous, she went off to join her husband.

Billy rubbed one palm against the other, then looked down to see what she had left. Would you believe it, he muttered with dis-

...71

gust, a lousy fifty cents. For all his effort, a goddamn lousy fifty cents!

Melinda caught Nick Martin's eye as he stood waiting patiently in the lobby. With the assurance of one who knows what she wants, she walked across the plush carpet never once breaking stride or taking her attention from his face. She knew a good find when she had one.

"I'm not late."

"No." She was one of the most striking women he had ever laid eyes on. "Shall we indulge?"

"In everything," she said, taking his arm and leading him past the nightclub toward the party.

Jonathan watched them enter the Gold room, checked to see that Ellen was where he could find her and went over to greet the two of them. Neither seemed happy at the intrusion.

"Good evening," he said, holding his hand out to Nick. "Glad you could make it." He turned to the lady at his side. "And good evening to you too, Miss—"

"This is Melinda Kaplan," Nick interrupted. "Melinda, this is Jonathan Lawrence, general manager of the Congress."

Melinda was both impressed and curious. Here Nick had only been at the hotel a few hours and already he knew the general manager. Mr. Lawrence had a reputation for avoiding guests at all costs. Whenever there were personal problems or complaints, he was known to leave the patching up to Mrs. Golden or Magda. "How did you ever get into the hospitality business, Mr. Lawrence? I understand you really don't like people very much." Melinda was nothing if not direct.

Jonathan felt his Adam's apple begin to throb, the way it used to when he was a kid and his stepmother discovered he had wet his bed again. "Not exactly, Miss Kaplan."

"It's Mrs. I'm divorced."

"I'm sorry. Mrs. Well, Mrs. Kaplan, it's not that I don't like people. Rest assured that I do. It's just that I have more important things to do than run around like a social butterfly. Hotels don't operate by themselves," he added pompously. "They need someone to control things behind the scenes, to make them work smoothly and efficiently so that people like you get the feeling the establishment runs itself." He had not been aware he had raised his voice and now as the music stopped he found himself, much to his embarrassment, the center of attraction. He cleared his throat quickly and turned to Nick.

"Mrs. Golden is across the room. Would you like me to introduce you?"

Nick looked in the direction Jonathan indicated, looked back at the nervous general manager, and shook his head. "No, I think not. This is no atmosphere for a serious conversation." His attitude toward Jonathan was distinctly peremptory. "I'm not interested in thirty-second cocktail chitchat."

"Um, yes, of course," Jonathan stuttered defensively. "You're quite right. We'll make it another time." Before he could finish his sentence, Nick and Melinda had already made off toward the bar.

Damn it, he muttered to himself, gulping down a glass of champagne. What the hell is happening to my control? Of all the times to . . .

"Hey," he said, spotting one of the bellhops at the entrance leaning against the wall, his jacket unbuttoned and hanging lopsided on his chest. He was talking to a teenage girl. "What do you think this is, a pool hall? Straighten up your uniform and find something to do." The girl gave Jonathan an icy stare. He moved on, feeling for the moment relieved.

"Excuse me one minute," Charlotte said, giving Bruce's forearm a little pinch. "I've got to go to the little girl's room." As she giggled and walked away, Fern had an immediate sense of panic. Charlotte had dominated the conversation until now and suddenly she had no idea what to say.

Bruce rubbed his arm and moved to her side. "Your friend's quite a character. Is she always this lively?"

"I don't really know. We don't hang around together all that much. It's our parents who are friends."

"I see." Bruce nodded slowly. "Is this your first trip to the Catskills?"

"Yes. I've never been to a place like this before." She sipped nervously at her drink.

"Me neither," he said, lighting toasting her champagne glass with his. Fern felt herself relax. This guy wasn't at all as pushy as she

. . . 73

had come to expect. There was something very unassuming about him, something quite natural and easy.

"I suppose it's still one of the best vacation values around, considering you don't have to pay extra for meals and entertainment," she said. "What was it you said you do?"

"Medical research. Lab work."

"That's a lot more interesting than what I do . . . bookkeeping."

"It may sound like it is, but most of the time it's like everything else—routines, filing, paperwork." He took a better look at this girl. She had such an attractive face, almost Levantine in structure. If only she wasn't so afraid of calling attention to it. Her lack of confidence was so obvious his heart went out to her. He felt an urge to hug her in his arms. If only someone could wake her up. He caught himself. He was at the Congress on business, not to play Pygmalion. "Would you like another?"

"Oh my," Fern said, looking down at her empty glass. "I think I'm drinking this stuff too fast."

"Don't fret. It'll help you loosen up. First experiences are always unnerving."

So he understood the way she felt, she thought, almost giddily. How lovely. "How can people eat so much," she asked, pointing to the couples going back for refill after refill, "with a full course meal waiting for them right around the corner?"

He laughed and shook his head. "Beats me. I guess they're making sure they get their money's worth. So," he went on, "where exactly do you live in the city?"

She answered and he asked another question. She began to talk more openly, about how she hated it when she lived with her parents, how she loved to listen to WOR's "Metropolitan Opera of the Air" on Saturday afternoons, and how much she liked Chinese food. They walked aimlessly around the Gold room, watching the people flirt and listening to the Latin music. It suddenly occurred to her that Charlotte was spending an awfully long time in the bathroom. She was glad.

Charlotte, in fact, was upstairs in the dining room trying to chase down the maitre d'. One of the headwaiters had gone in the kitchen to get him as she stood cooling her heels and watching the staff prepare for the invasion that would take place in a matter of minutes. The room was enormous, but thanks to a strategic placement of mirrors and balconies, it gave off an undisputed feeling of warmth and intimacy. The china and crystal glistened in the candlelight as the busboys and porters continued to make last minute gestures, polishing the silver, filling the relish and bread trays, putting the fresh flowers in vases, and setting up the coffee and tea service. The captains continued to see that the stations were in order and finally the elegant Mr. Pat, uncharacteristically harassed, hurried down the middle aisle. "I'm sorry to have kept you waiting," he said as he took Charlotte's hand in his and brushed it up to his lips. "We had a little confusion in the kitchen. A couple of dishwashers forgot to show up."

"I'm sorry to hear that. I'll only keep you a moment. Actually, I'm here for a favor. My girlfriend and I just met an old friend at the cocktail party whom we didn't know was going to be here. I was wondering if you could arrange for him to be seated at our table."

"Let me see," Mr. Pat said, looking at the chart on the top of his desk. "You are—"

"Charlotte Fein. And my friend is Fern Rosen."

The maitre d' perused the chart slightly longer than he needed. He knew the girls were already slated to sit in Siberia, the area furthest away from the kitchen and serviced by the least experienced help. He also knew they would not complain.

Seating arrangements at a Catskill resort were never left to chance and after many years Mr. Pat of the Congress had it down to a science. Most couples and families preferred to dine with each other, not too close to the entrance and not too far from the kitchen. Old timers were happiest right in the center or on the first balcony where they could oversee all that was going on. Older people preferred tables with younger folk, a desire not reciprocated by the younger ones. Singles only wanted to be with each other, even in Siberia, and if the chemistry at the table was right, they didn't mind if the service was slow. It gave them more time to get to know each other. Also, and not a matter to be taken lightly, they knew they would be able to get away with tipping less than their counterparts in the more distinguished areas.

Mr. Pat had a unique method for making the arrangements. Some time ago he had built a large peg board with large circles that represented the location of tables in the dining room. Using different colored pegs—blue for unattached males, pink for females, and yellow for couples, he would work up his strategy every Friday afternoon after getting copies of the check-in slips, balancing sexes, marital statuses, sometimes even geographical backgrounds to set up tables. He was firmly convinced that as many romances, affairs and marriages were due to the placement of his colored pegs as they were to Magda, the hostess's introductions.

"And the gentleman's name?"

"Solomon. Bruce Solomon," Charlotte said, stepping close to the desk and slipping a folded five-dollar bill in the hand closest to his pocket.

"There'll be no problem," he said with a smile, moving a blue peg from one circle to another a few inches away. "No problem at all. You'll all be at table 21."

"Thank you," Charlotte said. "It sounds just fine."

The jingle of the phone jarred Grant out of his trance. It was a trance built out of anger. Melinda had actually suggested that he take his meals in the Children's Dining Room. "You just wouldn't have a good time eating with a group of adults, Grant. You'll feel out of place." It wasn't enough that she had totally ignored him since the moment they arrived. Now she didn't even want him near her at dinner. Why the hell had she brought him up there in the first place?

"I'm not going to eat in any Children's Dining Room," he screamed. "I'm not going to eat at all if that's my only choice!" Finally she compromised and gave him money for the coffee shop.

Now the phone was ringing and his first thought was that she was calling to say she had changed her mind. Well, it was too late. He didn't care. Now he wouldn't eat in the dining room if she got down on her knees and begged.

"Yeah?"

"Yeah? What kind of way to answer the phone is that?" Sandi asked.

"I thought it was my mother."

"That's a heck of a way to talk to your mother."

"So what do you want?"

"Jesus, you're a hell of a conversationalist."

He leaned back, pressed his back to the wall, and slid down to the floor. "I'm just not in a good mood right now. Sorry."

"Forget it. I just called to find out what table you're at in the dining room."

"I'm not going to eat in the dining room. I'm gonna grab a hamburger in the coffee shop."

"How come?"

"It's a bore—sitting with all those stupid adults who just blah, blah, blah all over the place."

"You're still going to meet Alison and me later anyway, aren't you?"

"Why should I?"

"You'll see. It'll be fun. Be in front of the Teen Room at nine, okay?"

"Maybe."

"We'll cheer you up, I promise."

"Maybe," he said again. He hung up abruptly. How the hell did he know what he'd be doing in three hours? He wasn't even sure where he'd be in the next ten minutes. He walked over to the double windows and looked down at the cars lining up one behind the other. They seemed almost human to him. Where were they coming from? Where were they going? And why didn't anybody care about him?

seven

Billy Marcus literally lifted Sandi off her feet and turned her away from the pinball machine in the Teen Room. The half dozen kids watching the game looked up in shock.

"Hey, what are you doing?"

"Your mother wants you in the office," he said, a look of disapproval on his face.

"I've got to finish my game."

"Not any more," he said and leaned over to tilt the machine. Sandi marched sullenly out of the room and followed him into the lobby.

"Your mother's been looking for you," the receptionist hollered as she passed the front desk.

"You don't have to yell. I know. Big deal." She entered her mother's office and slammed the door behind her. Ellen looked up from her desk.

"What kind of way is that to come into the office?"

"Well, I was right in the middle of a pinball game and Billy Marcus tilted it."

"A pinball game? That's what you're in such a huff about?"

Sandi gave her a dirty look, then walked over to the couch and flopped backward, her skirt flying up past her knees. Ellen had been rehearsing her words all evening, wanting desperately to say the psychologically correct things, but one look at the obstinate expression on her daughter's face made them just tumble out.

"Where the devil were you this evening? I don't think there was one old-timer at the cocktail party who didn't ask for you. Mr. Teitelbaum was actually going to walk over to the farmhouse to get you."

"I wasn't there."

"I know. I called. Where were you?"

"Just walking around."

"Just walking around. I see. I thought we decided you'd be with me in the Gold room."

"We didn't decide. You decided. I said maybe."

"Do you think it was easy for me, standing all by myself, greeting all those people?"

... 78

"You weren't by yourself. Magda was there."

"You know I love Magda very much, but is she family?"

"Well, not exactly . . ."

"This was the first Fourth of July in fifteen years I've been without your father. We've always spent it together as a family and that was how we welcomed our guests at the start of the season. It was a tradition we started when you were three years old."

"I don't give a damn about tradition," Sandi said sarcastically.

Ellen struggled to keep her emotions under control. "Then just what exactly do you give a damn about? Pinball machines? Band singers? Is that all you care about?" She swiveled in her chair and looked out the window at the young couples strolling arm in arm on the terrace, seemingly without a care in the world. Then she turned around.

"I don't know if you understand," she said softly. Sandi caught the change in her mother's tone and looked up. "I'm going through a very difficult time now. I miss your father very much. To make things worse, I'm not even sure I'm capable of taking his place, being all things to all people here like he was. Most important, I'm afraid of losing you, too. And nothing means more to me in the world than you."

Sandi felt her eyes well up and looked away.

"I hate this hotel," she said angrily.

"Not really, honey," her mother said sympathetically. "I just think that right now you blame it for taking your father away from you. Sometimes I feel the same way, but then I think back about what Dr. Bronstein said. Remember?" Sandi shook her head. "That sometimes people die before their time and there's no logical explanation. It has nothing to do with their physical history or their work, it just happens, and there's nothing we can do but be grateful they were with us for as long as they were. Like Mrs. Teitelbaum was telling me this evening, sometimes we just have to accept things as God's way, no matter how difficult it is. It would be unfair to just blame the hotel."

Her daughter ran her fingers up and down the gold locket her father had given her for her thirteenth birthday. After a moment of silence her feelings erupted. "I was afraid to go to the cocktail party. I was afraid people would keep talking about daddy, saying how sorry they were he had died and all of those things." The tears started pouring down her cheeks. "I knew it would make me feel bad because it wouldn't bring him back and I didn't think I could stand to listen to them." Suddenly she bolted and ran into her mother's arms. Ellen held her as if her life depended on it, which, for the moment, she felt it did.

"I'm sorry, mama, I'm really sorry," she sobbed. "It's just that sometimes I get so confused. I don't even know what I'm feeling half the time."

"Hush baby, it's all right. Just cry and get it out." Their tears intermingled.

When Sandi finally pulled herself together she decided to ask her mother something that had been on her mind for days. "Maybe we ought to sell this place and get away . . . go somewhere where no one ever heard of the Catskills or the Congress."

Ellen laughed in spite of herself. "It's not that I haven't thought of it," she said, "but I don't think there's a place in this country where someone hasn't heard of the Congress, and for that you can be very proud of your father. Besides, I feel I have an obligation to his memory to at least try to keep it running the way he would have wanted it. It meant so much to him and he put so much into it. It just wouldn't be fair to walk away."

"But wouldn't daddy want to see us happy?"

"More than anything else in the world . . . but we're still not sure we can't be happy here. Let's make a deal," she suggested. "I'm not sure I can do it but I'm willing to give it a try under one condition."

"What's that?"

"That you give me a helping hand."

"Me? What can I do? I'm only thirteen."

"I'm not sure yet, but we'll figure something out. Right now what I need most from you is just to know you're on my side—that the Goldens are a team. If it doesn't work out here, we'll look into something else. Is it a deal?"

"Okay," she said tentatively. "I guess so." She stood up to leave.

"What are you going to do now?"

"I don't know. Go back to the Teen Room, I guess."

"Fine. And if you decide to go to Champagne Hour, let me know. Maybe I'll join you for a few minutes. As a matter of fact, why don't you check in anyway with me from time to time. Just in case I need you," she added with a wink.

"Will do," Sandi said as she left to meet Grant and Alison. For a moment, now that her mother was going to give her responsibility, she almost felt grown-up.

Ellen was just beginning to relax where there was a knock on the door.

"Sorry to disturb you, Mrs. Golden," her secretary said, "but I thought you'd like to know."

"Know what?"

"I was just talking to Buzzy Sussman, one of the porters. His sister is a Pink Lady up at Community General. They don't get paid, you know, but they help out around the hospital, bring juice to the patients and—"

"I know what a Pink Lady does," she said, trying hard to hide her impatience. "What does that have to do with me?"

"Well, Buzzy says his sister told him that the Chinese man who was sick died."

"What Chinese man?"

"A guy by the name of Tony Wong. He was one of the new custodians." Ellen recalled a vague reference Magda had made in the coffee shop, something about a new employee being hospitalized.

"What happened to him?"

"Buzzy's sister didn't know. All she said was that he was dead and his doctor told everyone not to talk about it."

That's odd, she thought. "Has Dr. Bronstein called?"

"Not since I've come on duty. Do you want me to call his office for you?"

"No," she said, looking at the small clock on her desk. It was 9 P.M. "We'd only get his answering service now. I'll make a note to call him in the morning. Thanks."

Ellen was pensive as her secretary left. It had been a long, hard day. The meeting with Jonathan, going through her rites of passage at the cocktail party, the scene with Sandi, now the death of an employee. It was almost too much for one person. More than anything else she wished she could just go home, put on some Bach, pick up a book, maybe even light the fire and have a pony of Courvoisier. Unfortunately, the night was young, even if she didn't feel she was, and there was more work to be done. The only saving grace was that by the time she was ready to lay her head down on her pillow, she'd be so physically and emotionally exhausted she'd drift off to sleep—that soft, gentle escape she'd welcome with open arms, if only for just a few hours.

* * *

The music in the Flamingo Room was so loud it could be heard two floors above. Garishly designed by an over-eager Francophile who thought tinsel, glitter and murals of Can-Can girls showing off their rear ends was the epitome of good taste, the nightclub was the one facility of the Congress that needed remodeling—fast. Phil had, in fact, already interviewed a number of architects and was about to make a decision shortly before he died.

Bruce, Charlotte and Fern sat high up at a corner table in one of the multileveled sections reserved for singles. They had been joined by a man they met at dinner, David Oberman, a twenty-eight-year-old CPA from Forest Hills.

David was a soft-spoken, unobtrusive man with large facial features, hair that was thinning prematurely, and a soft chubby frame that reminded them of the comedian Buddy Hackett. From what they had gathered at dinner, he came to the Congress often in hopes of finding "the right girl" but had never yet found anyone his mother thought good enough for her only son, the certified public accountant.

Bruce couldn't help noticing how Fern identified with Oberman, his awkwardness with people, his obvious lack of confidence, and it surprised him to discover he was jealous. The more Charlotte dominated the conversation, the more he felt it important to win Fern's attention. Charlotte, in turn, sensed Bruce's lack of interest and took it philosophically. It wouldn't be the first time and, rather than brood, she turned her attention to the newcomer. If not exactly her knight in shining armor, at least he was there.

"With all the times you've been here, David, I'm sure you've entered Champagne Hour at least once."

"Me? You've got to be kidding. I wouldn't enter a contest like that for a million dollars!"

"What kind of contest?" Bruce interrupted. He looked questioningly at Fern but it was obvious she didn't know any more than he.

"After the dance teachers finish their exhibition, they call for volunteers. Five couples to go on stage and do the tango, merengue, mambo, peabody, whatever they think they do best. When they're done, the instructors hold their hands over each couple and we, the audience, bang our 'knockers' on the table."

"Our what?" Fern almost fell out of her chair.

"Our knockers," Charlotte said, lifting the orange and purple sticks from her cocktail napkin. "What did you think I meant?" She directed her question coquettishly at David.

Fern looked the other way. "And then?"

"The winners get a complimentary bottle of champagne."

Bruce laughed and tapped his knockers rhythmically on the table. "Here, here!"

"So what do you say, David?" Charlotte asked, shaking him by his shoulder pad. "Are you game to take a chance with me?"

"You mean enter the contest?"

"Well, there are other things, but we can talk about them—later!"

Bruce and Fern looked at each other in mock exasperation.

"Well, I'm really . . . not much . . . good. I mean—"

"I won't take 'no' for an answer. There's nothing to it," she said. "All you have to do is follow my lead." She grabbed him by the hand. "C'mon, let's go down to the dance floor and practice."

Reluctantly, Oberman permitted himself to be pulled from his seat. Bruce and Fern sat for a few moments in silence, each wondering what the other was thinking. Finally he signaled a waiter and ordered more drinks. "She's something else, that Charlotte. Doesn't she ever get embarrassed?"

"She's really not that bad," Fern said. "You've got to understand her . . . her desperation. It affects different people different ways. Some pull back, others plow ahead like gangbusters."

"I'm not sure I understand."

"When you are a woman and you reach a certain age," she said, fingering the top of her glass, "there are certain pressures. People—sometimes it gets unbearable. I mean—" she looked at him directly and intensely for the first time. "You're never considered an individual, a complete person, unless you have a man. People think of you as something unfinished. That's why Charlotte is so desperate. She wants to feel complete." She took a sip of her drink. "I often wonder if there'll ever come a time when a woman can be respected for what she is, a real human being, just for herself." Bruce was staring at her with a half-frozen smile on his face. "I guess I'm not making any sense."

"On the contrary. You just amazed me, that's all. I guess I never thought of it that way before."

"It's why I didn't want to come up here in the first place," she continued, encouraged by what seemed to be genuine interest.

"Sometimes I get a feeling it's like a cartoon. Young girls come up looking for husbands and husbands come up looking for young girls. People are expected to play certain roles, be caricatures of themselves, and a woman isn't supposed to have a mind, just a bosom, ass and hips."

"Why can't you have them all?" Bruce asked. "I've never enjoyed going out with a mannequin who has cabbage for a brain, but I also have too much respect for the human body not to realize that needs are biological as well as emotional."

"I guess it's a matter of priorities," Fern said, verbalizing her feelings to a man for the first time. "I want to be appreciated intellectually before I give myself physically. With men, I guess it's the other way around."

"Don't be too sure," the researcher said with a smile. He didn't want the conversation to get too serious. "Sometimes we men can fool you. For instance, I bet you even think I know how to dance." He extended his hand and she took it. "Now, what is that," he asked, leading her onto the crowded dance floor, "a mambo or a cha-cha? I never can figure out the difference." He enjoyed the way her eyes twinkled and pulled her body tenderly close to his.

She didn't say a word. Somehow it just didn't seem necessary.

"So I'm here," Grant said. "What's the big deal?"

The girls had been waiting for him in front of the Teen Room, Sandi as sophisticated in her navy jersey and heels as Alison was dowdy in her dirndl and flats. "I win the bet. Alison said you wouldn't show up," Sandi said.

"What's the prize?" Grant asked, trying hard not to stare at the two little mole hills trying to erupt from her chest.

"You'll find out soon enough. It's a surprise."

"Okay. Surprise me."

Neither girl made a move.

"Well, are we going to stand around here all night like a bunch of idiots or are we going to do something?" he asked impatiently. He hated not knowing what he was doing.

Sandi looked around to make sure she wouldn't be overheard, then whispered. "Wait just a sec. Then we're going down to my secret hideaway."

"Hideaway? What kind of hideaway?" He was intrigued.

Sandi waited until the last elevator opened and nobody she

knew got off. "Okay, follow me," she said, leading them through the passage that connected the boutiques, dance studio, barber shop, makeup concession and beauty parlor. At the end was a door marked Exit that opened to a flight of stairs. Sandi and Alison entered quickly and waited for Grant to catch up.

"Hurry up," she chastized him. "The basement is off limits to anyone who doesn't have permission. My mother would kill me if she knew I was here."

"So would mine," Alison piped up.

Grant remained silent. His mother probably wouldn't give a damn.

"I have a secret room," Sandi said, starting down the stairs. "It's a storage room with a few old mattresses in it, but it's never used anymore. Except by me when I need to be alone."

"I'd be in there all the time," Grant said, but Sandi was too far ahead to hear him. Alison and Grant were both affected by her surreptitious behavior. When she got to the bottom, she put her hand up and they stopped on the last two steps. She looked down the long, gray corridor. The low, indistinct murmuring of custodians could be heard.

Other than that, the corridor was deserted. She gestured for them to follow as they passed various storage rooms, some used for dry goods, sacks of flour and barrels of powdered soap, others filled with tools and parts of worn-out machines. Grant looked up and stared at the steel girders running along the ceiling. Pipes and wires were crisscrossed all along the hall. He shifted his attention to the wide metal ducts that were turned up and through the ceiling of the basement. He imagined they were used for air-conditioning and heat.

About three quarters of the way down, Sandi stopped at a closed door and took out a key. Grant presumed this must be the hideaway she was talking about but his curiosity was even more aroused by what looked to be a carpenter's workshop at the end of the hall. Stage scenery, wooden horses, cans of paint, brushes, styrofoam cutouts of wells, animals and trees and hundreds of crepe paper ornaments were stacked next to and on top of each other.

"What's all that?"

"That's where they make the stage scenery for the nightclub shows," Sandi explained. Grant studied it for a moment as Sandi opened the hideaway door and snapped on a light. "Get in quickly," she urged, closing the door quietly behind them.

Grant could hardly hide his disappointment. The hideaway consisted of two rather dirty double mattresses on the floor, a half dozen more of the same stacked along one of the walls, two folding chairs, a few cartons, three shelves of comic books and old newspapers and a crumpled stack of what looked to be used wallpaper. Alison stood dumbly by, she, too, not quite sure what to make of it.

"So this is the big deal hideaway?" he sneered. "Jesus, what are we supposed to do now, somersaults?"

"Relax," Sandi said. "Wait a minute." She walked over to the mattresses stacked against the wall, knelt down and reached in behind them. Grant watched with interest. Alison stood by nervously biting her lip. In a moment, Sandi's hand came back out holding a giant bottle of Concord grape wine.

"I've got a few other surprises back here too," she said, putting the bottle down beside her on the mattresses. She reached in again and this time pulled out a pack of Lucky Strikes. Grant grabbed one eagerly and looked around for a glass for the wine. Not seeing any, he put the bottle to his lips and took a deep slug.

"Shit, I don't have any matches," Sandi said. "I forgot about them."

"Don't worry," Grant said, kneeling down beside her. "I have some." He smiled broadly for the first time.

"Close the door," Jonathan barked as he had done so often in the Marines. Gary Becker stifled the impulse to salute and proceeded to obey the order. "Well?"

"I did what you told me, Mr. Lawrence. Took the three of them straight to the Hotel Coolidge in Manhattan. The two Puerto Rican guys jabbered in Spanish all the way down and from what I understood, I don't think they were too happy about it."

"You just don't know your Spanish, Gary. I'm sure they were happy. Is that all?"

"I had problems with Margret Thomas."

"What kind of problems?" He looked up sharply and sat straight in his seat. The hotel chauffeur automatically shifted into a position of attention.

"At first she was just bitchin' a lot, snappin' at the Puerto Rican guys, cursin' them, you know. Then she started actin' funny. Said she had stomach pains, wanted me to pull into the first service station, so I did. She went to the can and when she came out she looked kind of

... 86

awful. Then I don't think we went more than ten miles when she says she has to go again and makes me look for another bathroom." He shifted his weight from one foot to the other. "You mind if I sit down, Mr. Lawrence? It was a helluva lousy trip."

Jonathan pointed to a chair.

"So I pulled into another place. Naturally, the Puerto Rican guys start complaining about all the stops. She curses the hell out of them and goes into the ladies' room. We wait and wait. It takes her a lot longer this time. She comes out looking a lot worse too."

"You made it into the city though, didn't you?"

"Oh, yeah, Mr. Lawrence. Like I said, we finally got to the Coolidge, but not before she made me pull over two more times. Then, coming over the George Washington Bridge, all hell broke loose. I think she messed in her pants because it stunk something awful. The Puerto Rican guys were screaming bloody murder and she was too weak to even talk back. Thank God by that time we'd reached midtown."

"You can skip the rest of the details, Gary. Most important, did you see her go into the hotel?"

"I was just getting to that," he said. "The Puerto Rican guys went in, I'm positive of that. But I could have sworn that as I pulled away, she was headed up the street away from the place. What the hell is this all about anyway?" he blurted out. "I mean, why did I drive those three into the city without any of their belongings?"

"I'm paid to ask the questions," Jonathan said brusquely. "You're not." He pulled out a black leather wallet from his pocket. "Here's an extra fifty for what you had to put up with."

"Gee, thanks, Mr. Lawrence, but . . ."

"And if Monday comes and you've kept your mouth shut, there's an extra twenty-five where this came from."

"Mum's the word," Gary said, getting up to leave. "I can't even remember where I went myself."

"That's fine." Jonathan rose and walked him to the door. "If anyone should ask, just say you took them to the bus depot and dropped them off. You have no idea where they went after that. Simple as that."

"You're the boss. Whatever you say." He opened the door and slipped out quickly, his thoughts spinning. First he had taken Tony Wong over to Dr. Bronstein's and then the Chinaman's roommates were whisked off to New York with a chambermaid. By the time they got there, she was sicker than anyone he had seen in a long time. Something about it didn't make sense. As he started the engine of his car, he wondered if he should dig around some, maybe even make a call to Dr. Bronstein. Then he remembered the extra seventy-five dollars. Better to leave well enough alone.

eight

    Breakfast at the Congress was often as elaborate as dinner in a fancy metropolitan restaurant. Besides the fresh fruits and appetizers one would normally expect, there were eighteen different varieties of herring to choose from, pickled, marinated, kippered and matjes the runaway favorites, every conceivable kind of smoked fish and lox, freshly baked Danish, bagels, bialys, matzos, onion rolls and cinnamon rolls, imported jellies and marmalades, cheeses of all nations, cereals, pancakes, waffles and a selection of egg styles to satisfy the most fickle of morning stomachs. Busboys and waiters, themselves somewhat subdued from a night of partying, moved in a mechanical, trancelike manner, taking orders quietly and walking robot fashion through the swinging doors to the kitchen. Each time the doors opened, those seated nearby were treated to a cacophony of sights and sounds. Dishes clanked, chefs screamed and waiters jostled for position, anxious to be the first to get their orders filled and diners fed and out so they could catch up on their sleep before setting up for lunch.

    On this particular Saturday morning, even the guests seemed unusually quiet. The conversations were down to a whisper, the laughs few and far between. Elderly people sat like tolerant monarchs sipping their hot water and prune juice and listened with a quiet wisdom born of similar experience to the tales of the night before told by the younger people at their tables. Married couples hardly exchanged a word as they picked lackadaisically at their food.

    At the head of the dining room, Stan Leshner reached under the desk for his hand mike. The six-foot four ex-New York Knick had been Director of Activities at the Congress for six years. Though not classically handsome, more a Charlton Heston type than a Paul Newman, his piercing green eyes radiated an excitement and energy that was electrically contagious. He was a man of action, never walking when he could run, rarely standing still, and moving with the fierce determination that flows from a sense of purpose. He was almost obsessed with the idea of making people happy, with making sure they had a good time, and he was extremely successful at what he did.

    His main job was to encourage, cajole and, if he had to, harangue even the most reluctant guest to participate in the myriad activities offered by the hotel. He also scheduled athletic competitions, conducted "Simon Says," arranged for and introduced guest lecturers and artists, ran an athletic and recreational department larger than many public schools and oversaw a staff of counselors who directed the children's day camp. It was the kind of job that left little time for social life.

"Looks like some of our guests had too much Champagne Hour last night," he said to Mr. Pat.

Pat looked around at the half empty room. "Maybe you should delay your announcement a few minutes."

"Can't," Stan said. "If I do, I'll mess up my schedule and I'm running late as it is." He plugged the microphone jack into a cable and checked the papers on his clipboard. After blowing into the mike to make sure it was on, he began to speak.

"Good morning ladies and gentlemen, may I have your attention please. I'm Stan Leshner, your Director of Activities, and I'd like to give you a quick rundown of what we have in store for you this morning." There were some loud groans from tables on the first balcony. "In half an hour, we'll be gathering on the Grand Patio on the front terrace for a vigorous twenty minutes of calisthenics and after that, I'll be leading you in a session of the worlds famous "Simon Says." Those interested in golf and tennis lessons . . ."

Fern stopped in the lobby just outside the entrance to the dining room and looked up at the small sign that indicated the direction of the beauty parlor. "I think I'm going to make an apointment," she said to Charlotte. "Right after breakfast."

Charlotte studied her friend with amusement. How things had changed in the last twenty-four hours! She noticed that Fern took much more time with her makeup and hair this morning, showing impatience and dissatisfaction when it didn't come out the way she wanted. She had borrowed Charlotte's off-the-shoulder top that was tapered at the waist and showed off her bosom to great advantage. That, together with the white striped bermudas that hugged her hips in a most affectionate way, proved that she did indeed possess quite a lovely figure.

"This wouldn't have anything to do with a certain Bruce Solomon, would it?" Charlotte asked. "You two did seem kind of cozy on the dance floor last night."

"I just thought I'd take a little of your advice, Charlotte dear," Fern said, mimicking one of Charlotte's frequent postures. "If you want certain things to happen, sometimes you have to make them happen!" They both burst out laughing.

"Welcome to the female race!" Charlotte beamed. "Now let's get going. I promised David I'd meet him at breakfast and I don't want to keep him waiting."

Upstairs in his room, Bruce jumped out of the shower to answer the phone. It was Sid Bronstein and the sound of the doctor's voice shattered the memories of the night before with Fern. It took a few seconds to switch gears.

"At least we made it through the night," Sid was saying. "I can't tell you how nervous I was every time the phone rang."

"Maybe we nipped it in the bud," Bruce said. "The only people who apparently had significant contact with Tony Wong have been shipped to a New York hospital for observation and I'll put in a call to the city after breakfast to see if there are any results on his specimen. If we're lucky—" If we're lucky, no cholera, no epidemic, and the rest of the weekend free to spend with Fern.

"Yeah, if we're lucky," Sid echoed. "You know, maybe Jonathan was right after all. Incidentally, have you seen much of him or Ellen?"

"Haven't even met her yet. She was at the cocktail party last night but he made no attempt to introduce us."

"That's strange. Anyway, I'm glad you went to the gala. After all these years, it's about time you saw how the other half lives."

Bruce laughed. "Figured I'd enjoy what I could while I had the chance." He was about to tell him about Fern, then thought perhaps it was best to keep it to himself.

"I'll try to drop by later," Sid said, "so we can get together and see where we stand. Call me as soon as you hear from the lab."

"Will do," Bruce said, his thoughts suddenly turning to Margret Thomas. If Wong's specimen was positive, they'd have to get that information to Ellen's New York doctor immediately. As a potential carrier, every second counted. But what if he couldn't locate Jonathan? It grated on him that the manager was acting as an intermediary; it seemed such a stupid waste of time. But then again, the Congress was really Sid's bailiwick. His cousin had always been as good a politician as he was a physician, expert in finessing people and complicated situations. Bruce could only presume he knew what he was doing. He reached for a towel.

"Good morning," Jonathan said, speaking into the phone box on his desk. "How'd you enjoy—"

"Have you gotten a response from Ellen Golden yet?"

"Why no. I told you yesterday it might take a little time."

"Well, I've decided I don't have a little time. Set me up with her in an hour."

"But I don't know—"

"Know. If you still want to be part of our operation, that is."

"I'll get right on it." He switched the phone box off sharply. Damn! He needed to locate Ellen fast. There was no time for sweet talk. He'd have to sit her down and paint the blackest, bleakest picture of the hotel's finances that he could, even exaggerate, if need be. Then he would lead her to Nick Martin, who he'd present as a savior. In the end, they would both be grateful to him.

When he got to her office he found her in conference with Artie Ross, the entertainment director for the hotel. It was apparent from the way they both looked that they had been discussing the house band's negotiations for a new contract. Artie had been with the hotel nearly twenty years now and it was the first time he had had trouble with either the unions or management.

"I was just going to send for you," Ellen said. "Artie says Phil promised the new musician's contract would be signed before the Fourth. He and the boys didn't feel right about pushing for it these last few weeks, and I appreciate the sentiment," she added, nodding to Artie, "but I don't understand your procrastination."

"The house band has been talking about playing only one set for dancing if they have to play for the show," Jonathan said, "and frankly, I vetoed the concept. It's not fair to the Latin dance band to have to play three straight sets. It's also not fair to us because according to union rules, if they do we have to pay them double."

"But you vetoed it without discussing it with me first," Artie said quietly. "Without even seeing if there was some way we might compromise."

"There can be no compromise when expenses are at stake," Jonathan said. "In fact, Ellen, that's why I'm here. I was hoping we could have a brief conversation about the economic situation. It's extremely important and perhaps if I explain our circumstances to you in greater detail, you'll understand what we're up against and why I sometimes have to do the things I do. I'm sure Artie will excuse us." He turned peremptorily to the entertainment director.

Artie looked to Ellen for instruction.

"Maybe he's right, Artie," she said somewhat hesitantly. "Let me meet with him now and I'll get together with you sometime this afternoon. I promise."

He gave her a smile of encouragement. "Okay, I'll call you after lunch. I'm sure we can work something out."

"Before you start, Jonathan," Ellen began as Artie closed the door, "it's important to me that you know how I feel about certain things. I'm not saying I have any special expertise in financial matters or any of your experience in management. But one thing about this place I do know is that it has been as successful as it is largely because the Goldens have always treated their staff as members of their own family, with courtesy and respect even when they disagree. It means looking at both sides of an issue and it also means not making decisions without discussing the pros and cons with the people involved, like with Artie just now or Moe Sandman yesterday. The end result is loyalty and it's one of the most valuable cogs on which the hotel runs."

"That attitude might have to be compromised somewhat, Ellen. Happy families and loyalties don't always pay off, especially when money is concerned. There comes a time when we have to face up to reality." He spoke with great confidence. "Last year wasn't as great a season as most people think, as you well know. I don't want to list all the mortgage notes and creditors right now but on top of what we owe, we've already committed ourselves to more expansion—"

"Jonathan." She held up her hand in an attempt to stop him, but he continued to speak.

"We don't have to debate hotel philosophy right now but you've got to face the facts. We need a financial transfusion and we need it badly. If not, there's a possibility we'll go broke." He stopped to let the words sink in.

"Broke?" she asked incredulously.

"That's right. Broke. Out of business. Kaput. Our old sources have either dried out or they've given up on us." From the look on her face he realized she had never known how serious things were.

"We need a new well to draw on and if there's one thing I can take credit for, it's knowing where to turn in an emergency. I've found some investors willing to speculate on us, to take a chance. One of their representatives is right here on the grounds and if it's possible, he'd like to meet with you now."

"Now?" Jonathan nodded. "Who? I mean, representative—of what?"

"Let him explain himself. Phil knew about him, was planning on meeting with him." It was, of course, a lie, but he was shrewd enough to know the effect it would have.

"I don't know. I—"

"Just listen to him Ellen, please. There's no harm in listening." He came the closest he ever had to pleading and she was genuinely touched. Perhaps, in his own way, he was more loyal than she had given him credit for. Besides, she had just lectured him on listening to both sides. Now, perhaps, it was her turn.

"What's his name?"

"Nick Martin. He's a businessman from Manhattan and as I said, he has a proposal even your husband was interested in."

"What about Artie Ross?"

"The nightclub is one of the few areas of the hotel where we're making money. If we have to pay overtime to the musicians, it will cut back our profit margin. From a budgetary point of view, it just doesn't make much sense."

"All right," she sighed. "I'll talk to him about it later. Maybe we can have the Latin band back the dance and novelty acts and the house band back the singers. Then no group plays straight through and everybody gets to take a break."

"Sound fine with me. Now I'll go find Nick Martin and bring him in."

Ellen took a deep breath and slumped down in her chair, drained of even the little energy she had had earlier in the day. And it's only the beginning, she realized. She looked up at the display of pictures on the right wall. Some were of Phil alone, others of him or the two of them with celebrities, still others of celebrities alone. But the picture dearest to her heart was taken on the day they were married fifteen years before. No superstars, no Broadway or Hollywood celebrities, no famous politicians or authors, just the two of them on the threshold of sharing a whole new experience together. Well, now there was just one. And somehow she knew she'd have to find the strength to carry on.

"What are you going to do, Grant, sleep right through breakfast?"

Her son turned over and pulled the cover over his head. Melinda slammed a dresser drawer and slipped into her new one-piece tennis outfit, the one with the abbreviated shorts. Satisfied with the way the material clung to her body, she went into the bathroom to put the finishing touches on her makeup and hair. He lowered the cover enough to peek out.

A small, pin-like pain made its way across the lower part of his forehead just above his eyes. It felt better when he closed the lids but the moment he raised his head, an explosion like a time bomb going off occurred at the top. His mouth was unbearably dry, his tongue and lips the texture of sandpaper. He presumed it was now Saturday morning. He had no idea how much he had drunk the night before in Sandi's hideaway, though he was sure it must have been a lot. Alison, he remembered, had left shortly after they arrived. It all came back to him in a haze.

"I'll smoke a cigarette," she had said, "but I don't want any wine. It always upsets my stomach."

"You don't know what you're missing." He grabbed the bottle from her chubby fingers. It looked so revolting, the way he slobbered over it when he drank, that Sandi was almost reluctant to put the same bottle to her mouth. When Grant passed it over, she wiped the neck with the hem of her dress and from where he was sitting, he could see straight up to her crotch. The sight of her cotton panties made quite an impression. In his mind's eye he saw it as a piece of adhesive, barely covering her adolescent vagina which he fantasized as having little or no pubic hair around it.

She took a short sip and passed the bottle back. He fell back against the stack of mattresses and straddled it between his legs, his right hand firmly grasping the neck. The two girls sucked at the cigarettes with such intensity it made him smile.

"Do you have a girl friend?" Sandi asked.

"Lots of them," he said with false braggadocio. "I don't stay with any one girl."

"My mother told me I couldn't go steady until I was a senior in high school," Alison said. She was just holding her cigarette now, letting it burn away between her fingers.

"Goin' steady is for kids," Grant said.

"How far do you think kids our age should go?" Sandi asked. Alison wished they could talk about something else but Sandi held her gaze steady. Grant's eyes darted quickly from side to side, as if he felt trapped. His fingers moved up and down the neck of the wine bottle nervously. He took another sip.

"It depends on the situation. I know some girls who go all the way on a first date."

"Really?" Sandi turned to Alison, who in turn looked horrified.

"Oh yeah. Of course none of us go out with them more than once," he added and laughed. He drank again. Over half of the quart was gone.

"Let me have some," Sandi said. Her face was beginning to

flush, as were all the nerve endings in her body. She threw her head back and took another swallow. Alison played nervously with her cigarette.

"Aren't the girls afraid of getting pregnant?"

Grant shrugged and took a long drag of his smoke. "The way I see it," he said, not looking directly at either of them, "that's not my problem. If they want to go all the way, they gotta worry about the consequences."

"That's not fair," Alison said. "They can't get pregnant by themselves."

"Nobody's forcing them."

"You ever wondered if you were an accident?" Sandi asked, looking from Grant to her girl friend.

"I know I was," Grant blurted out. Both girls grew wide-eyed. He rambled on. "My mother didn't want any kids. She always tells me how I nearly ruined her figure. My father says she kept her weight down so low when she was pregnant I nearly had brain damage when I was born."

"When did they get divorced?"

"About three years ago." He took another slug of wine. His eyes were glassy now. Sandi thought he looked as though he might cry at any moment. "He caught her with another man."

"Oh, my God," Alison said.

"That's really tough," Sandi said sympathetically, touching his shoulder ever so lightly. "Really tough." For a long time no one spoke.

"I think I'd better get upstairs," Alison finally said, realizing from the looks Sandi and Grant were giving each other that they probably wanted to be alone. "I told my mother I'd meet her at Champagne Hour."

"You're kidding."

"No, I really gotta go." She stubbed out her cigarette on the floor.

"Don't let anyone see you going out of here."

"I'll be careful," she said. "I promise."

Sandi closed the door behind her and noticed that the bottle of wine Grant held in his hand was now almost empty.

"Want another cigarette?"

"Not right now."

"Alison's a little immature."

"Not up here," he said patting his chest. He smiled widely.

Sandi laughed, uncrossed her legs and sat back on her hands. He thought about her vagina again, once again imagining it denuded of pubic hair. He knew that a girl her age would have to have at least some, but he could only think of the female sex organ in terms of his mother's. Someday he would have to ask her why she shaved herself down there if he could just figure out a way so that she wouldn't know he watched her undress and studied her body so carefully.

Sandi, at the same time, was thinking about Margret Thomas and the scene she had witnessed the night before. "You ever read *Lady Chatterley's Lover?*" she asked.

"Naw. I don't read much."

"It's got some great parts in it. I'll show you tomorrow." He didn't reply. He was too dizzy. "You sure drank a lot of that wine."

"Huh?" He held the bottle up to his face. "Yeah, so what?" He took a final sip to empty it and fell back on the mattress.

"You're all right, aren't you?"

"Sure, Sandi-handi," he giggled.

She wished he hadn't had so much to drink. She wished it hadn't got so late. Obviously this wasn't going to be the best time to experiment with sex. "You're not too drunk to walk, are you?"

"Shit, no. I just don't feel like moving."

"I'd better put that bottle back," she said, taking it abruptly from his hand. He looked up at her with a wide grin, reached over and grabbed the back of her lower leg.

"Gotcha," he said, laughing loudly.

"Shh. Someone might hear us and I'll be up the creek." She took his hand away from her leg but held it in hers for a moment. "Let's take a walk outside. You'd better sober up before you meet up with your mother."

"Hell, I won't meet up with her until morning."

Sandi stood up, tugging gently on his arm. He pushed himself forward and let her lift him to his feet.

"Whooooeeeeee. Why is the room spinning?"

" 'Cause you're having a good time," she laughed, slipping his arm around her shoulder.

He remembered thinking she was pretty. The gardenia scent of her hair, and the softness in her face. She was delicious in a delightful, but confectionery, sort of way. When he looked at her he wanted to twirl her hair around one of his fingers, to brush her forehead repeatedly with his lips. He wanted to press the tips of his fingers into the lines of her neck until he sensed the pulsation of her blood.

They left the room, giggled together and walked out of a side basement door that opened on the lawn between the pool and the main building. He stumbled stupidly beside her for a while until the dizziness passed and he was left with only a dull pounding in his head. They parted with a promise to have another rendezvous in the hideaway the next night, this time without Alison whom he had drunkenly nicknamed "Alison Tits."

Now, the morning after, as he lay snugly under the blanket, he resurrected images of Sandi, the way her nose curved up slightly at the tip, the candy-coated lipstick, the suppleness of her budding breasts. His fingers moved to his penis but it didn't stir into the erection he anticipated. He held the limpness between two fingers of his right hand and moved them up and down, back and forth. The only reaction was a slow, very slow, tingling sensation but still no hardness at all.

Then Melinda came out of the bathroom, bubbling and talking a mile a minute. She was going down to breakfast and then she'd play a game or two of "Simon Says." After that, she was scheduled for a tennis lesson. When the lesson was over, she was coming back to the room to change into her bathing suit and go to the pool for the buffet.

"How do I look?" She turned to check herself in the mirror. The skirt of her tennis shorts barely covered the bottoms of her cheeks.

"Great. Just great."

"You could sound more enthusiastic. Now get up and have some breakfast," she said as she waved and walked out the door. He listened to the silence. The scent of her perfume lingered. He sat up and dangled his legs over the bed. For a few moments, he just stared into her bedroom. Then he went to her dresser and reached into the top drawer to scoop out a pair of her bikini panties. It was a struggle to get the silk material over his thighs but he had a slim build and finally succeeded.

The tightness growing in his crotch felt good. He closed his eyes and fell forward onto her bed. Then he took her pillow and shoved it down between his legs. He moved slowly at first. Then an exquisite heat started to build in his loins.

He stopped, as if to tease himself. This is wrong, he thought. It's not only wrong, it's sick.

But I can't help it, he replied to the Puritan voice, and what's more, I don't want to.

He moved faster and faster until he came in short, magnificent jerks.

As usual, his first reaction was guilt. How many times had he promised himself, made deals with himself that this wouldn't happen again?

A shower brought a bit of relief. The feeling of cleanliness quieted his conscience, but it didn't erase the memory. He put the pillow back in place and tried to smooth it out.

Tonight, he thought, tonight she'd put her face against it. It was crazy, but the very realization brought a new excitement to him.

"Just a minute," Charlotte said. Bruce and Fern stopped, then moved to the side of the aisle as she approached the maitre d'. Bruce thought both girls had been markedly different during breakfast— Charlotte had been uncharacteristically quiet and restless, shifting her attention to the entrance every time a guest walked in and Fern suddenly complained of little appetite and seemed to be forcing herself to pay attention to his conversation. The little life that came to the table was sparked when Fern mentioned her intention to go to the beauty parlor and visit the cosmetician.

"She's going to pull a *My Fair Lady,*" Charlotte said. "I think she thinks you're Professor Henry Higgins."

"I've been called worse," Bruce said, his mouth widening in a grin. Fern's face lit up for the first time that morning. "And remember, we have a tennis date after lunch."

She nodded but he didn't sense the enthusiasm he had hoped would be there.

"Excuse me," Charlotte said. Mr. Pat looked up and smiled, remembering her kindly from the night before. "Did a Mr. David Oberman, by chance, make different arrangements for his seating?"

"David Oberman?" He picked up his list. "No, he's still down for your table, table 21. No change."

"That's curious. He hasn't been down yet." She looked over her shoulder to see if he had come in while she was talking.

"There's nothing unusual about that," Pat said. "Guests often sleep late when they enjoyed themselves the night before. That's one of the pleasures on vacation and one of the reasons why we serve until eleven."

She looked down at her watch. "But it's almost a quarter of."

. . . 99

"What can I do?" He shrugged, looking at Bruce and Fern. "It must have been some night." He called over a captain from a table nearby. "It's been kind of spotty all morning."

"Is that unusual?" Bruce asked, moving closer to the desk.

"Well, now that you mention it, yes. There are a lot of people who don't like big breakfasts but most manage to drop in for at least a little something."

Bruce turned and looked back over the dining room, noting the many empty seats and setups that had not been disturbed. He felt a surge of suspicion.

"Why don't you give him a call, Charlotte?"

"Who me? Chase a man? No way." She thanked Mr. Pat and they went into the lobby.

"Are you sure you don't want to check his room?" Fern asked. "Just to make sure he's all right?"

"No. It really doesn't matter." She tried unsuccessfully to camouflage her hurt. "I'm going back to the room for a minute. You run ahead to the beauty parlor and tell them you want to be stunning! She will be, too," she said, turning to Bruce. "You're in for a treat!"

"I can't wait," he said as he waved the two of them off. Then he went directly to one of the house phones. The operator came on in a matter of seconds.

"Connect me with a Mr. David Oberman, please. I don't know his room number."

"Just a moment, sir." He gazed around the lobby as he waited, watching the men and women with tennis rackets, bathing gear and golf clubs slung over their shoulders make their way to the fresh outdoors. He wished he could be one of them. After a moment he heard the line ring. He let it buzz five times and was about to hang up when Oberman finally answered.

"Hello," he said weakly.

"David?"

"Yes."

"I didn't wake you up, did I, buddy? It's Bruce Solomon. From last night."

"Oh yeah. No, I wasn't asleep."

"The girls were kind of wondering what happened to you this morning. I think Charlotte was disappointed when you didn't make it down for breakfast."

"I know. I promised to meet her there but I gotta tell you, I'm feeling pretty rotten. Must've been something I ate at dinner or the drinks or something. I've been throwing up all morning."

Bruce held the receiver so tightly against his ear he felt pain. For a moment he didn't utter a sound.

"You still there?" David asked.

"Yeah, sure. What's your room number?"

"Four-twelve. Why?"

"I'll be right up."

In two seconds he was in front of the main elevator which looked like it was stuck on the third floor. He was about to run up the back stairs when the doors finally opened and he barged in, bumping clumsily into two overdressed elderly dowagers on their way to the art class. They glared at him angrily and he muttered an apology. He banged the "four" button hard with his fist. "Let it be too much to drink," he repeated. "Let it be too much to drink."

nine

"No one plays cards 'til four in the morning!" Flo Goldberg slammed the bathroom door behind her. Manny groaned as he bent down to put on his shoes. The layers of fat rippled down his abdomen, spiraling into wider and wider circles as they descended. Naked from the waist up, his upper body seemed to contain an old inner tube, deflated and soft, running over itself. His excess flesh dropped over his pants waist. In order to tuck in his undershirt, he had to press the palms of his hands firmly against his abdomen and take a deep breath. The material strained at the seams. He stood up and ran his fingers through his hair, looking like a man in a daze.

The shrillness of her morning voice lingered in his ears. From the moment his eyes opened, she was at him. After the Champagne Hour was over he had left her to go to the Card Room. She had gone up to their room without him. He promised it would only be an hour. Despite the fact that he was quiet when he came in and didn't put on a single light, she was awake the moment his overweight body hit the bed.

"It's four in the morning, Manny." He grunted and turned his back to her. "Bastard," she said, but it was already too late. He was in a deep sleep. In the morning, she picked up the argument.

"I've come home late after playing cards before," he said, turning to the closed bathroom door. There was no response. He went to one of the opened suitcases and took out a shirt. As he put it on, he thought about that beautiful blonde bar waitress with the small birthmark just above the cleavage of her breasts. Before the night was over, he had probably stuffed over a C-note's worth of five-dollar bills into that valley of promises.

"How much does it take?" he had asked.

"How much do you want?"

Everybody roared. That's my kind of broad, he thought, not out to put you down, not teasing and then turning you off, but a straight put it on the table, lay it on the line, broad. He'd stand in line for that one.

His wife opened the bathroom door. Dressed only in her bra and panties, she sauntered to the closet. Still thinking about the barmaid, he came up behind her and cupped her ass in his palm. She jumped away instantly, as if his hand was on fire.

"What's the matter?"

"Why didn't you find your way in early enough last night if you wanted some of that?"

"Aw shit," he said and turned toward the bathroom. She smiled to herself. It had always been good strategy, always good technique. Most of her girl friends did it too. The rule was that if you were having affairs, fooling around, you continually accused your husband of the same thing, made something out of every possible opportunity he had, and read something into everything he said. Then he'd be so busy defending himself, he'd never have the time to spot your own little escapades. So far, knock wood, it had worked.

She slipped into her beige-and-brown pinstripe pinafore, the one that was the rage for women in their twenties, and stepped back to admire herself. Not bad for a forty-four-year-old woman, she thought, a woman with a married daughter and a son in his first year of law school. Sure, she was a little chunky at the thighs and a small flabbiness had begun to form under her upper arms, but continuous exercise and dieting kept her from slipping away and falling into the netherworld where dwelled "the women of no return." It was her way of categorizing so many of her female friends who had gotten careless and let their bodies go to pot.

She knew they still looked at her with envy and she was proud of that. Indeed, her vanity was one of her rationalizations for her extramarital relationships. If it weren't for those periodic affairs, she might easily lose her self-image and neglect her figure. She certainly wouldn't have kept it up for Manny's sake. Look at him, look at the physical mess he had become. He was so out of shape that whenever they did indulge in one of their infrequent sessions of lovemaking, he moved like a man recovering from a coronary.

Thinking about lovemaking brought a flush to her face. Just once she'd like to be able to be casual with a man as vibrant and virile as Billy Marcus, the young bellhop, instead of rushing to find a meeting place, rushing to have a climax, and then rushing to get back to her husband. But that was one of the sacrifices one had to make when one had a demanding husband and son.

When she thought more seriously about it, she was always intrigued by the mysterious way offspring could escape the worst in their parents. How she and Manny had ever produced such a genius as Bernard she'd never understand. It must have had something to do with the genes of their forefathers. It certainly wasn't handed down from them. She had been little better than an average student in high school and Manny had barely graduated, yet Bernard had the IQ and aggressive personality of a man destined to succeed in whatever he chose. She sensed that Manny was somewhat uncomfortable with his son, even resented him in many ways because the son was everything the father was not. No matter how Bernard tried, the lines of communication were closed, yet Manny loved him probably more than life itself.

She suddenly became aware that she was scowling at herself in the mirror. Her eyelids drooped and her mouth soured at the corners. She took a deep breath and forced herself to smile. Later she would get a mud pack treatment and sauna at the health club, maybe have a session with the cosmetologist too. She'd buy all the help she could get.

Flo Goldberg had always thought of her body the same way she thought of her wardrobe. It was adjustable, changeable, and something to be manipulated. She could take it in here, tone it up there, color it differently at one spot, trim it at another. It wasn't quite yet the era of disposable parts, but there were certainly ways to rejuvenate what one had. Concern about her body and her looks took up an enormous part of her daily life. Bernard accused her of being vain but he was still too young to know how it felt to cross the one-way bridge into middle age.

"What am I doing?" she mumbled as she looked at herself in the mirror. Without thinking, she had pressed her palms against her breasts. She dropped them and spun around quickly, in anticipation of Manny's entrance from the bathroom, but he wasn't coming out. The noise she heard was strange. "Manny?"

She walked to the doorway and listened. It sounded almost as if he was choking. She knocked on the door.

"What the hell are you doing in there?"

"Nothin'." he croaked in a raspy voice. "Go down to breakfast without me. I'll be along in a while."

"Really, Manny, are you throwing up?"

"I just got the dry heaves, that's all. I'll take a bicarb."

She lingered for a moment, thinking. Then she checked her watch. The dining room was due to close in ten minutes.

"Some card game," she yelled into the door. She picked up her purse from the small table near the bed and headed out. She heard him heave again, hesitated, and then thought "serves the bastard right."

After that, she left.

Ellen stood up behind her desk and reached over to shake hands with the tall, attractive Nick Martin. Jonathan, who had just introduced them, stood at his side, looking more like an interpreter and translator than a general manager. Finally he sat down on the black vinyl couch to the right of her desk. Nick took the seat to the left. He tapped a cigarette out of his gold-plated case and offered one to Ellen. She shook her head and sat back.

"Jonathan describes you as an investor, Mr. Martin," she said. She hoped her voice didn't betray the nervousness she felt. Business negotiations were still one of the areas of the hotel's management where she felt insecure.

"Call me Nick, please." His smile reminded her somewhat of Richard Conte's, confident, bordering on cocky. There was something about him that made her feel uncomfortable. Suddenly she was reminded of something Mama Golden used to say. "First impressions may not be de best, but dey remain mit you de longest." Her first impression left something to be desired.

"Let's come right to the point," she suggested, holding herself tensely in the chair. Instinctively she felt bluntness was the best tack for someone who felt unsure of herself. Bluff him with a facade of toughness. "Why are you or the people you represent so anxious to pour money into the Catskills at this particular time? The whole area is in a state of decline. We've been hurt by jet travel, packaged tours, the growing popularity of Mexico and the Caribbean, everything."

"Let's just say I represent people who specialize in bringing places back to life." His eyes twinkled, the smile freezing on his face. There was only the slightest movement of his head toward Jonathan who sat back, trying to look nonchalant and relaxed.

"I hope you understand, Mr. Martin . . . Nick . . . that even though the Congress, despite its popularity and reputation is somewhat of a marginal operation at the moment . . ." She paused, congratulating herself for the use of the term "marginal operation," "I am not out in the market actively soliciting investors."

"I understand that completely," Nick said. "And we're not out actively soliciting just any hotel." He sat back to let that sink in. "I'm thinking of the future and I'm sure you are too. If certain situations come to pass, it just might be important for you to be able to get financing so you can expand and take advantage of them."

"I assume you're talking about the possibility of gambling coming to New York State."

"Precisely."

"The most logical place to have it would be in the Catskills," Jonathan butted in. "It's already got the reputation and its own built-in hospitality industry."

"You have all the basic facilities needed to make the Congress the showcase of the state, possibly the entire country," Nick said. "Now I don't want to give you, or you, Jonathan," he said, turning to him, "the impression that the people I represent are in the habit of throwing their money around. We've done a good deal of preliminary research and a number of marketing studies." He smiled again. The smoke traveled up from the cigarette between his fingers. Ellen noted the strong, yet at the same time casual way he conducted himself. Do I look like an easy mark, she wondered? He made her conscious of her nervous foot movements under the desk. She stopped them immediately.

"Almost all of the hotels in the Catskills are in a transitional state. Those that don't make the appropriate changes, open themselves up to new customers, will be out of business before the decade is over."

"Some of them are already on their way out," Jonathan added.

"You need to prepare for the possibility of gambling, Mrs. Golden, no matter what your personal reservations about it are. Until then, you need to expand, update, and construct more facilities—luxury suites, auditoriums, rooftop dining rooms, things that will attract convention groups. It's a vast market, one that you people in the Catskills haven't even begun to tap."

"I'm not sure I agree with you that gambling is the wave of the future for us, or conventions either," Ellen said, her eyes growing smaller. "Our operation may well be marginal at the moment, but somehow or other I'm sure we'll come through. You may consider us old-fashioned, Mr. Martin, but we're a family operation and we're proud that we've built on a foundation of tradition. Why, my in-laws—"

"But that's exactly why my people have chosen you," Nick interrupted. "We want to buy a hotel that combines the best of the Catskill's past with the potential of the Catskill's future."

"You want to *buy* a hotel?" She wasn't sure she had heard

correctly. She looked at Jonathan but he was mute. Then she turned to Nick. "Am I to understand that you're interested in buying out the Congress?"

"There is that possibility, yes. It is one option, if our offer to become silent partners doesn't appeal to you."

She was nonplussed. Why hadn't Jonathan prepared her for this? Of course she'd had her fantasies about selling out, right after Phil died. She'd said as much to her daughter the night before, but. . . At the same time, somewhere deep inside there was a voice speaking. It said that, in her position, no one would blame her for taking the easy way out. After all, it declared, it wasn't her background and tradition. She had just married into it. It wasn't in her blood the way it was in Phil's.

And what about Sandi? Her precociousness, the continuous exposure to all the sexual hijinks going on at the hotel . . . all of it crying out for strong parental guidance, guidance she might not have time to give as long as she had a hotel to run. Was it worth more to her than bringing up and guiding her own daughter?

Then another voice took over, reminding her how much she loved the hotel. It had been her home, a good one, for over fifteen years. The staff, the guests, were like a family to her. The Congress, whether she wanted to admit it or not, was a part of her life too. Perhaps not as longstanding a part of hers as of Phil's, but a great part nevertheless.

She was faltering. The longer she remained silent, the weaker she knew she appeared. For a few moments she was unable to speak.

"Well, I . . ." she smiled wanly and shook her head. "I honestly don't know what to say. This comes as quite a surprise, as you can well imagine. I don't want to close the door on either of your offers but at the same time . . ."

Even that was more than Jonathan had led Nick to expect. "I don't want to push you," he said. "It's not like walking into a department store to buy a suit of clothes. We both have to look into a lot of things. I just wanted to make my intentions clear and give you something to think about. In the interim, you might have some loans or notes that you can't handle." He shot a quick look at Jonathan. "To protect our potential investment, we might be persuaded to extend money to you at a lower than usual rate of interest. Just to keep the vultures away," he added, smiling. She was confused about the reference to loans she couldn't handle and was beginning to hate his smile.

"Ellen doesn't know all of the economic details yet," Jonathan cut in. "She's had to move in rather quickly and our accountants are still preparing an analysis for her perusal."

"We're also in the middle of the biggest weekend of our season," Ellen added.

"Of course. I know this is a busy time for you and I don't want to take any more of your time. Why don't we set a date for another discussion, say the middle of next week? I'm sure both of us will have many questions we'll be wanting answers to."

"All right," Ellen said. "Make the arrangements with Jonathan and he'll keep me informed."

Nick nodded and stood up. Jonathan practically jumped to attention.

"It's been a pleasure meeting you, Mrs. Golden. Not only do you and the Congress live up to your reputations, you surpass them." He certainly knows how to turn on the charm, Ellen thought as she stood up and reached out to shake his hand again.

"Thank you," she said, turning on some charm of her own, "If there's anything you need to make your stay more comfortable, please feel free to call on me anytime."

Nick nodded to Jonathan who followed him out. They stopped just a few feet from the main desk.

"Not such a tiger after all," Nick said. "More like a pussycat. I thought you said she'd never even entertain the idea of selling out."

"She surprised me," Jonathan said. It was an understatement.

Nick eyed him suspiciously and reached for another cigarette. "Here I expected to be up against a brick wall and I find myself talking to a very gracious lady who is quite open to suggestions." He shook his head disapprovingly and Jonathan did not miss the message. "I hope your business acumen is better than your evaluation of people. I'd hate to think we were considering investing in someone who . . ."

"I swear to you, a week ago the woman barely tolerated discussions about conventions and legalized gambling, much less. . . Something must have happened—"

"Well, perhaps you should get to work and find out exactly what. In the meantime, send that file you prepared on the hotel's financial situation up to my room. When the time comes to talk to her again, I want to be totally prepared."

"Of course."

"And no more mistakes," he added pointedly, crushing his butt into the rug with his heel. Before Jonathan could respond, he moved away and headed toward the elevator.

"Let's go sit under that tree over there," Sandi said. Grant put his head down and followed the two girls as the three of them crossed the driveway and walked toward the old, sprawling maple tree near the chain-linked fence that divided the highway from the hotel's grounds. Much to his displeasure, Phil Golden had had to fence in the Congress more than ten years ago. It was the only way he could guarantee his guests exclusiveness. Without some sort of security, too many outsiders could simply walk in and take advantage of the hotel's facilities without paying.

Not too far away, they were able to see a group of nearly eighty people gathered on the terrace about to begin a game of "Simon Says." Stan Leshner stood on a small wooden platform, mike in hand, and explained the rules. "All commands preceded by the words Simon Says, you will obey. All others you will not." Sandi and Alison stopped walking when they noticed Grant had slowed down to listen.

"What a dumb game," he said. "My mother won last time we were here."

"Then she can't be very dumb," Sandi countered. "It's not as easy as it looks. It takes a lot of concentration and coordination." They continued to watch as the director of activities, placing his hands on his shoulders, ordered "Simon Says hands on shoulders. Hands on shoulders place!" His audience dutifully placed their hands on their shoulders. He waited five seconds. "Okay, hands down."

He pointed to a fat lady in the first row who had dropped her hands to her side. "See, if we were playing for real, you'd be out because Simon didn't say to do it. Got it?" There was some nervous laughter and kidding from others who had dropped their hands, the kind, though you could never tell from his face, Stan had heard countless times before.

"Look at them," Grant sneered, "a bunch of idiots. Monkey see, monkey do."

Sandi studied his face for a moment. "They're just trying to have a good time. What's wrong with that?" He didn't bother to respond, just stuck his hands in his pockets and continued walking toward the tree. Alison shook her head.

"I think he's a little crazy. Maybe we shouldn't be hanging around with him."

"He's not crazy, he's just got some problems, that's all," Sandi said. She suddenly turned on Alison, her eyes ablaze. "Not everybody's got it as lucky as you do . . . with a mother and father and everything. . . ." She turned and started after Grant.

"What's that supposed to mean, Sandi? Sandi?" Alison rushed to catch up with her.

Sandi couldn't say what she meant or really understand why she had turned so angrily on her friend. All she knew was that she felt a strange kinship to this weird, new boy who walked around the hotel with a continuous scowl on his face, ridiculed everything that was going on, and resented just about everyone he met. She recognized the anger in him but in a curious way, she felt she understood. Being at the Congress made Grant feel like a nonperson. It was obvious even his mother didn't want him around. Sandi was luckier. She knew her mother loved her, but even she wasn't quite sure what kind of person she was at the Congress. Being the daughter of the owner affected the image everyone had of her, including her own. School was the worst.

She hadn't planned it that way but she did have more facilities at her disposal than the average kid could even contemplate. Not only that, she met celebrities with the same frequency her friends met each other. She had letters and autographed pictures, and almost every day she came across tidbits of information gossip columnists would give their eye teeth to have. But whenever she mentioned these to her friends at school, not out of a desire to brag but from a need to share her everyday life, she was accused of name dropping and met with envy that often bordered on downright hostility.

By the same token, these same so-called friends would vie for her favor in subtle and not so subtle ways. Who would she invite to the hotel this weekend? Who would be able to swim in the indoor pool in the middle of winter? Who would get to eat in the hotel dining room? Who would be lucky enough to spend an afternoon in the hotel's Teen Room? But there was no one around to answer her own question. Who could she trust to like her for herself and not for what she had to give?

As a result, not surprisingly, she began to resent the hotel and talked against it to anyone at school who would listen. She complained about the lack of a real home life, bitched about the guests and wished out loud she had a normal childhood like everybody else. When she discovered the kids were laughing behind her back, she began to withdraw.

Only recently Ellen had been warned about her daughter's changing personality. "It's not terribly serious right now, Mrs. Golden," Keith Spier, the guidance counselor at the local school, began during the informal hour after parents' night, "but a number of teachers have remarked about Sandi's way of relating, or not relating, to the other students. She doesn't seem to be able to trust anyone, to get close. She's become more of a loner than we think is healthy for a youngster of her age. It's a bit strange, considering she's exposed to so many people at the hotel."

Ellen was very disturbed that she didn't noticed it earlier. At the Congress, as far as she could see, Sandi had no trouble adjusting and seemed to have friends. When she repeated the conversation to Phil he nodded, tucked in his lower lip and promised to direct more attention to her. But it was like so many other promises, heartfelt though they may be, destined never to be kept.

Grant sat back with his back against the tree and began pulling out clumps of grass. Sandi lowered herself to sit beside him. Alison remained standing, staring off across the hotel's lawn. The parking lot was located just across the road and they all turned as a carhop spun the wheels of a guest's car, spitting up gravel and burning the rubber so hard they could smell it from where they were.

"I bought the book," Sandi said. Alison had a question mark on her face. Grant began chewing on a blade of grass. She took it out of the back pocket of her jeans. It was wrapped in brown bag paper so no one could see the title. Grant made a grab for it and pulled the paper off.

"*Lady Chatterley's Lover.*" He looked up at Alison. "I think my mother wrote this book." Sandi and he laughed but Alison, feeling very left out, turned away, shaking her head. "These the pages, where you got the corners turned down?"

"Uh huh."

" 'And she held the penis soft in her hand,' " he began.

Alison began to blush. "Stop that," she said. "You're not supposed to read that kind of stuff out loud."

He looked up at her and then turned to Sandi, who now wore a wry smile on her face.

"What's with Alison Tits?"

"CUT THAT OUT!" Alison stamped her foot. Sandi looked up, fighting to subdue her laughter. Grant continued to read.

" 'And she quickly kissed the soft penis. . . .' "

... *111*

Alison was disgusted and trotted off, heading back to her parents in the main building. She moved awkwardly over the lawn, the small heels of her shoes sinking too deeply into the sod, causing her legs to wobble. Grant laughed very loudly.

"She'll never talk to me again," Sandi said.

"No loss."

"And she'll tell her mother, who will go and tell my mother."

"Big deal."

"I'm beginning to think she's right. You're nothing but a juvenile delinquent."

"So? Why don't you run off too?"

She wasn't sure. She found herself staring at him, both thrilled and frightened by his anger. Part of her wanted to go, but a stronger part of her, the part stimulated by the words in the book, by the mysterious urges in her young body, wanted to stay. Before she could reply, they heard a strange sound coming from behind them, in the parking lot. They turned to see what it was.

One of the gardeners had his hand braced against the side of an automobile as he leaned over. He was retching up his guts. It had the deep, hollow sound of a clogged sink drain.

"Ugh." Sandi stood up. Grant laughed again.

"Too bad Alison had to miss this."

"Let's get out of here," Sandi said, starting away. "C'mon." Grant watched the gardener a moment more, fascinated with his misery. Then he closed the book and stood up. After a moment's hesitation, he followed her.

It took David Oberman an extraordinarily long time to come to the door of his room. Bruce was conscious of the fact that he was practically pounding on it. An elderly man and woman down the corridor stopped and looked his way. He tried to relax, reminding himself that he had a responsibility to keep calm. The moment Oberman opened the door, Bruce knew they were in trouble.

The chunky man's face was so pale his lips had practically lost all hue. His eyes were glassy and bloodshot and it obviously took great effort to keep them open. The lids hung as if ready to spring shut at any moment. He was dressed in a very faded white tee shirt and an obviously hastily put on pair of pants—the zipper undone, no shoes or socks. His hair was disheveled, strands of it sticking out like porcupine quills. He backed away from the entrance, swaying slightly as he did. Bruce stepped in quickly and closed the door.

"I . . . guess I . . . fell asleep since you called."

"Since I called? I just called!" Bruce reached out and took his arm. "C'mon, you'd better get back to bed. How many times have you thrown up?"

"Five, six, I've lost track. But now nothing comes up, it's just dry heaves. Ohhhh . . . my stomach. . ." He made an attempt to rub it and he stumbled. Bruce kept him steady, guided him to the bed, and helped him lie back. Then he went to the phone.

"This is Bruce Solomon. I'm in Mr. David Oberman's room. I want you to get hold of Dr. Bronstein and have him call me at this extension immediately. If you can't reach him, call me back and let me know." He spoke so quickly, Rosie didn't have a chance to deliver her messages. Finally he paused for a breath.

"Mr. Solomon, Dr. Bronstein has been trying to reach you too. We paged you only a few moments ago."

"Well, call him back."

"I can't. He said he was on the way from his office to the hotel to see a guest."

"A guest? What guest? Who?"

"What guest? Just an ordinary—"

"Who?"

"I'm looking at the message, Mr. Solomon. Yes, here it is, a Mrs. Bluestone, room three fifteen."

He hung up before she could continue and just as quickly, the phone jingled again.

"Mr. Solomon?" Rosie asked.

"Yes."

"You hung up before I could give you the other message."

"Other message? What other message?"

"The one from New York. I don't know what it means but someone named Burt from your lab called long distance, no last name, just Burt, and he simply said to give you one word."

"What word?"

"Positive." There was a moment's silence. "Mr. Solomon? I'm sorry, but that's the whole message. Positive. I did ask him twice if there was anything else, but . . ."

"No, no, that's all right. Unfortunately, it's enough." This time he lowered the receiver more slowly, staring ahead at David Oberman who lay back on his bed, his eyes closed, clutching his stomach and moaning.

Somehow, Bruce thought, the world had gone haywire. Suddenly a series of events had occurred, despite the odds and percentages against it being overwhelming; a modern, twentieth-century resort had been thrown back through time, and delivered into the grip of an ancient plague that makes its home in the midst of poverty and degradation—everything the Congress was not. The irony was not lost on him, but he had no time to ponder its meaning.

ten

"I'm very worried about her," Mrs. Teitelbaum said as she came out of the bedroom, her hands clasped tightly and pressed against the bottom of her chin. Her husband looked up from the small cushioned chair. He bit his lower lip gently and nodded. His thick, bright white hair glistened under the light of the standing lamp on his side. Upset though he was, he was still a striking gentleman, one whose age, if anything, had added character to his robust facial features. At seventy-one, he was the patriarch incarnate, fatherly and authoritative; the kind of man who never publicized his wisdom, but whose advice was regularly sought.

"We've already called the doctor. We can't do much more than wait."

She shook her head and sat down on the small couch across from him. In contrast to her husband, she was a study in fragility, petite and delicate where he was sturdy and strong, but in her case, the appearance was deceptive. Although long retired from the leadership of many clubs, organizations and causes, her accomplishments on behalf of the underprivileged were documented at length in *Who's Who* and other respected anthologies. Hers was a history of dynamic action, and unlike many of her contemporaries, she refused to let age slow her down.

"I feel responsible," she said.

"That's nonsense," he chided. "How could you be responsible?"

"I was the one who talked her into coming up here in the first place."

"You did it as an act of charity. It was the only solution. You saw how enthusiastic Tillie and Harry were when you made the suggestion. If she didn't get away for a few days she would have driven them crazy. After all, family is family, but," he lowered his voice, "I'm sure it hasn't been a bed of roses for them. You know yourself that Martha Bluestone was never easy to live with. Did you forget all the aggravation she gave Gordon, he should rest in peace?"

She shook her head. "There's no point in dredging up the past. You think it's the flu maybe?"

"How should I know? I'm not a doctor. I never called one to

...115

help me try a case in court and no doctor ever called me for advice with a patient."

"I'm surprised," she said, not unkindly. "You have an opinion on just about everthing else."

He chuckled and shook his head. Mrs. Teitelbaum looked toward the bedroom.

"She's so exhausted from vomiting, poor dear, she can't even lift her head off the pillow."

"So quickly it happened. Yesterday afternoon she was full of vigor, wanting everything her way, as usual—screaming at the bellhop for handling her luggage too roughly, demanding a table in the dining room with the young people. Suddenly—"

"You think it could be food poisoning?" his wife interrupted.

"Bite your tongue. That's all Ellen needs now, someone spreading such a rumor in the hotel."

"I'm not spreading a rumor. I'm talking to you. Talking to you is not spreading a rumor," she said.

"We all ate the same things," he said in response.

"She said it started very early this morning."

"So there you are. If it was from the food, the two of us would probably have come down with it by now too."

"Then what could it be?"

"Patience, my dear," he said. "The doctor will be here soon and he'll tell us, I'm sure."

They heard a moan from the bedroom and looked at each other anxiously. Mrs. Teitelbaum quickly got up and went in to her friend. The old man stood up slowly, wishing there was some way he could alleviate some of her pain. His wife reappeared before he could even prepare to act.

"She's messed the bed something awful and has terrible stomach cramps. Call again for the doctor." He nodded and went to the phone.

"Good morning. This is Mr. Teitelbaum in room three fifteen. I called earlier for a doctor for Mrs. Bluestone and . . . good." He hung up the receiver. "She said Dr. Bronstein is in the hotel and on the way up."

When he heard the knock on the door he seized the knob quickly and opened it. Bruce Solomon stood there nervously, dressed in a sweatshirt and slacks. Blanche Teitelbaum stepped forward.

"You're the doctor?" she asked somewhat incredulously.

... *116*

"No, I'm his cousin. I'm meeting him here. My name's Bruce Solomon. I'm . . . a lab technician and I thought I might be of some assistance."

"Thank you, but the operator just told me the doctor should be here at any moment."

"Who's sick?" Bruce asked, ignoring Mr. Teitelbaum for the moment.

"Our friend, Mrs. Bluestone."

"Stomach trouble?"

"Yes," Sam said quickly. He looked at his wife and then back at Bruce. "Why? Are there other people here with the same problem?"

Before Bruce could reply, he heard the elevator doors open and stepped out to intercept Sid. The moment he saw the expression on Bruce's face, he knew the worst had happened.

"I got my call from New York ten minutes ago. You were right about Tony Wong. The lab confirms he died of cholera." Bronstein nodded without speaking and entered the room.

"She's in there, doctor," Mrs. Teitelbaum said, opening the bedroom door. Bronstein went in quickly without speaking and closed it behind him. Sam sat down restlessly on the couch but Blanche remained standing, staring at Bruce.

"Is there something going on here we should know?" she asked straightforwardly.

He motioned for her to sit down, then said quietly, "Very possibly . . . but we won't know for sure until Sid finishes his examination."

Blanche's eyes grew narrow. She could smell trouble a mile away. Slowly she moved to the couch and sat next to her husband.

"We're all in some danger, aren't we?" she asked, but without the slightest note of panic in her voice. Bruce was impressed with her control.

"Yes," he said, his voice full of sadness, "yes." They all turned as Bronstein reappeared.

"Call down for an ambulance," he said, looking at Bruce and shaking his head sorrowfully.

"There's another one in room four twelve," Bruce said. "His name's David Oberman."

"Another what?" Mrs. Teitelbaum interrupted. "Exactly what is going on, Dr. Bronstein? Mrs. Bluestone is our best friend. We brought her up here with us. Certainly we have the right to know." Bronstein hesitated. "We are also close, longstanding friends of the

Golden family, doctor. If there's food poisoning at the hotel, I can assure you we're not about to announce it on the public address system."

"I'm not sure it's food poisoning," Sid finally began. "It might be something worse." He tried to choose his words with care. "I won't know until we run some tests. I just received the necessary antisera . . . but someone on the staff has died of cholera. Your friend's symptoms, unfortunately, are quite similar to his."

Mrs. Teitelbaum brought the palms of her hands to her cheeks. Her husband opened his mouth as if to speak but it occurred to him that, for maybe the first time, he didn't know what to say.

"There are two precautions you must take," Bronstein went on, looking first at Mr. Teitelbaum and then at his wife. First, I want you to go back to your room right away and scrub your hands vigorously. Secondly, and this is very important, we don't want to do anything that will set off a panic. I'm sure you understand how important that is. I'm asking you, for everybody's sake, not to say a word about this to anyone until we have a chance to contact the proper authorities. They, in turn, will take whatever actions are appropriate."

"But . . . is it contagious? How widespread . . . are my wife and I in any danger?"

"We're not sure," Bruce said in all candor, "but we'll be in constant touch." He lifted the phone to call the ambulance.

"I'll go up to Oberman," Bronstein said, picking up his bag and moving toward the door.

"I'll meet you there. I left the door unlocked. Hello," he said to the operator, "this is Bruce Solomon. I'm calling for Dr. Bronstein."

Sam Teitelbaum reached for his wife's hand but she quickly pulled it back.

"I've got to wash up."

Bruce caught the look of terror in her eyes. He knew it was about to begin.

As Nick Martin came around the corner of the hall corridor, he reached out and instinctively caught the two-year-old tow-headed youngster just as she was about to fall backward on the carpet. Her giggling stopped the moment his hands braced her forward.

"Whoa there," he cried. He lifted her straight up and then down again. She was silent until her feet touched the ground. Then she started to cry.

"What are you crying for, Amy?" her mother asked, walking

toward them quickly. "The nice man stopped you from falling. I'm sorry," she said, her eyes widening as she looked at the dark-haired man in front of her. She tugged down on her slipover blouse and reached out blindly for little Amy's hand. The baby hugged her mother's leg, but continued to stare up at Nick.

"No harm done," he said. He tapped the little girl softly on the top of her head and walked on. The instant he moved away, she broke free once again and toddled merrily down the corridor.

Nick stopped in front of Melinda's room and checked his watch. For assignations like this he preferred being late. Better they should wait for him. He paused, then knocked at the door.

She was standing there wrapped in a large beach towel, the ends tucked in loosely at her breasts. The skirt of the towel ended just above her pelvis. Her face was still flushed from her last set of tennis, but it hardly detracted from her beauty. On the contrary, it created a sexiness all its own. She smiled and stepped back to let him in.

"You did say your tennis lesson would be finished at eleven-thirty," he said. "If I'm early . . ." Damned if she wasn't playing the same game as he.

"No, not at all . . . it's just that things got so backed up at the courts we ran late. I haven't even had a chance to shower." She looked at the clock on the end table and smiled at him warmly. "Please, come in. There's a draft."

He moved in quickly and closed the door behind him.

"Looks like you got in a lot of exercise," he said, touching his hand to her wet cheek.

"It was great. Too bad you couldn't join me." She pushed her hair back with both hands and the towel slipped, revealing more of her breasts and the crevice between them.

"I had some business to take care of," he said. He was going to reach for a cigarette but changed his mind. His attention was riveted on the little tuck in the towel. There were more exciting ways of getting gratification.

"Just what is your business, Nick? You make it out to be so mysterious."

"It's nothing mysterious," he said smiling. "As I just said to someone this morning, you might say I make a profession out of bringing things back to life."

"Do I look like I'm dead?" She was challenging him and he loved it. He stepped forward and brought her body to him. She lifted her face to meet his lips. As they kissed, she undid the tuck in her towel. The terrycloth material dropped quickly. Her naked body felt small but comfortable in his arms. She moaned as she twirled the bottom of his earlobe in her fingers. He knelt down and scooped her up in his arms to carry her into the bedroom.

Gazing down at her as he began to undress, it occurred to him that she was one of the most delicious packages of sensual pleasure he had ever seen. Her firm, full breasts quivered only slightly as she turned to greet him. Her small waist turned with gentle lines into hips that were slim and perfectly proportioned. But something was out of sync. It eluded him for a full five seconds. Then he realized, almost with a shock, that she had no pubic hair. Much to his astonishment, it turned him on.

As he kissed and fondled her body, the strangest images formed in his mind. He was king of the universe and she his nubile slave, a vestal virgin who had never been with a man before. It was like making love to a fantasy, she was so compliant, so in tune with his directions and desires. He was able to mold her into whatever sexual experience he wanted.

Her left hand cupped his balls almost as if she were weighing them. Her forefinger and thumb encircled the top of his prick and began to move up as far as the tip, then down to the bottom. The friction hardened him, swelling him to his full size. She was kissing his neck, working her way down to his chest, moving with even more energy and intensity than he. The inexperienced partner of his imagination had suddenly turned into a professional, and although he hadn't been in a whorehouse for more than twenty years, he found himself recalling, with great gusto, one of the most exciting experiences of his life.

By now Melinda had turned their lovemaking around so that it was she who was doing the molding. He wanted to draw back and assume control again but she wouldn't permit it. Instead she clung to his torso with desperation, intertwining his thighs with hers and pressing her pelvis forward. He felt the moistened vaginal lips and became aware, once again, of the surprising smoothness. She must shave every damn day, he thought, and fantasized about the scene.

Finally he mustered up enough strength to push her back so he could mount her the way he wanted to. She relinquished, this time without resistance, and he entered her swiftly, easily. She brought her legs up and wrapped them tightly around his lower back. They fell into a vigorous steady rhythm. She closed her eyes and wagged her head from side to side, moaning softly. Her lips parted, her tongue sought contact. He brought his fingers to her lips and teased her by running them along the rim of her mouth. Then he touched her tongue and she took his forefinger between her lips and sucked on it.

She screamed with each climax. His power to bring her to such a pitch of excitement turned him on even more. He tried desperately to hold back and keep himself from coming but they were into such a perfectly synchronized movement his body simply flowed on. He exploded in long, deeply satisfactory spurts, pressing and pushing forward with each one.

When it was over he turned on his back to catch his breath. Her eyes remained closed but the look on her face was a testimony to how pleasing and satisfactory their lovemaking had been. The throbbing in her neck continued.

"Tennis always get you in such a mood?" he asked.

"Everything gets me in the mood."

"I'll have to remember that." He looked at her seriously. "You know, I really don't know much about you."

"About as much as I know about you," she said, sitting up.

"But I do know I need a shower." She stood up and turned to him, beckoning him with her finger. "C'mon, I'll wash your back."

"Sounds good to me," he said, letting her help him to his feet. "As they say in my business," he gave her a pat on the rear, "one hand washes the other."

When Grant opened the door, a few seconds later, he was confronted immediately by the sight of Melinda's bath towel, crumpled on the carpet. He stared for a moment, then listened. He heard the shower going but intuitively knew something unusual was going on. He walked further into the suite until he was confronted with a man's slacks and jacket draped over the chair near the bed. By now he didn't have to strain to hear the muffled laughter and whispers emanating from the shower.

He pushed the bathroom door open ever so slightly and through the transparent shower curtains saw the silhouettes of his mother and a man. She was kneeling. He was leaning over, his hands on her shoulders. Suddenly her head started moving back and forth. Grant wanted to get closer, but the realization of what she was doing enraged him. He felt a flush come into his face and he was unable to swallow. Choking from anger, he ran hastily from the scene.

Once out in the corridor, he experienced a series of chills. A salty taste brought the realization that he had bitten down hard on his tongue and drawn blood. He spit out at the wall.

He looked about with the panic of a cornered animal and focused on the stairway that led to the next floor. In a spurt of anger and frustration, he lunged at the steps and took them in threes. When he got to the next floor he ran to the next, and the next, and the next, until there were no more stairs to climb.

At the top, though he could hardly catch his breath, his energy, insane as it was, increased. Standing there, looking to see if there was a window he could fling himself out of, images of the sex scene began flashing before him again. The man's erection, his mother's mouth . . . the same mouth she used to kiss him goodnight.

He buffeted himself from one side of the wall to the other. Suddenly his wild gaze focused on the fire extinguisher hanging near the stairwell. Satisfied there was no one else around, he moved forward and ripped it off the wall. Cradling it in his arms like a baby, he carried it until he reached the far end of the corridor. Every floor of the hotel had at least one or two small rooms set aside there for the storage of fresh linen, vacuums and ironing boards. Grant had noticed them the first time he had come to the hotel.

Almost without thinking, he brought the nozzle of the fire extinguisher to the largest bin and pointed it in. Then, as if to destroy everything that was neat and clean, he pressed the extinguisher. The white foamy liquid shot out first in short, then in long spurts. Grant blinked his eyes and gasped with each spurt. When the extinguisher was spent, he checked the hall again and carried it back.

Then, almost as if possessed by a demon, he ran down to the sixteenth floor, the fifteenth, then the fourteenth, and thirteenth and twelfth, until he was finally on the second, as spent and drained as were all the fire extinguishers he had emptied.

The only thing he wanted to do now was to curl up in the warm sun and go to sleep.

Fern had never been so happy that something had ended. The whole time the cosmetician and beautician had been working on her, her stomach churned in despair. Probably just nerves, she thought. No one had ever pummeled her face and pulled her hair like that before, and it made her uncomfortable. She was grateful when it was over and she could get up and walk away.

Having arrived early for the hairdresser, she decided to stick her head in next door and see what was happening at the makeup class. She rarely paid attention to what she used on her face but today, to her amazement and amusement, she found herself fascinated by the different kinds of moisturizers, powders, lipsticks, eye shadows and eyeliners. She even let herself be talked into being the demonstration model for the class.

Funny, she mused later as she headed to the lower level to meet Charlotte, what's happening to me is exactly what so many other women, single women, dream about when they come to the Catskills. They will meet their version of Prince Charming, fall in love and maybe even live happily ever after. The funniest part, it occurred to her, was that she hadn't even sought him out. She really didn't care one way or the other whether she met a man over the weekend or not. And in spite of all this—it never occurred to her it might be because of this—Bruce, Prince Charming, had come to her.

Charlotte. That was another thing. She was discovering another side to her roommate. She would have expected her, under the circumstances, to be jealous, even bitchy. Instead, she appeared to be genuinely happy for her, lending her unlimited encouragement and support.

Instantly, Fern felt some regret. She wished that Charlotte would have some romantic luck too. David Oberman couldn't really be considered a find, even though he seemed to have been having a good enough time the evening before. Obviously he had changed his mind when he got to his room and that's why he hadn't joined them at breakfast as he had promised. He probably couldn't take any more of Charlotte's coarseness, and it bothered her that her friend might never understand.

Unfortunately, Fern realized, there was nothing she could do about it. Charlotte was old enough and experienced enough to take care of herself. She shifted her thoughts to the kind of new dress she should buy. Her wardrobe didn't contain anything suitable for the Saturday night extravaganza where everybody wore their very finest accompanied by whatever jewels they could beg, borrow or steal. Maybe a pale lime ankle-length strapless set off with a tasteful pearl choker and matching earrings. She should have paid more attention to the sun the day before. A tan would have done wonders for her complexion.

Is this really me? she asked herself. The smile that must have crept over her face caught the attention of a number of guests as they walked on and they returned it with enthusiasm. It had never happened to her before—people she didn't know reacting to her like this. Wasn't there something just a teeny bit vulgar about being so vain, spending so much time thinking about makeup and clothes? She paused at a mirror and looked at herself once again. For a moment it was like looking at a complete stranger. The blond streaks were magnificent. The two curls at the cheeks were so perfectly placed they looked painted over her skin. A teeny bit vulgar, perhaps, but she liked what she saw.

She was wearing a darker lipstick than usual because the cosmetician had advised that "Ruby Red" was in style and it contrasted "in a very flattering way with your translucent skin, my dear." She realized now, as she studied her "new face," why she had avoided eye shadow in the past. Whenever she had tried to put it on by herself, she somehow ended up looking either ten years younger or ten years older than she was, but now, with the professional's touch, it didn't look that way at all. On the contrary, it made her eyes look large and lovely and at twenty-four years old, she was more attractive than she had ever been in her entire life.

If only she felt a little better. Her stomach continued to complain and for the life of her, she couldn't understand why. She had eaten so little at breakfast and was the only person at dinner the night before who gorged herself on salad instead of double desserts. Again, she concluded it was nerves. It's a lot like playing a part in a play she decided, puffing her hair up over her ears. This isn't actually me . . . and yet if I play the role long enough, maybe . . .

When she reached the boutique she stopped and looked around for Charlotte. After a moment, she realized her friend was standing just a few feet away. Their eyes met and Charlotte let out a whoop.

"Honest to God, Fern, honest to God," she squealed, giving Fern a big hug, "I was looking right at you and didn't recognize you."

"Oh, come on."

"I'm serious. Jesus, they really did a job on you." She turned her around to inspect the back of her hair. "You look absolutely gorgeous. Wait till Bruce gets a look at you. You'll have him in bed in fifteen minutes!"

"Charlotte, please," Fern said, slightly embarrassed, "lower your voice. People are starting to stare."

"Let them. Who cares?" She looked her over once again. "I knew it, I just knew it. The potential was always there. You just needed someone to encourage you to get off your duff and do something about it."

"Actually, I feel a lot like one of those mannequins in the window. They can't do anything unless someone manipulates them."

"You'll get over it," Charlotte said. "Come on, let's go inside and find something smashing, that will make people drop dead at the sight of you."

"There must be a better description," Fern protested, but she followed Charlotte willingly. If only I can get my stomach to calm down, she thought, maybe I'll even enjoy shopping for the first time.

"Smile," Charlotte said as they stopped at the first rack. "The rest of this is going to be easy." Suddenly she looked at Fern's face. "Hey, what's the matter? You look pale as a ghost even with all the makeup. Are you sure you're okay?"

"Yeah, sure," Fern said wanly. "It's probably the odor of the hair spray. It's making me a little nauseous."

"Then we'll get you some toilet water to overcome it."

The thought made her even more nauseous but she looked around, thought of the look on Bruce's face when he saw her all dressed up, and took a deep breath. She forced herself to concentrate on the garments Charlotte was pulling off the rack.

The first ring of the phone made Sam Teitelbaum jump. If it was bad news, he didn't want to hear it. It rang again and, embarrassed by his selfishness, he rushed over to answer it. Bruce was standing in the open doorway, waiting for the appearance of the ambulance squad.

"It's for you," Sam said. Bruce moved quickly to the phone.

"Thanks. Hello?"

"Bruce, it's Sid. I'm in room four twelve to see your friend Oberman but there's no one here."

"That's impossible. I just left him fifteen minutes ago and he was too damn weak . . . holy God, he's probably wandering around in some kind of delirium. We've got to locate him fast!"

"Meet me in the lobby right away," Bronstein said.

"Can you handle things here, Mr. Teitelbaum? It's another emergency and I've got to catch up with the doctor fast."

"Of course, young man. Don't worry, I'll take care of everything. They know what room to come to, right?"

"Right. Just hold together." He squeezed the elderly man's upper arm. "We're praying for the best." Then he rushed to the elevator.

It struck him as curious, knowing what he did, that the hotel should be carrying on as usual. Here he stood, after the doors opened, gazing out at this mass of humanity, guests in bermudas and

...125

polo shirts carrying tennis rackets, guests sitting casually over drinks talking in quick excited, happy voices, guests in robes and sandals going out to the pool. He was tempted to scream out to them, "Stop you idiots. There's a germ called vibro cholerae, a potential killer, on the loose, maybe even nesting in your guts. And all you're concerned about is enjoying yourselves and having a good time!" Wouldn't that go over big, he thought. The elevator beside him opened and Sid stepped out ahead of the crowd.

"Any sign of him?"

"None whatsoever. We better have him paged. I can't believe he was able to get out of the room. You should have seen the shape he was in."

"He probably panicked and it set off his adrenalin. Come on." They ran down the stairs to the switchboard. "Rosie, put out a page immediately for a David Oberman, please. It's important."

"Doc, I'm glad I found you. Mrs. Golden's been looking all over for you." Her voice lowered a decibel. "We're bringing the ambulance around the back . . . where the staff entrance is. You know how seeing this sort of thing disturbs the guests."

He shook his head. "There's no time for that baloney now," he said. "let them come right through the lobby. Every second counts."

"But Mrs. Golden said . . ."

"Where is Ellen now?"

"She just went down to the health club . . . some sort of emergency."

"Call her back. But page David Oberman first. When you reach Ellen, tell her we'll be waiting in her office and to get there as fast as she can."

"But . . ."

"*Quickly,* damn it." He slammed his hand on the switchboard. Rosie quickly rearranged her earphones and signaled for the pageboy across the hall.

"What's this business about the ambulance going around the back?" Bruce asked.

"Guests on holiday don't like to see any signs of illness around them when they're on vacation," Sid said, leading his cousin toward Ellen's office. "They like the idea that medical attention is available nearby but they don't want to see anything that reminds them of sickness or of death. A lot of elderly people vacation in the Catskills."

"So they sneak in the ambulances where nobody can see."

"That's about it. Don't laugh. I've been to hotels where they've made the ambulance attendants don jackets and ties in the evening before they could walk through the lobby to get to a sick person. About two years ago," he went on, opening the door to the office, "a man collapsed at the desk in this very lobby. I was upstairs treating a woman who picked up poison ivy in the woods behind the staff quarters. She never did tell me what she was doing there though I can guess. Anyway, by the time I came downstairs, the man was dead as a doornail. I looked up at Phil Golden and he looked down at me. There was nothing to be said. We sent for an ambulance and when it arrived, we put an oxygen mask on the dead man's face. As long as it appeared there was still hope, you see, people were satisfied. But to let them know that death had already arrived . . ."

"What the hell is going to happen around here when we let them know the truth about the cholera?"

"I shudder to think of it."

They both took seats in the office, Sid at the easy chair to the right of Ellen's desk and Bruce on the couch.

"What about Jonathan Lawrence?" Bruce asked.

"What about him?"

"Shouldn't he be here?"

"Let Ellen handle him. He works for her," Sid said.

"You're obviously not particularly fond of this guy. How come you placed so much trust in him?"

"As they say, he was the only game in town."

"What about the health authorities?"

"When you meet the health officer, you'll see why I tried to avoid bringing him in unless I positively had to."

"I don't understand," Bruce said, trying hard not to sound critical. "Personality notwithstanding, shouldn't he have been notified right away?"

"If you go by the book, I suppose so. But life doesn't always go that way."

They were interrupted by a gentle knock on the door. It was Rosie.

"Mrs. Golden's on her way, but your David Oberman isn't answering the page."

"Please keep trying, Rosie. It's very urgent we locate him."

"I'll send some bellhops down to the lake and the golf course if you think it will help."

"I can't see him going out there, Sid."

. . . 127

"Let her do it anyway. Who knows how far he was able to go."

Rosie hesitated, waiting to see if the doctor would say anything more, something that would give her a hint as to what was going on. He looked at her sharply and she backed out, closing the door behind her.

"To get back to why you didn't call the public health office on Thursday?" Bruce continued.

This time they were interrupted by Ellen Golden opening the door. Both men stood up as she acknowledged them and continued into the office.

"Hello, Sid." She looked at Bruce.

"This is Bruce Solomon, my cousin."

"Sorry I didn't get to meet you earlier," Bruce said quickly. She looked at him curiously and then back at Sid.

"Does this have something to do with the woman in three fifteen?" Ellen walked to her desk slowly.

"Everything, I'm afraid."

"Oh?" She sat down, staring at Bruce. The two men took their seats. "Rosie told me how you wanted to handle the ambulance. Is it that serious?"

"We're practically positive that she's got it."

"Got it? Got what?"

Sid shot a quick, very frightened look at Bruce who bolted up so quickly for a moment Sid feared he'd go through the ceiling.

"You know why Bruce is here at the hotel, right?"

"I'm not sure I understand," Ellen said. "You did say he had something to do with the woman in three fifteen."

"Didn't Jonathan tell you about Bruce?"

"Jonathan? No. What was he supposed to tell me?" She kept looking from Sid to Bruce.

"I'm getting very bad vibrations," Bruce said. Sid felt his own stomach churn. The blood rushed to his face. A wave of panic caused a sudden shudder.

"Ellen, you do know about Tony Wong, don't you?"

"Tony Wong? Oh, yes." Sid relaxed a little. "He was the Chinaman who passed away. I've been meaning to call you about him, in fact, but you won't believe what's been going on around here. I just came from the health club where they tell me a man walked right into the steam room with all his clothes on. I didn't stay around because Rosie called to say you had an emergency back here but I told Sven to get that man out of there as fast as he could, even if he had to carry him out bodily. Can you imagine?" She stopped talking because both men were staring at her so intensely.

"Ellen," Sid said quietly, marking every word with precision, "didn't you know that there was a possibility you had cholera in this hotel?"

Somewhere in the greatest recesses of her mind, where her thought and words were in the embryonic stages, where images were conceived, where memories of pain and fear lay dormant until resurrected, a scream was struggling to free itself and travel down the highways of communication. She struggled to subdue it calling on all her strength and all her control.

"What in God's name are you talking about?" she said, her voice strangely hollow.

"I knew it," Bruce said, getting up and pacing the floor. "I knew somehow this was going to happen." Before anyone else could speak, the phone rang. Ellen found it took all of her might to reach out and lift the receiver. She wasn't even sure she had said hello. Then she listened.

"Dr. Bronstein will be right there," she said and hung up. "The man in the steam bath . . . they just carried him out . . . they think he's dead."

"David Oberman," Sid and Bruce said in tandem. "My God."

The phone rang for the second time.

"Yes? Right." She hung up once again. "The ambulance squad is here. They're on their way to three fifteen."

"I'll meet them there," Sid said, standing up. "Bruce, you go down to the steam room. See if it's Oberman and if there's a chance he's still alive. I'll send one of the ambulance guys over right away."

"Will do."

"One thing," Ellen asked. "Jonathan. Sid, you say he knew all about this?"

"Everything."

"I see," she said. "Does anyone else know?"

"No. Just the three of us . . . and now you. I suggest you get your general manager down here right away. We'll be back as soon as we can."

The two of them rushed out of the office, When the door closed, Ellen sat back in her chair. It was as though she had been punched in the very center of her existence. She lifted the receiver. She felt a stranger to the new sound in her voice.

"Get me Jonathan Lawrence. If he's not in his office, call security and have him located immediately. I want him in this office in five minutes."

Her rage began to subside but she wouldn't permit it.

"I'm too frightened," she thought. "I can't afford to stop being angry."

eleven

The day camp was an inglorious mixture of cherubs of all ages. One of the counselors carried a three-year-old in her arms and pleaded with him to stand on his own two feet. He was having none of it. The minute she lowered him in the earth's direction he set up such a howl she was forced to lift him back to her level. Grateful and content, he brought the nipple of his juice bottle to his mouth and began to suck.

Most of the children were working industriously on various arts and crafts projects—finger painting, weaving, belt making and clay sculpture. Others were playing games like checkers, Parcheesi, Monopoly or simply reading or coloring under a tree.

Half a dozen counselors circulated among them, most of them teenage girls and boys from town who worked the season for a minimal salary plus whatever tips they could wangle from the parents. Those who were more experienced made it their business early in the summer to find out which kids came from wealthy families so they could seek them out for special attention.

Because there were more children this weekend than expected, the counselors were overwhelmed by the number of children in their charge.

Sandi stood in the arts and crafts section of the rec hall dishing out globs of sticky clay into eagerly awaiting hands. Only an hour before, against her better judgment, she had let Magda cajole her into lending a hand. It was something she hated to do, especially today when she wanted to spend more time with Grant, but it was hard to turn Magda down when she asked a favor.

"It's not for the entire summer, Sandi. It's just for a couple of days. You don't want your mother to have another problem to worry about, do you?"

No, she didn't. Not after last night's conversation. She remembered her mother's words the last time she was asked to pitch in two or three months ago. "A little work won't kill you now and then, honey. Your father started helping out when he was still in short pants and he doesn't look any the worse for it, does he? Besides," she'd added, "it will give you character."

How the hell working with screaming, nose-dripping, spoiled

brats gave her character, Sandi never quite figured out. All it did for her was give her a headache.

Nevertheless when she got to the day camp she saw that Magda had been right. It was like a three-ring circus, the counselors running around in circles surrounded by little armies of noisy, dirty, three-to-eleven-year-olds all demanding immediate attention. Stan Leshner, the director of activities, was overjoyed to see her.

"You're an angel in disguise," he said, lifting her off her feet. "I don't have the time to break in someone new. Let me have your attention everybody," he shouted, clapping his hands loudly. "Everybody hold it down a minute, okay? Now listen boys and girls. After lunch your counselors are going to take you for a nature hike in the woods behind the staff cottages. Then you'll come back and change for a swim. After rest hour, there'll be a puppet show in the rec hall." There were a lot of oohs and ahs. "So everyone behave and give your counselors your full cooperation, okay?" The children nodded seriously. "Good, I'll see you all later."

He withdrew quickly, grateful that at least one situation was under control. Sandi went to her station by the clay and after seeing that her charges were occupied, began to mold something for herself. At first it began as a long, thin scarecrow but gradually it began to look more and more like a long phallus. One of the counselors, Mary Dickson, a bright redhead with a heavily freckled face, stared at the way Sandi was working the clay up and down her hand.

"What is that?" she asked, looking up from the small group of children seated around her. Sandi snapped out of her daze.

"Huh?"

Mary laughed and turned back to her kids. Sandi studied her creation and then crushed it quickly, pounding it with vicious energy. Suddenly she felt a tug on her jeans. She looked down at a four-or five-year-old girl with an expression on her face that told all.

"Shit," she said, louder than she meant to. Much of the action around her stopped and other children looked up from their work. "Glady, GLADYS," she screamed at the head counselor who was working with the older kids. The tall, excrutiatingly thin eighteen-year-old turned around impatiently. She had dull brown hair and a plain, homely face.

"What is it?"

"We've got a problem here. One of the kids made in her pants."

"Well, can't you handle it?"

"Not if I'm not getting paid." Whether her mother liked it or not, there was a point where she drew the line.

...132

Glady frowned and came across the room, weaving her way in between a maze of little bodies. When she saw who it was she gasped in amazement and put her hands on her hips.

"Not you again, Miriam."

The little girl nodded softly and began to cry.

"Nice work, Gladys," Sandi whispered sarcastically. "Now you've got her crying too."

"Well this is the third time I've had to take this kid to be changed."

"My stomach hurts," the little girl sobbed. Both counselors stared down at her. She really did look terrible.

"Didn't you tell her mother?"

"I couldn't find her. I got the room key from the front desk and took her up myself. The first time I just changed her panties and let her come back. The second time I made her put on a different dress. But this time it's splattered all over . . ."

"You better find her mother before it's too late. The kid looks awful. When you see her, don't forget to remind her that the hotel has a doctor she can call if it gets really bad."

"Thanks, I'll do that. Watch my side, will ya?" She started to embrace the child, then thought better of it. Instead, she took her hand and led her once again toward the main house.

It wasn't more than fifteen minutes later when Mary Dickson let out a scream. The sound of the counselor's voice was enough to bring the entire camp to silence. She stood up quickly, holding her skirt away from her body. The little boy seated beside her had suddenly, and without apparent warning, begun regurgitating. He was still throwing up and spitting on the floor.

I don't believe it, Sandi thought. What the hell did I get myself into?

"Everybody get up and go outside while we clean things up in here," one of the other counselors announced. "Let's go over and sit under the apple tree and sing some songs," another one suggested.

The children rose obediently, their faces reflecting curiosity and surprise. They were unusually cooperative and quiet as they filed out of the hall. Mary Dickson, still holding her skirt up and away from her body, yelled out for a rag. The little boy began to cry.

"I'll take him back to the hotel," Sandi said, helping him up to his feet. She took his hand in hers and started him out of the building. "It's all right, little boy, don't cry," she said. "You'll feel better in no time."

"My stomach hurts," he replied. She stopped for a moment and looked over at him. He sounded exactly like that little girl Miriam. Odd, she thought, two children in the same morning.

Just outside the steam room, the men's health club had three rows of lounges on which guests could nap and relax. The walls of the health club were made of a heavy, slick aqua tile. The floors had recently been relaid with an inexpensive indoor-outdoor darker blue carpet. On both sides of the lounge area there were shelves of towels and racks of current newspapers and magazines. Further in, just past the steam room, was the shower section consisting of a dozen stalls. Small cakes of soap could be taken from wall dispensers spaced out evenly along the outside walls. To the left of the showers were two small rooms used for massages. Four men dressed in see-through tee shirts and white pants slapped and stirred the flesh of groggy guests sprawled out like corpses in a pathology lab. Legs juggled and stomachs growled as muscles were stretched and the blood around them stimulated.

Bruce Solomon knelt down beside the end lounge on which the limp and now dampened body of David Oberman had been placed. Marco Romano, the men's health room attendant, stood beside him looking down. Marco had been a professional wrestler, a fact still testified to by his thick, muscular shoulders and forearms. Only his lower stomach had surrendered to time and lack of exercise. He had almost grotesque facial features with wide separations between his teeth. A piece of his left eyebrow was missing, the result of an old wrestling injury that never healed properly. In his time, he had been a popular performer going under the name Marco the Magnificent. When he worked he wore a centurion costume and carried a spear into the ring with him.

"Sven told me he couldn't get this guy to move but I didn't want to use force on him till we contacted Mrs. Golden. It could be he's drunk or maybe just a kook. We get our share around here, you know."

"Look," Bruce said, noticing the small crowd that was beginning to form around them, "you'll have to clear out one of those massage rooms so we can put this man in there until the ambulance comes."

"Clear one out?" He looked in their direction. "But . . . the guests are paying for their time in there." One look at Bruce and he knew he wasn't kidding. "Okay, I'll take care of it right away."

"What's the matter with him?" a man asked.

"I'm not sure. Probably passed out from too much heat." He remembered Sid's description of how hotels handled their sick in front of their guests.

"O.K.," Marco said, coming back. "let's just lift him lounge and all. It'll be easier."

"Right."

The two of them carried David's body into the massage room. Marco left and Bruce closed the door, shutting himself off from the onlookers. He studied the dead man's face. His mouth was opened slightly, but his eyes were sealed so tightly they looked like they'd been sewn shut. His identity had already begun to seep out of him. Death was replacing it with that anonymity that characterized all corpses. How quickly a man or woman became a thing, an object only good for scientific curiosity. It was difficult to relate the voice and the gestures of the David Oberman he had met the night before to this cold and clammy body sprawled before him.

"Is it Oberman?" Sid asked, coming into the room. Bruce hadn't heard him enter. "Bruce?" He tapped him on the shoulder.

Bruce whirled around. "Huh? Oh, Sid. Hi."

"Is that the man?"

"Yes, it's him . . . or I should say was him." Bronstein moved forward and lifted an eyelid. He felt for a pulse and pinched the skin.

"When you wipe off the condensation from the steam room, you see how dry the skin was."

"I noticed that when I spoke with him earlier but it didn't occur to me he was near death."

"The Bluestone woman is in a very bad way. She must've been rundown to start. Dehydrated quickly. She's already into uremia."

"A really vicious strain."

"That's my guess now. We'd better get back to Ellen's office. There's nothing else we can do here."

Bruce nodded and they left the room. Marco approached quickly. "How long's that guy gonna be in there?"

"The ambulance should be along any minute," Bronstein said. "In the meantime, it's essential that no one goes into the room."

"Sure, sure."

They walked out of the health club quickly and headed up the stairs to Ellen's office. When Sid opened the door they were confronted by a cool, neatly composed Jonathan seated on the couch, a file folder in his hand, his pipe held comfortably in his fingers. Ellen's face looked flushed but there was a surprisingly controlled calm about her. She leaned forward, eager to hear what they had to say.

"The man in the health club is dead," Sid reported. "I'm sorry. He turned to Jonathan and pointed his finger. "Dead, Jonathan, okay? What you were so sure was impossible a day and a half ago is cold reality today. Damn it, I never should have listened to you in the first place!" He stood up and started pacing around the room. "And why the hell didn't you tell Ellen like you promised? You knew how important it was. . . ."

"He claims he was trying to protect me," Ellen interrupted. "That there was no reason to upset me over something that would probably prove to be a false alarm."

"False alarm? He knew I had very serious suspicions that Tony Wong had cholera. And that you had to be alerted to all of the potential danger. I'm sorry if I'm getting carried away, but. . ."

"You're the doctor, Sid. Why didn't you tell me yourself if it was that important?" Ellen asked quietly.

There it was. The question he always knew he would have to face along with why he hadn't called the health authorities immediately. To say he had faith in Jonathan was little more than half truth. To say that he would have done anything to avoid bringing Ellen news of another death, this time perhaps the death of the Congress itself, was not the whole truth either. No, deep down he knew he had acted in a cowardly way. He hadn't wanted to rock the boat, disturb the status quo, or be the least bit responsible for participating in a disaster that could have caused his father-in-law to lose his investment and put friends and associates out of business. And disturb his pleasant life style, too, he admitted. At this moment, he didn't particularly like himself very much.

The pained look on his face aroused great sympathy in Ellen. She pushed him no further. "What do we do now to protect our people? Do we send them away?"

Sid was grateful for the chance to get back to medicine. "No. First I have to call Gerson Kaplow, the public health officer. The procedures are pretty well outlined for Class I communicable diseases. Quarantine is mandatory where there is a possibility of an epidemic and they don't know what's causing or who's carrying the disease."

Ellen's hands flew involuntarily to her face. "Quarantine? You mean keeping all the guests restricted to the grounds?"

"Everybody, guests and staff alike. All deliveries will be stopped at the gate and no one will be permitted in or out without official authorization."

"Oh, my God. It's like keeping hostages in a prison."

"Not exactly," Sid said, managing a smile for the first time. "No prison I've ever seen has such elegant meals and facilities."

Suddenly Bruce interrupted. "There's something we've got to do right away," he said. He looked directly at Jonathan. "The New York doctor you sent the dishwashers and chambermaid to. You've got to call him immediately and advise him of the status of things. There's a possibility they are infected and—"

"There's no one to call," Jonathan whispered, staring down at his patent leather pumps. The enormity of what was happening was finally sinking in. He let out a deep breath and tapped out his pipe. His shoulders began to sag.

"What are you talking about now?" Ellen asked.

"Hold it," Bruce said, ignoring her question. It suddenly all become clear. "You didn't send those people to a medical facility either, did you? Did you?" The room was silent. "Just where the hell did you send them?" He reached down toward Jonathan, grabbed him by the collar of his jacket and pulled him to his feet.

"Get your fuckin' hands . . ."

"Hold it, Bruce," Sid said, pulling them apart. "Fighting isn't going to solve anything." He turned to the general manager. "Just what exactly did you do with them, Jonathan?"

"I gave them some money and sent them into the city to have some fun until the weekend was over."

"You sent them into the city to walk the streets when they might have been contaminated because you were afraid the hotel might get some negative publicity? Why you son of a . . ." Bruce pushed Sid away and lunged for him again.

Ellen stood up. *"Enough,"* she said sharply. In the midst of the three raging men, she suddenly took on new strength and control. "Now sit down, all of you." Bruce glared at Jonathan and retreated to a chair. "Bruce, I want you to go to Halloran and see if he has any information regarding where the dishwashers and Margret Thomas went. Sid, I know you have your hands full. Jonathan," she turned with undisguised bitterness to her general manager. "I have nothing to say to you right now. When this is over, if there's anything left after the damage to our reputation and finances is computed, we'll discuss whether or not you have a future with the Congress."

"There won't be any need." He backed toward the door. "There won't be any hotel to discuss. I'm getting out while there's still a chance."

"I advise you not to try to leave," Bruce said.

"He's right," Sid said. "By the time you're finished packing we'll be in quarantine."

"And," Bruce added, "as hard as it may be for you to believe, Mr. Holier-than-Thou, you too might already be infected. Knowing what kind of a scum you are, it probably feels right at home." Jonathan didn't wait to hear what anyone else had to say. He turned and rushed out of the office.

"You'd better start making your phone calls," Ellen said. Sid nodded and reached for the phone.

"I'm sorry Ellen," he said quietly. He lifted the receiver but before he could get the operator, Rosie came barging into the office.

"Oh, Dr. Bronstein, hurry. There's a pregnant woman with stomach pains, terrible stomach pains, and they just took her out of the dining room. She's afraid it might be a miscarriage."

Bronstein followed her out of the office.

"Cholera can do that," Bruce said softly. Ellen Golden reached for the phone to make some of the calls herself.

When Flo Goldberg came back to her room after breakfast, she found Manny in his undershirt and shorts sleeping on top of the bed. His mouth was wide open and he was snoring. For a few moments she stood staring at him in disgust. Then she tiptoed across the room to her dresser, took out her bathing suit, and went into the bathroom. She changed, put on her robe and sandals, gathered her body oils and lotions together, found her copy of *McCalls*, scooped up her sunglasses and headed out of the room.

They were giving mambo lessons at the pool and she was the first to volunteer. All of the others who joined the class came up in couples. Since she was alone the dance instructor used her for his demonstration. That was all right, but when he was finished illustrating the steps, he left her to give the couples individual attention. For a few moments she stood there with a bemused expression on her face looking about for a partner, someone who would step forward and rescue her from this absolutely foolish stance in between the dancers. No one came over so she went back to her chaise.

She tried to read her magazine but the words kept flying off the page. When she looked around the pool, it seemed to her that everyone else had someone to be with. Of course, this wasn't true. There were other women who were unescorted, but most of them at least had other women to talk to. She was completely by herself. She stared at the lifeguard and tried to think about his body and the way he would move in bed, but even those thoughts became unglued.

Gradually the mambo rhythms, the voices of the people, the sound of splashing in the pool, and the laughter all around turned annoying. She didn't understand why, but she was suddenly feeling miserable. She thought about ordering a drink, then remembered what drinking in the daytime usually did to her. If anything, it made her groggy and gave her sinus headaches.

She even considered writing a few postcards, then realized how stupid that would be. After all, she was only spending an extended weekend in the Catskills. It wasn't like a trip to Europe or the Far East. Besides, Bernard hated the Congress and everything he thought it stood for. He certainly wouldn't be interested in any details. In some ways he was a terrible snob. She wondered if it was a terrible thing for a mother to sometimes dislike her own son.

With her daughter it was just the opposite. It was Linda who had come to dislike her. They saw so little of each other now and somehow she had come to realize it was better that way—a mutual truce, an unspoken understanding. The love, the respect, it just wasn't there—despite the years and the attention, the meals and the doctoring. It had never taken, like a skin graft that failed. Perhaps she wasn't cut out to be a mother in the first place.

As the late morning wore on, Flo lay there thinking. She felt very small and alone. Her affairs, her two minute episodes, were really not very satisfying. She could dote on them for a while but in the long run they were like aspirins. The thought made her laugh but she could see that the analogy was true. The aspirin took away the symptoms of the headache but didn't really get to the cause.

What was the cause? If, for a moment, she would give her life serious thought, she was certain to grow depressed. Here she was over forty years old without close friends, without any family that really gave a damn, without any purpose. In some ways she envied Ellen Golden. Her husband had died and left her with too many problems and too many responsibilities to feel sorry for herself. She thought about her, wondered where she was right now, imagined herself in Ellen Golden's place, saw herself greeting people, issuing orders and overseeing glamorous projects. It didn't take her long to see how ridiculous a picture that would make. She had a hard enough time running a house for her husband and son, much less a hotel like this.

The sound of a man and woman laughing together drew her attention across the pool. She saw a young couple, with a pair of young children about them. It made her maudlin. They looked impregnable, happy, complete. They were continually aware of each other, almost as if invisible spiderlike threads were strung between them, holding them together.

Why couldn't she have loved someone that way? Why couldn't she have enjoyed her children and her marriage instead of continually thinking of them as an ordeal? Her self-pity was making her feel old and tired. She tried to fight it off but couldn't. It turned into bitterness. Those husbands would stray from those wives soon enough, she mumbled, and the wives would do the same. Their children would grow up to be self-centered and ungrateful just like hers. They were no different. Why, she thought, I bet Manny and I even looked that happy once upon a time. She tried to resurrect the images but no such memory existed.

It made her angry and she took relief in the change of emotions. Where was that idiot? How long could he sleep? Did he have to spend so many hours drinking and playing cards? Their vacation always turned out this way, him going along his own way and leaving her alone. She'd fix him. She'd make it as miserable for him as he was making it for her. Maybe she would do the drinking tonight and not come back until 4 A.M. How would he like that for a change?

None of these vengeful thoughts really satisfied her. They left her even more miserable than before. Now the sun was getting too hot. Her shoulders felt sunburned. She was thirsty. The straps of the lounge were cutting into her back. Those damn little kids were splashing water. The band was playing too loud. She reached for her robe, slipped into her sandals and scooped up her belongings. Then she stood up abruptly and started back to the room. If that son of a bitch was still asleep . . .

A large group of people at the end of the pool had turned their attention to something going on down the path. It drew her curiosity so she followed the crowd to see what was happening. It was disgusting. What looked like a teenage boy was throwing up into one of the small ponds by the rock garden. Two of his friends stood nearby laughing.

An elderly man on a bench looked up at her.

"I'll bet you anything," he said, "that young whippersnapper

. . . 140

drank too much *shnapps* last night. Such a shame to have to drink so much in order to be happy."

She thought about Manny.

"You're probably right," she said and walked on.

Sandi opened her mother's office door just enough to peer in. Ellen had just put the phone down and sat back. Sandi walked in further because she didn't see Bruce seated to one side. The moment she did, she stopped.

"Oh, I'm sorry. I thought you were alone, mom."

"That's all right, honey. Come in. This is Mr. Solomon. Bruce, this is my daughter Sandi."

"Hi," Bruce said. He winked and smiled at her. Cute, she thought, moving to the desk.

"I just stopped by to take a breather."

"Oh?"

"I was helping out at the day camp."

"I know. Magda told me. I think that's just great."

"The counselors took the rest of them on a hike."

"Rest of them?"

"Yeah. A couple of the kids had accidents."

"My God, I hope nobody got hurt. What kind of accidents?"

"They got sick," she said, looking at Bruce again. His face changed completely. "One made number two in her pants a few times and the other kid threw up. Right on Mary Dickson!"

"Where are these children now?" Bruce asked.

"We took them back to their parents."

"We?" Ellen said. Sandi stared at her. Her mother's face suddenly had a look of genuine fear. She didn't know what to say. "*You* did?"

"Take it easy, Ellen," Bruce said. "There are very limited ways in which this thing can be spread."

"What thing?"

"Oh, Sandi."

"What is it, mama?" Sandi moved around the desk to her mother's side.

"We have big trouble, baby. Big."

"It's essential you understand this thing." Bruce went on, very much tuned in to the mounting hysteria forming in Ellen's voice. Sandi took her mother's hand. "Wait a minute, Sandi," he said leaning forward and extending his right hand. "Did you have any contact with . . . the mess the children made?"

"Contact?"

"Did you accidentally touch any of it or did any of it get on your clothes that you might have touched?"

"No." She shook her head. "The head counselor took care of the little girl and the boy threw up on someone else. I just brought him back to the hotel."

"Do you know if he or his counselor touched anything he threw up?"

"I don't think so. Why?"

"You haven't eaten anything since you brought him in, have you? Even a stick of gum?"

She shook her head and looked at Ellen, who seemed to be holding her breath.

"All right," Bruce went on, relaxing some and leaning back. "Just to be on the safe side, go wash your hands real good, lots of soap and hot water, will you?"

"I don't understand."

"Just listen, Sandi." Her mother spoke in a quick, clipped command. She let go of her hand and backed away. "Go on."

"Isn't anybody going to tell me what this is all about?"

"Just go wash up and come back. Then I'll tell you everything, I promise."

Sandi looked at Bruce again and then turned and left the office.

"You see," Bruce began as if he had just been interrupted, "direct contact with contaminated material is our major concern."

"There's so much I don't know about this. Actually, I barely know how to spell the damn word. All I do know are all sorts of horrible stories . . ."

"I know. That, and misinformation, lack of information, confusion—will be out biggest problems for the next few days."

"Days? How long will the quarantine last?"

"Well, if my memory serves me correctly, we're talking about five or six days. It's the length of the incubation period, you see."

"Five or six days," Ellen murmured softly. "An awful lot can happen in five or six days."

. . . 142

twelve

The State Police car was parked inconspicuously just outside the main gate. From the main building no one could see it, let alone the two uniformed men standing beside the regular Congress security guard at the small booth. Equally hidden was the police car at the side entrance usually used by the staff and a third police vehicle parked at the entrance to the guest parking lot.

The first confrontation came with the arrival of a telephone repair truck. One of the state policemen at the gate held up his hand and brought it to a halt. The driver leaned out of his window, annoyed at not being waved through.

"What's up?"

"You can't go in."

"Whaddya mean I can't go in? I have a repair order for a couple of pay phones in the coffee shop," he said, shaking some papers at him.

"Not today." The tall highway patrolman had a stern, military demeanor and the repairman wondered what he was doing there.

"What 'dya mean, not today?"

"The hotel grounds have been closed off. Those are our orders."

"You're kiddin'?" He looked at the other policeman but he offered no encouragement. "Jesus," he said, "they sure as hell ain't gonna believe this back at the office."

He slammed his shift into reverse and backed the truck out. The policemen watched him go in silence. A few moments later, a light blue Chevy four-door turned into the entrance and came to a stop. There were two nurses in the front seat and three others in the back. The driver flashed some identification to the officer.

"Looks like you have your work cut out for you," he said.

"That's what they tell us" the nurse who was driving said. They drove on into the grounds, winding slowly down the driveway toward the main house.

"The place seems quiet enough now," one of the patrolmen said.

"I guess the people don't know about it yet."

...143

"When they find out, all hell's gonna break loose."

"You better believe it. The sheriff's department's supposed to send more cars as backup in case we run into trouble."

"Helluva thing, turning a resort into a prison."

"Hey," the hotel security man said stepping out of his booth. "What happens to me?"

"Happens?"

"I'm off duty in about twenty minutes. Do I just leave?"

"Hell, no," the taller patrolman said. "You turn your ass around and go right back into the hotel. You had lunch in there today."

"So what? I got a home in town to go to."

"Maybe so, but until you get authorization, you have to stay inside the grounds just like everybody else. Sorry."

The security guard stared at them for a moment and then slammed his clipboard down on the small table inside the booth. He sat on his chair and sulked.

In the distance they could hear the siren of yet another ambulance. It had a sobering effect. Even the birds in the woods across the way seemed to have retreated deeper into the shadows.

Ellen's office resembled the Pentagon war room. Two large portable blackboards borrowed from the hotel's day camp were wheeled in and set up on the left. On one, a basic outline of the hotel complex had been drawn with all the exits and entrances circled in red. This was the guide to setting up barriers so that no unauthorized persons would be able to enter or exit without being checked. Rafferty, the security chief, was going over it inch by inch, marking off breaks in the fence and crossing out the areas with x's where forest rather than fencing bordered the grounds. Sheriff Balbera stood to one side and studied the map. He had come to the hotel directly from a speaking engagement at the Concord where a contingent of law enforcement agents had gathered for the weekend. He was a tall, hard-looking man with a lean ruddy face and strong jaw, a man one would imagine more at home in a checkered shirt and jeans sitting on top of a horse somewhere than stuffed into the business suit he had on.

"Once the guests get the full story, we'll have to expect a few of them might take to those woods there," he said, pointing to one of the Xed out areas.

"With luggage?"

"People in a panic will do anything," he said. He spoke with the quiet authority that automatically begets respect. Rafferty nodded. "We'll need some men in that area patroling."

"I've got my hands full with the main building already and I'm understaffed at that," the hotel chief muttered.

"Lieutenant Fielding from the Ferndale State Police barracks should be here any minute. We'll see if we can borrow some manpower from him." He turned and looked at Bruce Solomon, who was seated to the right of Ellen's desk. Bruce was taking notes as the sheriff spoke. Sid Bronstein, already exhausted and haggard, his shirt unbuttoned at the throat, his tie loosened and hair disheveled, sat behind the desk talking to his office. He was telling his receptionist to cancel all appointments and post a notice stating there would be no office hours for the rest of the weekend.

Gerson Kaplow, the local public health officer, sat on the couch seemingly detached from the events taking place around him. In fact, he was anything but. It was an open secret that medicine was not his primary interest and that the *Wall Street Journal* was infinitely more important to him than any issue of the *Journal of the American Medical Association*. Kaplow was a speculator in real estate, having sunk most of his income into syndicates that bought up Catskill acreage for resale to hotel and motel chains and land and housing developers. With the possibility of gambling coming to the area, he considered it a good risk and in the last few years his medical practice had dwindled in almost direct proportion to his business activity.

He was the laughing stock of the medical community and more than once they had tried to get him ousted as public health officer. "He's so damn stupid that if we ever had a real emergency it would turn into a tragedy, simply because he was in control." "C'mon, fellows," the county supervisor countered, "when's the last time we had a real health emergency up here? Besides, he's politically connected and there's no way I can oust him from the board." So he stayed.

When Bronstein had called him to the office earlier, he tried desperately to extricate himself from the involvement. First, he knew that for him it was going to mean economic suicide. Second, he wasn't even sure what he was supposed to do in a situation like this. Cholera? He hadn't even thought of the word for the past thirty years. Fortunately, the story had already broken at the hospital and arrangements for special facilities made. Also, the public health nurses had been contacted and the sheriff's office informed. Ellen, in a quick, deliberate action, had contacted the police herself. She had an instinctive understanding that law and order would be serious considerations in the hours and days to follow.

There was no point in trying to fake it. The situation was too serious. "What am I supposed to do now?"

"First you have to contact the state authorities." Sid found it hard to hide the contempt in his voice. "Then you formally have to place the hotel in quarantine."

Quarantine. The word stuck in his throat. The word he had buried in his mind. The word he didn't want to hear. Sweat started to pour from his face. All his investments, his entire economic future, going to hell with one brisk directive.

"You've got to do it," Bronstein repeated. "You've got the authority."

Authority, shit, Gerson thought. I've got nothing.

So now he sat half an hour later still in Ellen Golden's office, a man watching events over which he had no control, caught in a violent downstream there was no way to fight. All he could do was be carried along like everybody else.

"I don't consider it the source of the problem," Bruce said, looking up from his papers, "but just to be sure, you are running a thorough analysis of the water, aren't you?"

"Samples are being taken from every major outlet," Kaplow said, almost by rote.

"Good. Jonathan Lawrence, the general manager, was supposed to have sent some out for analysis, but the way he's screwed up everything else. . ."

"When's Ellen going to announce all this?" Sheriff Balbera asked as Sid hung up the phone.

"She's in the process of gathering the executive staff together right now. When she's finished with them, she'll start working on the guests."

"What about the food for dinner?"

"It's all been ordered fresh," Bruce said, "and to be on the safe side we're getting it from different sources."

"Are you so sure the people who died picked it up from the food?" Kaplow asked. He realized he knew nothing about cholera at all.

"We're not sure about anything at this point, but we've got to get at the bottom of this somehow. All we know right now is that in the first instance the janitor was in his room all the time, and yet guests who had no association with him have come down with it, too.

"What about those people Jonathan sent into the city?" Bronstein asked.

"I talked to Halloran," Rafferty volunteered. "Jonathan mentioned the Hotel Coolidge to him and I was able to locate the two Puerto Rican dishwashers. They've been sent to a New York hospital for tests."

"And Margret Thomas?"

"She never checked into the hotel. The guys don't know a thing about her."

"It's damn important that we find her," Bruce said, looking at the sheriff. "She cleaned up the Chinese guy's room and maybe . . ."

"We'll contact the New York police immediately."

Bruce nodded. There was a short moment of silence. Then he got up and walked over to the blank blackboard.

"What I want to start doing," he said, picking up a piece of chalk, "is see if I can determine any coincidence, no matter how farfetched, tying the people we know to have been contaminated together." He wrote Wong's name on the board and then added Oberman and Bluestone.

"Those two children from the day camp either have mild cases," Bronstein said, "or nothing at all. It's not unusual for me to see kids with nervous stomachs on holiday weekends. Usually comes from too much excitement. Right now they're resting comfortably in their rooms so I'm going to give them a little more time. No point in scaring the hell out of their parents."

"Sandi said the little girl's name is Myers. And the boy is . . ."

"Feigen. I think his parents are friends of Ellen."

Bruce added their names and put a question mark next to each. Kaplow shook his head. The sheriff bit down on his lower lip and stared at the names as if straining to see beyond them. Just then the public health nurses arrived. The sight of them encouraged them all. Allies had joined in the fight. They wore everyday clothing but carried their uniforms in small bags, having been asked to arrive incognito in order not to alarm anyone. Lillian Sokofsky, a short, blonde woman in her early forties was recognized as the titular head of the group. She had a sympathetic, motherly face, the kind any patient could trust, but the moment the door closed behind her she was all business.

"Okay, let's have it," she said. "Tell us where to start and when."

Sid and Bruce looked at each other and breathed a collective sigh of relief. These no-nonsense medical Wacs were just what the doctor ordered.

Ellen Golden sat at her bedroom vanity table in the old farmhouse and looked out the window. From that particular perspective she had a panoramic view of the outdoor tennis courts and the last two cottages. All of the courts were in use and a number of guests were waiting nearby, watching the action, anxious to get their turn. On the far court the tennis pro was demonstrating the correct way to hold a racket. He had the attention of a half dozen people. For a moment it appeared totally ridiculous to her. For anyone to be worrying about such nonsense in light of the situation exploding all around seemed almost insane. On the other hand, she reminded herself, there was no way they could know. The explosions that had already occurred were silent and only slightly noted.

She had come back to the farmhouse to think. It wasn't that she was running away from responsibilities and decisions—there was hardly the time for such luxury—but she needed to surround herself with things familiar, to have some privacy, to cry if need be, to finger mementoes and look at Phil's picture in hopes it would give her the courage she needed to go back and take charge.

It was at the farmhouse that she had made the major decisions of her married life and it was here that Phil and she had done their most intimate and significant talking. The house itself was an anachronism. Surrounded by the most modern of resort facilities, the turn-of-the-century structure looked like the home of a reluctant old-world tenant who refused to give in to progress. Guests who came to the Congress for the first time found it an object of curiosity. When told it was the private home of the Goldens they became even more curious. Why would a family who owned such a big resort have such a dilapidated old house? Surely they didn't really live in it. They must maintain a penthouse apartment at the top of the main building.

Turning around in her swivel chair, Ellen couldn't help wondering what Phil would be doing if he were in her place. Beyond a question, his first concern would be the safety of the guests and staff. He had a certain resiliency about material things. "They can all be replaced." And as far as money was concerned he was convinced that what the hotel lost one year, it would regain the next. In this instance it was likely he'd have been proven wrong, but . . .

The irony that everything the Goldens had created and everything her husband had worked for and probably died for was on the brink of collapse due to events beyond anyone's control was not lost on her. All along, from the moment she had had to take the symbolic reins, the one thing she was most afraid of was that she, herself, would do something that would bring the hotel to ruin. That was why she began with a soft voice and a gentle hand, why she leaned on her staff so much, and why she maintained her dependence on Jonathan despite her instinctive dislike for the man. And now . . . her grandmother would probably have called it *beshert*. Fate. The only word Ellen could think of was sad.

The one emotion curiously missing from her reaction was self-pity. Pity for the people who were sick, definitely. Pity for those whose financial future might be at stake, of course. Pity for those who had given so much of themselves to the Congress only to see it all possibly fall apart, yes. But for herself, no. She was comparatively young, healthy, please God, and no matter what, she and Sandi would make a life for themselves. Of that she was sure. But she wasn't yet ready to give up on the Congress.

She thought of the men who were waiting for her in her office, probably expecting her to crumple, withdraw, fall apart. She was determined not to let it happen. Yes, she would be afraid, and in the privacy of her bedroom she might even cry, but this was *her* hotel, hers and Sandi's, and she would be in on every damn decision that affected it and the people in it. She would be visible everywhere as much as possible. She'd even sleep in the damn lobby if she had to. She was a Golden too and no one was ever going to accuse her of being a coward.

She was just getting ready to leave when the phone rang. It was Magda.

"You wanted me to come to the farmhouse?"

"No," she said quickly. Originally it had been her intention to ask Magda to come over so they could commiserate together. Magda would pat her on the hand and they would both be dramatically distraught. She had looked forward to the comfort and consolation of that mutual mourning but now there was no time, or need, for such indulgence.

"What is it?"

"We have a serious problem. I'd appreciate if you could be in my office in ten minutes."

"Billy Marcus told me he saw Sheriff Balbera here. Does he have something to do with it?"

"Yes. I'll see you soon," she said and hung up.

She went over to check her face in the mirror, brushed some loose strands back over her ear, wiped away a smudge on her cheek, and started to leave.

She opened the door the exact minute Sandi opened hers.

"Do I have to stay here?"

"Yes. At least until we straighten things out."

"But you're going over there."

"I'm not exactly excited about the idea, but you know I've got to go."

"I should be there, too. That's what daddy would have wanted."

"That's the last thing in the world he'd have wanted, and you know it." She shook her head. "It'll be better for both of us if you stay. You'll have to have dinner here, too."

"Oh, mom."

"Don't you understand? I'm not trying to punish you. But they think it may have something to do with the food."

"But I heard Mr. Solomon say he was ordering all new food for the dining room."

"Even so, there's no sense in taking any chances. It's going to be bedlam over there anyway. You'd only get in the way."

Sandi slammed the door and Ellen hesitated outside. She was about to ask if she wanted Alison or maybe her new friend Grant sent over but thought better of it. If possible, she didn't want her near any of the guests. At least until it was safe. By that time, she thought, unfortunately, there probably won't be any guests hanging around. She tapped lightly on the door.

"If you want," she said softly, "call Mike's Taxi in Ferndale later and have him pick up some Chinese food for you. He can leave it at the gate and I'll ask one of the guards to bring it over."

"I don't want Chinese food."

"Sandi, please, don't add to my problems. I'm only doing this for your own good." She picked up her alligator bag and started down the stairs. "I'll call you in an hour and let you know what's happening. Whatever you do," she yelled over her shoulder, "don't go out and don't invite anyone from the hotel over here."

"Yeah," Sandi grumbled.

Ellen decided not to say anything else. There wasn't time anyway. Instead she hurried out of the house and rushed back to her office.

* * *

"Shit," Bruce said. He had just realized he was twenty minutes late for his date with Fern. No one in the office had any idea what he was referring to and chalked it up to the frustration they were all feeling. He looked about self-consciously but everyone had gone back to what they were doing. I better call and make some excuse, he thought, but I won't tell her the real reason until later. He made a mental note to catch up with her before Ellen met with the guests, then picked up the phone and asked the operator to ring her room. When no one answered after a dozen rings, he assumed she had gotten tired of waiting and left.

In fact, she had gotten such an intense attack of stomach cramps it was all she could do to get her entire body onto her bed. She had been lying like this for nearly fifteen minutes, clutching her abdomen in agony and praying for the pain to subside. It didn't—and each time she tried to straighten up or stand it intensified. It felt like a workman's pneumatic drill riveting from within, the tip of it ripping and cutting at the insides of her body. Waves of nausea swept over her and her face grew alternately flushed and dry. Her eyes seemed to want to roll back into her head and whenever she opened them, the room started to spin.

It took what seemed hours to turn her head so she could look at herself in the mirror. When she did, what she saw was almost comical. Dressed in her brand new tennis midriff with the bright yellow trim, her hair cut into its new style and frozen into place with sprays and pins, she looked like a twisted gargoyle. Her arms were flung askew over her stomach, her legs drawn up unevenly to her chest. Her skin had taken on a newer and even sallower shade of white and the mascara was smudged all over her eyes.

When the phone began to ring she assumed it was Bruce and tried with the very little strength she had left to get to it. She straightened out her legs and with great effort pushed her upper body off the bed. For a moment she sat dazed. Then she tried to put her full body weight down but her feet buckled under. The phone was still ringing and she made another effort to stand. The strength it required made extra demands on her stomach muscles. The pain increased tremendously but this time she didn't even care. She just wanted to talk to Bruce, to tell him . . . Then it happened.

It happened so quickly and came so unexpectedly she panicked. It was as though her entire body had opened up, as if her entire bowel system was flushing out. She had no control. The demonic forces working within had assumed full management of all her physical powers. Her digestive and excretory systems were in total revolt.

And still the phone kept ringing. With the little energy remaining, she screamed her outrage and frustration but it made no difference at all. The backs of her legs, extending down to her sneakers, were soaked with a smelly brown liquid. Her hair, her face, her tennis outfit were totally ruined. Desperately she lunged forward in the direction of the bathroom. At one point she was actually forced to crawl. When she got there she stripped away as much clothing as she could. The pain seemed to have subsided somewhat but she was too frightened to be grateful.

Unable to pull her panties down, she stepped into the shower. For a few minutes she started to feel better and was relieved enough to begin telling herself that everything would ultimately be all right. Somehow she would fix everything up and it would be good again. She told herself she should have paid more attention to the stomachaches she had all morning. She should have taken an Alka-Seltzer or something. But now the worst was over. Whatever it was, would pass.

"I'm going to be all right," she mumbled. "I'm going to be all right." She let the water hit her face. Then she opened her mouth and drew some in as she washed her back and legs. After that she sudsed her stomach and ran the soap under her breasts as she continued the chant. "I'm going to be all right. I'm going to be all right."

Then the pain started anew, rising from the tips of her toes and centering in just below her waist. This time it came like a hammer, pounding, pounding, crashing against the inside of her stomach. She clutched at herself with both hands. The soap slipped out of her fingers. The pain made her crumple again. She squatted in the shower stall and then, despite her every effort to prevent it from happening, the deluge reoccurred. It was impossible to maintain her balance and she fell backward against the tile. The shower poured down over her limp body and she realized she had no choice. She closed her eyes and surrendered totally in the direction her body insisted on taking her. In the recess of her mind, she vaguely realized the phone had long since stopped ringing.

After Bruce hung up, he stood wondering if perhaps he shouldn't take a quick walk out to the tennis courts, find her and apologize. It bothered him that he had stood up this girl. He knew that she would take it a lot more seriously than others might, and he didn't want that to happen. He cared for her too much. Then again, he realized, it was a matter of priorities. Somehow he would find the time later to make amends. He nodded to himself and went back to the blackboard.

Jonathan opened the patio door that led out to the terrace of his penthouse apartment, stepped out and looked over the railing, and glared down at the activity below. He was both angry and terrified. Why were they all so furious with him? He still couldn't figure it out. He hadn't hired the Chinaman. It wasn't his fault the poor bastard died. All he was trying to do was protect the hotel and the Golden family name. Did that make him a son of a bitch?

Turning back to his bedroom he recalled Bruce's final threat. He, too, could be a victim of the disease. Possibly, but he hardly considered it likely. He hadn't associated with anyone who had been stricken. No, it wasn't the thought of cholera that terrorized him. What terrorized him was the thought of Nick Martin. Nick Martin. The hit man who kept asking "are you sure there's nothing you're not telling us?" The gangster who didn't like to lose. He thought about all he had done to bring the hotel and Nick's people together, the loan he had engineered, the expansion he had committed. They were here now because he, Jonathan, had convinced them this was the place to be. He had promised they would make a fortune and now . . .

He went into the bathroom to collect his shaving gear. Somehow they'd find a way to put the blame on him. He knew the way those people worked. In their minds you're just as responsible for the bad luck as you are for making the good. They weren't going to let him off the hook.

Got to get out of here, he thought. No sense hanging around for the funeral, the hotel's or mine. He remembered what Sid had said about a quarantine and realized there was no time to pack. He just threw a few things in a suitcase.

Leaving the apartment, he took the service elevator down to the basement. When the door opened, he checked the corridor, found it empty, and took the side exit to the VIP parking lot. There was no one around there either. He threw the suitcase in the Caddy's trunk and drove out quickly but as he approached the driveway to the exit, he slowed down. He checked the rearview mirror. No one seemed to notice him. He smiled confidently and kept going toward the main gate.

As he came around the small turn in the drive, he saw the back

. . . *153*

end of a state police car. The sight of the two patrolmen made him freeze. George Briggs stepped out of the security booth and put up his hand in stop-traffic fashion. For a quick second Jonathan actually considered surging ahead but the looks on the cops' faces changed his mind.

"What are you trying to do, Mr. Lawrence?" Briggs asked after he walked over to the driver's side. "I'd figure you, of all people, would know about this crazy order not to let anyone in or out."

For a moment Jonathan had trouble gathering his thoughts. The policemen were staring at him from a distance. He never expected the action would be taken so quickly but the reality of it drove home the significance of the situation. He should have left the moment he walked out of Ellen's office instead of going to his office and gathering up his documents.

"Yeah, I know," he said, "but I've got some hotel business to tend to in town. It can't be put off. I'll be back in an hour."

The state police, noting that he wasn't backing up and turning around, started for the car. Briggs shrugged and turned to them.

"This is the hotel's general manager, Jonathan Lawrence. He says he has some important business for the hotel in town and has to leave for a while."

"Out of the question, Mr. Lawrence. No one's notified us you can go. You'll have to conduct the business by phone."

"But I have important documents to deliver."

"Sorry sir, but until we're given orders to the contrary, we can't permit it."

"We're not even sure ourselves what's going on," the other patrolman said.

Jonathan stared at them for a moment. The first trooper had his right hand resting softly on the handle of his pistol. It was most probably an unconscious act but it had an intimidating effect on Jonathan. He nodded without a further word and put the car into reverse. They all watched as he backed up and turned the car in the direction of the hotel. As he headed back, he looked in the rearview mirror. The three of them remained where they were, looking in his direction, silent.

He had to get out of there, he said to himself. He had to find a way. It takes more than a couple of cops to hold Jonathan Lawrence back. He'd think of something in a minute or two. Only thing was, when he lifted his hand off the steering wheel, he couldn't prevent it from shaking.

...154

thirteen

An ominous stillness came over the group as Ellen stepped through the doorway of the conference room. Magda was close behind and they were flanked by Sid Bronstein, Bruce and Gerson Kaplow. Behind them came the Sheriff, Rafferty and Lieutenant Fielding of the State Police. They walked behind the conference table and remained standing. Ellen looked out at her fifteen department heads. The director of engineering coughed. A chair scraped against the floor. The auditor dropped his pen on the carpet. Bruce put his clipboard on the table. Everyone appeared to be uncomfortable.

"I don't know if there's any right way to begin all this," she finally said. She held herself erect and spoke without notes. "So I'm just going to state the facts as I understand them and then let the experts tell you what has been done and what remains to be done." She paused for a second to look at Magda. "Some of you already know that a staff member, a very new one, Tony Wong, was taken to the hospital Thursday evening. He died there yesterday morning from what has been positively diagnosed as cholera."

For a moment the silence was overwhelming. Then everyone started talking at once. "I don't believe it." "Jesus Christ," "Holy shit," . . . and much indistinguishable mumbling.

"Unfortunately all of this occurred without my knowledge. Mr. Lawrence took too much on himself and made certain promises to Dr. Bronstein. The promises were never kept, and as a result, Jonathan no longer serves as the general manager of this hotel. But that is a side issue, and I don't have the time or inclination to get into it now.

"The initial hope was that Wong was an isolated case, a freak thing, but it turns out, unfortunately, we're not that lucky. This morning a male guest became seriously ill and died in the health club. Not long after that an elderly woman, apparently a cholera victim, died in an ambulance on the way to the hospital. One woman has had a miscarriage, and a few other guests, including two children, have complained about minor intestinal problems. Fortunately, none of them seem very serious."

"I've got a gardener who's taken pretty sick," Bob Halloran said.

"Where is he?" Bronstein asked.

"Dungeon. First room on the right."

"Anybody else know of someone sick?" Bruce asked.

"Suddenly I don't feel so great myself," Mr. Pat said. There was an outbreak of nervous laughter.

"Anyway," Ellen went on, "the end result of all this is that by order of the public health department, the hotel is in a state of quarantine."

"Quarantine!" The word echoed through the group.

"What exactly does that mean?" Stan Leshner asked.

"It means that no one can leave the hotel and only certain people, mainly those associated with the health profession, will be allowed in," the Sheriff said.

"No one can leave? For how long?" Moe Sandman wiped his hands on his apron. "I mean most of us don't live at the hotel." There were a number of seconds from the floor.

"I guess I can help answer that," Bruce said.

"Oh, I'm sorry," Ellen said. "I should have introduced everyone before I started. My head's still spinning. This is Bruce Solomon. He's Sid—Dr. Bronstein's cousin and he's had experience with tropical diseases. He works at Mt. Sinai in New York. I'm sure most of you know the Sheriff and Dr. Kaplow, the town's public health officer. And the man on the far left is Lieutenant Fielding of the State Police. Go on, Bruce."

"Thank you. First let me explain, ladies and gentlemen, that we're not quite sure how the cholera was transmitted to the guests although we're quite certain it was brought in by Tony Wong. Just to be sure, we're doing analyses on the water and examining milk supplies. The odds are that somehow it was spread through the food, though at the moment we have no idea how. To prevent it from happening again we've ordered an entirely new supply. What's puzzling," he continued, "is that apparently Wong had no contact with the food that's been served the past few days, so in a sense we're back to square one."

"But," Halloran interrupted, speaking quickly with the excitement of someone who thinks he's found an answer, "his roommates were dishwashers."

"That's true," Bruce said.

"Then that's why they were shipped outta here last night," he continued excitedly, suddenly seeing the pieces fit together. "You guys knew some thing was up as far back as yesterday!" There was a loud murmur through the group. "What's he talking about?" "What the hell's going on?"

"We had suspicions," Bronstein said, "but they were far from conclusive. Your men were supposed to have been sent to a hospital in the city for tests, for their protection as well as our own, but . . ." He didn't want to go any further.

"Regardless," Bruce broke in, "I've pieced together things chronologically and it doesn't seem likely that Tony's roommates could have contracted the disease or passed it on. They were away from him and their room during the time he was sick and they weren't there during the incubation period. I don't think they had anything to do with spreading it."

"What you're saying then is that the source is still right here in the hotel," the publicity director said.

"Possibly, but we very honestly don't know. I realize this isn't a very satisfactory answer but I'm asking you to bear with us. We just found out about the latest cases an hour or so ago and haven't had time to track anything down. We're going to start just as soon as we're through meeting with you and the guests."

"You still haven't answered the question Moe asked," Artie Ross said. "How long is the quarantine?"

"The incubation period can last as long as six days. Since it's possible that some people contacted the disease today, we'd have to say . . . six days from today at the least."

"Six days!"

There was an explosion of raised arms, loud voices and cries of dissent. Ellen sat herself down and Magda followed suit. The men remained standing. Bruce cupped his hands around his mouth and shouted for order. He was finding himself more and more thrust into the leadership role, and although there wasn't any formal decision about it, he accepted it without argument. No one seemed to mind, least of all Sid. Gradually a semblance of order returned to the meeting.

"I'm sure Mrs. Golden is going to make a similar request," he began again, "but the point is we're meeting with all of you because we need your help. There's going to be enough chaos as it is when the guests find out what's going on."

"You can say that again," Kaplow said. Everyone looked at him as though they had just realized he was there. The stout doctor took a seat and maintained a look of total disgust.

"Wouldn't it be better just to get everyone outta here?" Halloran asked. "At least until we're sure it's all clear?"

"No," Bruce said. He continued as spokesman. "We'd be unleashing the contagion into all the communities these people went back to. Besides, the quarantine is a public health decision, not the hotel's."

"How are you going to keep them on the grounds if they want to leave?" the superintendent of service asked.

"That's our job," the Sheriff said. "Mine, Rafferty's and Lieutenant Fielding's. We'll explain our security measures when we meet with the guests and I'm hoping to have everyone's cooperation. Especially yours," he added, throwing them a no-nonsense look.

"I don't know who else I speak for," Netta, the reservations manager piped up, "but the truth is I don't know a damn thing about cholera, so I don't know what kind of help I'd be." There were many voices of agreement. "All I know is my grandmother used the word to represent any and all tragedies. Sometimes it was even a curse."

"All right," Bruce said. "You've got a point." He picked up his clipboard, looked at his notes and put it back down. "Let me simplify it as best I can, and Sid or Dr. Kaplow can add what they think is important. The symptoms include diarrhea and vomiting along with severe muscle cramps. The danger lies in dehydration and uremia. When we treat a case early on, the percentage of complete recuperation is over ninety-five percent."

"And the treatment is not terribly involved," Sid said.

"Cholera is not contagious in the sense people usually think of when they think of a contagious disease. The organism is generally transmitted only in food or water and not from person to person." There were many audible sighs of relief.

"Chances are," Sid broke in, "that since all-new food will be used from now on, those of you who are not feeling any symptoms by now are probably not in danger."

"Unless we picked it up last night or this morning, and it hasn't had time to show up," the maitre d' of the Flamingo Room said.

"Yes," Bruce said quietly. "There is still that possibility. If you'll permit me to change the subject . . . Dr. Kaplow has brought with him pamphlets about the danger signs of cholera and what to do about them to be passed out by you to the guests and your staff. Please read them carefully so you can serve as buffers and help maintain a certain degree of calm over the next few days.

"There's no sense in our getting any more technical here," he went on. "Mrs. Golden's office will serve as headquarters. We'll call some of you in from time to time to ask questions if we think the answers will help us in any way. I don't know if there's anything else I can say." He looked toward Sid and the Sheriff.

"I just want to repeat," the Sheriff said, "that we're only going to be able to beat this thing if we pull together. We'll need each other's help as much as possible."

There was a very short, very somber silence. Then Ellen stood and everyone focused his attention on her. "I want to stress that my primary concern is for you, our staff and our guests, but you all know what the impact of this is going to be. I didn't get much of a chance to grow in my job and, as you all know, I didn't assume it under happy circumstances." She hesitated a moment and swallowed. "Now I'm almost glad Phil isn't here. It would have broken his heart. In any case," she added, throwing her head back and brushing a tear away, "I need your support more than ever. Those of you who don't live on the grounds will be taken care of. Halloran will make the arrangements. Please, do what you can to keep everyone calm. Panic can cause more problems than the cholera. I'll be speaking to the guests in the nightclub in about twenty minutes so you can use the time to notify your departments."

"If this hotel's going down," Moe Sandman said, rising to his feet, "It's going down with a hell of a fight!" There were cheers and some applauding, but most faces reflected fear and concern.

"Thank you, Moe."

"If I could just add one thing," Bruce said, "we are especially interested in the whereabouts of a chambermaid named Margret Thomas during the early afternoon hours yesterday. If you or anyone in your department can help us with that, please let us know immediately. Also, if you have any specific questions, you're welcome to stay now and ask them."

For a moment no one moved. Then slowly, one by one, they began to exit, each going over to Ellen first to offer comfort and consolation.

"I'm heading over to the dungeon," Bronstein said, "to check on that gardener."

"You know, I don't even know what the hell I'm supposed to do now," Gerson Kaplow said.

"You're supposed to supervise the quarantine," Bruce said. He had little patience for stupidity. "Why don't you check with the reservation desk and see if there are any doctors in the house? We're going to need all the help we can get."

"Just think of all the medicine you're about to learn," Bronstein added, but this sarcasm was lost on the deeply worried and dejected fellow physician.

Sam Teitelbaum and his wife climbed out of the hotel station wagon very slowly. It took more effort than it ever had before. Gone for the moment was the youthful vigor that contradicted their actual age. They clung to each other with that desperation characteristic of the elderly, a desperation borne out of fear of the future and fear of the here and now. Suddenly nothing made sense. In a matter of hours a journey that had begun as a happily anticipated holiday had turned into a terrifying trip to horror and death.

They had just identified their friend Mrs. Bluestone's body for the coroner.

"Let's go right to Ellen's office," Sam said when they stepped into the lobby. His wife remained mute. She permitted herself to be directed like a somnambulist. "We want to see Mrs. Golden," he said when they reached the front desk.

"Oh, just a moment," the girl said. She stepped into the receptionist's area and whispered. There was a short conversation and another girl got up and came to the desk.

"I'm afraid Mrs. Golden's at a staff meeting right now. Can I be of some assistance?"

"No, Please," Sam said. "We *have* to speak with her. Is it all right if we wait in her office?"

"Well, I . . ." She looked at him curiously. "Do you have an appointment?"

"You don't know who I am? Sam Teitelbaum? I've been coming here every Fourth for thirty years and we're close friends of Mrs. Golden and her late husband, may he rest in peace."

The girl became flustered. "I'm sorry. I just started working here last week. Besides, Mrs. Golden's office . . . well, there are some people in there already waiting to see her."

"Let's just go up to the room, Sam."

He looked at his wife and nodded.

"You'll have her call me the moment she comes back?"

"I certainly will, Mr. Teitelbaum." She scribbled some words on a memo pad. "What room did you say were in?"

"We're in room 315."

"Fine." She added the numbers to the paper. "I'll get the message to Mrs. Golden as soon as she's free."

"Thank you," he said. If he had been wearing a hat he would have tipped it. They turned from the desk and went to the elevator.

"I want to go home," his wife said. "I want to be in my own house."

"We'll see," he said. Her voice was so thin, so small and birdlike it frightened him.

"Her sister-in-law blames us. I knew this morning she would do it. I heard it in her voice."

"That's silly. How can it be our fault that for some reason only God can understand she was taken with cholera?"

"I don't know. But they hold us responsible anyway. We're the ones who talked her into coming up here."

"I think you're reading into it." He put his arm around her protectively. "They're shocked and upset. We all are. Nobody's thinking straight. When we see them at the funeral Monday . . ."

"I want to go home, now, today," she repeated. "I don't want to wait until Monday." The elevator opened and they stepped in.

"We'll see," Sam said again. They both looked out at the lobby, their faces frozen in similar expressions of bewilderment and emotional fatigue. They stared ahead with dull, lifeless eyes. The elevator doors closed effortlessly in front of them, shutting them away from the world like the lid of a five-hundred-pound coffin.

Charlotte stopped at the top of the carpeted stairway and studied the lobby. He was nowhere in sight. She had looked everywhere—the tennis courts, the pool, the lake, even the baseball diamond. Finally she even succumbed and called his room but he didn't seem to be there either. Now she was caught between the frustration of not being able to find him and feeling like an idiot for spending so much time and energy trying to track him down. It was degrading enough to chase around after any man, but a shlump like

David Oberman? It bothered her that she cared so much. Maybe a quick cup of tea at the coffee shop would calm her down. Besides, maybe she'd find him there.

She had just started down the corridor when she spotted Bruce walking with a tall, strong-looking man in an obvious hurry. He saw her, said something to the man, and approached. She waited, a half smile on her face.

"I thought you'd be with Fern."

"I think I messed things up. I got stuck somewhere and didn't call her on time. When I did, there was no answer and I assumed she was either with you or at the tennis court."

"Oh, no," Charlotte said, now curious where Fern was, too. "And I know she's not playing tennis because I just left there. Actually," she said, almost pathetically, "I've been running all over the place trying to locate David. You haven't seen him, have you?" Bruce felt his body tense. "You have, haven't you? I can tell by your face. What is it, he didn't want to see me any more?" She was deflated. "You don't have to say anything," she finally said, "that's obviously it. I can tell."

"Oh, no. No," Bruce said, "That's not it at all. I'm sorry. I was thinking of something else. I haven't seen David all morning." It bothered him to have to lie, but he didn't think he had the right to confide in her before Ellen's meeting with the guests. It was better that she learned the truth along with everyone else.

"I'll bet," she said, sulking. "Anyway," she went on, looking over his shoulder at a dark-complexioned man in tight jeans, "I have no idea where Fern is either. Maybe she's back in the room."

"I doubt it. I just called again and nobody answered."

"In that case, maybe she's out under a tree reading a book or taking a walk somewhere."

"Think so?" He looked back and saw the Sheriff growing impatient. "Listen, I've got to run. If you find her, please, tell her I'm really sorry I was late. I'll explain it all to her later, okay?"

"Sure, sure."

He walked off quickly and rejoined Balbera. Charlotte watched the two of them hurry down the hall. Very mysterious guy, Bruce's friend, it occurred to her. Great eyes. Maybe I'll get Bruce to introduce me. She started on again, heading for the coffee shop, but as she thought more about what Bruce had said she slowed her pace until she came to a complete halt. Where the hell was Fern anyway?

. . . 162

Why hadn't she come looking for her when Bruce didn't call? Also, it wasn't like her to give up on someone she obviously cared about just because he was a few minutes late. She had gone to too much trouble to make changes for him. Her curiosity got the better of her. She turned and headed for the elevators.

As soon as she opened the door to their room she heard the sound of the shower. Odd, she thought. Why would Fern be taking a shower so soon after getting a makeup job and having her hair done? She crossed over from the dressing room to the bathroom. The door was wide open. "Fern?" She stepped inside.

The sight she confronted was so shocking that at first she was tempted to run out and make sure she was in the right place. Her roommate was slumped on the floor of the shower stall, her knees turned away from her body, her head bowed, her chin bobbing against her chest. The water pounded down rhythmically over her head, down her back, creating a steady stream under, over and around her. Charlotte's first thought was that she must have tripped and hit her head against the tile.

"Fern!" This time she screamed the name.

There was no answer. Charlotte reached in tentatively and turned off the water. Then she knelt down and tried to lift her head. Her eyes were closed and she was apparently unconscious.

"Oh my God. Fern, FERN!" She slapped her face, first once, then two and three times. There was a stirring under her closed eyelids. Charlotte put her arms under her friend's, braced her against her body and tugged her out of the shower. Her feet bounced over the floor as Charlotte grunted and pulled to get her out of the bathroom. Finally she succeeded in dragging her into the bedroom where, in two strenuous moves, she got her onto the bed. Instinctively she felt for a pulse at her wrists. She found none. Her panic grew.

She groggily stared around her and began to shout "Help, help, somebody help." She lunged for the room phone. It seemed to take the operator forever.

"Hello? This is Charlotte Fein," she finally said. "My roommate's seriously ill, and I need a doctor right away."

"What seems to be the problem?"

"I don't know. I think she hit her head in the shower. All I know is that she's not conscious and I can't feel a pulse. Please, help, do something!"

... 163

"I'll do what I can, Miss. Try to stay calm. Our doctor's already in the building and I'll put him on page right away. As soon as he answers, I'll send him up."

"Hurry . . . *please* . . . it's an emergency!" Tears started streaming down her cheeks.

"I'll get him right away."

Charlotte held the phone in her hand for a moment, then looked back at Fern's half-naked body on the bed. Gently she walked over and covered her with her bedspread. There were brownish stains on both the spread and the carpet. The trail led to the bathroom. Following the traces with her eyes, she spotted the white yellow trimmed tennis outfit, also spotted with brown, crumpled messily on the floor.

What the hell went on here? Something didn't make sense. If Fern fell in the shower, why were there stains on the bed sheet and the floor? She went back to the bed and sat beside her, taking her hand in hers and rubbing vigorously.

"Fern. It's me, Charlotte. Can you hear me?"

She detected a definite stirring again. Fern's eyelids began to flicker. Thank God, she was still alive! A very slight, nearly inaudible moan emanated from the mouth. Her lips quivered. Then her eyes parted slowly.

"Fern?"

"Charlotte," she moaned through parched lips. Charlotte had to bring her head very close to hear.

"What is it? What happened? Did you hit your head?"

"Charlotte . . ." she said again.

"Yes Fern. I'm here. What is it?"

"My stomach . . . the pain . . ." She tried, in vain, to lift her hand. "I don't think I'm going to make it. . . ."

"Oh my God!" Charlotte shot up and ran back to the phone. It made no sense to her at all. Her roommate thought she was dying. She screamed hysterically into the receiver.

"Where the hell've you been?" Manny Goldberg asked. Flo closed the door without replying. She took off her robe and draped it over the chair, then turned and glared at him. He was dressed in a baggy pair of bermuda shorts and a striped yellow and green jersey. It was tucked only halfway in, making him look even sloppier than usual.

She unclipped the snaps that held the top of her bathing suit securely to her bosom. The bit of sun she had gotten earlier caused her skin to grow pink over the top of her breasts. It caught his attention and he felt a stirring inside of his shorts.

"What did you expect me to do, Manny, wait around all day for you to recuperate from your hangover?"

"It wasn't a hangover. I told you. I was sick to my stomach."

"Sure, Manny, anything you say." Not only didn't she believe him, but by this time she didn't even care.

"How come you're back so quickly?"

"I got bored. Besides, it's about time for lunch." She watched him put his wallet in his pocket. "Are you going to join me?"

"Naw. I thought I'd take in some golf. I'll get a bite at the club house."

"Then you're obviously feeling better," she said dryly. "Amazing how the body recuperates."

"Not exactly," he said, pulling up his socks. "But I'm sure not getting any better here. Maybe the fresh air and exercise'll help."

She began stripping off her suit and he watched with admiration as her naked body emerged from the confines of the tight material. He was aroused. Her breasts suddenly seemed particularly cool and inviting. He wanted to nibble around their softness and take her nipples between his teeth.

"Of course," he said, "I could just as easily stay here and get some exercise." She recognized the tone of his voice and turned and looked at him as though he were out of his mind.

"You'd give yourself a hernia, Manny."

He wasn't sure whether she was joking or not but to be on the safe side, he laughed.

"Jesus, you're crude. And to think you call me crude?"

Crude, she thought. Yeah, she was crude sometimes. It was the story of her life. Damn it, she just couldn't shake her depression today.

He came up to her and tried to put his arms around her but she pushed him away.

"I'm not in the mood."

"Not in the mood? When the hell are you ever in the mood? There used to be a time when you couldn't get enough of me." She shook her head and hung up her bathing suit. Yes, there used to be a time. But that was a long, long time ago.

Now, during the infrequent times they made love, their foreplay was short and he was always too quick entering her. Instead of their lovemaking being something beautiful, something mutual, it was merely self-satisfying, always on his side. She remembered a line of her friend Mimi Englewood. "My husband only sees me as someone to masturbate into." How true that was of Manny.

"Not in the mood," he muttered. He shoved a cigar into his mouth and twirled it with his tongue. She simply walked into the bathroom and slammed the door.

For a moment he stood staring at it. The anger built from his loins up. He stood next to the door.

"Next time you're in the mood," he yelled, "let me know. I'll have them announce it on the public address system."

With that, he left.

Bruce looked up as Lillian Sokofsky and her coterie of nurses slid through the doorway of Ellen's office. They had all changed into their uniforms and were standing by waiting to be introduced to the guests.

"One false alarm, thank God," Lillian said.

"Who? The guy in the dungeon?"

"Yeah. Cheap wine and beer, that's all it was. Dr. Bronstein found the bottles piled in his room."

"I'm afraid we're going to have a lot of that kind of confusion. Anybody with a simple ache or pain is going to be convinced he has cholera."

"Panic turns people into hypochondriacs," Lillian said. "You know that." She settled on the couch while the others walked around looking at the photographs. "I worked the polio epidemic up here in '51 and I remember the hysterics. That's why it's so important we get the proper information out right away. We certainly don't want someone with a heart condition frightening himself into an attack just because he gets a gas pain and thinks he got 'it.' "

They stopped their conversation as the public address system came on.

"LADIES AND GENTLEMEN, MAY WE HAVE YOUR ATTENTION. YOUR ATTENTION, PLEASE." He recognized Magda's voice. "ALL OF THE GUESTS ARE ASKED TO CONGREGATE IN THE FLAMINGO ROOM IN FIFTEEN MINUTES. I REPEAT, FIFTEEN MINUTES. THIS IS AN EMERGENCY MEETING AND IS OF EXTREME IMPORTANCE.

EVERYBODY MUST ATTEND. ONCE AGAIN, THIS IS AN EMERGENCY. FIFTEEN MINUTES. DOWNSTAIRS. A MEETING IN THE FLAMINGO ROOM."

"It begins," Bruce said dejectedly. "Where's Sid?"

"He didn't get halfway across the lobby before he was called to another room. Something about a guest hitting her head in a shower. It's funny . . . but when you have an outbreak like this you forget that people have other problems too."

"Old woman?"

"Don't think so. The roommate called for help."

"Roommate, huh?" It made no impression, and he turned back to his papers. "You know," he said without looking up, "in 1849 there was a terrible cholera epidemic in London. This was before they knew anything about the existence of germs. A doctor by the name of John Snow, through painstaking backtracking, determined that most of the victims drank from a specific water pump on a specific street. He had the pump handle removed and the epidemic subsided."

"Fascinating."

"Yeah," he went on with an enthusiasm characteristic of one who enjoys his work. "Not long afterward it was scientifically proved that the water, which had been contaminated by sewage, was indeed the culprit. What they learned from this was twofold; there was something that everyone with cholera had in common, and that once proper sanitary conditions are instituted, the disease becomes practically nonexistent. That's what gets me here. The sanitary conditions at the Congress are exemplary. This means it had to be carried through the food."

"But I understand Wong had nothing to do with the kitchen."

"That's what's driving me up the wall. It's almost as if someone literally took the damn bacteria out of his room and released it in the kitchen."

"You don't really believe that, do you?" Her eyes widened in surprise.

"No, no," Bruce said. "Of course not." Actually it was the first time he had thought of it but. . . , "That would presuppose that someone knew his condition in the first place. Besides, what kind of an idiot would do something like that?" He saw that the other nurses were looking at him strangely. "I'm sorry girls, I'm not serious. I just got carried away. It's been that kind of day."

"So where does that leave you?" Lillian asked.

"I don't know. What I figured I'd do," he said, "is use old John Snow's tried and true method of backtracking. Somehow, somewhere, the victims did something in common. Now it's a question of zeroing in and finding out what."

The sound of the phone interrupted the conversation. He leaned over and picked it up.

"Hello?"

"Bruce." Sid was practically whispering.

"Yeah. What's up?"

"Listen, I've got a serious case up here."

"Cholera?" He looked at Lillian who sat forward in her seat. "I thought someone hit her head in the shower."

"No, you were right the first time." He didn't want to say cholera in front of Charlotte. "Apparently you know the girl. Fern something or other. Her roommate's been babbling and she said something about an appointment. She mentioned your name. I . . ."

"Rosen? Fern Rosen? Is that the girl you're seeing?"

"Yeah, Rosen. That's it."

"I'll be right there." He jumped up and slammed down his clipboard. "Tell her I'm on my way." He left the receiver dangling on the desk.

"What . . . ?"

He was out of the door before Lillian could finish.

fourteen

By the time Bruce reached Fern's floor, Sid was standing outside the room waiting. It was obvious he was upset and concerned. Bruce felt the blood rush to his face.

"How is she?"

Sid shook his head.

"She's in shock. Gone into a coma. I've sent for a stretcher. We can't afford to wait for an ambulance. Having her taken to the hospital in the hotel wagon." His staccato comments were driven in like nails. "Where do you know her from?"

"I just met her here. Last night. But I like her a lot."

"Her roommate's pretty upset. I gave her a sedative."

"You didn't mention Oberman, did you?"

"No. Why?"

"The roommate was . . . well, sort of interested in him. I want to go in." He reached for the door. Sid followed.

Charlotte was seated on her bed, staring at Fern who was flat on her back, her eyes closed. The white linen pillow and matching cover sheet framed her face in a shroudlike background. Her face looked drawn, so much so that her features seemed distorted to Bruce. Her hair, the permanent pounded out of it by the driving shower, fell listlessly around and under her head in clipped uneven strands. Her lips were slightly parted.

Bruce turned to Charlotte. She stared back at him with tired, empty eyes. Her lips quivered, her shoulders slumped. He saw her fingers opening and closing against the palms of her hands, moving with a crab's slow, constant rhythm. She started to shake her head.

"I don't know what's . . . wr . . . wrong . . . with her, Bruce."

"Just take it easy."

"I thought she hit her head but. . . ." She turned back and looked at Fern again. Bruce moved to her side and squeezed her hand. She didn't look up.

"She's being rushed to the hospital. She'll be all right."

Charlotte didn't reply. Bruce turned back to Sid and they walked out of the room. They stood by the doorway in the hall.

"I'd better ride over to the hospital with her," Bruce said. "Her roommate's in no condition . . ."

"Don't be surprised when you get there," Sid said. "It's total bedlam. You can't imagine . . . we don't have anywhere near the capacity we should for a major resort area. In the summertime this county swells to a population of hundreds of thousands and what do we have to service it? A two-hundred-and-eighty bed facility. Not even enough for the off-season. And now that they have to isolate anyone we send over, they'll have to set aside an entire wing and . . ."

"You'll have to start shipping some patients down to the city, won't you?"

"Those we can, sure. But who knows how hard or fast we're going to get hit?"

"That's an aspect that's going to require some coordination. Dr. Kaplow . . ."

"That asshole."

"Where did he disappear to after Ellen's meeting?"

"I haven't the slightest idea. Probably ran to the newspaper stand to get a copy of *Forbes*."

Bruce looked at his watch impatiently. "Where the hell's the stretcher?"

"I'm sure it'll be here any moment," Sid said, looking back into the room. "Listen, I won't be able to leave the hotel now. I called a colleague of mine, Julie Elias. He's a good man and he'll be at the hospital waiting for you. You can't get much better up here."

Just at that moment, Gary Becker, the hotel chauffeur, and a bellhop stepped out of the elevator. They were carrying a folding stretcher. When Dr. Bronstein waved, they walked quickly down the corridor.

"This way," Bruce called. He wanted them to run.

"What's going on?" the bellhop asked. "What's that announcement all about?"

"I'll explain later," Bronstein said. "Let's take care of this first. The girl inside is pretty sick."

"I've got the wagon pulled up to the side entrance," Gary said.

Charlotte stood up when they entered. Bruce and Sid lifted Fern, top sheet and all, on the stretcher. Then Bruce tucked a pillow under her head. Her eyes quivered slightly.

"What the hell's wrong with her?" Gary asked. Sid looked up sharply. "Hey, she doesn't have whatever Tony Wong had, does she?" The driver got so scared he almost dropped the end he was carrying.

. . . *170*

"Hey, take it easy. We've got a sick lady here," Sid admonished. They moved toward the door. Bruce turned to Charlotte. She had her hand to her mouth.

"You try to take a nap. As soon as I get back from the hospital, I'll come up and let you know what's happening." He was glad Sid had given her a sedative. Better to knock her out than to chance her getting hysterical at the meeting.

"Is she going to die?" she asked tentatively.

"No," Bruce said quickly. He wanted to push the thought out of his own head as well. Then he rushed out to follow Bronstein.

"What the hell's going on here?" Gary asked as they left the elevator.

"I'll tell you all about it in the wagon," Bruce said.

They carried the stretcher, out of view of the guests, to the side entrance. The back door of the wagon was opened and the back seat folded down, making it into a makeshift ambulance. Bruce got into the passenger side after the back door was closed.

"Listen, doc," Gary said, pulling Sid to the side of the car. "I don't know whether this is important or not but Jonathan Lawrence made me take Tony Wong's roommates and a chambermaid into New York yesterday."

"We know all about that, Gary, and we'll be talking to you about it later."

"Yeah, but this chambermaid, Margret Thomas, she got pretty sick on the way down."

"Hey," Bruce yelled, leaning over and honking the horn. "Let's get a move on!"

"Look, Gary, tell Bruce everything. He's . . . he's sort of in charge of that now."

"What's going on?"

"Just go ahead. Tell him on the way to the hospital."

"I don't like the sound of this," Gary said. "Am I in any danger driving that wagon? I mean . . . I took Wong to your office in it and . . ."

"No, you're safe, Gary. Honest."

The driver moved to the car and got in with obvious reluctance. Slowly he shifted into gear and started away. Bronstein and the bellhop watched them go.

"So what the hell's wrong with her, doc?"

"Huh? Oh, I'm not completely sure yet. Gotta take some tests." He started back into the building.

"I forgot to tell you, doc. Rosie said your wife called and she wants you to call her back right away."

"Thanks." Better I don't call her back, he thought. That's just what I need. More *tsures*.

Ellen knocked gently on the Teitelbaums' door. It was a long moment before Sam opened it and when he did, she saw the terror and tragedy of what was happening in the hotel written all over his face.

The wrinkles and lines had sunk deep in his skin. His once sparkling, teasing eyes were now glassy and dull. Nevertheless he was still dressed immaculately. Men his own age often looked lost in their clothes—buttons misfastened, belts too small for their pants, faces dotted here and there with stubble missed by an uncertain razor, nudged and badgered continually by their wives to zip their flies, tie their laces, and tuck in their shirts. But not Sam.

He still dressed like a man with a strong grip on life. His posture was erect, his gait certain and definite. He was very much in control, except, perhaps, today. Because he was a contemporary of Papa Golden, whom she loved, Ellen had always looked up to him as one of the last survivors of an era populated by men who were rugged, sturdy and strong. They had been the true pioneers, the ones who didn't know from comfort and easy living, from inheritances and going by the book. The only thing they knew was work, hard work, and Ellen had a great deal of respect for them.

Sam took one look at her and hugged her tight and close.

"Blanche is lying down," he said, stepping back and starting for the bedroom.

"No, let her sleep."

"She's not sleeping, just resting. And I know she wants to talk to you."

Ellen sat down in the arm chair but stood up again as Sam brought his wife in. Her eyes were streaked with tiny red lines and she looked as though it took all her strength to walk. Ellen gave her a kiss and the three of them sat down.

"I came up as soon as I could."

"We appreciate it," Sam said. "We know how busy you are. Blanche is upset because the Bluestone family blames us for what's happened. I keep trying to tell her they're in shock and don't really know what they're saying."

"I know what they're going through," Ellen said. "It's only natural. When there's trouble people always look for someone or something to blame. Right now, for example, in the eyes of most people, the hotel is responsible for what's happening. It's so ironic. You know how we've always prided ourselves on a clean kitchen. Why, we spend twice for staff in that department what any other hotel in the mountains does."

"You could eat off the floor in that kitchen," Blanche said. There was a silence. "So, Ellen, what are you going to do?"

"It's mostly out of my hands now. I'll be meeting with the guests right after I leave you to explain what's going on. The health authorities have taken control. The hotel's in quarantine."

"Doesn't that keep people in as well as out?" Sam asked.

Ellen nodded.

"But we have to leave tomorrow," Blanche said. "There'll be the funeral, and . . ." She looked at Sam but he said nothing in support.

"I'll see what can be done," Ellen said, "but I can't make any promises. Like I said, the situation's out of my hands. But you know I'll do everything I can."

"Don't worry about us," Sam said. "You've got more important things than us old folks to think about. You know, it's curious how the past has a way of coming back at us," he said, leaning back on the couch. "I remember the panic up here in 1916. That was the bad summer of infantile paralysis. Papa Golden and I sat up many nights sweating out tests and examinations of children who got sick when this was nothing more than a small tourist area. You can imagine what would have happened if one of those kids contracted polio while at the Congress."

"No one would have stayed and no one would have come back," Blanche said.

"But as luck would have it, thanks be to God, no one got sick."

"And what about the Spanish flu?" Blanche asked, getting caught up in his reminiscences.

"That was two years later. I remember it was in August. Barber shops, stores in town and hotels had to close at six P.M. each day. People were afraid to mix with each other and everybody walked around in a perpetual state of terror. But once again we were lucky and no one at the Congress got sick."

"Nevertheless, can you imagine what's going to go on here after Ellen meets with the guests?" Blanche said.

"Come, dear, don't make her any more frightened than she is."

"It's all right," Ellen said quietly. "I'm resigned to the fact that this is probably the end of the Congress."

"How can you *say* such a thing, young lady?" Sam Teitelbaum's face took on some of his old energy. "Do you know what went in to building this place? Why I worked on my hands and knees side by side with Papa Golden long before you were even born. How can you be so quick to give up?"

Ellen remained mute.

"No one thought the hotel industry would survive the polio epidemics. And no one thought they'd survive the flu. But the important thing is that they did. And you're going to survive this, too. Just wait and see."

Ellen reached for his wrinkled hand, brought it up to her lips, and kissed it. "Thank you for that." She looked first to him and then to Blanche. "I love you both. You said something earlier, Sam, about the past having a way of coming back. If it could just happen one more time . . . if we could just see this tragedy through . . ." She blinked a tear away as she checked her watch and realized it was time for her to leave. "Incidentally," she said, standing up and getting her pocketbook, "I also came here to tell you that if you wanted, you could stay over with us at the old farmhouse. I thought it might make you feel safer and . . ."

"No, no," Sam said. He stood up too. "Why take a chance of spreading things? We don't know, maybe this thing's in us too."

Ellen knew there was no reassurance she could give. "It's an open invitation. Think about it. If you change your mind, just let my secretary know and she'll make the arrangements." She kissed them both again and hurried out of the suite.

The moment the door closed behind her, she wanted to cry. It wasn't rational, she knew, but still somewhere deep inside she did feel responsible for what was happening. After all, it was at her hotel that all these people had been exposed to cholera. A few had already died, others had gotten sick, and they probably still hadn't seen the last of it.

If old Mrs. Bluestone hadn't come through the main gate of the Congress, she might have lived to see her grandchildren grow up. And what about that young man Oberman? And the kids at the day camp? She suddenly found it hard to swallow. We've got to beat this thing back, she thought. We've *got* to. She straightened and moved to the elevator, determined to speak with confidence when she faced the guests.

When it was over, she would go somewhere and mourn.

There was no way to deaden the impact of that announcement over the public address system. Those who were able to hear it were thrown into a frenzy. Some imagined it some sort of hotel prank. Was it a mysterious new July Fourth activity? Their confusion and anxiety was compounded by the fact that many of the lower echelon staff members seemed to know nothing and looked just as confused. The front desk was mobbed. The girls were polite and patient, but some guests resented their "we really don't know" reply and responded with nasty looks and remarks.

Mimeographed messages on slips of paper were run off in the print shop and the bellhops were given stacks, assigned floors, and told to knock on doors. If there was no response, their orders were to slip the messages under the doors and go on to the next room.

Other bellhops were sent outdoors to pipe the announcements on the golf course, tennis courts, at the pool, down by the lake, on the baseball fields and wherever guests might be. The worst reactions came on the golf course and at the pool. Some guests were abusive and refused to leave. When the bellhops couldn't give them any details about the meeting in the nightclub, they disregarded it altogether. However, most guests were surprised by the unusual request and dutifully obeyed.

The noise in the lobby was intense as the people milled around. Some were angry they hadn't been permitted to finish their lunch. Children, pulled along reluctantly by their parents, cried and whined. Guests shouted questions to each other to discover what they could. For some the general ignorance created a carnival atmosphere. Over near the card room practical-jokers tried to outdo one another by screaming ridiculous reasons for the gathering.

"They've run out of borscht!"
"Someone's been caught stealing towels!"
"There's a virgin loose in the hotel!"

Magda stationed herself in the center of the crowd, reassuring people, calming children, smiling, squeezing hands, kissing cheeks. Old-timers pulled at her, first-timers flocked around. She gave no one any specific information but her presence, her smile and her warmth helped lower the level of insecurity, especially for the elderly.

Rafferty and two of his security men gently moved everyone toward the nightclub. Although they were firm, they neither pushed nor shouted. Some of the department heads helped out. Stan Leshner brought people in from the courts. Moe Sandman cleared out the coffee shop. Netta, the reservations manager, made sure everyone was out of the beauty parlor and boutiques.

Sandals slapped against the floor. Some guests still carried their tennis rackets. Many from the pool wore nothing but their bathing suits with a towel wrapped around their necks or tied around their waists. As the parade of vacationers moved through the club's wide double doors, their voices dropped immediately. Instinctively, the earliest arrivals had avoided the front tables. Most had congregated toward the rear. Artie Ross and Mr. Pat pleaded and begged them to move forward. Wives took their husbands' hands and pulled their children close. The nightclub was never designed to be a highly illuminated place and even though all the lights were on, the effect was still somewhat subdued. To compensate for that, all the stage lights were activated.

The sight of Ellen, Bronstein and the five public health nurses in uniform, had an immediate effect on the crowd. Although Bronstein was not known to most of the guests, almost all had seen the large portrait of Ellen and Phil in the main lobby and a great many had met her at the cocktail party the night before. It was the public health nurses that caused the greatest stir. The uniforms even stifled the jokers. Something serious was up. This was obviously no joke.

As more and more people came in, Ellen moved toward the microphone on stage. In a calm, steady voice she asked them to please take seats. "It'll help if more of you move down and make room for those entering. Please."

Bar waiters acted as ushers, directing people in off the aisles. Gradually, those who had reacted angrily about having their recreation disturbed became less belligerent and more interested in what was about to take place. Eager guests started shouting at others who were taking too long to get seated.

"The quicker we all get settled, the quicker I can begin," Ellen said.

"When we're ready to start," Sid said, partially covering his mouth with his hand so no one out front could hear, "introduce me right after your opening remarks. Hopefully, hearing from a doctor will calm some of them down."

"Shouldn't Gerson Kaplow be here?"

"He should, but I don't know where he is. I can tell you this much, I sure as hell don't want to have to be the one to deal with the press. That should be his responsibility as public health officer."

"The press," Ellen said, repressing an urge to slap her palm against her forehead. "I've been so preoccupied I haven't even given it a thought."

She turned and looked out at the nearly filled Flamingo Room. The noise level had grown again, but most of the guests now had their attention fixed on her and the others on stage. She saw Magda walking down an aisle, reaching over tables to pat hands. Amazing woman, Ellen thought. She always comes through.

She looked down at her notes and realized her hands were sweaty. Despite the air conditioning, the nightclub still seemed stifling. It was time to begin, she thought. No point in putting it off any longer. Visions of an hysterical mob flashed through her mind. She imagined people trying to rush out, men leaping over tables, women screaming, children crying. Oh God, she thought, I hope my voice doesn't crack.

There were only a few people moving through the doors now. She looked over at Sid. He and the nurses had stopped talking; their eyes were fixed on her. Sid nodded and then she began.

They were just about to go down to the Pelican Lounge for a drink when Nick noticed a slip of paper under the door.

"What is it?" Melinda asked.

"I'm not sure." He leaned down to pick it up. "Something about a meeting in the Flamingo Room that everyone is requested to attend."

"Sounds more like some kind of prank," Melinda said. She didn't add it sounded like something Grant would do if he were bored. She decided to call the front desk and check.

"Well, it's true," she said, hanging up. "They confirmed it."

"What the hell could it be?"

"They didn't seem to know themselves."

Nick walked to the window and looked out. He saw people,

alone and in groups, converging on the main building in various states of dress.

"Maybe another country attacked us," Melinda said. "Like Pearl Harbor."

"Stop kidding. I don't like this," he said. "C'mon, we better get going."

He took her by the arm and she locked the door behind them. At the same time, Grant was bounding up the stairs in twos and threes, excited by the news and eager to tell his mother. When Melinda saw him fly around the corner and into the corridor, she turned white as though she'd just seen a ghost.

Even from down the hall, Grant recognized her reaction. He had seen it often enough before. Sometimes, if he wanted to be nice to her, he was accommodating and pretended he didn't know her. Not that she had actually come out and suggested he do that, but he knew she appreciated it. But now, as he came upon her accompanied by this sharply dressed, dark-complexioned man, he felt resentful and angry. This was obviously the same man he'd seen in the shower and here he was, holding her arm, looking cool and cocky as if he had gotten away with something.

Melinda turned back to the room.

"You forget something?" Nick asked.

"No. Yes," she said quickly. It might work, she thought, if I get back there fast enough and pretend he has the wrong room. But Grant stopped her with a shout.

"Ma!" God, how she hated the sound of that word.

"Ma?" Nick took on a half smile. He looked from the approaching Grant to Melinda, who had stopped dead in her tracks.

"Yes," Melinda said. "That's my son."

"You know," Nick said, "I thought I saw a pair of pants too big for you draped over a chair. So," he said, looking at the gawky youth in front of him.

"Grant, this is Mr. Martin. Nick, this is Grant."

"Hi," Nick said, extending his hand. Grant looked at it but didn't shake. Nick brought it back, the smile frozen on his face. "I guess I'll learn about you through surprises, huh, Melinda?"

"Grant, don't you know enough to say hello?"

"Hello," he mumbled, his eyes fastened to the floor.

"I didn't see you in the dining room," Nick said.

"That's because I wasn't there."

"Where are you going, Grant?" Melinda broke in, eager to find out what was on his mind. "Why were you running up the stairs like that?"

Grant hesitated a moment. He couldn't understand it, but suddenly he felt like flaring out wildly. He wanted to scream and yell and break something apart. She looked so good, he thought, so fresh and clean. Why did she give it away so easily? This man was good-looking, but he was a damn stranger, just like all the others. There was never anything lasting between them.

"Something important's going on," he said. "They're telling everybody they have to go to the nightclub. I wanted to make sure you knew."

"We already do. Someone put a note under our door. What's up?"

"I don't know. I was outside walking by the big fence and one of the bellhops told me, but just before that, I saw a bunch of cops lock a gate."

"What cops?"

"He must mean the hotel security," Nick said.

"No, they weren't hotel security. I know hotel security. They were state policemen."

"State police locked the gate? Why?" Nick asked. Grant chose to ignore him.

"Is this one of your stories, Grant?"

"Shit! I don't care if you believe me or not!" He started to walk away.

"Grant! Stop it! Either go down to the meeting or go back to the room and take a shower or something."

The word triggered his ire.

"Is that what you did? Do you want me to take a shower just the way you did?" He gave her a dirty look and stormed away.

"Now you know why I don't talk about him," Melinda said. She took Nick's arm as if to insure he wouldn't run away. "He's always been a problem."

Nick's mind was not on Grant. "This is damn peculiar," he said, looking again at the mimeographed message. "Let's get a move on."

"Maybe there's a killer loose in the hotel," Melinda said.

That's all this place needs, he thought, publicity like that. Well, there was only one way to find out.

* * *

There was a button outside the emergency room door. Pressing it signaled the attendant or nurse inside to open it to receive patients. Bruce practically pounded on it. Every second could be crucial. An attendant opened the door and a nurse came up behind him.

"You'll need a roller," Bruce shouted. The attendant went to get it and the nurse came to the wagon.

"Is this Dr. Bronstein's patient from the Congress?" she asked.

"Yes, it is."

"Good. We've been waiting for her."

The attendant came back pushing a rolling stretcher and with Bruce's help, lifted Fern onto it. Then Bruce pushed it into the hospital.

"Should I wait?" Gary asked.

"Definitely," Bruce called back. "Don't dare leave without me." The door closed behind him and he looked about frantically.

"In here," the attendant said, pointing to a large wooden door to the left. They rolled her into a small emergency room. The nurse went to take Fern's blood pressure.

"Call for Dr. Elias," she told the attendant. "You'll have to wait outside," she said to Bruce. He hesitated a moment, then walked out. The moment he came back into the hall, he was approached by a man in a suit and tie.

"Did you just bring a woman in from the Congress hotel?"

"Yes. Why?"

"Jesus, how the hell did you get out of there? Are you a doctor? What's happening up there, anyway?"

"Who the hell are you?"

"Name's Bert Young." He flashed a press card. "I'm with the *Times Herald.*"

"I'm sorry. There's nothing I can tell you."

"C'mon, buddy, give me a break. You're the only one who's gotten out of there since that quarantine's been slapped on. I'm trying to get a scoop."

"I don't have any scoops," Bruce said. He noticed a stout gray-haired man hurrying down the corridor.

"How are the people taking it?"

Bruce ignored him. "Dr. Elias?" he called.

"Yes."

"I'm Bruce Solomon, Sid Bronstein's cousin." He reached out to shake his hand. "I'm with the patient from the Congress. Her name's Fern Rosen."

...180

"Yes, I've been expecting you. Let me take a look at her and I'll speak to you as soon as I'm through." He walked into the emergency room.

"Is she a cholera victim?" the reporter badgered. "How many have there been?"

"Look, I'm sure they'll have a news conference, and then you'll have a chance to ask all the questions you want."

"Yeah, but why can't you . . ."

"Listen, damn it," Bruce said, pushing him back with his forefinger. "I'm here because I'm concerned about that young woman in there. My mind has no room for any scoops or news or sensational details. What are you anyway, some kind of parasite, hanging around emergency rooms? Buzz off."

Young shook his head.

"I'm just another guy trying to do his job," he muttered and walked away. Bruce felt some remorse, but his mind centered back on what was taking place in the emergency room. It seemed at least half an hour before Dr. Elias finally came out.

"It's going to be a battle," he said. "She's lost a great deal of body fluid, and she's still in shock. There's no point in waiting around. It'll be a while." He put the chart down on a nearby desk. "How are things going at the hotel?"

"By now the guests are being told and I expect all hell's breaking loose. You're right. I'd better go back. Can I reach you here later?"

"I'll be here until seven."

"Thanks," Bruce said. He looked at the closed emergency door for a moment, debating whether or not he should step in. He decided against it and walked back to the hospital's emergency exit. When he stepped outside, he was shocked to find that the hotel car and driver were no longer there.

fifteen

"I have met many of you personally this weekend," Ellen began, "and some of you know me from previous visits to the Congress. I'm Ellen Golden," she explained for the others who might not recognize her, "and I've called this meeting because I'm afraid we have a very serious problem. I should say, a crisis." She paused. A loud murmur rippled through the audience. "Before I give you the details, I want to assure you that every possible precaution is being taken, and that we have the best medical personnel available for your consultation."

Sid tapped her on the shoulder.

"Don't let them know anyone's died," he whispered. "Not yet."

"But . . . all right," she said. She turned back to her audience. "Three people, one a member of our staff and two guests, have come down with what has been positively diagnosed as cholera."

For a short moment there was complete silence. It reminded Sid of the hushed moment right before a tornado hits. He was sure the response resulted from a mixture of things—disbelief, ignorance and delayed reaction. "Now," Ellen started, but the eye of the storm had passed. People began to scream and a few of them even cried. Hundreds of people shouted questions at her. A few had backed toward the doors. Ellen put her hands up and gestured for quiet.

"Please, we have to remain calm," she said. "If you'll give me a chance, I'll answer whatever questions I can. Those I can't, will be answered by the professionals up here with me."

"Why did you bring us all together?" a man in the first row shouted. There were many, many seconds.

"There is no danger whatsoever in your being together. That is not how the disease is spread. The doctor will explain more about that shortly. First, let me bring you up to date on what is happening. Please." There were attempts to quiet one another and calm the children. The noise subsided. "Public health authorities have been brought in and certain actions, under their direction, have already been instituted."

"We all just better get the hell outta here," someone shouted. The seconding began again.

. . . 182

"NO, YOU CAN'T," Ellen's voice bounced off the walls. The speakers had been turned up to maximum just at the right moment. It held back a mass exodus. "THE HOTEL HAS BEEN PLACED UNDER QUARANTINE."

"Oh my God!" The words reverberated like in an echo chamber in an amusement park.

"We will explain exactly what that means in a few minutes. But first, I want you to know what's being done to protect you." The noise did not subside. "Please, won't you let me speak?" Her sincerity, her composure, her firm determination to stand her ground gradually won out.

"Please, let me continue. If not, you'll frighten yourselves unnecessarily." She paused dramatically, seizing more control of the crowd by forcing them to grow even quieter.

"The disease is not spread through the air you breathe. It is spread through contaminated food or water. You have to take it into your mouths."

For a good moment, Ellen had control of their attention. Then a woman fainted. She simply fell over her chair near the center aisle. All hell broke loose again.

"She must have it," another woman screamed. Those closest to the fallen woman pushed back. Others, too far in the rear to see exactly what had happened shouted for information. Exaggerations were passed along the way. The hysteria mounted in a chorus of shouts and warnings as people got up to leave. Ellen turned with a pleading look to Sid. Two of the public health nurses had gone down to treat the woman who had fallen.

"These people are going to trample each other," Sid said. They both looked down at the Sheriff who had taken a position in the front. He stepped forward, drew his revolver from his shoulder holster and fired a blank at the floor just where the musicians' pit met with the stage. The blast echoed off the nightclub walls in a thunderous reverberation. Everyone grew still; even the bawling children paused.

"YOU'VE GOT TO GET A HOLD OF YOURSELVES," Ellen screamed. "WE HAVE PROCEDURES DESIGNED TO PROTECT AND HELP YOU, BUT IF YOU DON'T LISTEN, YOU WON'T KNOW WHAT TO DO."

"Let her talk," a man shouted.

"Give her a chance."

"Shut up, everybody!"

"We've got to prevent this kind of hysteria from taking hold," Ellen said, composed again. "Now let me tell you what has been done. First, all-new foodstuff has been ordered and received. All of the old food has been disposed of. Every piece of kitchen equipment is being sterilized again and again. And our water has been analyzed and found germ free."

"She's holding them now," Sid said to no one in particular. The public health nurses had brought the woman in the audience back to consciousness and had her sitting up in a chair.

"On the stage with me here are members of the county's public health nurse department and Dr. Bronstein, our local physician. There are other doctors in the hotel as well. They will be available to you at all times to answer questions or to examine anyone who thinks he might be ill."

"What about this quarantine?" someone shouted.

"Quarantine is standard procedure when cholera is discovered. We're simply not sure who might have been contaminated and who might not have been," Ellen said. Her honest reply had a sobering effect. "The quarantine will last for the next six days."

A roar went up from the crowd. Some people were shouting their absolute refusal to cooperate. Others were expressing reasons for having to leave on schedule. Still others were reinforcing and supporting those who vocalized their dissatisfaction.

"We better get into specifics," Sid said and went to the microphone. The sound of a new voice drew back the audience's attention.

"Please, let us have your attention a little while longer. My name is Dr. Bronstein. Mrs. Golden's statements are correct. The law is very specific, and it must be followed not only to protect you, but to protect other people on the outside who could possibly be infected. The hotel has been sealed off. Local and state law enforcement officers are serving as security.

"You've turned this place into a damn prison," a man shouted. There were many shouts of agreement.

"I assure you," Ellen said, taking the microphone again, "that none of the hotel's facilities or services will be shut down. Of course, and I'm sure I don't even have to say it, the expenses for the extra days, as well as yesterday and today, will be borne by the hotel. You must know that we regret what's happening as much as any of you do. It's small comfort, I know, but the bars in our lounge and nightclub will be open twenty-four hours a day and the drinks are on the house. Rest assured we will do everything possible to make this as inoffensive as possible.

"Now if I may," Bronstein said "let me just briefly explain what we have set up in the way of medical facilities. The director of activities' office and adjoining health office will be utilized as examination rooms. Anyone suffering any discomforts should come there for a preliminary examination. The public health nurses will be circulating among you, visiting your rooms when you request it, and they will answer whatever questions you have. Pamphlets are also being distributed at the main desk which will give you more information about the disease, its symptoms and the precautions that must be taken. I'm sure you'll see that we have taken all the necessary precautions.

"Cholera has a very small fatality rate when treated early and we are not anticipating any serious problems. If we all stay calm, I'm confident we can keep the situation quite under control."

He backed away from the mike and Ellen moved to it quickly before the audience had time to break out into conversation again.

"I know many of you have personal problems with this quarantine. Magda and other members of my staff will be stationed in my office to help you deal with them. And now if I may get personal for just a moment." She cleared her throat. "I can't tell you how sorry I am that this has happened to you. I would give all that I own for it not to have happened, but it seems tragedy has stationed himself at our gate. For those of you who are interested, Rabbi Gordon has scheduled a prayer service in the synagogue one hour from now. I know it will be difficult," she said, her voice now nearly cracking, "but as Dr. Bronstein said, we must all try to stay as calm as possible. Thank you and God bless you all."

She stepped away from the front of the stage. Sid put his arm around her shoulder.

"Very good," he said, kissing her lightly on the cheek. The crowd began drifting from the club. Their voices were still loud and there were occasional shouts and hysterical arguments, but for the most part, the crowd sounded like an audience emerging from a Broadway show. They moved out single file in an orderly fashion. Most faces wore looks of utter confusion. Older people clung to one another in a new desperation. Mothers held the hands of their small children so tightly that they complained.

Guests who had come in from the golf course, the tennis courts and the pool moved out to the lobby with indecision. Should they simply go back to what they were doing? How could they frolic in the sun after hearing all that? It seemed a little indecent. Everywhere people were questioning their slightest aches and pains. A large group had already gathered around the main desk to get the pamphlets. Many wanted to go outside to see just how tight the security really was around the hotel's entrances and exits. Others sought the safety of their rooms. There was a rush on all the available phones. Small meetings were being held throughout the premises. Opinions were being voiced and discussed. Statements were announced in headline style.

"They're not telling us everything."

"The water must have been bad no matter what they say. Don't drink it."

"If they think I'm going to eat anything from their kitchen, they're crazy."

"They ain't keeping me here for six days. I don't give a damn what they say!"

Ellen and Sid retreated through the stage's back entrance. The public health nurses waded through the crowd. The lights on the nightclub's stage shut off as though a performance had just ended. At the back near the bar, some people had already started taking advantage of the free booze. Others looked at them as though they were totally insane.

"We should have told them everything," Ellen said, as she and Sid followed a corridor that would take them back around to the front of the hotel. "They're going to find out one way or the other that people have died and then they won't believe anything we tell them."

"If you had mentioned death, you would never have been able to hold them together long enough to get anything out. Believe me."

"Maybe," Ellen said. Then she stopped walking. "But that's the last time. I will not tolerate a single additional half-truth around here any more. No matter what the consequences."

Sid nodded. They walked on.

Manny Goldberg's face was flushed. When the mass meeting with Ellen ended, he dashed out of the nightclub so quickly that Flo got lost in the crowd behind him. Finally, she caught up with him in the lobby.

"What's the big rush? You're running like you've got somewhere to go."

"I can't stay here," he murmured. "There's no way." He looked about as if to see if there were escape routes hidden behind the chairs and couches.

... *186*

"You didn't feel well before, Manny," she said, touching the palm of her hand to his forehead. "Maybe you should go for the examination."

He brushed her hand away roughly. "I'm all right. I'm all right." She shook her head and followed him outside.

"Where the hell do you think you're going?"

"I've got to get back to the city," he whispered. She studied his face. His eyes were wide and excited. His mouth was open, the lips straining at the corners. She stepped back. He looked as though he had gone berserk. For a moment she wondered if he had indeed contracted cholera and this wild and strange reaction was one of the symptoms.

"What's wrong with an extra few days on the house? We'll call my brother. You know Mike can be trusted to handle the business. Besides, you heard them. There are policemen all around to make sure we don't get out."

"I still gotta go," he repeated, as if he hadn't heard a word she said. He brought his hands out from his waist and began slapping the sides of his legs. Carrying on a tantrum like that, dressed in his ill-fitting tee shirt and sloppy bermudas, he looked almost comical.

"Manny, get hold of yourself, for godsakes. Everyone's looking at you."

He turned around and glared. "Look," he said. "Look." He took her arm brusquely and led her on to the patio. "I lied to you."

"When? What lie?"

"When I told you Mike was selling out his partnership in the firm to raise money for debts. It wasn't true. It's the other way around."

"I don't follow you, Manny. What are you trying to tell me?"

"I made a bad investment. I . . . I gambled on something that didn't come through." He began to slap his legs again.

"But . . ."

"I had to borrow some money fast to cover myself so I put up our piece of the business as collateral."

"That's impossible," she said. "I'd have to sign documents too. Don't try to bullshit me about this, Manny. My father took great pains to explain things to me. I may not be a genius but—"

"I . . ." He looked away from her. "I forged your signature."

"You did what?" She couldn't believe what she was hearing.

"I had to. It looked like a sure thing. There was this prime land. A fast food chain was supposed to buy it. I had inside information." His face strained with every sentence. He looked as though he would explode at any minute. "I gambled a hundred thousand dollars. If it went through, I coulda made a half million, but . . ."

"The food chain didn't buy it," she said quietly.

"Yeah. That's about it."

"So what's going to happen now?"

"The guys I borrowed from want their money back. Mike said he'll be able to raise fifty thousand dollars on my share of the company. That's the amount I need to hold them off. If I don't get there by Tuesday . . ."

"So they'll wait."

"No," he said, shaking his head, "they won't. They're not the type who wait."

"What do you mean they're not the type who wait. Just who are these people anyway." She raised her voice. "Tell me, who?"

"What's the difference who? I borrowed money and I've got to be there Tuesday to repay some of it. That's the only thing that's important. There are papers I have to sign." He started muttering to himself. "You don't understand. You just don't understand."

"And Mike," she said. "What happens to the business if my brother can't come up with the fifty thousand dollars?" Manny stared at the grass beneath his feet. "You asshole, you dumb . . ." She started to get hysterical. "My father worked all his life to build that business and now Mr. Bigshot here . . ."

"Your father, your father."

She was at him in an instant, like a wild animal. For a few moments his body absorbed all the pain, all the agony, all the tension she'd ever experienced. She swung out indiscriminately, her hands clenched into small fists. She kicked and pounded at him. He tried to fend her off, holding his arms up to serve as an umbrella.

"Stop it, you crazy . . ."

A small crowd began to gather. Two men stepped forward and tried to hold her back. She cursed and spat at them as well. One man's arm was badly scratched. Manny retreated, waving his fist at her.

"You do that again and I'll belt you one in the mouth. I swear it."

"Bastard," she screamed. He walked off toward the side of the building. She relaxed and the men let her go.

"Take it easy, lady. We've got enough troubles around here as it is."

"Go fuck yourself," she said. They moved away from her

quickly and the crowd dispersed. She looked in the direction of Manny's retreat and then went back into the hotel.

Sandi looked out her bedroom window and watched the guests emerging from the main house. She had seen and heard them all being gathered inside and she knew what must have taken place. So this was the "partnership" her mother had designed for her. This was the way she would be treated like an adult—told to stay home, kept away from the hotel. It had all been words, meaningless adult words again. In her mother's eyes, she was still a little girl.

She certainly didn't want to stay alone at the farmhouse for the next six days but she didn't know what else to do. Alison was pretty mad at her so she doubted she would come over. She thought about calling some of her friends from school and seeing if she could visit, but then she remembered she couldn't get off the grounds. God, she really was a prisoner.

Grant Kaplan, she thought. They had made a vague agreement to meet again, but he probably had forgotten all about it by now. He was so strange—yet thinking about him seemed even more enticing than it was before. In the midst of all the turmoil, all the new restrictions and confinements, the thought of a rendezvous took on added danger and intrigue. She wondered what he was doing and how he had reacted to what had happened.

She went to the phone and tried to call him but all the lines were tied up and they stayed that way for as long as she tried. Finally she gave up in disgust and flopped on the bed. For a while she just lay there, thinking about different guys who she thought were cute. Included in her list was this new man, Bruce Solomon. Wouldn't it be fun to be over at the office working alongside him? She began to fantasize. Together they would solve the crisis. Afterward they would walk in the moonlight, holding hands, laughing and talking softly. Then he would take her in his arms and kiss her passionately. His lips would travel down her neck. She'd let him run his fingers under her blouse. Maybe they would sit on a bench in the darkness. Maybe . . .

The ringing phone shattered her fantasy. For a moment she resented it. Then she realized it was contact with the outside and she practically lunged for the receiver. It was Magda.

"Hi, Sandi. Are you all right?"

"Of course I'm all right. Why shouldn't I be?" She was a little put out that it wasn't Grant.

"I just wanted to make sure. Can you make supper yourself or would you like me to come over later and do it for you?"

"I'm not a baby, Magda."

"No one said you were. I just thought you might want some company. What will you have for dinner?"

"I dunno. I'm not very hungry."

"You're feeling all right, aren't you?" There was obvious concern in her voice. Sandi debated whether or not to plant some doubt in Magda's mind. She felt just mad enough at her mother to do it, but then she realized they'd send Dr. Bronstein over and she'd have to go through some sort of medical examination. She changed her mind.

"I'm fine. I'm just bored."

"Be grateful for that," Magda said. "I've got to go back to work. I'll call you later."

"Magda, wait."

"Yes?"

"I want to call someone in the hotel but the damn lines are tied up."

"I guess all the guests are calling home. You can imagine what's . . ."

"Can't you get me a line? Please?" Her plea was hard to refuse.

"Okay, I'll try. But remember, don't invite anyone over to the farmhouse. Your mother . . ."

"I won't."

"Good girl. Hang up and I'll have them ring you as soon as a line's free."

"Thanks, Magda. You're a peach."

She sat back and waited. Less then five minutes later, the switchboard operator called. Sandi asked for Grant's room. When the phone didn't answer on the fourth ring she was ready to give up. Then he picked up the receiver.

"I'm confined to the farmhouse," she said. "It's Sandi."

"I know. Whadja do, rob the cookie jar?"

"Very funny. Don't you know what's going on at the hotel?"

"I didn't go down to that meeting, if that's what you mean."

"Why not?"

"I took a shower instead."

"I don't believe it."

"Honest. The faucet's still drippin'."

"Grant, people at the hotel got cholera. It's a bad disease. The hotel's under quarantine." He was silent. "The police won't let anyone in or out for six days."

"So that's why they locked that gate," he said, suddenly making sense of what he had seen earlier. "I told her but she didn't believe me."

"Who?"

"Never mind. So you can't come out of your little farmhouse, huh?"

"I'm not supposed to but I can if I want to."

"Sure, sure."

"I mean it. Remember, we have a date at the hideaway at nine o'clock tonight."

"Okay," he said, "but I'm warning you, I'm not going to wait more than five minutes."

"I'll be there. You'll see." She wanted to say good-bye but he had already hung up.

For a few moments she debated the sense of keeping the rendezvous. How could he not have been curious enough to go to that meeting? What was wrong with him? And did she want to be alone with a kid like that? The prospect carried an element of fear with it, but that same fear began to create its own excitement, and the way things were going right now, confined as she was to the house, she sure could use some real excitement.

I'll be there, she decided. I'll be there.

"I certainly can use that drink now," Melinda said. "Why don't we go to the bar?"

"You go on. I'll join you later. I have to make some calls."

"Don't be long, sweetie. I'll be waiting for you." She ran her fingers through his hair.

Nick recombed it as soon as he was out of her sight and made his way to the nearest house phone. Where the hell was Jonathan Lawrence? How come he wasn't on that stage with Ellen?

Nick had been seething the entire time he was in the Flamingo Room. All this just didn't happen by itself, obviously. Jonathan must've known something about it when they spoke. Why didn't he warn him? Why hadn't he leveled with him from the beginning? Nick felt like a fool, and not only because Jonathan had withheld critical information from him. Just yesterday he had reported back to his bosses, even though it wasn't completely true, that it looked like a fait accompli. By now the news must surely have broken back in the city. His suspicions were verified when the telephone operator informed him there were messages waiting for him.

"You've had two calls, Mr. Martin, each asking you to call back immediately, but unfortunately all our lines are tied up at the moment."

"These are urgent."

"That's what everyone is saying, sir."

"Do you have the times of those calls?"

"One came in an hour ago, Mr. Martin, and the other ten minutes later." Damn, he thought, while I was in Melinda's room. I should have left a referring room number. "I might suggest you try the pay phones down by the coffee shop, sir, although I assume there'll be a wait there, too."

"Where's Mr. Lawrence?" he demanded.

"Mr. Lawrence isn't taking any calls. He is no longer in his office."

"Can you tell me where I can find him?"

"I really can't say, sir."

Odd, he thought. Had Jonathan already left the hotel grounds? Gotten out before Nick had a chance to set the record straight? He hung up and headed down to the coffee shop. When he got there he saw the long lines waiting for the pay phones. It was terribly frustrating. He just hoped his bosses would understand. He'd have to wait and explain it to them later. Right now it was imperative he find Jonathan.

He walked quickly to the carpeted stairway and headed for the mezzanine. Maybe the operator had been giving out the story about Jonathan's not being around so he wouldn't be bothered by guests. Well, he'll see me, Nick thought, whether he wants to or not. When he got to the general manager's office, he found the secretary packing papers into a carton.

"Deserting the ship?" he asked, smiling.

"Oh, no sir. This is just some papers Mrs. Golden requested I send down to her office. Are you looking for Mr. Lawrence?" She stood up straight.

"Yes, I am. We have some unfinished business to take care of."

"He's no longer in this office, I'm afraid." The secretary looked kind of sad. For a moment Nick thought Jonathan might have been one of the cholera victims Ellen talked about in the nightclub.

"No longer in this office? I'm afraid I don't understand." He perched on the end of her desk.

...192

"He . . . he was fired, I think." She shook her head. "It's just incredible. I'm still spinning from all this."

"Fired? You mean Mrs. Golden fired him?" She nodded. "Has he left the grounds then?"

"I doubt it. No one is allowed to leave the premises. He's probably locked away in his apartment."

"I see. His leaving, did it have anything to do with what's going on in the hotel? I mean this cholera thing?"

The secretary hesitated a moment and then let it all spill out. She was almost grateful for the opportunity to talk to someone. It had been a very trying afternoon.

"I'll say it did. All the time I worked for Mr. Lawrence, I knew he wasn't a very decent man, but this was the most despicable . . . he never even bothered to tell Mrs. Golden about Tony Wong."

"Tony Wong?"

"The janitor. The first guy who died. All the while he kept . . ."

"Died? First person?"

"Oh, my God," she said, bringing her hand to her mouth. "Weren't the guests told that?"

"That little detail was left out."

"Please, please don't tell anyone I told you."

"It's all right," Nick said. "Mum's the word." He looked down at the desk, his gaze falling on the phone. "Wait a minute. Lawrence had his own trunk line, didn't he?"

"I beg your pardon?"

"His own private telephone line. One that doesn't go through the switchboard."

"Well, yes."

"I must use it. It's urgent." He headed for Jonathan's private office.

"But . . ."

"Now we have a little bargain, don't we? I'm keeping my mouth shut about the guy who died, and you're letting me use Jonathan's private phone." She nodded slowly and he went in. He wasn't eager to make the call, but he knew they would have instructions for him. The sooner he got them, the better it would be. At least for him.

"You'll have to let me off here," Bruce said as the cab approached the main gate of the Congress.

"That's fine with me, just fine." The driver pulled to the side

. . . 193

and Bruce got out, paid him, and walked to the security booth. Two state policemen converged, but the hotel guard reminded them who Bruce was.

"What happened to the house car?" the guard asked. Bruce explained that Gary had disappeared.

"I didn't have time to call anyone about it. I figured I'd tell the Sheriff when I got back."

"Get in the patrol car," the cop to his right said. "I'll drive you around to the front."

As they cruised down the driveway, Bruce noted that a lot of guests had obviously gone back to their recreations, though not as many as usual. From a distance, the Congress looked as peaceful as any other Catskill resort. There was nothing on the golf course, on the tennis courts, or at the pool that would suggest panic. For a moment, as Bruce looked out the side window, he imagined that none of it had really happened, that it had all been some strange dream. The new and interesting girl he had met the night before was not lying critically ill in a local hospital. Over a thousand people had not been exposed to a horrible disease. His moments of false euphoria were ended with the sight of the Sheriff's car parked in front of the main entrance.

"Anyone try to sneak out since they were told?" Bruce asked the police officer.

"Not from here. A few did approach the side gate that leads to the parking lot but when they saw our guys patrolling, they headed back quickly enough."

"After a while some might decide to forget their cars and try it on foot."

"Lieutenant Fielding and the Sheriff have coordinated a round-the-clock surveillance of all the adjoining highways. They'll go after any hitchhikers. And all drivers are being warned not to pick up anybody on the road."

"Sounds tight enough."

"Except for something like that chauffeur with the house car."

"Yeah," Bruce said. "Nothing's ever 100 percent. Thanks for the lift." He got out of the car.

Groups of guests were still involved in highly emotional arguments as he entered the lobby. An elderly woman, her head back, her eyes closed, was seated on a couch. She was being fanned and comforted by her daughter and son-in-law. A middle-aged couple walked around with handkerchiefs over their mouths. The main desk was still overwhelmed with guests asking questions. Bruce spotted Lillian Sokofsky coming out of Ellen's office.

"How's it going?"

"About as expected," the nurse said. "The hypochondriacs are coming out of the woodwork. Fortunately for us, there were eight other physicians in the crowd this weekend and they're lending a hand. We've set up a medical area near the athletic director's office. There were three pretty definite new cases since you left, but I think they're milder than this morning's. I put their names up on the board for you."

"Thanks. I'm going to check in with Sid and then go see Fern Rosen's roommate. I'll be back in the office later."

"How's Miss Rosen doing?"

"It's critical right now. The next few hours will tell."

"Oh, someone named Halloran was looking for you."

"Did he say what he wanted?"

"No, but he looked worried. Maybe he thinks he has it, too."

"Maybe," Bruce said, but for some reason he didn't think that was the reason. He made a mental note to see him as soon as he could.

sixteen

The Pelican Lounge filled slowly. People were tentative about gathering around a bar, even an "open bar." Some wondered if the cholera could be passed to them from the glasses. "Alcohol kills all germs," the bartenders told them. Gradually initial fears diminished. The temptation of free drinks won out. The bartenders were emphatic in their demonstrations of cleanliness. Glasses were held up to the light and inspected with dramatic interest. Early on, everyone took notice of it, but as the drinking became more intense and increased, the crowd lost its desire to participate in the sterilization process.

What they sought instead was a way to forget. A new attitude began to develop among the drinkers—a bizarre joviality built out of tension and fear. Statements made in jest became refrains for the late afternoon. "It's too late now, so what the hell. . ." "I came up here for a good time, and I'm going to have it come hell or high water. . ." "If I'm going to die from something, it might as well be booze!" The celebration became louder. If the Angel of Death indeed hovered about, then this might be their one last fling. It was stupid to sit around and brood. "What the hell," someone yelled, "you only live once." The more they drank, the more they felt justified. Newcomers were chastized for wearing long faces and letting free liquor go to waste. "It's party time, everybody. Enjoy!"

The music started up. The three-man combo was cheered. Laughter and applause gave way to people shouting requests and singing along with the band. The Pelican Lounge began to look and sound like a New Year's Eve party. Although the bartenders were working harder and faster than usual, they too contributed to the atmosphere of frivolity, keeping up with their customers drink for drink. After all, even they might as well eat, drink and be merry, for tomorrow. . .

At the center of all this was Melinda Kaplan. She had grown impatient waiting for Nick, and after her third drink began flirting with every available man. The small crowd that had gathered around her grew larger. She encouraged them to join her, led them in song and soon looked like a queen holding court. Other women, jealous of the attention she was commanding, tried to compete. They soon settled on imitating whatever she did. If she called out a song for the combo, they joined in with the men to demand it. If she began dancing, they did too. At one point, she was lifted onto a small table while the men around her cheered. She bumped and ground her hips suggestively to the rapid beat of the bongos and everyone applauded.

Melinda's vivaciousness stimulated the other women, and soon many were permitting themselves to be fondled and caressed in ways they seldom tolerated in private, much less in public. Someone started to imitate Bronstein making his speech about cholera only he substituted the word "syphilis" instead. The ensuing laughter was contagious, the conversation raw. The noise grew so loud it spilled into the lower lounges, attracting passersby. A few of them, mostly straight-laced and generally older people, gathered at the entrance and looked at the revelers as though they were witnessing a party conducted in an asylum. They muttered and shook their heads.

Thirty minutes later when the combo went on a break, some feared the party was over and melancholy began to creep in. Some of the men stepped outside for a breath of fresh air while the women sat at the small tables and looked exhausted. Even the bartenders began to slow down. Melinda felt the change but she didn't want it to end. If it ended, what else would there be? Suddenly she raised her arms and stepped on a chair.

"Hold it everyone, hold it."

What little noise there was subsided. Even the bartenders stopped what they were doing. The titular head of this spontaneous insanity was about to speak

"I say we make our own good time. The hell with the music. There'll be a party in room fourteen sixty-five right after dinner tonight!"

"The hell with dinner," someone shouted. There were cheers of affirmation.

"Who wants to take a chance eating their food anyway?" someone else said.

"Now, now, keep the party going now." A chant developed. Melinda clapped her hands. Why not, she thought. "Now, now, keep the party going now."

"NOW!" she screamed.

Two men helped her down from her chair. Others demanded bottles of liquor and glasses from the bartenders. The momentum was such that there was no resistance. It seemed like a good idea to get these crazy people out of there anyway. Not everyone followed Melinda and her entourage out, but enough did to create a wild parade through the lobby and to the elevators. When Melinda got into the first one, she seemed to be the only woman, surrounded by a dozen men. They sandwiched her into the middle and cheered as the doors closed. Others took to the stairs, despite the number of flights.

The lobby once again took on the air of gloom that had pervaded it ever since Ellen's speech. The bartenders in the lounge began cleaning up the mess. A few guests remained to drink, but the atmosphere was dark and dreary. The bartenders cleaned with quiet exhaustion. Guests who had heard about the hilarity peeked in and searched for evidence of the so-called bacchanal. Obviously there had been some exaggeration. Who in his right mind would carry on like that in the midst of a crisis anyway?

Ellen and Sid had just stepped out of the elevator when they were approached by a frantic woman about forty years old.

"You've got to help me, Mrs. Golden. It's my mother . . . my mother."

"She's sick?" Dr. Bronstein asked.

"No, but she refuses to come down to dinner. She won't eat or drink a thing. She says she'd rather die from starvation."

"All right," Ellen said, "I'll have one of the nurses go up and talk to her. What room—"

"No, she won't believe anyone but the doctor, and even that's somewhat doubtful. She remembers cholera from the old country, she says."

"I'd better go up to see her," Bronstein said. "I'll catch up with you in a few minutes."

"Thank you, doctor, thank you." The woman practically pulled him back into the elevator.

Ellen went up to her office. Sheriff Balbera was on the phone at her desk. When she entered he stood up, but she waved him back into the seat. After a moment, he hung up.

"Your chauffeur took off."

"Took off?"

"Dropped Bruce Solomon and a patient at the hospital and then drove away. The hotel car's been located at the South Fallsburgh entrance to the thruway but no sign, so far, of the driver. One of my men is bringing the car back now."

"Where's Mr. Solomon?"

"He just went up to see someone."

"Not another victim?" She moved to her desk.

"No, I don't think so. Just a roommate of one. Incidentally, Gary wasn't the only guy on staff to run away, Mrs. Golden. There's a confirmed report about two of the carpenters climbing the fence. We located them in that rundown apartment house nearby, the one everyone calls the Bowery."

"I can't blame them. I feel like running myself." She looked down at a phone message left on her desk. It indicated that an emergency meeting of the Catskill Hotelman's Association was to take place at five o'clock. It was now ten to six. Oh well, even if she could pull rank and get off the grounds, it was too late to attend. Besides, what was the difference? The difference came via a phone call ten minutes later. It was Bernie Jaffe from the Ambassador. He was the current president of the association.

"We were sorry you couldn't make it, Ellen, but we understand your situation."

"You do? That's good, because I hardly do."

"Things are that bad, huh?"

"Well, thank God we haven't had as many serious cases as was feared, but we're still in no position to be optimistic."

"You know we're all here if you need anything. This, on top of Phil's death, why it's just too . . ."

"Thank you, Bernie. Thank everyone."

"A couple of things though, Ellen," he said quickly, anxious to get to the point "We've been discussing the situation at length, as I'm sure you understand. Being that you're kind of cut off from the world up there, you're probably not aware of the tremendous publicity you've had. The story's broken in all of the major papers. The press should be coming up in force."

"Well, I certainly don't intend to get involved in that aspect. Gerson Kaplow, the public health officer . . ."

"Forget Kaplow. He's worthless. I can't think of anyone who'd want him for a spokesman. No, what I was getting at is this. We, as a hotel association, have come up with a sort of unified response to the situation. I don't know if you've had a chance to consider the impact of all that has happened—not only on the Congress, but on the entire industry. . . ."

"It's occurred to me," she said, dryly.

"Yeah, well, the thing is this, Ellen. We've already heard comments like 'the disease came from some peculiar kosher food served only in the borscht belt' or 'What do you expect from Jews. They always try to cut corners! They probably bought cheap meat'." He tried to laugh. "Of course, that's ridiculous, but nevertheless, we have to deal with it. So what really has to be done . . . you see, it's for the best, even for the Congress because, eventually, you'll come out ahead of this, and . . ."

"What have you come up with Bernie?" She tapped her ball point impatiently.

"Everyone feels we must isolate the situation, Ellen. Listen," he said, lowering his voice, "you know as well as I that we don't all follow the sanitary requirements to the letter. It's a physical and financial impossibility. And the kitchen staff we hire, most of it is transient anyway. If the government decided to enforce every law, if every one of these people was examined, given chest X-rays . . . let's face it, we'd all be in a financial bind."

"So?"

"So our position has got to be that the Congress has a very unique problem. It has nothing to do with the resort industry up here as a whole."

"In other words, we are the only hotel that might not have been sufficiently diligent with our sanitary or health procedures. Our kitchen might not have been as clean as everyone else's."

"Now, I'm not saying that, Ellen."

"But the implication is there."

"All we're asking you to do is to take the whole picture into consideration. What good would it do anyone if the reputation of the entire Catskills was smeared because of this? Surely you can understand . . ."

"I understand only too well, Bernie. You just go on out there and save your own rear ends and I'll," she made some notes on her memo pad, "do here what I have to do. And oh," she said, sarcastically as an afterthought, "don't forget to thank everyone for offering help." She hung up before he could respond.

For a moment she just sat there, staring ahead. So this is the business Phil gave his life's energy to, she thought. This is the business she inherited. If only Nick Martin would walk in here right now and offer to buy the place . . . but that's ridiculous. Even people like those he represented wouldn't want anything to do with the Congress at this point. It all seemed so hopeless.

She thought about the preparations for dinner, the new produce, and the extra efforts they were taking to sanitize everything. Everybody was trying so hard. She might as well go down to the kitchen, she thought, and help out in whatever capacity she could. As long as she kept on working, there was a possibility she'd be all right.

Charlotte had sounded groggy on the phone when he called, so Bruce knocked loud and hard on the door. When she opened it, she looked like a woman coming off a drunk, seemingly dazed and without perspective. She rubbed her right cheek with her fist. Creases from the linen were imprinted on her face. She stepped back and Bruce entered. He closed the door.

"Are you all right?"

"Yeah," she said, somewhat slowly. "Oh Jesus." She lost her balance and stumbled backward. Bruce reached out and took her by the arm. He led her to a chair.

"Relax a minute," he said. "You're still suffering from the effects of the sedative." He got her a glass of water.

"What about Fern?" she said.

"We took her to the hospital."

"I know that. But what's wrong with her? Is she going to be all right?"

"She's going to be fine" he said with such assurance he almost convinced himself. Charlotte began to relax.

'What happened to her?"

"Listen to me," he said, taking her hand. "This might be a little hard to digest when you're not feeling very well, but I think its time you knew the truth. Do you feel up to it?" She looked at him quizzically and nodded.

"I didn't come up to the Congress for a vacation like I told you last night. My cousin is the doctor who takes care of guests up here. About two days ago one of the guys on staff came down with a disease called cholera. Sid, the cousin I mentioned, asked me to come up and help him out. Things came to a head this morning."

He paused, wondering if it was wise to tell her everthing else but decided it was better she hear it from him than piecemeal from any of the guests. "It began with David Oberman," he said hesitantly.

"David? What do you mean it began with him? What began with him?" She was beginning to think the unthinkable. She struggled to get up from her chair and when that didn't work, slumped back.

"I called him after he didn't show for breakfast. He was sick. . . There's no point going into all the details."

She could tell by his face. "He's dead. David's dead, isn't he? He died of cholera." Bruce nodded. Tears started streaming down her face. "Oh my God." She brought her fingers up to her mouth and bit down.

"I can't believe it. Last night he was so happy and now . . . so fast . . . it's almost like a time bomb going off when you least expect it."

"Yes, in a curious way it is like a bomb. But in this case you don't even know where it's located. To go on, an elderly woman passed away shortly after that. She was on the way to the hospital. We had some scattered cases later in the morning and then Fern. . ."

"Fern has cholera, too?" He stared at the carpet. "She's dead," Charlotte screamed, "SHE'S DEAD! You lied to me. You said she was going to be all right. But she's not. She's dead. Just like David."

"No, no," Bruce said, grabbing her by the shoulders. "I promise you. We got her to the hospital in time. She's going to be all right."

"I DON'T BELIEVE YOU!" she shouted, mustering all her strength so she could stand. She went at Bruce with her fingernails.

"Charlotte!" He slapped her face on both sides, and she started to cry. He sat her down again. "It's all right, believe me when I tell you. Fern's going to be all right. I'm telling you the truth." She calmed down and leaned against him for support as he took out his handkerchief and wiped the tears from her cheek. Her sobbing gradually subsided.

"I'm sorry," she said, blowing her nose and coughing.

"It's all right. I understand how you feel. I felt the same way when I heard. But she really is going to be all right." He managed to smile for her sake. "The hotel's been placed under quarantine."

"You mean no one can leave?"

"That's right. Not for six days. All of the food capable of carrying the organism has been replaced, of course, so chances are you aren't in any real danger."

"But I could be carrying it from something I ate yesterday."

"Yes, but . . ."

"I mean if Fern has it and David had it . . ."

"But I don't have it, and I had dinner with them too. Right now there doesn't seem to be much logic as to who comes down with it. There aren't any predictable patterns. That's one of the things I'm trying to look into now . . . but if you feel the slightest bit sick, I want you to call me right away."

"Thank you," she said, "I will." She sat up straighter. "Actually, other than still being groggy from the pill, I think I'm okay. My stomach feels fine."

"That's good."

"When can I see Fern?"

"I'll let you know." He stood up to leave. "I'll be in touch with you after I speak to her doctor later on. Maybe you should take a short nap to sleep off the rest of the pill and then if you're up to it, go downstairs and mix with other people. It might do you some good."

"But isn't that dangerous?"

"No, not at all. I promise."

"Okay, if you say so." She went to look at herself in the mirror and frowned. "Don't worry about me," she said. "Go do what you have to do. I'll be in touch."

"Good girl. I'll see you later." He touched her shoulder and walked out.

Damn, he was good-looking, she thought, and a *mensh* too. Fern was a lucky girl. Then she thought about David Oberman. The tears started flowing once again. No good, she said to herself, no good. Crying doesn't do anyone any good. The hell with the nap. She went to the bathroom and started fixing up her face.

Nick straightened his tie but left his jacket unbuttoned. Jonathan's secretary once again stopped what she was doing as he came out of his inner office. He nodded at her without speaking and proceeded out to the corridor. When his gaze fell on the elevator, there was no longer a charming softness about his eyes. His expression had totally changed. Even his posture was different. The gracefulness was missing from his gait. He moved with a firm, more intense determination, quite unlike the man who had walked into the hotel the day before as a quiet observer. The Richard Conte smile was gone from his face and indeed, anyone looking at him now would have difficulty imagining such a smile ever having settled there. His fingers were tightened into fists. His body was taut, ready to explode. He poked impatiently at the elevator button, no longer tolerant of delays, however small or reasonable.

When it finally arrived and the doors opened, he was grateful for its emptiness. He had no desire to speak to other guests. He could think of only one thing. He hardly blinked as the doors closed. The silence inside served to amplify the voice in his mind. It was as though the phone conversation he had just finished had been taped and was now being played over speakers piped into the elevator.

Over the last few years he had been just on the brink of making it big, no mean accomplishment for a kid who had started as a "gofer" running errands for nickels and dimes for the right people in the streets of Little Italy. He was bright and observant and it didn't take him long to figure out that the front men had it better than the goons. They lived well, women flocked around them, and they got what they wanted wherever they went. He wanted the same for himself. He started small, took business courses at night school, worked for nothing just so he could learn how things operated from the "inside" and attracted the attention of all the right people. He took advice gratefully and listened and waited patiently. Soon enough the powers that be began to give him more responsibility. Finally, a few months back, they gave him permission to initiate a project on his own. The Congress was his first time out. It was on this hotel that he had decided to gamble his future with the syndicate. He had studied it, analyzed it and concluded that the risks for making a fortune were small and the potential great. And it would have turned out that way if only . . . yes, it was a freak situation and yes, it was incredible bad luck, but his bosses weren't interested in freak situations or bad luck. Somehow he felt Jonathan could have been straighter with him. He knew what he had to do.

When the elevator doors opened, he paused only a moment. Today's unfortunate circumstances notwithstanding, the experiences of his past had turned him into a professional, and a professional never telegraphed his intentions. A professional was a man who could create whatever facade was necessary and discard it when it was no longer needed. He took a deep breath and unclenched his fists. When he stepped out of the elevator he looked exactly like the easy-going Nick Martin who had checked in at the main desk twenty-four hours before. This would be the man Jonathan Lawrence would confront when he opened the door to his penthouse suite.

After his scene with Flo, Manny wandered aimlessly around the hotel grounds, muttering and cursing under his breath. It was just like a woman to take a narrow view of things. Here he was, trying to branch out into a new area, real estate investment. He was sick and tired of the garment business. He wanted to try something else. You'd think she'd congratulate him for having some ambition, taking an initiative but no, all she could do was harp on his losing some money, money he'd quickly make back next time around.

Her father's business. What was it when he came into it? A half-assed outfit working from one month's accounts to the next. Whose idea had it been to move the factory to South Carolina so they didn't have to hire union help? Who had instigated selling to chain stores? And who thought up the idea of creating an advertising campaign? He had a right to gamble with the money, for crissakes. He was the one responsible for making it in the first place. Her brother, the *shlep,* just went along for the ride.

By the time he had snapped out of his resentment he found himself near the back of the hotel. He noticed what was probably the delivery entrance and moved closer to it. On each side of the gate there was a chain spread as far as the eye could see with locks set up at various intervals. He saw the state police car parked on the road and realized that the guest parking lot was located on the other side of the road, away from the hotel. All he'd have to do was somehow get through the chain fence and he'd be home free. His car was parked on the far side of the gate, away from where the police were patrolling.

When the policemen spotted him, they stopped chatting and stared. He pretended not to see them and continued along the pathway. There didn't seem to be an end to that damn fence. A mile or so beyond, he realized it ran into an undeveloped wooded area at the north end of the hotel's property. There was a good four acres of forest there. Eventually the forest led out to another highway that ran into some of the small towns and villages in Sullivan County, but Manny didn't know this. To his urban eye, the forest seemed endless and wild. He was frightened of the idea that he could enter it and somehow get lost. He might wander about for days without food or water before a search party could locate him. And what about wild animals? He had heard rumors about bears and wildcats, but didn't know if they were true.

Nevertheless, to Manny, it looked ominous. As he drew closer to the woods, however, he saw that the link fence was changed into an approximately five-foot-high barbed wire border. It would be easy to lift up the bottom strand and slip under. His spirits lifted. If successful, all he would have to do was turn to the right, cross over the road, and he'd be at the guest parking lot. And because he'd be entering from the rear, the state police would never know he was there.

The planned escape rejuvenated him. He walked quickly back to the main building. When Flo learned what he was going to do, maybe she'd get off his back and stop nagging him. Maybe she'd even forgive him. He would go back to the city, take care of the money problems on Tuesday, and then make arrangements for another vacation somewhere else, somewhere where people didn't get sick from crazy diseases.

She wasn't in the room when he returned. He found his little carryall and filled it with what he considered his essentials. He wasn't going to be able to carry a whole suitcase if he was going to sneak under barbed wire. Thoughts about the escape began to excite him. He saw it as an adventure. He would prove he knew how to beat the odds. He picked out his darkest pants and shirt, aware of the importance of not being seen. He looked at his watch. It would be a good two and a half hours until enough darkness would fall.

He heard the door opening and looked up at Flo. Her face was still red and her eyes puffed up. When she saw him, she slammed the door behind her.

"I called Mike," she said. "He thought I knew everything all along. He's pretty pissed off at you, Manny."

"Big deal. So your idiot brother's pissed off."

"You call him an idiot? Look who's talking."

"Now don't go getting all worked up again. I've got it all figured out." He waited for her to ask how but when she didn't, he continued anyway. "I'm going to sneak out of here tonight, before they tighten things up even more." She didn't reply. "Honest, I've got a plan."

"Knowing you," she said, "it's bound to fuck up. From what I hear, they'll enforce this quarantine any way they have to and that might even include shooting someone."

"You're crazy. They'd never . . ."

She walked into the bathroom. He stood there for a moment, thinking. They'd never. . . . He imagined himself getting hit with a bullet in the back of the head. Ridiculous, he thought. Nevertheless it made him tremble.

Screw it. He was ready to take his chances. He'd get out tonight, hell or high water. He went back to his preparations.

seventeen

Jonathan sat in an oversized white velveteen easy chair and felt close to tears. After his aborted escape from the hotel he returned via the same clandestine route he had taken to leave. No one but the security guard at the gate and the state police knew of his attempt, but by now he was sure that the story had spread and many people rejoiced that he hadn't made it. He sat with his right cheek braced against his closed fist and stared down at the antique white shag carpet. White had always been his favorite color, projecting as it did a sense of simplicity and order.

His apartment had been decorated, at his own expense, with these thoughts in mind. The long, white couch, was placed at a right angle to the easy chair and the small, matching love seat. The end tables and center round marble table were all evenly spaced from each other and every other piece of furniture. Only the table had anything on it, a small, heavy Steuben glass ashtray, spotlessly clean. What bright color there was in the room came from the large Mondrian on the wall above the couch. It was a print of *Composition with Red, Yellow and Blue,* chosen, not for its hues, but because its perfect rectangles and large and small squares reinforced the mathematical logic of Jonathan's mind.

Sitting there in utter dejection, he thought about his life—all the business opportunities he had passed up, including one as a top level executive with the Holiday Inn chain, in order to get involved with the Congress. God, he'd never forget the first time he had met with Phil Golden over coffee and heard an elderly guest order prune juice and hot water. What was it the waiters called it?—Ex-Lax in a glass. And all that bastardized lingo, those idioms, those Yiddish expressions. He had never even heard the word *shmuck* until he had come to the Catskills. Sometimes he felt that he needed a translator at his side twenty-four hours a day. But he stayed with it, and he tolerated it, and he smiled and nodded at the appropriate times because he believed that at the end of the rainbow, even if it was a Jewish rainbow, there was the proverbial pot of gold. And now? Now he felt like an American who had learned Swahili to work in Africa, only to be banished from the country. What good was all of his knowledge about the Catskill resort world now?

He took a deep breath and was stricken by a pain in his side. What was that? Was it just gas or . . . ? Once again he recalled Bruce Solomon's warning. "Even you . . ." He remembered that cholera could pop up any time in the next few days and started to think back about the food he had eaten over the last day and a half. He felt another jab of pain. What if he did get cholera? Would Sid Bronstein even treat him?

He felt the beads of sweat along the top of his forehead and around the back of his neck. Whenever he perspired, memories of childhood returned. His father, always working late, never home to take him to ball games . . . his stepmother seeing to it that, no matter what the weather, he carried a warm sweater so he wouldn't get a chill, telling him he couldn't play football, he might get hurt, and making him drink warm milk before he went to bed. His stomach churned. Was it nerves? He pressed down on his abdomen. Was he nauseated? Yes, a little. But maybe something else.

He jumped up in panic. My face, he thought, got to check my face. His reflection in the bathroom mirror was as white as his rug. What was happening? Should he take something? What? Would aspirin antagonize it? Maybe a glass of warm milk? The thought of warm milk make him think of his stepmother once again, and once again sweat started pouring from his body.

He considered going down to the coffee shop for some tea but then thought about all the questions, the snickers, the looks. Everyone would want to know why he was no longer the general manager. Well, he wouldn't give them the satisfaction.

His mind began to race. What would he do about dinner? Actually, it was a moot point, because he had absolutely no appetite. He worried about that too. Wasn't loss of appetite a symptom? He should have paid more attention to what Bronstein was saying, but. . . .

These and other thoughts were interrupted by the sound of a knocking at the door. Because it was such a rare occurrence, he sat frozen for a moment. Then he shook his head. Why hadn't whoever it was phoned up in advance the way he was supposed to? Damn them all!

"Who is it?" He straightened his tie and walked toward the door. There was no answer. After a moment, the knocking continued. He opened the door. "Oh."

"Hello, Jonathan. You weren't in your office." Nick's smile was inscrutable.

"I'm not feeling too well."

"No, no, I don't imagine you are." Nick entered the apartment and closed the door behind him. "Nice place you have here. Or should I say 'had.'"

"Then you know all about it," Jonathan said.

"Yes. Everything I need to know. Mrs. Golden's speech was most enlightening."

"She's handled the situation like an asshole. If it had been up to me, I could have worked it all out so that no real harm was done to the hotel's image . . ."

"But you're leaving out one small point. It wasn't up to you." Nick moved further into the suite. He ran his hand over the soft material of the settee. "I'll tell you what my problem is now, Jonathan. My people want to know why I wasn't informed about this from the start. They want to know what's going to become of the money they've already invested." His face became hard. "And they want to know how they can trust my judgments in the future, seeing as I gave you such a buildup and all."

"This has nothing to do with my capability and you know that. It was a freak thing. An accident. It could have happened anyplace."

"Except that it didn't. It happened here. And you knew about the Chinaman and the possibility of an outbreak before we met yesterday afternoon and I made an offer to buy the hotel. Before I reported back to my superiors that it looked like we probably had a deal."

Jonathan shook his head. "The reason I didn't tell you was because the chances were so remote. The doc gets nervous easily, and I thought . . ."

"We like to think that the people we're dealing with are totally up front with us. When you brought Phil Golden to us for that loan, we were open, receptive and gave you every cent you asked for. There were no mysteries, no secrets."

Jonathan felt a chill run down his spine. "Wait a minute. I think I know what you're getting at, but I'm not a Golden, remember that. I don't have any legal responsibility for that loan."

"There are responsibilities and there are responsibilities," Nick said. "As far as we're concerned, the loan was extended because of you. We didn't know Phil Golden from a hole in the wall. And if you aren't going to be good for it, it looks like we're going to have to write most of it off, something we don't particularly enjoy doing." He moved a few steps closer and though his face remained calm, Jonathan sensed a threat; he backed up instinctively.

"So what do you want from me?" He abhorred the whine in his

own voice. It made him indignant. "You're not the only ones suffering some loss, damn it."

"We don't care about your losses. We only care about our own."

Their eyes locked and Jonathan had less than a second's warning, barely enough time to bring up his arms. Nick's left hand sprang to his neck. His long forefinger and thumb caught him just under the jaw. He closed his fingers tightly. Lashing out, Jonathan seized Nick's wrist, but because he was concentrating on pulling him down with the little strength he had left, he didn't hear the small click.

In his right hand, Nick held what looked like an ordinary fountain pen, but when he pressed its clip, a six-inch steel stiletto, the thickness of a knitting needle, popped from its top.

With a quick movement, he drove it into Jonathan's heart. Once it penetrated, he turned and twisted it, tearing across the aorta. Jonathan's eyes widened with surprise and pain. He let go of Nick's wrists, moved his mouth open and closed and then slid down the wall, landing in a sitting position on the floor. He died with his eyes wide open.

Nick went into the bathroom, washed the stains of blood off his needle-knife, reinserted the blade in the pen case, and clipped it back on his suit jacket. A large round blood stain had formed on Jonathan's white shirt. Nick looked around the suite. He took out his handerchief and wiped off the faucet handle in the bathroom. Then, wrapping the handkerchief around his hand, he opened the door and walked out into the empty corridor.

He moved with the calmness and precision of a man who had been in this situation many times before. The only disgust or emotion he felt came from the fact that he had had to do his own dirty work. He had grown to think of himself as above that, but in this situation, he accepted the unwritten assumption of his associates that everyone was responsible for correcting his own mistakes.

At the very least, he was satisfied that retribution was made and some face saved. There would still be disapproval and unhappiness with his judgment but he would have shown himself capable of evening things up. With patience, he would be given other opportunities.

He stepped out of the elevator. The sight of blood, the power he had evoked, the Godlike decision of life and death he had made all conspired to stimulate his carnal lusts. He went back to his room to change. He longed to find Melinda and make love to her again and again, make love to her like she had never been loved before, until she begged him to have mercy and stop. His body strained with desire and he hurried to seek her out.

When Ellen left her office to inspect the preparations for dinner, she spotted Bruce coming back from his talk with Charlotte. Although the events of the day had precluded their having any lengthy discussions, she had developed an instinctive liking for this young man. In fact, when she compared him to Sid or any of the other medical people now involved in the situation, she found herself automatically looking to him for guidance. She had particularly liked his indignation in the scene with Jonathan when all his deceptions were exposed. He had a moral sense, a clear view of responsibilities, and his suggestions seemed devoid of the usual compromises. She was glad he was there.

"Where's Sid?"

"He had to go calm an elderly woman who refuses to eat. I was just on my way to check out the new food situation. Care to come along?"

"Sure. I'm on my way to see Halloran. He was looking for me before but I guess I can reach his office just as easily through the kitchen. Besides, it will give me a chance to have a look at the cooking facilities. Might help me trace this thing faster."

"All right, then, I'll make it a guided tour."

They entered the dining room through the front door. She stopped at Mr. Pat's desk and picked up a new menu. Despite the fact that so much had had to be reordered, it was basically as previously planned; a choice of fruits or juice, matzo ball soup, garden vegetable soup or clear broth *en tasse,* an appetizer of grilled sweetbreads on toast and a choice of several main dishes including prime ribs of beef, goulash Hungarienne, stuffed breast of veal, and the perennial favorite, chicken in the pot. Served with it, of course, were relishes, breads, salads and an assortment of vegetables topped off with six mouthwatering and highly caloric desserts.

"Nice menu. Even your most cautious guests will be tempted," Bruce said.

They continued on through the dining room toward the kitchen. Busboys and waiters were making last minute preparations. Every station was spotless. Not a crumb, not a speck, not a piece of dull silverware or china would be tolerated. The water goblets glistened.

The linen was starched and crisp. The carpets had been revacuumed and the wooden floors rewaxed. The captains and Mr. Pat were going from table to table checking things. It reminded Bruce of the barracks inspection at boot camp. The busboys and waiters waited eagerly for approval as they approached.

"We're making that extra effort tonight," Ellen said. They walked through the swinging doors and entered the kitchen. For a moment all the clatter and rushing around stopped. Everyone looked Ellen's way. Then it all started again.

"You know," Bruce said, "my problem here is I've never been what one might call a 'practicing Jew.' Exactly what does it mean when a Catskill hotel advertises that it's 'kosher?'"

"The term we use is *glatt kosher*. Twice in Exodus and once in Deuteronomy it says that Jews are forbidden to boil a kid in its mother's milk. This evolved into a prohibition against eating any milk product where meat is served. Since meat and dairy food can't be prepared together, our kitchen, as you can see, is actually two kitchens, thirteen thousand square feet, each with its own dishwashing and silver-cleaning machines, steam tables, soup kettles, walk-in freezers and refrigerated storerooms. Two completely different china and silver services are used; one for the dairy breakfast and lunch meals, and the other for the evening meat meal."

"What time do they start preparing dinner?"

"The chef and his assistants usually get started around noon."

"It's as though you're feeding an army."

"Well, our guests have a big appetite," she said smiling.

"I can't believe some of the figures I saw on your desk! For one week two hundred seventy-five standing ribs of beef, nine hundred fifty pounds of poultry, five hundred pounds of Nova Scotia salmon."

"She's not here at the moment," Ellen interrupted, looking toward the far corner. "We buy 27,000 eggs a week and we have someone on staff who spends her entire day sitting in front of two barrels cracking them open. She deposits the whites and yolks in one barrel and the shells in another."

Bruce recited more statistics. "Over seventy cases of fresh oranges for breakfast juice and seven hundred pounds of coffee every seven days? I bet some coffee shops in New York don't go through that in six months."

"If you're counting, don't forget our bakery. Every day we produce something like eight hundred portions of cake and pie, and there's a minimum of three for each meal, so that's four thousand eight hundred portions a day and nearly four thousand rolls and an equal number of Danish pastries. The only thing we buy locally is the bread.

"Well, it looks like I'm learning something new every day." They walked past the pantry. "Is this where you prepare the salads?"

"No, they do that in the cellar below. I can show it to you if you wish, but first I have to have a few words with my chef. They're all understandably upset. No professional likes the thought that a disease is suspected to be coming from his kitchen, no matter how little responsibility he has for it."

"Sure, sure. Look, the salad thing's not important. I'd better go look for Halloran see what was on his mind. Then I want to get back to the office. Thanks for the tour."

"No. It's I who should be thanking you, Bruce. You don't have the economic stake in this thing that so many others have, yet you're pursuing the problem with more vigor than most."

"Maybe that lack of vested interest is exactly why I can," he said.

"I think I understand what you mean. I was somewhat disappointed in the way Sid handled things initially but. . . ." She shrugged her shoulders.

"Onward," Bruce said. He was happy to see her smile at him. He hadn't spent that much time with her, but he had sensed her insecurity. He wanted to tell her she had no reason to feel it. She had handled herself better than most people would have and considering the family tragedy she had recently endured, she was holding together incredibly well. He wanted to say all these things, but said nothing. He merely squeezed her hand and left.

There was no time now for dramatic statements. He had already gone out on a limb when he practically guaranteed the department heads that the possibility of their coming down with cholera now was nil. There was always the unaccountable and unexpected to contend with. He had to be ready for anything.

The noise announced them long before they arrived. Grant opened the door and looked down the hall. They were singing by the elevator. "For she's a jolly good fellow, for she's a jolly good fellow. For she's a jolly good fellow . . ." A half dozen men were jostling each other for position. The idea was to transport Melinda in style.

Finally, two men lifted her up, balancing her on their shoulders. There was loud applause and cheering as they started toward her suite.

Grant slammed the door and backed up. They were on the way here, to his own room. His mother was taking on the whole damn hotel now! He looked around in a panic. He didn't want to open the door and run past them. He was afraid they would laugh. What was he going to do, hide under the bed and be an unwilling witness to it all? Escape, he needed a means of escape. His eyes fastened on the corridor fire escape. Of course. What more natural way?

He rushed to the window, opened it and stepped out onto the iron grate landing. He stared out over the hotel grounds. Being outside and so high up was exhilarating. He stood there a moment, considered walking down, then looked up and changed his mind. Why not? He turned onto the stairs leading upward. He moved slowly, stopping at each landing and looking down.

When he reached the seventeenth floor, he surveyed the scene. From this particular height, the highways in the distance were quite visible. The traffic was continuous, the Congress quarantine notwithstanding. The view gave him a good impression of the immediate area. Although there was some forest and undeveloped land around the hotel grounds, the Quickway, a strip of stores, gas stations and roadside taverns and restaurants, was really very close. In the distance, perhaps only a half dozen miles away, he could see the outskirts of a small village.

He turned to the penthouse window behind him. It wasn't his intention to be a peeping tom because he really had little interest in what other people were doing, but something odd caught his glance just as he was going to start back down. A man was sitting up on the floor. He wasn't moving at all and he seemed to be staring into space. Grant moved closer, pressing his face nearer to the window. Suddenly he saw the dark man his mother had been with in the shower. He came out of the penthouse bathroom and then went back in. He had what looked like a handkerchief in his hand.

Grant looked at the seated man again. What was that on his chest, that big red blob? How come he hadn't moved an inch all this time? He considered tapping on the window just to see what would happen and was about to do it when he heard someone yelling. Looking down through the grate floor of the fire escape landing, he saw a hotel security cop fifteen flights below, his hands cupped around his mouth, shouting up at him. He stood straight and moved to the stairway.

"HEY YOU. KID. WHAT THE HELL ARE YOU DOING? YOU DON'T BELONG THERE. GET DOWN FROM THERE IMMEDIATELY!"

Grant walked down the metal steps, slowly at first, but when he reached his own landing on the twelfth floor, the noise, the music, the laughter, drove him down faster. The cop was waiting for him when he stepped off the bottom.

"You weren't supposed to be up there. What the hell were you doing?"

"Takin' a walk."

"I see. Takin' a walk. What's your name, son?"

"Howdy Doody."

"A wise guy, huh?" He didn't really feel like getting into a confrontation with the kid, not with all the other problems he had. "Okay, Mr. Doody, have it your way. I just don't want to see you up on that fire escape again, hear?"

"Sure. I never go the same way twice."

The security cop glared at him, shook his head and walked on. Grant watched him disappear around the building, his face still smarting from being called "Mr. Doody." If the guy hadn't been such a bigmouth, he might have told him about that man up there in the penthouse, the man with what was probably blood dripping down his shirt. But the hell with him. The hell with him and everyone else.

He looked back up the fire escape and thought about his mother and all those men and all that noise. He wanted to get away. Now. But they wouldn't let him go. They had locked him in with everyone else, locked him in with his mother and her orgies, with Alison Tits and her smirks, with grouchy security guards and their big mouths.

He looked across the lawn at the old farmhouse and thought about Sandi Golden. She was the only thing that held out the slightest interest for him. He thought about going over to see her but then it occurred to him her house was probably guarded more than the dumb hotel. He'd wait to meet her in her hideaway. Maybe he'd tell her about that guy up there, sitting on the floor.

He started to walk away, but thoughts about his mother kept flashing back at him. All those men, all those hands touching her, mauling her. How many men would have her before the night was over? He wanted to put his arms around the building and shake it until it fell apart, to rip it into little pieces. It was practically the only thing that would give him any satisfaction. And he knew it couldn't be done. He thought about heaving a rock at his mother's window

...215

but he knew she wouldn't even notice. What would she notice? Anything?

He looked at the side door to the basement. All he wanted now was to be alone and not be hounded. He'd go down there, find a place to wait and think. Maybe he could force the lock to Sandi's hideaway. Maybe he'd even discover his own place. He checked around to be sure no one was watching. Then he went to the basement door. In a moment, he disappeared into the bowels of the hotel.

"Hear you're looking for me," Bruce said. Halloran looked up from his small desk, stood up quickly and went to the door. He closed it behind Bruce.

"I don't know if it means anything," he said, "but I figured I better tell you about it anyway."

"I'm all ears."

"There's this guy, one of the salad men, see. He's married to a cashier in the coffee shop. They got a couple kids and . . ."

"What are you getting at?"

"Well, you asked about Margret Thomas at that meeting we had with Ellen."

"Yeah? Go on." He sat on the edge of the desk.

"I'm not trying to make excuses for anyone, but Margret was about as easy a piece of ass as you can imagine . . . a real piece of community property if you know what I mean."

"Are you saying that you . . ."

"Hell, no. Not me. I wouldn't touch her. It was this salad man. He came to me a few hours ago, lookin' kinda mousey, like he had something to confess." Bruce flipped open his notebook and took out his pen. "I promised him I'd keep his name out of it. Can we do that?"

"There's no way I can make any promises. It depends on what he has to say." Halloran shook his head.

"Okay, I'll do what I can under the circumstances."

"Good enough. Now I'll get to the point." He brushed the hair away from his forehead. "Remember when we were first looking for Margret? When we rounded up the two Puerto Rican dishwashers? You were all excited about finding her after I told you she had cleaned up the mess in Tony Wong's room. Well, it seems that at the time we were looking for her, she was having a 'rendezvous,' if you

. . . 216

will, with the salad man in the cellar. He was down there soaking the dinner lettuce in the bathtubs."

"Bathtubs?"

"Yeah. I know it sounds crazy but there are so many heads to rinse, it's the only way that makes any sense. Anyway, Margret met him down there. It's kind of isolated in the early afternoon. They whacked away for a while and then . . ." He shook his head. "Then she helped him clean the lettuce so he could catch up with his work."

An alarm went off in Bruce's head. The water, the lettuce, the contaminated hands! Of course! He leaped off the desk.

"She put her hands in that tub of water containing the lettuce?" Halloran nodded. "Then that's how it got from Wong's room into the hotel! That explains why some people have already come down with it while others are perfectly okay. My God, man, do you know what this means?" He answered his own question. "It's like Russian roulette. Anyone who ate salad last night is a potential victim . . ."

"And probably everyone did."

"Shit!" Bruce shouted. "Look, I'll have to meet with the salad man and get a more detailed account and then notify the authorities. Send him up to Ellen Golden's office in fifteen minutes."

"He ain't gonna like it."

"Right now there are more important things at stake than whether or not he likes it. This new lettuce you just got in. Was it washed in the same tubs?"

"I guess so. Of course the water's been changed but . . ."

"No good. The cholera vibrios could still be clinging to the sides of the tubs, mixing in with the new lettuce." He rushed out of the office and took the stairway, sprinting up two and three steps at a time. Ellen Golden might be still in the kitchen. He'd need her to issue orders. The first thing they had to do was to throw out all the salad. When he came through the back door of the kitchen he was relieved to see she was still there, talking in placating tones to the steward. She turned with some surprise as Bruce barged into the large room. In fact, the look on his face caught just about everyone's attention.

Just to his right, huge bowls of tossed salad were being lined up for the busboys to take back to their tables. Bruce practically lunged at the line.

"NO," he screamed.

"What the hell . . . ?" The steward took a step foward. "Who is . . . ?"

. . . 217

"Bruce, what is it?"

"THE LETTUCE," he screamed. "IT'S IN THE LETTUCE!" The line of busboys washed back in one move. Bruce took the first bowl he could reach and dumped it into a garbage container. "Who touched this?" he asked. One of the chefs stepped forward.

"Just me. I prepare the salad. It's my special job," he added, both proudly and defensively.

"Did you touch anything else?"

"No, just the salad."

"Then go wash your hands as vigorously as you can in as hot water as you can possibly stand." The chef stared at him a moment and then looked to Ellen, who quickly nodded. He rushed out of the kitchen.

Bruce continued to dump the large bowls of salad into the garbage while the entire kitchen staff looked on in astonishment.

eighteen

The Teitelbaums hesitated in the doorway of the dining room. They had come down later than usual, but at first it seemed they might have come down too early. The dinner population was scattered. Some tables were empty. At others, there were only one or two couples. Busboys and waiters at serving stations stood by talking idly. At this point during a normal Saturday night dinner they would be moving so quickly they would hardly have time to do more than shout "coming through" or "get out of the way!" Mr. Pat stood by his desk greeting those who did arrive with such salutations and enthusiasm that they felt they were guests of honor.

Mrs. Teitelbaum tightened her grip on her husband's hand. He recognized the gesture of despair. Despite his brave words to Ellen upstairs, fear lingered in his mind too. At this age, he thought, a common cold was threat enough. Yet with it all, he was philosophical. He had led a good life, had a wonderful family, and at his age, what would be, would be. His wife shared his feelings and agreed that they should do whatever they could to contribute toward Ellen's effort to make things appear as normal as possible. Nevertheless, they understood why others had stayed away . . . and sympathized.

"Good evening, Mr. and Mrs. Teitelbaum. You're going to get service tonight like you've never seen," Mr. Pat said.

"I'm looking forward to it. I see many people are afraid to eat."

"They're coming, little by little. Their appetites will get the best of them sooner or later."

"I see there's no one at our table. They must have heard about Mrs. Bluestone."

Blanche gave her husband a little nudge. "So we'll have a peaceful meal for a change."

They walked on toward their table. Some of the staff who knew them waved and nodded. He could sense they were encouraged by each guest's appearance. Suddenly they felt someone slip her arms through theirs from behind. Ellen had come in between them.

"My most courageous couple."

"There's not a soul at our table, and I'm glad," Mrs. Teitelbaum said. "We're going to pretend its our second honeymoon." Ellen laughed.

"How's Sandi?" Sam asked.

"She's home playing housewife with a can of tuna. Magda volunteered to go over and make something for her but she said she wasn't hungry."

"Not sick, I hope?"

"No. Just sulking because I told her to stay away from the main building."

"You did the right thing," Blanche said. "She's just a child. She should be spared such problems." When they reached the table, the busboy and waiter helped them into their seats and then hovered a few feet behind.

Blanche looked around the table. "Where's the salad?" She turned halfway toward the waiter. Both he and the busboy looked at Ellen.

"There won't be any tonight," she said quickly.

"Oh?"

"It's one of those courses we weren't able to replace immediately. Fresh lettuce was sold out by the time we put in our order."

Blanche noticed the way her eyes moved away.

"Well, olives and celery will do just fine," she said. "In fact, it will be a welcome change."

There was a long, embarrassing pause. Then Ellen spotted Toby Feigen coming in with her daughter.

"I've got to see some people," she said. Blanche grabbed her by the wrist.

"If we ate the lettuce last night we aren't in any danger, are we?"

Sam studied Ellen's reaction. The blood had drained from her face. "You're feeling all right, aren't you?" she asked, avoiding a direct answer to the question.

His lawyer's instincts told him something was wrong. They also told him to avoid further questions. "Blanche is fine and so am I," he said. "She was just curious."

"You're not fine," his wife reminded him. She leaned over and whispered something in his ear. Ellen was only able to hear the last word. "Constipated."

Sam laughed out loud. "That, my dear, is the exact opposite of

...220

what happens when you have cholera. But you've reminded me. Young man," he called. The waiter snapped to attention. "Maybe you can get me a glass of prune juice."

"Sir," he said with a grin, "it will be my pleasure."

Still somewhat stunned and subdued, Charlotte had come down to dinner, not from any demands of appetite, but rather from a need to be with people. Just as Bruce had suggested, it was better to be where there was noise and activity. She had asked to be transferred to another table in order to avoid having to answer questions about Fern and David, but the more the conversation at her new table centered around the topic of cholera, the more she thought about them both. At one point, the young couple seated to her left stopped talking abruptly. For a moment she had no idea why.

"What's wrong?" the young girl asked.

"Wrong?"

"There are . . . there are tears streaming down your face."

She brought her palms to her cheeks. The feel of the teardrops shocked her. She stood up immediately.

"I . . . I'm sorry," she said, excusing herself from the table. She ran hurriedly back up the aisle and out of the dining room. For a few moments those remaining at her table were speechless. Then they all started talking at once.

She got hold of herself in the lobby. Then she saw Bruce talking on a house phone and hurried to his side.

"Charlotte!" he said, hanging up the phone, I was just about to look for you. That was the doctor at the hospital. Fern's completely out of danger. She's responded well to the treatment."

"Oh, thank God," she said. He put his arm around her shoulders.

"You all right, kid?"

"Yes, yes. I just need to catch my breath. Can I talk to her?"

"She's kind of out of it for tonight. Call her first thing in the morning. Going in to dinner?"

"No, I don't think so." She looked back at the dining room entrance as though there was a ring of fire around it. "I'm not hungry."

"C'mon, you've got to eat something."

"Later," she said. "Right now, all I want is a drink."

"Well, take it easy on an empty stomach. Remember, you still probably have some after-effects from the sedative."

"Right doc, I'll keep that in mind. Care to join me?"

"Maybe later. Believe it or not, all this work has given me an appetite."

"From the look of things in there, there'll be enough food for you to have thirds." She hesitated a moment, then leaned forward and kissed him on the cheek. Then she headed for the Pelican Lounge.

There were more people in there than she expected and one man at the bar was particularly busy fortifying himself with liquid courage—Manny Goldberg. He had come down for a cocktail with Flo but she left him to go to dinner. He sat there alone, staring at the small neon light that pulsated the word BUDWEISER. He was practically hypnotized by it and at first didn't notice Charlotte take a seat two down from him on his right. She ordered a rum and Coke because she thought she wanted something sweet, yet something that would have a jolt to it, too.

The combo was on a break but the juke box was on and Frankie Avalon was singing his hit song "Venus." The subdued lighting, a relaxed atmosphere and the music all worked to calm her down. She clutched her drink with both hands and brought it to her lips like a construction worker taking a beer break on the streets of New York City in the middle of July. Then she sat back and opened her pocketbook to take out one of those menthol cigarettes she had bought just for this trip. Vacations, she had figured, were always a good time to experiment with something different.

The flame of her cigarette lighter caught Manny's attention. She looked familiar to him but then again, half the girls up here looked familiar to him after a while. Right now, he couldn't think straight anyway. Charlotte blew her smoke to the side and turned to see him staring at her. She smiled nervously and took another sip of her drink.

"Don't want to eat either?" he said.

"I'm too nervous. What'll probably happen is I'll wake up at two in the morning starving to death and eat my blanket."

He laughed and finished his drink. Then he quickly ordered another. What was he so afraid of? He could do it; he could do anything, even escape from the Congress. Look how easy it was for him to start with a woman. Confidence, confidence—the man with confidence wins the day.

"Me," he said, moving off his stool and taking the one beside her, "I don't trust 'em here."

"What do you mean?"

"They say they're giving us new food, but how do we know for sure?"

"Oh, I don't think . . ."

"You don't, huh? Do you have any idea how much food they would have to throw out? You know what it takes to feed a crowd like this? C'mon, we're talking about tens of thousands of dollars."

"Yes, but there are health inspectors here and doctors and . . ."

"Whadda they know?" He paid for his new drink. "I don't go in for this quarantine idea. I think it's the dumbest thing they coulda done. I mean, what did I do to get locked up like this?"

"Locked up?"

"If you can't go out when you please, you're locked up, ain't ya?"

"I wasn't going anywhere for the next couple of days anyway."

"Yeah, but they're talking about six of them."

"I gather it's what has to be done."

"Yeah, well not to me," he said, "not to me."

"Really," she said, turning fully toward him for the first time, "why don't you just relax and enjoy yourself? You're at a famous resort. There are a lot worse places to be quarantined."

He studied her for a moment. Damn it, he did know this girl from someplace.

"You don't work in the garment district, do you?"

"No, but I'd like to. I'd be able to get clothes at a discount." He laughed and reached into his pocket for a business card.

"Here," he said. "You're ever in the neighborhood, drop in. I'll see what I can get for you wholesale."

"Thanks." She looked at the card and put it in her pocketbook. He checked his watch again and took a big gulp of his drink.

"Well," he said, "I gotta get goin'."

"There's no need to hurry. They'll be serving dinner for another hour easy," she said, suddenly not wanting to be alone.

"I'm not going to dinner. Nice meetin' you, Miss . . ."

"Fein. Charlotte Fein."

"Miss Fein." He rubbed his hands together vigorously. She looked at him with a curious expression.

"Where are you going, bowling?" He laughed and started out.

. . . 223

"Yeah, in a sense. I'm going to knock some kings off their pins." He laughed again and disappeared through the door. She motioned to the bartender and ordered another rum and Coke.

Despite Flo's tough and bitter reaction to what Manny had told her, in truth she was frightened. The prospect of bankruptcy terrified her. What would they do if they lost all their money? What about all those outstanding charge accounts she had run up, accounts Manny wasn't even aware existed. And the house . . . they were down to the last few years of the mortgage. Did that mean they could lose that, too? She cursed herself for not taking more interest when her father had tried to explain the financial complexities of the business. All she really knew was that nothing could be sold without her signature, but how the profits were made and how they were spent, she had no idea. She didn't even know how much money Manny had in the bank. As long as there was always enough to buy what she wanted and go where she wanted, she had no reason to care. But now, to think they might end up paupers, maybe have to borrow money from the children . . . it was something she couldn't bear to contemplate.

Her dinner table was only half filled and, as at most of the others, everyone was talking about Ellen's speech and the quarantine. She listened, but contributed little and ate sparingly. At times, she found her hands shaking and looked to see if anyone noticed. She wondered if Manny had tried his escape yet—wondered if she should hope he made it. If he was able to get back to the city in time, it might at least forestall financial disaster.

She declined dessert and left the table early. She was much too nervous to sit there and talk. The others sensed her reluctance to get involved and proceeded to ignore her. They barely noticed when she left. When she got to the lobby, she felt even more confused. She knew she didn't want to go to the bar or the card room where she might bump into Manny's friends, but by the same token, she didn't want to sit at the end of the lobby and watch television with the old biddies either. The prospect of going back up to her room and lying there alone was even more distasteful. She desperately needed to get her mind off things, if only for a little while.

She was standing uncertainly when she spotted Billy Marcus coming from the Pelican Lounge carrying a tray loaded with ice and glasses. He didn't see her until he was nearly on top of her.

"Where's all that going?"

"There's a wild party up on the fourteenth floor."

"Party? Someone's having a party now?"

"You wouldn't believe it. It's more like a carnival. They took the furniture out of one of the suites and put it in the hallway to make room for themselves. When I left before, they had put two mattresses down on the floor in one of the bedrooms." He leaned toward her and whispered. "It's like a community bed, know what I mean?"

"Can anyone go to this party?"

"Guess so. No one knows who anyone else is anyway. Excuse me, but I gotta get this ice up there before they tear the roof off."

"Wait," she said, moving toward him. "I'll go along with you. I've got nothing better to do right now anyway."

"I don't think your husband would approve, Mrs. Goldberg."

"That never bothered you before," she said dryly. He laughed and she followed him into the elevator.

The noise from Melinda's party had shattered the privacy of every room on the floor. The dancing and frolicking spilled out into the hall, and some guests were seated on the floor of the corridor, their backs to the wall, drinking and laughing. Women sat with their thighs spread apart, their panties long ago removed. Couples kissed and petted openly. It was a bacchanal the likes of which Flo had never even imagined.

Although most of the people were young, there were more older people than she would have expected. It occurred to her she knew many of the men's wives and wondered what they would say if they knew what their husbands were doing right now. Billy Marcus's tray was literally attacked. He could barely keep it in balance as hands reached out from everywhere to grab glasses and ice. She saw what was happening and quickly took one for herself. Then she started through the crowd in search of some booze.

"Be careful, Mrs. Goldberg," Billy called with a wink.

Melinda's bedroom had been stripped clean—dresser, bed, vanity tables and chairs. In their place, as Billy had said, were mattresses. People walked around barefoot. The normal heat had been so increased by the presence of so many bodies and so much activity, that many people had begun to strip. Two women had their blouses completely unbuttoned, their breasts practically popping out of their bras. The music was so loud everyone had to shout to be heard.

Melinda herself was sprawled in one corner, a man on each side of her, a third man squatting at her feet. Her skirt was nearly up to her crotch; her open blouse left nothing to the imagination. From this most ludicrous position, like some Queen of Sheba, she proceeded to shout out perverse commands. It was a pornographic version of "Simon Says." As a result of her personal magnetism, she had been successful in turning grown men into court clowns. They danced around in bras, zipped down their flies and made complete asses of themselves, all as a result of "Melinda Says."

At the very moment Flo came to her doorway, Melinda had a man of about fifty doing a strip tease a few feet away from her. It had attracted the attention of everyone in the room. The man, obviously quite drunk, was so clumsy about unbuttoning his shirt he nearly strangled himself taking off his tie. He fell over once and was helped up by two other men. Then, to the rhythm of the music and shouts of "take it off, take it off," he dropped his pants. Standing in his boxer shorts, he moved his body from side to side in an awkward and silly attempt to mimic a bellydancer. Suddenly two ladies, friends of the men who had helped him up, came from behind him and, each taking one side of his shorts, yanked them down to his knees. There was an explosion of laughter. The man was stunned by his own nudity.

His penis drooped between his thighs. He bent down to pull his shorts back on but a man at his side slapped his hands away. All the women in the room, including Flo, seemed hypnotized by the thick, jiggling organ. He struggled again in a vain attempt to regain his shorts but two other ladies, also drunk and encouraged by the audience, put their arms under his and pushed him in the direction of the eager crowd.

Two men picked him up, pulled his legs apart, and began rotating him toward each side of the room. The onlookers pointed, jeered and clapped as the man made desperate attempts to find something to cover himself with. Each attempt only brought on more and more laughter. Finally the audience grew bored and let him drop to the floor. Someone helped him to his feet and directed him toward the bathroom. The couple in the tub made no attempt to leave, but by this time the drunk neither noticed or cared. At the same time, people were screwing on the mattresses in various combinations of threes and fours.

All this turned Flo on in ways she had never thought possible. For all her carrying on, she had never even been with two men in the same bed, much less participated in an orgy. She was curious to see what it was like. She chug-a-lugged what was left in her glass and went to look for more. The booze had been set up on the small dresser in Grant's room, the only piece of furniture tolerated because it served as a makeshift bar. Turning around, she recognized the pool's stunning lifeguard, the one she had ogled earlier in the day, pouring drinks for two young women. He looked even sexier out of the sun.

"Hi," she said, "Can you do that for me too?"

"Sure." He smiled. "I can do anything you say."

"Sounds promising. I think I'll take you up on it."

He laughed and filled up her glass. Then she felt someone pinch her ass and hoped that it might be Billy Marcus. If not, anyone would do. In this instance, three would definitely not be a crowd.

"I've got some good news and some bad," Bruce said, intercepting Ellen as she left the Teitelbaum table. "Fern Rosen, that friend of mine, is finally out of danger."

"Thank God."

"And the Feigen boy is responding well to treatment, too."

"Oh, I'm so relieved. I was just on my way to his mother's table. She'll be so happy to hear." Then the smile on her face disappeared. "What's the bad news?"

"The doctors have identified three other likely cases, one quite acute—an elderly gentleman. It doesn't look very promising."

"Oh, no." For some reason she had thought the worst was over.

"They've all been sent to the hospital and of course they'll get the best treatment available." Bruce looked around the dining room. "Doesn't look too good. What would you say, half full?"

"Not even. I've asked Mr. Pat to keep the dining room open an hour longer than usual. Maybe later in the evening, from boredom if nothing else, people will come in. I know the public health nurses are doing their best to convince everyone that the food is perfectly safe."

"Um. Tell me something. Where does Jonathan usually sit when he comes to dinner?"

"Up over there," she said, pointing to the empty table on the far end of the balcony. "At the executive table. Why?"

"Just curious. I haven't seen him since we had that showdown in your office. Have you?"

"Now that you mention it, no, and I've spoken to his secretary a few times, and I remember her saying he hasn't been in his office either."

"You don't think that guy got out of here somehow, do you?"

"It wouldn't surprise me," Ellen said. "He's capable of anything." She saw Toby Feigen wave at her. "Let me go over and give my friend the good news about her son. I don't want to waste any more time talking about Jonathan."

Bruce nodded and watched her walk away. For a moment he considered whether or not he should go back out to the lobby and try to locate him but his hunger pangs won out. He sat down and began to eat his melon. Later, when he was finished, there would be time enough to check and see what happened to Mr. Lawrence. It didn't really surprise him, though, that the man wasn't showing his face. If he were Jonathan, he thought, he'd have crawled into a hole too. He looked up from his plate with some interest when Ellen was stopped by a sharply dressed, dark-skinned man before she reached the Feigen table. He didn't know who he was but he could see, even from this distance, that the conversation wasn't a pleasant one.

It was Nick Martin, and he wore that same enigmatic smile.

"Too bad we didn't wrap up a deal earlier, Mrs. Golden. You would have unloaded a big headache. Or, should I say, stomach ache?"

"That has the earmarks of a real sick joke, Mr. Martin."

"I'm beginning to understand now why you and Mr. Lawrence were receptive to my offer. Sort of a chance to bail out before . . ."

"Certainly you don't think . . ."

"It doesn't really matter now what I think, Mrs. Golden. But take heart. Luck has a way of turning around." He gave her a sly wink and walked on to his table. She looked after him a moment and then she turned and looked at Bruce. He gestured as if to say "What's up?" She simply shook her head and continued on her way.

Sandi put on Elvis's "Heartbreak Hotel" for the fifth time. The song seemed to fit her mood perfectly. Then she went back to the window and looked out at the main building. It had grown considerably darker, but not dark enough. When she left, she wanted to be sure no one spotted her and reported back to her mother. She looked at the musical alarm clock the Teitelbaums had brought her from Italy three years ago. It was 8:30, the tail end of the dinner hour, or at least what usually was the dinner hour. She figured her mother was still in the dining room, circulating among the guests.

Every time she thought about meeting Grant, her heart began to pound. She knew he wasn't what anyone would describe as handsome. He certainly was no Bobby Grant or Fabian or even Frankie Avalon. But there was something definitely, well, something very sexual about him, at least to her. It was in his eyes, part of his anger, the wild rage he always seemed to be supressing. Being around him was like being around a stick of dynamite ready to explode at any minute. And it excited her.

Other boys she could think of, boys in the local junior high, paled and dimmed beside the thought of him. Sure, they were wild in their own way, with their black leather jackets and duck tail haircuts, smoking cigarettes openly in the school basement and defying the teachers to give them detention. Once she had even found them fascinating, but now they just seemed dirty, unattractive and ignorant.

Not like Grant who would probably be just as bored in the company of those leather jacketed jerks as she was. He was too restless to belong to anything organized, and it was just this impulsiveness that appealed to her. She wondered what it would be like to kiss him, to feel his tongue moving around in her mouth. The glow of light in the window of one of the small cottages brought back the memory of Caesar Jiminez and Margret Thomas making love. Was it only two nights before? She recalled the color of their flesh, the eroticism of their movements. She wondered what it would be like if Grant did all that to her. Her thoughts was abruptly disturbed by the ringing of the phone.

"Hi, Sandi, what are you doing?"

"Just sitting and listening to records." She could hear the fatigue in her mother's voice. "Are you going to come home soon?"

"I don't think so. I've got to stick around a while longer. Some more people got sick and I should be here in case anyone needs me."

"You want me to do anything?"

"No, baby."

"I'm not a baby," she snapped and regretted it instantly. There was silence on the other end of the phone.

"No, you're not," Ellen finally said, softly. "And I'm sorry. I didn't mean to make it seem I think you are. What did you have for dinner?"

"I ate some of the tuna and mixed it up with mayonnaise and stuff. It was delicious." She hoped her mother would realize it was her way of apologizing.

"I'm glad. If you get hungry and want anything else, just let me or Magda know."

"All right," Sandi said. "I will."

"Go to sleep early. I'll look in when I get home."

"Okay," Sandi said. She let her mother hang up first.

For a few long moments afterward, she felt almost as sad as she did the day her father died. She fought back her tears, went back to the window and looked out at the hotel. It was wrong for her to meet Grant and she knew it. She was betraying her mother who loved and trusted her. A good girl would stay at home and not complain, no matter how bored she was.

Then she thought again about Grant, what it would be like to feel his hand on her breast, his lips close to hers, and once again changed her mind. What was so bad about just spending a couple of hours with him? What danger was there in going over to her hide-away? She wouldn't be exposed to any of the guests except Grant and besides, she had spent part of the morning with him anyway. She really wouldn't be doing anything that wrong.

Sandi promised herself she'd get back before her mother came home. That way, Ellen would never have to know. She looked out the window again. It was just about dark enough—just about time. She went to the mirror and put on more lipstick. Then she sprayed some perfume on her neck and down her bra the way she had read about in *Lady Chatterley's Lover*. She was so excited, she nearly forgot to turn off the phonograph.

She joined Elvis on the last line of "Heartbreak Hotel," turned off the machine, and improvised the last three words to sing on her way out.

"It's down at the end of lonely street . . . my hide-a-way."

nineteen

Manny stayed within the shadows until the couple ahead of him disappeared down the path. Then he crouched low and began to move. Lights from the main building threw long, twisted fingers of illumination over the grounds. He had had too much to drink and the alcohol was clouding and distorting his vision. He wobbled and wove a zig-zag path to the back of the main building. The sound of a siren in the distance brought him to a halt. He had an immediate vision of being caught, handcuffed and marched degradingly back into the hotel to be used as an example for anyone else contemplating breaking out of the quarantine.

The siren passed on. He listened intently and heard the muffled footsteps of some people walking back to one of the cottages. He looked behind him to make sure he hadn't been spotted, then stumbled on. When he entered the darkness away from the reach of the hotel's lights, he began to feel safer. He checked his pants pocket for the feel of his car keys and, confident they were his passport to freedom, went into an even deeper crouch. In this posture, he began to run toward the woods. Once he tripped and flew forward, catching himself on the palms of his hands. Even so, he scraped his knees and though he couldn't see it, picked up dark green grass stains on his pants and shirt. He cursed, rubbed his legs and moved on, this time more carefully and slowly.

When he got to where he could see the wide entrance to the main gate, he stopped and listened once again. Though there was absolute stillness, it was obvious that the police stationed on either side, sitting patiently in their cars, were ready to move at the slightest sound. It was at this point that Manny took the greatest care, practically tiptoeing away from them and toward the forest over five hundred yards away. When he finally got to the barbed wire fence he felt elated. The only problem now was how, in the darkness, to know exactly where he should slip underneath. He moved a few feet down to see if there was a natural opening, but he couldn't find one and rather than waste precious time searching, chose a spot at random, lifted the lowest tier of wire and began sliding under. The wire was a lot tauter than he had imagined and it kept a continuous pressure on his hand. He was terrified of catching one of the rusty metal points on his face so he turned his head into the earth, pressing down as hard as he could. It seemed to take forever to work his body under. It was at times like this he wished he had taken Flo's advice and lost thirty pounds, but, incredibly, he was finally able to do it. His face and clothing were smeared from all the dirt, but his appearance was the last thing he was worried about now. There'd be plenty of time to wash and change when he reached the city.

Once he was able to stand on the other side of the fence, he felt sure he was almost home free. He shook himself off and picked up his little traveling bag. Sneaking into the parking lot was going to be a piece of cake compared to what he had just been through. He began moving through the woods in a northerly direction. Branches and bushes caught his pants, and he had to stop and untangle himself from time to time, but his adrenalin level was so high it didn't phase him.

Finally, he could see the road ahead. In his eagerness to reach it, he neglected to study the way the earth dipped and failed to see the ditch. He fell forward once again, this time landing on his side. He knew enough not to moan, shout, or do anything that would attract attention, but for a moment, the pain was almost unbearable. Finally it disappeared.

He rose, crossed the road quickly and hurried toward the parking lot. When he reached what he figured was the back entrance, he suddenly pricked up his ears. The chatter from the patrol car's two-way radio at the main gate could be heard quite distinctly. He could see the silhouette of the car a couple of thousand yards down the road, but he believed that as long as kept out of the reach of approaching car lights, they wouldn't be able to see him.

After he acclimated himself, he scooted into the lot. Now he had a new set of problems. How to locate his own car among the rows and rows of other parked vehicles. His certainly wasn't the only blue Chevy there and in the darkness, there was no way to read the license plates. Suddenly he thought of Flo and for the first time, blessed her for using the front seat as her personal beauty parlor. That was it! When he found a car that resembled his, he'd check the windshield area. If there were lots of hair rollers and eye makeup scattered about, he'd know he'd hit pay dirt.

He was only halfway down the first row when he heard a deep male voice shout "Hey!" His heart nearly stopped as he debated whether to simply ignore it, hide or run. There was no time for a decision. A uniformed patrolman opened the door of a car in the second row and walked toward him. He couldn't believe it. Had they actually stationed a man or men in parked cars in the lot?

"Where do you think you're going?"

"Just taking a stroll. Thought I'd get some fresh air."

"It's a curious place to take a stroll. Are you a registered guest?"

Manny hesitated. What was he supposed to say?

"Listen, buddy, I gotta get outta here. It's worth a great deal to me." He reached into his pocket and pulled out his money clip.

"What you're trying to do is a serious thing," the patrolman said.

"And I'm offering serious money." Manny peeled off five twenty-dollar bills but the cop ignored him completely. He raised his right hand to his mouth and blew down hard on a whistle. The piercing sound made Manny shake. Once again he considered the possibility of running, but the patrol car at the main gate had already responded to the whistle and quickly pulled up beside them. Two state policemen got out. To Manny, they looked enormous.

"Got a live one," the patrolman said. Manny quickly shoved his money back into his pocket.

"Sorry sir," the nearest state policeman said. "We must enforce this quarantine until otherwise advised. You'll have to go back with us."

"Do you mind telling us how you got out of the hotel proper?" the other state trooper asked.

"I flew over the fence."

The trooper stared at his mudstained face. "You're the first angel I ever met with a dirty face." He managed to smile. "Right this way, sir." The patrol car's back door was opened for him. When he sat inside, he noticed there were no handles on the inside of the door. The only way he could get out was if the door was opened from the outside. He was trapped again, just as he was trapped in that damn hotel. The state patrolmen congratulated the uniformed cop and then got into their car.

No one spoke as they ran Manny back through the main gate and drove him to the front entrance of the hotel. One of the officers got out and opened the back door for him, as guests standing nearby looked on with interest.

"We hope you understand that we're serious about the quarantine, sir, and that you won't make another attempt." Manny simply grunted, gave them the finger, and scowled back at the people who had stopped to stare. Then he walked back into the hotel and headed for the bar. He was furious, frustrated and angry. He had blown all the money he had in the world and right now all he wanted to do was to strike out at someone, anyone. He thought about having to face Flo again and swore to himself that if she bugged him even a little bit, he'd haul off and belt her right in the mouth. That image was the only thing that brought the slightest degree of consolation. Otherwise, he was just plain miserable.

For a reason she couldn't quite fathom for the moment, the basement had suddenly taken on new and ominous vibrations. The shadows loomed darker and longer, the hum of the motors was threatening, and the muffled conversations of distant custodians scared her. She lingered at the entrance as though standing on the brink of disaster. It was as if she had crossed an abyss into the setting of a recurring nightmare lingering in the deepest crypt of her memory. It was all there in her mind's eye . . . her father's shrunken face, the stiff and bony fingers, his glassy eyes staring up into space. The funeral cortege was winding its way slowly through the hotel with hundreds of people following the coffin. It ended up here in the basement. They were going to dump the body in her hideaway. Someone patted her on the head and said she was going to have a nice new playmate. She was about to scream at the images when Grant's voice shook her back to reality.

"Thought you'd never show," he said. He stepped out from behind a column, both hands in his pockets. A toothpick dangled from his mouth.

"You scared me. What were you doing behind there?"

"Playing tiddleywinks with manhole covers." He laughed and came closer to her. "What do you think I was doing? I was waiting for you. Everyone else is running around the place like it's the end of the world."

"Doesn't look like it from the farmhouse. From there it looks like everything's about normal." She was so happy to see him she began to relax. "I was just listening to some records. I got a new Elvis album."

"Yeah, I like him."

"C'mon," she said. "Let's go to the hideaway before someone spots us."

"What did you do with Alison Tits?" he asked as she unlocked the door.

. . . 234

"She hasn't spoken to me since this morning. I think she's mad at both of us."

"No loss."

She closed the door and put on the light. He went behind the mattress leaning against the side wall and pulled out what remained of another bottle that Sandi had hidden. There was barely a quarter of it left.

"I think that's the last one I have. I shoulda gotten another one but I was afraid . . ."

"That's okay. There's enough."

"Gimme a cigarette," she said. She sat herself down comfortably and leaned against the wall. He took out his pack and pounded one out. "Light it," she said when he handed it to her. He smiled and put it in his mouth. The he took out his matches and lit it, taking two long puffs. He passed it over. She inhaled sharply and nearly choked. He laughed sarcastically, took a drink from the bottle and offered it to her.

"You're not going to get drunk again, are you?"

"On this little? Never happen."

"Whaddya want to do?"

"What do you want to do?" Even his response was loaded with sarcasm.

"Play strip poker," she said, half to reply in kind.

"You wouldn't have the guts."

"Would too."

"Big talker with no cards." He took another drink. She looked around for something she could substitute for playing cards but then got a better idea.

"Got any money on you?"

"Money? Sure. Why?"

"I mean change."

"Yep." He reached into his pocket and came out with a handful of nickels, dimes and quarters. "Got it for those dumb pinball machines in the Teen Room."

"We'll use a quarter." She reached over and took one out of his hand. He looked at her with curiosity, a half smile on his face.

"I don't get it," he said, putting the rest of the change back.

"It's very simple. I'm heads and you're tails. We'll take turns flipping. If I win, you take something off. If you win, I do."

He held the bottle in his hand frozen near his face and looked to see if she was serious. It was obvious she was. He thought about

. . . 235

her supple body under all those clothes and then about his own nudity.

"What if someone comes along?"

"No problem. The door's easy to lock." She got up and turned the latch. He felt a curious anxiety building from within, but he wasn't sure whether it stemmed from excitement or fear. When she returned, she kneeled directly across from him, her buttocks leaning down on her ankles for support. "We'll flip to see who flips first." He still hadn't said anything or moved. "Well, are you game or not?"

"Sure I'm game," he said. "What do you think I am, a baby? Go ahead." She tossed the coin in the air. It fell with a dull thud on the mattress. It was tails.

"You win. You start." She picked up the quarter and placed it in his free hand. He took another swig from the wine bottle and put it down on the floor. Her eyes were intense and staring at him. He tossed the coin in the air and it fell heads up. She clapped her hands and looked at him expectantly.

"Big deal," he said and took off a shoe. Then she took it and flipped it quickly. It was heads up again. He smirked and took off his other shoe.

The next flip was tails up. He expected her to take off one of her shoes, just as he had done, but she surprised him. Instead of reaching for her foot she stood up, put her hands under her skirt, and pulled down her panties, taking great care to step out of them neatly. Then she tossed them to the side with mock bravado.

"Coin please," she said, lowering herself back to the mattress. She kept her skirt close to her body. "I said coin."

"Huh? Oh, yeah."

A half dozen flips resulted in his removing his socks and shirt and her removing both shoes and a sock. He drained the wine bottle empty and lit a cigarette. They had both grown strangely quiet. He thought his hand shook when he flipped the coin again, but she pretended not to notice. He won the next toss and she removed her second sock.

"Down to the nitty gritty," she said. The coin came up tails. She stared down at it. He waited a moment and reached out and put his hand over it.

"If you wanna quit, we'll quit," he said.

"No, that's not fair. Besides, it was my idea." She reached down and pulled her cotton blouse up and over her head without unbuttoning the middle or lower buttons. She held it in front of her for a moment, then draped it dramatically over the wine bottle. He stared

... 236

at the cups of her bra, noting how tight it was fastened. It looked as though it pinched her body. He wondered if it hurt.

"What are you going to do if you lose again?"

"You'll find out. Whatever I have to."

He shook his head and turned the coin over and over in his sweaty hand. Then he rested it on the nail of his thumb. "Here goes," he said and flicked it up in the air. This time it fell on its side and landed tails up. Sandi lost again. She hesitated only a second, then reached behind her back and unfastened her bra. It fell away from her body instantly. Her tiny bosom quivered as though she had gotten a chill. Slightly embarrassed, she folded her arms across her chest and her face turned beet red.

"You flip," he said, not sure whether he should smile or not. She reached for the coin. Her tits looked so tiny, not at all like his mother's. She tossed the coin quickly and won. He unfastened his pants without looking at her.

"It's neck and neck," she said. She looked for the fullness in his crotch and was surprised that it wasn't there. Odd, she thought. From everything she had read, he should be having an erection by now. That was what she wanted to see, why she had suggested playing this stupid game in the first place. More than anything in the world, right now she wanted to see his loose, smooth underwear tighten and strain—his thing, pushing against it with all its strength in its eagerness to get out and be near a girl, near Sandi, near her. She recalled a description in one of those cheap paperbacks a maid once left behind. A man's erection was pictured like an independent animal, its head rising toward the stars, its neck thickening like a bull. But none of this was happening with Grant and she wondered what was wrong.

"Wanna call it a draw?" he asked.

"Do you?'"

"I don't care."

"Well, it's not exactly a draw no matter what we do. I mean, I never let a boy see me like this before," she said.

He shrugged and leaned back against the mattress behind him. "I'll bet."

"No, honest." For a moment she wondered what it would be like to kiss him, her naked breasts rubbing against his naked chest. She wondered why he didn't have that same urge. He still seemed so disinterested, so removed from what was going on between them. Was it because she kept her arms folded across her chest? She thought about it and let them drop slowly to her side. Grant continued to stare at her, but it was as though he was looking through, rather than at, her body.

Her naked bosom had created a series of images in his mind, flashbacks moving in record speed, like a series of old-time movie cards being flipped. In each scene, he resurrected a picture of his mother—the time a few years ago when she had come into the kitchen with only a towel pressed against her chest. She reached across for something at the table and one of her naked breasts caressed his forehead. He was surprised and pleased at the softness. She didn't seem to notice his reaction . . . or the time he was nine and had a sore on his penis and she bent down to kiss it and make it better.

"Well," Sandi said, "are you just going to sit there staring?"

"You're asking for it."

"I think you're scared."

"Bullshit."

"There's the coin." She gestured toward it with her head. He remained immobile. "If you want, I'll flip it for you."

"Relax," he said, unaware of the sharpness in his voice. "I don't need your help." He grabbed it up in a quick action and squeezed it against his palm. Then he flung it against the far wall. It bounced off and landed a few feet away from them. She walked over to it and looked down. A smile formed across her face. "You lose," she said. He didn't move. "Come and see if you don't believe me."

His hand involuntarily went down to cover the fly of his shorts. "This is stupid."

"It wasn't so stupid when I had to take off my bra. I always knew you were chicken." He still didn't move. "If it was me who had to take something off again, you wouldn't think it's so stupid." He pretended not to hear. She leaned over and picked up her bra.

"I didn't say I wasn't going to pay up."

"Sure," she said with disgust. He watched her slip her panties up her legs and reach out for her socks. When she put on her first shoe, he stood up.

"All right," he said. "Hold your horses."

"Chicken," she mumbled again. He felt himself blush with anger.

"I'M NOT CHICKEN!"

She stopped with her second shoe and stared at him. He looked straight ahead, took a deep breath, and jerked his underpants down below his knees. His member peeked out from a patch of dark black pubic hair. It looked to be the size of a big toe. Contrasted with the enormity of Caesar Jiminez's cock, as far as Sandi was concerned it looked tiny. He could see the look of disappointment on her face.

"So? What's the matter?"

"You . . . aren't you supposed to be, uh . . . hard?"

He looked down at himself as if to see what was there. Then he took the tip between his forefinger and thumb. She realized he was squeezing it but wasn't sure exactly why. He continued to twirl it between his fingers, moving it back and forth, almost as if he were alone. She wondered if he was trying to masturbate in front of her. Nothing was happening and the look on his face turned from exasperation to sheer ugliness. She was frightened by the expression in his eyes. Something about this guy wasn't normal, and she should have known it from the start. She reached for the hideaway key in her shirt pocket and moved toward the door. He took steps to cut her off.

"You going somewhere?" he said.

"I gotta get back to the farmhouse. Magda's going to be calling." She rushed to the door lock, inserted the key and turned the handle. He grabbed her other hand and put it on his cock. "Stop that," she cried and pushed him against the wall. "There's something wrong with you. I don't know what, but you're sick, sick, sick!"

She flung the door open and ran out.

"Wait," he yelled, "you don't under . . ." but she was already down at the end of the hall. He closed the door and stood there, naked, inert and alone. Then he picked up the coin and heaved it against the wall. It fell near his feet, heads up. He would have lost again.

"Is that really you?" Charlotte said. She was on her fourth rum and Coke and beginning to feel the effects. She turned around completely to face Manny Goldberg as he entered. He smirked. There were only a half dozen people in the bar and Charlotte was at the same seat she was in when he had left to escape the quarantine.

"Yeah, it's me. In the flesh."

"What happened to you?" she asked as he stepped further into the light. He looked down at his clothing and for the first time since he had been escorted back from the parking lot, realized what a mess he was. Ordinarily he would have rushed right into the men's room and washed up but at this point he was just too disgusted to

...239

care. He brushed down his shirt and sat on the stool beside her.

"I had an accident."

"I'll say." She laughed and turned to the bartender. "I think this man needs a drink."

"Scotch and soda," he said. "Make it a double." He reached into his shirt pocket and took out a cigar. It was totally crushed. "Damn." He crumbled the bits and pieces in the ashtray.

"What did happen to you?"

He waited for the bartender to serve his drink. Then he leaned closer to her.

"I tried to get outta here, only they had a cop in the parking lot, sitting in a car."

"Really?"

"Yeah, really. The son of a bitch wouldn't let me go." He took a long sip of his drink and looked around. "How come this place is so dead? I figured all the swingers would be down here by now." He looked at his watch. "Dinner's over, isn't it?"

"I'm not sure. The bartender says it's been extended."

"Oh."

"But that isn't the only reason the place is so empty, right, Charlie?"

"Pardon me?" the bartender said, stepping over to them.

"I was telling Mr. . . . Mr. . . . ."

"Goldberg. Call me Manny."

"Goldberg, call me Manny," she tittered, "that there's a reason why this place is like a funeral parlor. Charlie says there's a wild party going on upstairs. Says it started here a couple of hours ago and then moved up to the fourteenth floor. Right, Charlie?"

"Right as the rain. And the bellhops who've been delivering the booze say it's the wildest party they've ever seen around here."

"That sounds like something I could use right now." Manny finished his drink in one gulp.

"I'm celebrating," Charlotte announced, apropos of nothing. He looked at her closely for the first time. Her eyes were already somewhat glassy from the rum. He left his gaze skim over her body and considered the possibilities. If he had to stay at the Congress and lose everything he had, he might as well go down with a bang.

"What are you celebrating?"

"My girl friend's gonna be all right."

"That sounds like something worth celebrating." He put his arm around her shoulders. "What was wrong with her?"

"She had the little buggers." She hiccuped loudly.

. . . 240

"Little buggers?" He thought for a moment and then moved back. "You mean she got the cholera?"

"Yep. The real thing. But the doctor says they caught it in time and everything's going to be all right." She lifted her drink in a mock salute and took another swallow.

"Shit. I'm tellin' ya," he said, "it's not safe for anyone to stay here. You never can tell . . ."

"There's nothing much we can do about it," she sing-songed, rocking back and forth on her stool. "You saw what happened when you tried to escape. We might as well just sit back and enjoy it." She tried to sit back and almost fell over.

He steadied her chair and looked at her again. She had the confused, vague, expression inebriated people sometimes get, as though her thoughts were stuck somewhere in her head like a broken 78.

"You're right," he said. "Maybe we should." He threw a five-dollar bill on the bar as a tip for Charlie. "C'mon, whaddya say we go up to that wild shindig and check it out." He took her by the arm.

"Huh?"

"The party. Let's go see what's happening."

"Oh, the party. I don't know. Maybe yes, maybe no."

"C'mon. What harm can it do?" He tugged slightly. "After all, you're the one who said we might as well enjoy."

She stood up uneasily to join him. "See you later, Charlie."

The bartender winked at her and continued to clean his glasses. Manny suggested they use the back stairs. He didn't want to chance bumping into Flo in the lobby.

"But that's fourteen flights."

"So what," he laughed. "The exercise will do you good." He patted her on the fanny.

"Hey, I didn't even eat yet."

"Don't worry. They probably have food up there anyway."

"Well, okay, but I'm not walking up any fourteen flights." She grabbed him by the hand and dragged him toward the lobby.

He followed her reluctantly. When they reached the elevators the door opened on a couple locked in a passionate embrace. Fortunately Flo was nowhere in sight. The duo turned and when they saw Manny and Charlotte looking in at them, they burst out in laughter.

"You didn't come from the fourteenth floor by any chance, didja?" Manny asked as they teetered out.

"You better believe it," the man said, giving him the high sign.

"You better believe." Manny pressed number fourteen hard and pulled Charlotte further into the elevator.

"I don't want to upset you, Ellen," Magda said, stopping her as she crossed the lobby toward the office. She was on her way to meet with Artie Ross to discuss the evening's entertainment. The quarantine had shut out their feature performer. What they would have to do now was build around Bobby Grant and utilize the dance instructors and other staff.

"What's wrong now?" She could tell from the look on Magda's face it was serious.

"I just came back from the farmhouse."

"Don't tell me. Sandi isn't there." She slapped her forehead with the palm of her hand. "I knew it," she said, shaking her head. "I knew she would never stay put. Has anyone seen her around the hotel?"

"I haven't and I know no one at the front desk has. Maybe she just went for a walk."

"But she promised she wouldn't leave the house. Please, put the service desk on it. Have her paged and send someone to the coffee shop and the Teen Room."

"I'll take care of it. I hate to bother you about this now," Magda said, her eyes saddened, "but I knew you'd be calling her eventually, and when I tried and there was no answer...."

"When there was no answer you knew how I would feel. A cholera epidemic I can handle, but a daughter who might be caught up in the middle of it, I . . ."

"I'll find her," Magda said and squeezed Ellen's hand. Ellen walked on, but was distracted by a signal from the main desk.

"We're having a lot of complaints about a party on the fourteenth floor."

"Party? You've got to be kidding. Someone's having a party on a night like this?"

"A lot of someones, apparently. What should I do?"

"Whose room?"

"A Mrs. Kaplan. Divorcee. She came up with her son."

"Well, send one of the bellhops up to ask them to calm down."

"I think it might have gone beyond that stage, Mrs. Golden."

"Call security then, but be sure to tell them not to create any incidents. Tell them to be polite, but firm."

"I'll pass on your instructions."

"Damn," Ellen said as she entered her office. Sid Bronstein was on her phone, his back to the door. He didn't hear her enter.

"You know, Sylvia, you talk as though you believe I brought this situation on single-handed. What the hell do you think I'm doing? And don't give me that crap about your father. Yeah, well . . ." He turned about and blanched the moment he saw Ellen. "I can't talk any more, Sylvia. There's a lot of work to be done here. Call Lois and go to dinner with her." He hung up and shook his head.

"Good old Sylvia," Ellen said.

"If anyone wants to know what keeps doctors from making house calls, just tell them it's doctor's wives. What's up?"

"Got a meeting with Artie Ross to go over the nightclub entertainment. We were supposed to have Buddy Hackett tonight, but under the circumstances . . ."

"Can't be of any help there. Listen, Ellen," he added, "I just want to tell you what a fantastic job you've been doing. You're absolutely incredible. Some women . . ." He looked at the phone. "Anyway, with the way Jonathan handled the preliminary situation . . ."

"Oh," she said, "speaking of Jonathan, no one's seen him since our little meeting here." She went to the phone and dialed the intercom number to his suite. "If he's there," she said, waiting, "he's not answering his phone."

Before Sid could respond, there was a knock on the door and Artie Ross peered in.

"Busy?"

"No, I'm just leaving," Sid said.

"Had two band members complaining, doc, but they both took bromos and said they're feeling better."

"Good. Let me know if there's any change." He started out. "I guess I'll try to grab a quick bite."

"Artie, you haven't seen Jonathan anyplace, have you?" Ellen asked as he sat down.

"Jonathan? Come to think of it, no."

She thought for a moment.

"Okay," she said, "first things first. What are we going to do about getting these people entertained tonight?"

Nick stopped dead in the hall the moment he stepped out of the elevator. What in hell was going on in Melinda's suite? He approached apprehensively, not quite sure what to expect. The music was extraordinarily loud, the people apparently unconcerned. Two couples were dancing in the hallway just outside the door and although the music was fast, they clung to each other's arms as if it were a foxtrot. When one of the girls saw Nick over her partner's shoulder, she licked her lips and smiled. He saw the half-naked crowd mingling in Melinda's rooms, shook his head and walked away.

It was obvious what was going on, but it wasn't what he was looking for. He didn't like group scenes. He wanted to focus all his attention on one woman, and in return, wanted all her attention on him. What angered him now was that he had lost his diversion. He was hoping to get his mind off things too. It angered him and he pounded on the elevator button. The doors opened immediately. When they closed, he banged the wall with his closed fist.

He was so deep in thought he didn't notice that the elevator had dropped past the lobby. The doors opened on the basement floor. He started out and stopped. "What the fuck . . ." He was about to press the lobby button when his curiosity got the best of him. What was down here anyway? For want of anything better to do, he decided to check it out. Almost immediately, the doors closed behind him and the elevator went up, responding to another demand. Nick studied the corridor, listened to the sounds and then took a few steps forward.

Suddenly something or someone moved along the basement wall, maybe a hundred yards ahead of him. All he could make out in the dim light was a shadowy figure clinging against the side and slinking forward. Whoever it was looked as though he was crouching. Why?

He wondered why it even mattered. The odor, dank and stale, didn't appeal to him at all. It would be nicer to go back up and sit in the bar and listen to soft music. The figure disappeared around the corner all the way down at the end of the corridor. He was about to leave when suddenly something occurred to him. Maybe there was an exit that led out of this place. If so, it would be nice to know about it. That way he could leave tomorrow if he had to. It certainly didn't make sense to stick around, especially once Jonathan's body was discovered.

He started forward in the direction of the shadow, slowly at first, and then quickly. But as he approached the end of the long corridor, he slowed down and made a great effort to move as silently as possible. It was always best to surprise the unknown. He stopped at the corner and peered around. As it turned out, it was a very smart thing to do.

twenty

Melinda's party had done more than simply spill out and into the corridor. It served as an inspiration for other festivities as well. Some couples who had met there, many for the first time, took their wild and frivolous flirtations down to more private quarters. Others spent their passions in whatever free spaces they could find. All caution had been abandoned.

When Manny came upon the raucous gathering, he experienced a rather childlike excitement. He wanted it all and he wanted it now. An older, rather buxom woman had stripped down to her panties. She stood on a chair just inside the suite where Manny could see her and did a beaten-down imitation of a fading burlesque queen at a second-rate roadside tavern. A half dozen men were at her feet, gazing up at her Jell-O-like breasts as they wobbled in the mold. Their shoulders and heads bobbed and weaved in drunken synchronization with her every move.

When Charlotte peeked in, her first impulse was to run away. It was as though she feared another sort of contamination. In the past few years she had seen some wild things at Catskill resorts but certainly never anything that could compare to this. Had everyone, including herself, gone mad? Manny laughed and held her arm even tighter.

"This is more like it," he said, licking his lips. "A man could forget his troubles for sure at a gathering like this."

For Charlotte, the noise and the activity was more than she had bargained for. Combined with the booze she had already consumed it made her feel wobbly, dizzy and even a bit nauseated. She continued to hesitate.

"C'mon," Manny said again, tugging her forward. He pressed between two dancing couples and pulled her along behind him. She stumbled over something and looked down at a naked man crawling along the floor laughing hysterically. No one paid any attention.

"Wait," she started to say, but Manny's grip was as fierce as his desire. They stopped in the middle of the crowd, just to the right of the woman doing her imitation. Manny stared up at her and studied her body with religious fascination.

"I want to get out of here," Charlotte said. The sweet rum and Cokes were beginning to get to her. She swallowed hard to keep the syrupy liquid down but the combined odor of cigarettes, sweat and pungent whiskeys was devastating. The acidlike liquid moved up into her mouth and burned her tongue. She began to choke on it but there was so much noise no one even noticed, least of all the hypnotized Manny.

The woman on the chair stopped her dance. Immediately one of the worshippers at her feet stood up, scooped her in his arms and carried her deeper into the suite toward Melinda's bedroom. As Manny's gaze followed, he saw a familiar dress, a familiar pair of legs and hips barely visible between some strangers. He looked harder toward the corner of the room and spotted her.

Flo was seated on the floor beside the lifeguard, his head planted comfortably between her breasts. Her slip was up well over her knees and the lifeguard had his right hand placed temptingly between her thighs. Flo's eyes were closed but the lifeguard's were concentrated on his fingers.

Manny dropped Charlotte's hand abruptly and pushed his way roughly through the crowd. Some people complained and one man even kicked him in the rear, but he was so obsessed he didn't notice or feel it. He pushed three people out of his path and finally stood just above Flo and the lifeguard. Fury overwhelmed him. The New York money problems, the frustration and embarrassment of his aborted escape and now this. The fucking, slut bitch, screwing around with a younger guy in front of all these people as if her husband—as if Manny Goldberg—didn't even exist. The fact that he was there for the same reason didn't make any difference.

His anger got the better of him. He kicked out and caught the lifeguard in the forehead, grazing it. The lifeguard jumped up in shock, for a second not realizing what was happening. Flo opened her eyes and looked up with a dazed expression.

"Get the fuck up," Manny screamed. His mouth strained at the corners, pulling his nostrils wide. All the veins in his temples were visibly outlined under the skin. His fists were clenched; his teeth bared.

"What the . . ." The lifeguard felt his forehead and looked for blood.

"YOU BASTARD!" Flo screamed.

Manny reached down and took a handful of her hair. He began pulling her to her feet. The lifeguard, his senses regained, grabbed Manny's wrist.

"Let her go."

"Bug off, schmuck."

The lifeguard responded with a well-aimed hard and fast swinging right. His fist crashed into the side of Manny's head, catching him in the left temple. His head practically spun around but he still didn't release his grip on Flo's hair. She screamed with the pain and bit into his wrist. Despite all the chaos, no one tried to break the fight up—they were too caught up in their own sexual pyrotechnics. Flo suddenly kicked her foot up and caught Manny's groin with her heel. He bellowed and released her, and the lifeguard took advantage of his pain and landed a fist in his kidney. "I'll teach you who to call 'schmuck.'" Manny toppled over to his right into a crowd of dancers, who immediately moved out of his way.

The fight was quick, but Charlotte had been close enough to catch it all. A very slight, thin line of blood had formed on the lifeguard's forehead and the sight of it plus Manny's rolling in agony on the floor finished off all her resistance. What remained of her rum and cokes came charging up and out. A woman standing nearby felt the wetness on the back of her stockings and turned in time to see Charlotte deliver another heave. The woman screamed and put her hands to her ears. Her action caught the attention of people nearby. Charlotte heaved a third time and the crowd began pulling back.

Flo and her lifeguard moved quickly to the exit. The bedlam caused by Charlotte's vomiting was just what they needed to cover their escape. Manny struggled to his feet but a group around him, annoyed that he had created a disturbance, formed a circle with him in the center and every time he tried to get up, pushed him back flat on his ass. Very little of this traveled into the second bedroom where Melinda was still holding court.

By the time Manny had bulldozed his way out, someone had already helped Charlotte out of the room and Flo had disappeared. He cursed and swung out wildly, making a path for himself. By the time he got out in the corridor, there was no one in sight. For a moment he considered running down the hall and smashing his fist on every door until he found Flo and her lover and made them pay for his humiliation.

But after a few minutes the impulse subsided and his rage settled down. Some loud laughter caught his attention. Another woman was up on the chair and this time the people around her were encouraging her to play with herself. She slowly let her fingers crawl down from her belly and was greeted with cheers and jeers. Manny wiped the side of his head. It still hurt, but it wasn't bad enough to take him out of the ball game. He looked back down the corridor, considered his options and turned back to the party.

He would take care of his bitch wife later, he thought, and worked to get a better position by the chair and the girl.

At first Nick didn't quite understand what Melinda's boy was doing crouched down like that. He was in the corner of the basement where all the stage flats and scenery were built and all the supplies stored. There was no one else around, the work on the staging for the July fourth weekend entertainment having already been completed. Various props and stage pieces were stacked and lined up near the wall. Shelves held cans of paint, dyes and rolls of crepe paper.

Grant squatted at the base of a cloth flat that had been painted and repainted many times. He held a lighted match to the material. The small flame seemed to leap off its tip as it quickly seized hold of the dry surface. Instantly a brown hole formed and began to expand. A steady stream of smoke rose up and Grant moved to another flat and repeated the maneuver. Although it, too, caught fire rather quickly, the flame was blocked once it worked its way from the material to the frame. Frustrated, Grant looked about frenetically for a way to satisfy his desire for a more demonstrable blaze; a way to symbolically send Sandi and his mother up in flames.

He spotted a rag in a dye pot and lifted it out. Holding it in his left hand, he lit it from the bottom. A blue-red flame rose so quickly it was as if the fire had been stored in the dirty rag itself, just waiting to be released. He was pleased with the way it looked and flung it into a cardboard wishing well a few feet away. It was at this point that Nick stepped out from behind the corner of the basement wall.

"What the fuck are you doing?"

Grant jumped back.

"Nothin'."

"Nothin'? You dumb little bastard. I've been standing right over here watching you. What the hell . . ." He stepped on the burning cinders that had resulted from the fire on the flats. "I think we better get you upstairs."

"Don't you touch me," Grant said as Nick stepped forward. Nick stopped and smiled at him, hoping the smile would allay some of the boy's anxiety. "I saw you. I saw you with that man upstairs."

Very slowly, the smile left Nick's face. Grant took another step back, his eyes fixed on Nick as though by magnetic force.

. . . 248

"What man?"

"The man in the penthouse. I was on the fire escape before and I looked in the window. I saw him and I saw you too. So you just keep away from me."

"What the hell are you talking about? What is it exactly that you saw?" Grant didn't respond. He simply continued to stare. "I think we'd better get you up to your mother. C'mon." Nick took another step forward and Grant backed further away. He looked behind him and saw his path was blocked somewhat by props, stage furniture and more flats.

"NO," Grant screamed. "If you touch me, I'll tell people everything I know."

Nick stopped again. He was beginning to get angry.

"I don't know what you're talking about, kid. I was never up in any penthouse. All I know is you tried to start a fire down here."

"You were, too, up in the penthouse. I saw you. There was a man in there sitting in the middle of the floor with blood on his shirt and he didn't move the entire time I was peering in. And you were there wiping stuff off the doorknobs with a handkerchief." Grant wasn't completely sure what it all meant, but he instinctively knew that it was enough information to place Nick Martin in fear of him. Nick's hesitation confirmed this. Grant began to be more confident. He relaxed somewhat and started to get cocky. "I coulda told the cop who caught me on the fire escape, but I didn't. I didn't tell nobody. Yet," he added, almost smirking.

"Well," Nick said, seeming to relax. Reaching nonchalantly into his pocket and taking out a cigarette lighter and case he offered one to Grant, who turned him down. Grant eyed the space between Nick and the wall. He considered making a dash past him and then down the corridor to the elevators. Nick put a cigarette into his mouth and lit it, moving just slightly toward the wall as he did so. It was if he anticipated Grant's idea. "You're quite a guy, aren't you? Quite the big shot."

"Go to hell," Grant said. Nick smiled and nodded.

"Okay then, let's make a deal. You keep your mouth shut about what you saw upstairs and I'll forget what you were trying to do down here. Whaddya say?"

"I'll think about it."

"Okay," Nick said. "You think about it."

The rag Grant had tossed into the fake wishing well had set fire to its bottom by now and the sides began to snap as the flames built up from within. Both stared at it transfixed.

"We'd better do something about that, though," Nick said. "See if there's a water faucet in there," he ordered, gesturing toward the boiler room a few feet away. Grant followed his gaze with his eyes but he didn't move. "C'mon, move it, or we'll get a load of people down here, and we'll both have a lot of explaining to do."

Reluctantly Grant moved toward the doorway of the room. He pushed the door open and looked inside. Nick moved so quickly and stealthily that when his forearm appeared under Grant's chin and pressed against his Adam's apple, the kid had no chance to react. In an instant, he was literally lifted off his feet.

The cutoff of air was immediate and complete, but it was the powerful and abrupt twist of the head that did the fatal damage. Grant's neck snapped like a piece of brittle candy. Unsupported, his head fell forward, his tongue extended. His last image was a dazzling, sparkling prism filled with neon stars. Death shut it off abruptly. His body sagged, and Nick let it fall to the floor.

He looked around quickly. The paper wishing well nearby was nearly burned out, its frame collapsed into its foundation. Sparks from the fire flew into nearby stacks of flats but nothing more had ignited. Nick looked at Grant's body and wondered what the hell the kid had been up to. He also considered the possibility that he had lied to him and maybe actually told someone else what he had seen in Jonathan's room.

But there would be time to think about that later. His first concern now was what to do with the body. He thought about the fire once again. If he hadn't come upon Grant, the kid might just have gotten a real blaze going. What if he had? That was a good question, and he repeated it to himself a couple of times before the answers began to come. He was pretty sure it wasn't what Grant had in mind, but the fact was that if there was a big fire, it would require evacuation of the hotel and that meant he'd have a way of getting the hell out and back to the city. And there was something even more interesting. He began to calculate. The hotel had fire insurance and that presented a real possibility for him and his people to retrieve the money they'd invested. Granted, relatively speaking, it wasn't a lot of cash but it added validity to their motto "We may not always win, but we try to never lose."

He would claim credit for engineering this recap of funds and restore his credibility. Surely he would be rewarded for his initiative. He smiled as he looked back at Grant's body. "Thanks, kid," he muttered. He studied the basement—the studded ceiling, the piles of ignitable material. He noted the flammable paints and cleaning alcohol on the shelves. Then he looked inside the room where Grant's body lay. There he saw the air and heat ducts that tunneled up through the ceiling leading to the very roof of the hotel. It was through these that the premises were heated or air conditioned. The metal surrounding the ducts was braced and framed by wood as old as the original building. The wood was matchstick dry. If he could get the flames to spurt high enough to reach the ducts in the ceiling...

He moved quickly, gathering the flammable liquids in both hands. Then he built a pile of flats, props and rags which he soaked with a can of makeshift starter fluid he found in the corner. He stepped back and listened. The basement remained eerily still—the day shift had long gone, the laundry room was closed because it was Saturday night and the stage crew was busy upstairs in the nightclub. Even most of the custodians had called it a night.

Without further hesitation, he moved the pile under the ducts, lit a rag soaked in paint thinner and threw the ball of fire onto his stack. Instantly, it ignited. He jumped back from the shock of heat that radiated outward. Flames flirted with the ceiling and the basement walls. He heaved on more material which caused the flames to flare even higher until they joined with the framework of the cooling and heating systems. There was a loud crack and then the fire shot up into the spine of the building. It followed the duct frames like an animal running a maze, a maze it knew by instinct, a maze it knew promised reward at the end.

At first the fire was narrow, confined by the diameter of the studs that served as its runway, but as it burned through the wood, it began to infect the very walls of the hotel's interior. Ropes of flame dropped into every available opening, widening every crevice. They joined with electric wires in an alliance of movement and speed. When the fire met with any installation that proved an obstacle, it hesitated as if it had a consciousness and was considering alternatives. Then it simply found ways to move around it enveloping it until it lost its support and fell out of the path. Nothing in the hotel's guts could stop the onslaught. It would be the most deadly of all possible blazes—working from the inside out.

As soon as Nick was satisfied that the conflagration had reached the point of no return, he stopped feeding material to the pyre. In the truest sense, that's what it really was. This was the hotel's funeral, whether the people upstairs knew it or not. Thinking of it in those terms gave Nick another idea. He took a full bottle of paint thinner and threw it over Grant's corpse. Then, in one great effort, he lifted the body and threw it on the fire.

His mission accomplished, he walked quickly to the nearby service stairway and left. If he was really lucky, he thought, the fire would even be damaging enough to destroy Jonathan's suite before anyone discovered his body. It could all be so perfect. He congratulated himself for his genius and actually considered going to the bar for a drink of celebration. But only if he was close to an exit.

Just a short time before Nick started the fire, the nightclub opened its doors. By now less than half of the hotel's eight hundred guests were inside. Despite the liveliness of the orchestra and the quick one-liners from the M.C., a wakelike atmosphere hung oppressively over the proceedings.

Jack and Toby Feigen, renewed and relieved by the good news concerning their son, got a babysitter for their kids and came down to the Flamingo Room to be entertained. They moved gracefully down the aisle toward their table, pausing only to greet some people they had met in the dining room. Most men turned to look in their direction. Toby looked as radiant as ever.

Although the M.C. continually invited couples to enjoy themselves on the dance floor, few took advantage of the offer. Because of the limited lineup of talent available for the variety show, a half hour of dancing had been scheduled to start things off, hopefully to get people in a congenial mood. From the looks of things, it wasn't working very well. Ellen had agreed with Artie Ross that Bobby Grant, the house singer, would be featured as the key act. It was the best they could do. Other members of the staff who had talent would follow. On any other occasion, it would have signaled the big break the amateurs had been waiting for. Tonight, however . . .

Ellen's intention was to pop in and out of the nightclub all evening. Right now, though, her thoughts were preoccupied with the whereabouts of Sandi. The bellhops had returned without finding her. Magda had grown concerned and decided to keep away from Ellen until she could bring her some definite information.

Bruce joined Sid in the kitchen for coffee. They sat alone at a small table in the corner, a table usually reserved for the chefs. A lone janitor was completing his cleanup around the stoves. There was a real sense of hiatus, a respite to contemplate the significance of all that had gone on the past couple of days. Sid and Bruce spoke in quiet and calm tones. Both showed signs of fatigue. For the first time since breakfast, they could relax somewhat and even make jokes. Each of them wondered out loud about the whereabouts of Jonathan Lawrence.

"He's probably sitting in his suite feeling sorry for himself," Sid said, "trying to figure out what hotel to inflict himself on next."

Upstairs, Melinda's party had slowed somewhat but there was still enough activity to keep it going. New people arrived periodically, many simply to look in on what was being described as the "wildest scene in the mountains." Manny Goldberg was singing in the corner near the spot where he had discovered his wife before. He had his arm around two women and the three of them were working over a chorus of "Roll Me Over in the Clover."

Flo and her lifeguard had slipped into the linen room at the end of Melinda's floor. That was why Manny couldn't find them when he looked down the hall. It turned out to be the craziest experience of Flo's life. The two of them stripped and climbed into the large linen cart stored in the rear. Then they rolled over and on top of each other in and around the soiled sheets and pillow cases, working to get into a comfortable position. Flo finally landed almost on her head, her ankles supported by the rim of the cart. The lifeguard mounted her by pressing his feet against the cloth sides and squatting on his knees. The wheels of the cart moved slightly back and forth in rhythm to their thrusts and returns, and they laughed and grunted simultaneously. Afterward, they collapsed against each other and dozed off in the softness of the linen.

Sam and Blanche Teitelbaum had decided to go to sleep early. They were both exhausted from the day's events. He sat on the edge of the bed, a half-dazed expression on his face and waited while his wife washed and prepared herself for bed. The music from the nightclub, although muffled and subdued, was audible. Neither he nor Blanche liked air-conditioning. It usually made him cough. They preferred fans and opened windows. While he was waiting, he got up and checked to make sure their window was open.

Most of the staff—Stan Leshner, Moe Sandman, Mr. Pat, Rosie the telephone operator, Halloran, Rafferty and others came to the nightclub to be supportive of the staff entertainers. The hotel family, threatened and desperate, had closed into an even tighter and stronger alliance. Like circus people, they came together in a crisis and lent each other comfort and support. They applauded when

Ellen entered the club. She joined them for a while and then went to see the Feigens, greeted other guests, and left to check the main desk for news of Sandi.

Charlotte talked herself into a short nap. Her head was still spinning from drinking on an empty stomach and throwing up and she knew she just had to sleep for a while. When she lowered her head to the pillow, she immediately passed out.

Outside, the hotel path lights flickered. A new shift of state police had come to the gates of the hotel. The driveway was empty, and there was an ominous quiet about the grounds. Some chambermaids were walking at a leisurely pace back to their quarters. They were talking so low their voices couldn't be heard. Although Sandi was not in the farmhouse, her bedroom lights were on. It was the only window lit in the old wooden building.

The night sky was moonless, clear and filled with stars. The humidity was somewhat high and the breeze had died down considerably. The tree limbs were so still it was as though they had been painted onto the scene. The silence was extraordinary, and because of this the music of the nightclub carried all the way to the main gate of the hotel. The two new patrolmen listened to it for a few moments and then continued their conversation.

The line of traffic going past the grounds was constant. Many local residents were curious and teenagers from the nearby towns drove by to get as close a look as they could at what was happening at the Congress. National radio and television networks had picked up the story. The Sunday morning headlines for the *News* and the *Mirror* had already been constructed!

**CONGRESS BECOMES PRISON FOR THOUSANDS
CATSKILL RESORT LOCKED UP BY CHOLERA.**

There were only thirty or forty guests in the main lobby. A group of bellhops were off to the right of the information desk bemoaning the fact that no one was tipping. The switchboard was active with incoming and outgoing calls, but the receptionist at the counter had little to do. When Ellen came back to the lobby, she remembered she wanted to send a bellhop up to Jonathan's suite to see if he was there and why he didn't answer the phone. She called one over, gave him instructions and sent him to the main desk for a master key. Then she went to her office to call the farmhouse again and see if Sandi had returned.

The bellhop got his key and went to the elevators. He pressed the button to command one and waited. His attention was drawn back to his buddies, who kidded him about the errand. Then he turned back to the elevator. When it didn't open, he pushed the button again. It was then that he noticed that the lights showing which floor the elevator was on were all off.

Sandi sat on the bench at the edge of the baseball field cloaked by the darkness. She was far enough away from the main building to escape the reach of its lights. After she had left the basement, she had wandered about aimlessly until for some reason this was where she had ended up. There was nothing deliberate about her choice but when she had gotten there, she realized it was on this very bench a couple of years ago that she had sat with her father and they had had one of their longest private conversations. He had told her stories about some of the things that had happened to him at the hotel when he was her age. She had laughed at the panorama of characters he resurrected—old Mrs. Rosenblatt, who pilfered entire meals from dining room tables and smuggled them out in her large pocketbook to share with the pigeons; Max Grossbard, the undertaker, who married and buried four wives, honeymooning with each at the Congress. "Imagine the confusion each time he introduced his new wife to Mama and Papa." Then there were people like the Rothenbergs. "Their son Danny was so lonely they offered me money to play with him. The first time I took their nickel, Mama practically cried. She made me give it back to them and I felt so bad, I ended up giving Danny a nickel of my own. Later he became one of my best friends."

As she sat there remembering, she could almost hear his voice. "Remember that no matter how busy I am, princess, I'm only doing it for you and your mother because you're the two people in the world I love most. And I'm so glad you're around to keep mommy company when I get involved at the hotel." Her throat ached from trying to hold back tears. Oh, God, she thought, what have I done?

Thinking about leaving the farmhouse against her mother's orders and Grant and that terrible scene in the hideaway made her feel terribly guilty. If her father were alive, would he still call her his little princess?

"Daddy," she whispered, wishing there was some way she could bring him back. "Daddy." She closed her eyes and embraced herself,

...255

rocking gently back and forth. "I'll be a good girl from now on. I promise."

She remained sitting like that for a while, totally lost in herself. Then the sound of an excited voice broke her spell.

One of the custodians was running from the basement entrance a couple of hundred yards away. She stood up on the bench so she could see better. He was waving his arms madly, desperate for someone's attention. It looked like his clothes were on fire.

"What is it?" she shouted, but he was too far away to hear. She struggled to understand what was going on.

She jumped down and took a few steps forward. The custodian fled around the corner of the building, heading for the front entrance. She had never seen a grown man in such panic. Then suddenly she caught on.

"Mommy," she said. It was practically inaudible. "MOMMY!" she shouted, and ran with all her might toward the main house.

twenty-one

Bobby Grant was understandably ecstatic. For him, the outbreak of cholera in the hotel had precipitated real opportunity. He was resigned to the fact that he would receive low billing all summer long even though some of the name vocalists who'd be entertaining didn't have half the talent, personality or energy he did. It was all part of paying his dues, something any beginner had to do; but that didn't mean he didn't feel frustrated or bitter sometimes.

Tonight it was going to be different. They had turned to him to headline the show. "In fact," Ellen Golden said, "we're asking you to be so good, you'll make the people forget why you're there in the first place. If you can, I promise to use whatever contacts I have to get you an audition anywhere you want."

"I'll give it my best," he promised. "You won't be sorry."

Now he stood anxiously in the wings. He brushed his hair back again and again, checked his face in the mirror, and shook his arms loose like he had seen Bobby Darin do when he played the Congress the last Fourth. He was going to sing some of Darin's songs too. The M.C. was finishing his introduction. The applause was hardly enthusiastic and although it was difficult to see past the first few rows because of the spotlights, it was obvious the nightclub was well under capacity. None of this, however, discouraged him. Tonight was his night and he was going to bring them to their feet.

He walked out to the band's last few bars of "Say It with Music" and took the microphone off the stand. It was crazy, considering how excited he was, but as the music started, he was remembering the advice a singer, he forgot which one, had once given him about how to deal with the mike. "Let it hang loose and forget about it. Concentrate on your audience. They're the ones you're playing to." He smiled at the bandleader, held the mike a few inches from his mouth, and took a deep breath. He was going to start with "Three Coins in the Fountain."

"Three . . ."

The screaming started from the left and then moved in a ripple across the center of the audience to the right. For a few seconds he and many of the stagehands thought they were screams of adoration. They had heard them many times before, especially when singers like Tony Bennett or Perry Como played the room. Maybe the kid really had it after all. But it took only a few seconds to realize that these screams were different.

Smoke had begun pouring in out of the air-conditioning vents in the nightclub walls, and a haze climbed quickly into the shadows of the lights. Only seconds later, the wall on the right behind the second tier ripped open to reveal a furnace. Chunks of ceiling adjacent to it began to rain down. A middle-aged woman who had stood up in panic was hit on the left side of her face. She raised her hand belatedly as the blood began pouring from her mouth. Some of the men disregarded women and the elderly and bulldozed their way through, knocking over tables and chairs in their way. The room became a symphony of high-pitched shrieks, crashing glasses, cries, screams and commands. A young woman became totally incapacitated, froze in terror, and stood by uncontrollably clutching the side of her face. She was unaware of how deeply she was scratching her skin. An elderly woman lost hold of her husband's hand and tripped over a broken chair. Fleeing couples behind her prevented her husband from getting back to help her to her feet. He was pushed dangerously near the tier and fell backward himself, his head smacking the side of an overturned table.

Those in the center of the room and to the left began rushing up the aisles toward the back, jostling and pushing each other on the way. The narrow aisles were obviously inadequate for such a mass exodus. Then a streak of fire broke out across the ceiling just above them, dropping cinders and sparks to the floor. This stimulated even more violence and alarm. More of the left wall caved in; more of the ceiling fell. The burlap scrim draped across the sides of the stage for decoration became a sheet of flame.

Jack Feigen, who was on the first tier, held his wife so close to him it was almost impossible to move. Neither of them spoke as they tried to make their way through to the back. Suddenly people behind them began to panic. One man fell and grabbed at Jack's leg. He had great difficulty shaking him off. Those behind him refused to wait and pressed forward with such force that Jack fell forward himself. Someone kicked him in the neck. Toby lost her grip on him and was spun around and forward. She started screaming his name: "Jack, Jack!" He became a raging animal and swung wildly at the people around him. Then he charged forward like a linebacker, knocking people out of his way until he was at her side again. They continued along with the excited crowd toward the exit.

The microphone had broken down as soon as the fire started

...258

and staff members stood up on the few tables that remained right side up and pleaded with people to calm down. Their voices were lost in the din. Stan Leshner lifted a small old woman off her chair and carried her like a trophy, over his head, up the aisle.

Flaming chunks of wall and ceiling ignited portions of the floor. As the fire cut across the electrical wires, the lights flickered and went out. The very air seemed to be burning. Sparks popped and snapped in blues, reds and yellows, making a July Fourth show of fireworks the likes of which few people had ever seen.

During all of this, Bobby Grant hadn't moved. He stood frozen in the center of the stage. A piece of the flaming curtain split and dropped only a few feet from him, but he remained immobile. Some of the stage crew yelled for him to come back and retreat through the rear exit, but he didn't seem to hear. All of his attention was focused on the mass of people backing away from him on the most important night of his life; literally attacking one another to get away from him.

Someone finally took hold of his arm and pulled him toward the wings. His last view of the audience was a man over six feet tall punching a woman in the face because she was clinging to the back of his jacket.

Halloran and Moe Sandman did the best they could to explain to people they had a better chance of getting out alive if they lined up in some orderly fashion—all the pushing and shoving was getting nobody anywhere—but it was to no avail. In return, they were pushed, shoved and cursed. Moe lost his footing and collapsed on the floor. For a few moments, he was dazed and tried to catch his breath. Halloran was driven further and further back by the charging audience. He tried to indicate that Moe should get up and follow, but Moe didn't have the strength to move.

Suddenly the walls in the rear of the club, where everyone was headed, gave way to the fire raging from behind. As the space became more and more engulfed in flames even those who had initially fought panic became totally uncontrollable and staff members and guests who had been contributing in a heroic way, suddenly thought only of themselves. The stage was on fire, the entire ceiling was burning down, the left, right and rear walls had caved in, and most of the floor furnishings and bar area were ignited. The nightclub had turned into an inferno.

Moe Sandman tried to stand up but a pain had developed down his left arm. His shoulder ached. It seemed impossible to breathe. He gasped and pulled himself forward, reaching out for tables along the way, but the pain in his arm shot up and across his chest. He reached straight up in the air. People shoved him aside as they tried to make their way toward the single exit that was not yet in flames. He offered no resistance. In vain, he mouthed the word "help" and then fell to the side, disappearing below chairs, taking a table over with him. No one paid the slightest attention. He was dead before he hit the floor.

The first indication Bruce and Sid had that anything was wrong came in the form of muffled shouting. They listened for a moment and then stood up.

"What the hell is that?" Sid walked through the kitchen and peeked into the dining room. The smoke has just succeeded in reaching the vents there and was beginning to pour into the area.

"That's smoke," he shouted. Bruce rushed to join him.

"Jesus Christ!"

They ran quickly through the dining room. The entrance to it that opened on the lobby was locked from the inside. Sid turned the latch and pulled the door toward him. To their shock and amazement they found themselves face to face with a mob fleeing the nightclub, hundreds of people who, because the front lobby was also on fire, didn't know where to turn. Suddenly they realized there might be a way out through the dining room and as if by command, turned in a wave and rushed inside. Bruce and Sid were shoved out of the way.

"WHAT THE HELL'S GOING ON?"

"FIRE, EVERYWHERE," one of the nightclub waiters shouted. They followed the crowd through the kitchen out the back exit. Bruce grabbed one of the bellhops. "What about the people upstairs?"

"Who knows?" He ripped himself out of Bruce's grip and ran on down the lawn away from the hotel. Sid was helping a limping woman. Bruce thought a moment and then rushed around the building toward the front entrance.

People were streaming out, many crying hysterically. Once out in the fresh air they walked about in small circles, confused, almost in a stupor. Clothing had been ripped and many were bleeding. Two men were carrying a woman who had fainted. They struggled with her weight, pounding her body on the lawn as they tried to move quickly.

. . . 260

Everywhere people were crying out names, moaning, babbling.
"MY HUSBAND. WHERE'S BEN?"
"DOROTHY!"
"GET ME OUT OF HERE! GET ME OUT OF HERE!"
"MY BABIES!" Toby Feigen cried, "MY BABIES ARE ON THE SIXTH FLOOR WITH A BABYSITTER!"

Bruce pushed his way through the crowd. Flames had already destroyed the lobby curtains. One of the chandeliers dropped to the floor, miraculously missing everyone. Another one dangled by a wire. A man's sport coat caught fire and he struggled to get it off his back while his wife screamed louder and louder. Bruce helped him remove it and then stamped madly on the burning garment. The man collapsed in his wife's arms. She struggled desperately to hold him up until Bruce helped carry him away. He set him down on the lawn, sufficiently far from the burning building. When he looked up, he saw the flames on the lower floors licking the ceilings, reaching out the windows, defiantly announcing their presence.

"Keep him quiet," Bruce said, "I've got to help others." He rushed to the residential side of the building and began guiding the people descending from the fire escape. Guests were jumping and hanging out from second and third story windows. When he looked up, he saw some screaming from bedroom windows many floors above.

For a few fleeting moments he thought about the people he knew: Ellen Golden, Charlotte, even Jonathan Lawrence. He had yet to see any one of them safe but he didn't have time now to think about it. A little boy, separated from his parents, was crying hysterically for his mommy. Bruce immediately lifted him in his arms and tried to calm him.

Those remaining in the building continued to break windows, push, jump, run, get out any way they could. The way the bodies tumbled out, it looked like a gigantic human domino chain that had just been knocked down.

When Sandi reached the front entrance after chasing the handyman she found herself driven back by the onslaught of people pouring out of the hotel. Frightened at first by the screaming and hysteria, she considered fleeing herself, but when she realized the gravity of the situation her first thoughts were for her mother's safety. It was impossible to get into the building through the lobby,

...261

so she ran to the side entrance that led in through the kitchen. A mob of people came tearing out of there, too. She didn't wait. Instead, she rushed around to the back where there was a little-used exit connecting with the Teen Room downstairs.

The fire hadn't yet reached this section of the hotel. The Goldens had added it on to the main building in the early fifties and it had a separate basement area and heating and cooling system. Nevertheless, the electricity had failed and Sandi entered into total darkness.

Fortunately, she knew her way and quickly wove in and out of corridors until she came up behind the front lobby. The scene that greeted her was like something out of a horror movie. There were large gaps over her head where the ceiling used to be, portions of the walls and supporting pillars had collapsed, and all the curtains and furniture had ignited and were in flames. When she saw the crowds massing at the exits, she tried to sight her mother but there were just too many bodies. Somehow she imagined her remaining in her office, directing the evacuation of the hotel, working like the captain of a sinking ship.

It was difficult, if not close to impossible, to push her way through the terrified people but she crawled, slipped and twisted her body until she got to the doorway of the office. When she looked in, she was shocked at how much of it was already destroyed. For a moment she considered the possibility of her mother being trapped. Then suddenly someone grabbed her hand from behind and pulled her roughly back.

"C'mon, you've gotta get out of here."

Bob Halloran, blackened with soot, his hair streaked with fallen plaster, his clothing torn, pulled her away from the office toward the crowd.

"My mother . . ."

"She's not in there," he said. "She's outside with Magda, and they're both safe." She stopped and looked around. The nightclub was now totally consumed. The exit through the Card Room that some enterprising people had found was blocked by the splintering walls and ceiling that had fallen in and now blazed away. The main entrance was still very congested with people trying to escape.

"Through the back," she motioned. "I came through the Game Room." He nodded and worked them that way, continuing to hold her hand as they made their way around the wreckage and away from the flames.

"I think Moe Sandman is dead," he said when they got to the

empty corridor, tears streaming down his face. He stopped for a second to cross himself. "Let's hurry. If anything happens to you . . ." He let go of her hand so they could move faster, but just before they went through the Game Room, a ceiling beam gave way, swung down, and caught him behind the head. The smack sent him reeling forward off his feet. He landed face down.

"Mr. Halloran! Mr. Halloran!"

She rushed to his side and shook him, but he didn't move. She turned his head to the side and his eyelids fluttered but then another chunk of ceiling flew down. The fire was starting to build a circle of flames around them. She tried pulling him by the arm, but it didn't work. He was too heavy for her to move.

"MR. HALLORAN!" she screamed. She stood up and shouted his name again and again, but there was no one close enough to hear. More of the Game Room collapsed. The glass tops on the pinball machines shattered, and all the buzzers went off at once. She looked down once again at the unconscious personnel director and then turned and fled, screaming all the way through the corridors to the back exit.

Outside, she fell to her knees on the nearby grass and cried. The flames pouring out from the sides of the second, third, fourth and fifth floors now lit the area, casting bright yellow and orange light deep into the shadows, driving the darkness back. She cried until there were no more tears. Then she shook herself and stood up. She looked back and thought about Halloran. The image of his fluttering eyelids repeated and repeated itself. She felt like throwing up. For a few moments, she was unable to get her legs to move. Then she stumbed hesitantly until she was finally able to break into a run. The first person she saw as she turned the bend that led to the lawn in front of the main house was her mother, directing people away from the building.

"MOMMY!" She threw out her arms, tripped, stood up again and continued to run. Ellen saw her come out of the shadows and ran toward her. They embraced instantly. Ellen held her as tightly as she possibly could. The glow of the fire washed over them, illuminating their tear-streaked faces.

"Oh, honey, where were you? I was so worried . . ." Her shoulders began to shake as she brought Sandi even closer.

"I thought . . ." She could only gasp her words. "I thought . . . you . . . were . . . you . . . were in there. Mr. Halloran . . . I think . . . I think he's dead."

Ellen ran her arms up and down her daughter's back. "Come

away," she said. "It's going to be all right." When Magda saw them, she ran over and the three of them embraced. "To the farmhouse," Ellen whispered. Sandi could only nod.

Dressed in loose, cotton pajamas, Sam Teitelbaum emerged from the bathroom. Blanche was already under the covers, the thin salmon-colored blanket drawn up to her chin. Sam turned off the bathroom light but then hesitated, keeping his finger on the switch. What was that funny odor? He turned the light back on and for another moment took a deep breath. A small but steady stream of smoke was pouring through openings between the pipes and the walls. At first he thought it might be some kind of steam coming from the pipes themselves, but that idea died very quickly. The odor was clearly recognizable.

"My God," he said to himself. He spun around. "Blanche, Blanche!"

"What is it?" She sat upright in the bed. He was in the bedroom doorway, his hands on his face, looking like a man who had just seen the Angel of Death.

"There's smoke," he said, trying to regain control. "Now don't get excited." He went to the closet and took her bathrobe off its hanger. She pulled the blanket away and stood up.

"What smoke? Where?"

"It's coming out of the plumbing in the bathroom. I don't know if it's serious or not." He helped her on with her robe as she searched for her slippers. "We'll just take precautions." He began leading her out the door.

"Sam, you know you can't go outside looking like that. You go back and get your robe and slippers too."

He rushed back. The smoke behind the walls and under the floor was now finding every possible route of escape. It flowed out from crevices in the walls, behind and through electrical outlets and around the framework of the air and heat vents. He thought about notifying the switchboard operator but quickly realized there was no time to waste. Whatever it was was growing every second. Suddenly they heard shouting in the corridor.

The hallway was already filling with black acrid smoke. A man struggled to get the fire extinguisher off the wall. He finally succeeded and turned the nozzle toward an air vent where smoke was pouring out. Nothing squirted out and he realized the extinguisher was empty. He cursed it and threw it on the floor. A woman dressed in a half slip and bra ran down the corridor, her hands on her ears as though she was trying to shut out a loud noise. She began pounding on the elevator doors but the heat emerging from under them quickly drove her back.

People came out of their rooms in various stages of undress and converged near the elevators despite the heat. It was the only familiar place they knew. The floor became total bedlam: children crying, men screaming orders, women waving their arms and pulling their kids back and forth. A young woman pounded her husband's back, demanding he do something. He stood stupidly for a moment and then tugged her toward the stairway. She was reluctant to move and for a moment it looked as though he might actually leave her there.

"NO," Sam shouted, pointing away from the exit to the stairs. "GO TO THE FIRE ESCAPE! THE FIRE ESCAPE. IT'S AT THE OTHER END OF THE HALL!"

Some people heard him and turned back. Others refused to listen. What did the old man know anyway? By now the smoke was thickening, blocking out any clear air. People were coughing and choking. Some were doubled up, leaning against the walls. They covered their eyes in an attempt to stop them from tearing. Blanche began to cough spasmodically. Sam followed his own suggestion and led her down the hall toward the fire escape, knocking on doors to wake people up along the way. The mesh and glass door to the outside landing was stuck and a small group had already gathered around.

"I can't get this damn screen opened," the man in the front said.

"Kick it out," yelled a voice from the rear.

"Hurry up. We ain't got all day!"

Two men began kicking the screen. It ripped and they pulled and tugged on the mesh until there was sufficient opening.

"Get the women out first," Sam suggested, but no one seemed to hear. "THE WOMEN," he shouted. "FIRST." This time the men in front reacted and pushed people aside so there was a path. A tall lean man with very bushy eyebrows and long forearms stood by the window and guided the women and children. His calm strength had a relaxing effect and the escape became somewhat orderly.

The people on the seven floors below had already started to go down their fire escapes but those on the flights above had yet to react. When Blanche got on to the landing, she wanted to wait for Sam, but the flow of people made it impossible. She started down the slim, iron steps, trying to move as carefully as possible. The hysterical guests behind her wouldn't tolerate her slowness, and there was some dangerous pushing. A little girl lost her footing entirely and almost fell over the railing. Her mother yelled and pulled her back by the wrist. The child smacked into the grating, scraped her legs, and began to cry. The tall man at the fire escape window continued to shout instructions.

"TAKE IT EASY. THERE'S PLENTY OF TIME. GO SLOWLY. GO SLOW!"

The frightened people who had remained on the floor, either in front of the elevator or in their rooms, now realized that the fire escape was their only chance. In a rush, they began to converge at the exit. Women and children were still given priority and Sam Teitelbaum found himself shoved further and further back. Everyone was jostling for a better position. The flow of smoke was now so intense that it was almost impossible to see beyond a foot or two.

Three flights down, Blanche Teitelbaum looked back and searched the line of descending people for signs of Sam but he wasn't to be found. Her heart sank. It was impossible to stop on the stairs. She could only go on and wait. Suddenly a closed window on one of the floors above exploded outward, raining pieces of glass on the fleeing line of people. Everyone covered his head. An elderly woman, not much older than Blanche, lost her footing and crashed forward into two people below. It started a chain reaction of slipping and falling, causing people to bang their bodies against the ironwork. The old woman was unable to get up and that stopped the descent of escaping guests. Dozens of people began shouting at her hysterically and that made it even more impossible for her to stand. Finally she was lifted to her feet and handed along so the line could continue.

Somewhere in the distance the fire sirens wailed but the sound was barely heard. Even if it had been, it would have brought little comfort.

twenty-two

As smoke seeped into the corridor and through the vents in Melinda's suite the party came to an immediate standstill. Someone shut off the music and others rolled off the mattresses. Suddenly there was a rumbling as if the building was falling apart. Because he was quite drunk at this point, Manny Goldberg had difficulty getting to his feet.

"What is it?" Melinda asked.

"FIRE!" some woman by the doorway screamed. "FIRE!"

One of the men beside Melinda threw open a window and leaned out. He could see the crowds streaming out of the building. There must have been over eight hundred people. Just then the hook and ladder trucks reached the hotel's main gate, their sirens blaring. Other people crowded about the window.

"Fire trucks," the man shouted. "This place is fucking burning!"

His announcement set off a mad rush. Almost everyone started out of the suite and rushed to the elevators, many of them stumbling over the furniture stacked in the hall. One man seized the fire extinguisher on the wall, realized there was nothing in it, and flung it down the corridor. People began pounding on the elevator doors and buttons. Someone shouted about the fire escape and the partygoers ran down toward it.

The moment the panic began, Melinda's admirers deserted her. For a brief moment she stood in the bedroom alone. A girl who had consumed too much wine huddled in a corner of the bathroom, babbling and crying like a baby. She clutched handfuls of her skirt and refused to move. Manny staggered to the doorway of the suite and watched. Idiotically, he began to imitate the movements of two hysterical women who ran up and down the corridor, arms flailing, not knowing where to turn. Finally he stumbled along and followed the crowd.

The entire group converged on the fire escape window which, like those above and below, had to be punched out and kicked away. The bedlam had a sobering effect on most but some, still suffering the effects of drinking, became belligerent. Men and women alike pulled and tugged against each other to get out.

Melinda stood back and watched with curious detachment. She still couldn't believe this was happening. Not the fire, specifically, but the fact that not one of the men who had previously vied for her favor now gave a damn about her. They had left her to fend for herself.

Manny struggled with a young man for a better position. Finally, the man punched him in the gut. He backed up and folded in pain. The crowd quickly filled in the gap.

Meanwhile, Flo and her lifeguard had awoken in a fit of coughing. Forgetting their nudity for the moment, they crawled out of the large laundry bin and peered into the hall. The sight was terrifying. Clouds of thick smoke were building in the little linen room as well. Without another thought, they joined the evacuation. The fire, the smoke, the screaming and the fear were so great that no one even noticed they were naked.

When Manny looked up from the floor, he saw his wife pressing and pushing to get to the fire escape landing. A man behind her put his arms around her waist and lifted her out of his way. Manny struggled to get to his feet. He was so dizzy he could barely stand, but he managed to take his jacket off and give it to her.

"Cover yourself, you bitch," he hissed under his breath. "I'll take care of you later." Everyone around them was choking now. It was becoming almost impossible to breathe. The group became even more violent. Women and children were flung back. The naked lifeguard had wormed his way to the side of the fire escape landing. He rapped the man in front of him in the neck and the man fell over on his side. The lifeguard quickly jumped over his body and pushed himself ahead and out of the window.

The floor around the elevator doors was the first part to collapse. The doors themselves became unhinged and shot downward into the black nothingness. Walls, rugs and the corridor ceiling began folding into the climbing flames. People were pounding each other to move faster. The stronger crawled over those in front. Most of the sixty people on the floor had by now crawled out of the window and onto the landing. Manny and Flo were among the last six.

Melinda got back on her feet and had to struggle with two women for position. They scratched and clawed at one another. She pushed them and shoved until she had the advantage and was able to get her hand on the fire escape window frame. One of the women took hold of her skirt. It ripped away from her body and she lashed out, catching the woman in the pelvis. The woman clutched her abdomen and staggered. Melinda crawled through the window on to the landing. She was right behind Manny and Flo.

The line of descending people was slowed by the hundreds of people escaping from the thirteen floors below. Everyone was shouting for the person in front to hurry. There was more pushing, even on the dangerously narrow iron stairs. Manny clutched the side railings tightly. The air, the noise and the excitement, combined with the booze, made him so dizzy he could barely see.

When the line came to a complete halt because someone on one of the floors below was injured, many people became undone. Melinda was struck in the back of the head. She fought with the woman behind her, struggling to keep from tripping. As a result, she fell back against Manny. The added weight came as a total surprise and he lost his grip on the railing. He fell against Flo and then slipped off the side of the stairway. For a few seconds he just dangled there, not quite sure of where he was. Flo screamed and pulled on his arm. It caused him to lose his grip entirely. She couldn't hold his weight and he fell. She watched his body crash into the ground below, and fainted. The man in front lifted her and the line continued its descent.

Charlotte awoke with a cough. The room was so filled with smoke that her eyes immediately began to tear. She sat up in the bed. She was barefoot and when she stood up, the heat from the floor was so intense she was forced to fall back on the bed. She picked up the phone to call the operator for help, but the line had long been disconnected. Frightened, she searched for her shoes, put them on, and then took the pillowcase off the pillow. Covering her face with it, she made her way to the door.

In the back of her mind was the vague hope that this was all a dream. In a moment she would awaken and the smoke would be gone. Where had it come from? What was going on? Why hadn't anyone told her? The moment her fingers touched the handle of the door, she screamed. Simply looking at it, there was no way she could have known, because it hadn't changed color. The knob was stovepipe hot, and it seared her hand. She ran to the bathroom to put it under cold water, but the smoke was so thick she had to turn back.

Trying to avoid panic, she wrapped her other hand in a pillowcase and tried the handle again. Even so, the heat radiated to her fingers, but this time she was able to hold on long enough to turn the knob. The moment the door opened, she knew she was in trouble. The corridor was completely in flames. The wall across from her room was half burned away, the ribs of the hotel structure visible and burning. She was a prisoner. There was no way to escape.

She slammed the door and backed into the bedroom, holding the pillowcase to her face. Then she knelt by the window to take deep gasps of air. That brought a measure of relief.

She worked the screen open and leaned out of the window. People were moving in a steady line down the fire escape far to her right. For a few moments she watched with quiet envy. They were on their way to safety. They would live. They would go on to fall in love and get married, to eat their favorite foods, watch their favorite movie stars and kiss, love and sit in the sun. They would have their hair done, buy a new dress, eat an ice cream cone in the shade, read a newspaper in the park. Nothing seemed too small or insignificant now.

She leaned further out of the window. Did no one down there even see her? Do no one even care? Where was Bruce? Strong, considerate, handsome Bruce. Did he wonder if she was still alive?

The smoke was getting black and thicker now. The realization of her impending death began to overwhelm her. She lost all control and screamed with all her might. Waving her hands frantically at the guests gathered on the ground below, she tried to get someone's attention, anyone, but from their vantage point, it was as if she didn't exist.

The flames were now starting to leap forward. The smoke was beginning to blind her. She crawled halfway out the window. It was a futile act. Her mind told her this, but she pushed the thought aside. She held on to the window frame and dangled for a moment.

"Mama," she cried. "Mama, mama."

She had the vision of her mother's face, smiling, gentle, the face that had comforted her whenever she was in need. The face she would never see again.

The smoke and fire began to surround her. It was as though they had predetermined their purpose, singled her out. She tried to inhale but couldn't. The pain throbbing in her burned hand forced her to loosen her grip. Her fingers ached and cramped.

Ironically, when she began to fall, she had a momentary sensation of being secure. It was as though God himself held her in his palm. Then she descended into the darkness, mercifully fainting before impact.

Fire departments in the Catskill resort area consisted of volunteer companies made up of ordinary citizens. Because of the magnitude of the blaze at the Congress and the hotel's central location in the county, practically every hamlet and village sent a truck. They were of little use once they arrived. The fire raged out of control, and about all they could do was extinguish the flames that spread with the falling chunks of the building and concentrate on getting the guests and staff as far away from the collapsing building as possible.

The lawns and surrounding grounds were strewn with debris and with people, over a thousand of them. Many had minor injuries—burns, cuts and smoke inhalation. Others were seriously hurt, half a dozen succumbing to heart attacks. Everywhere people were in shock. Children who had been separated from their parents on the fire escape were tearfully reunited on the ground. Husbands, wives, grandparents clung to each other with an enthusiasm borne of the need to confirm survival. As they looked back at the seventeen-story building, now totally lit up, the flames tearing at the very stars, they shook their heads in gratitude and wonder that they had escaped and were still alive. A good number of their friends hadn't been that lucky.

Ambulances began arriving on the scene. Police cars were all over the grounds. A mayday call had gone out to every doctor in the county. Interns, public health nurses, first aide squads, all circulated among the people, picking out the most seriously injured. The scene took on characteristics of a war zone after battle.

Bruce and Sid were everywhere, comforting and treating people, locating the ones who needed immediate transport to the hospital. The fire itself had reached such proportions that it drove back the night. A communal spirit, sad though it was, began to develop. People were helping one another, calming one another, becoming friends.

Magda and Ellen did whatever they could. They guided people away from the dangerous areas, brought what linen and toweling they could from the farmhouse, and assisted the doctors whenever they were asked. Sandi stood on the steps of the farmhouse and watched, trembling with the memory of what had happened inside the hotel.

Sam and Blanche Teitelbaum sat dejectedly on one of the lawn benches. Both had blankets wrapped around their shoulders. All who were safe now and quiet shared the same expression—stunned, shocked, anesthetized. They stared with empty eyes. Overwhelmed by all the misery, they retreated deeper into themselves.

Some people wandered around aimlessly, moving out of some reflexive need. It was as though they feared stopping would permit the fire to catch up with them. Those who had fled successfully out of the nightclub located themselves furthest away from the hotel. Dressed in their fine evening clothes, they looked like amateur actors staging a scene from the theatre of the absurd. They huddled together, bonded by the horrible experience. Now they were all telling one another what they had seen, when they had seen it and what they had done.

Not so the people who had been at Melinda's party. They fled from one another the first chance they got. Each had been totally concerned with his own welfare, and now it was difficult to face someone pushed aside in flight. Melinda stood alone. She held a blanket that had been handed to her since she lost half her clothing in the melee. As she watched the crowds moving around, the people being treated and stroked, she began to wonder about Grant. Her first vague thoughts were he must be safe; he was so damn independent, wiry and sly.

"Hey," she called and stepped forward to pull the arm of a first-aide squad member who was treating the burns on a man's leg. "Hey." He stopped what he was doing and looked up. "I can't find my son. Is there someplace special for kids?"

"I don't think so, ma'am. We're setting up a headquarters over by that trailer." He pointed to a small mobile trailer that had been sent over from the hospital. "Try that." She followed in the direction he pointed.

Flo Goldberg, now unconscious and covered by a blanket, lay on a stretcher awaiting an ambulance. Rescuers had been unable to retrieve Manny's body since it was so close to the burning building. Large portions of the structure had collapsed around it and by now it was no longer visible.

The Sheriff pulled Ellen away from the guests and led her to the command post. He had actually done her a great favor. She was very near total exhaustion—her hair falling dishevelled around her tear-stained face, her clothing smeared with blood, her body slumped with depression and fatigue. Chiefs of the various fire departments quickly joined them.

"We've got to get some kind of body count as soon as possible," he said. "Do you have any idea how many guests . . ."

"My reservations director, Netta . . ."

"I just saw her," the Sheriff said. He started away.

"She'll have an exact number."

"As soon as my sound trucks are set up, we'll begin announcing the names of those we've been told are missing. Maybe they're just lost in the crowd and will come forward. As for the others . . . Do you have someone who can run down the list of staff?"

She thought a moment. It seemed a gigantic task just to recollect names she had known for years.

"My department heads. They'll be able to help you. Call for them."

He nodded.

"You'd better get yourself a little rest, Mrs. Golden. No sense your collapsing on us now. We're going to need your help as soon as we get this under control."

"But the people who are injured . . . there are so many . . ."

"Volunteers are coming in from all over. They'll help."

"I can't leave," she said. "Got to get back . . ." She thought about walking away but couldn't. She looked back at the fire chief. He tilted his head slightly because she had such a strangely helpless expression on her face. Then she passed out.

Nick Martin hovered in the shadows some distance from the building. The immensity of the fire was awe-inspiring. To think he had done that in less than a minute and as a result, all his problems were solved. "So long, Jonathan Lawrence," he mumbled. "You creep." A fire truck screamed behind him as it turned into the Congress main gate. Police on the adjacent highway were forcing traffic to bypass the scene. Security was just about nonexistent. Every hand available was needed inside the grounds.

He lit a cigarette and watched a cop on the road directing the traffic in and out. No one seemed to be stopped from entering or leaving the hotel. His stomach churned in anticipation of his escape. Arrogantly confident, he had gone into the bar, ordered his drink,

. . . 273

and left before the pandemonium started. Now the taste of the alcohol was coming back to him. He attributed it to all the excitement. Then he felt himself flush. Was it from nerves, he wondered. Ridiculous. He was much too cool for that. But he might as well get started.

He flipped his cigarette into the grass and approached the main gate. The cop on the road below had his back to him, waving at approaching vehicles. Nick moved quickly off the hotel property, crossed the street, and began walking up the road. The first thing he saw was a traffic cop stationed at the far end, blocking the entrance of any unauthorized vehicles.

Nick wasn't sure what the status of the quarantine was now that the fire had broken out, but he didn't plan to stick around to find out. His plan was to get off the ancillary road to the main highway, hitch a ride to the nearest bus depot and go on to New York. Hell, if he had to, he'd hire a cab to get him back to the city. What did he care as long as he got there? Later on he'd send someone back for his car. There was no point in looking for it in that massive parking lot now. Besides, the keys had been left at the main desk, and they probably were burned into molten metal by now.

He tried to walk even faster but a sudden pain shot up from his abdomen. It was so sharp it took his breath away. He stopped, held his hands on his stomach and took some deep breaths. It made him feel better, but not much. He began walking again, but slower this time. The taste of the liquor took on an acid quality. He began to spit it up. Every once in a while, he turned back to be sure no one had noticed him. The traffic cop still had his back to him. The only problem now was going to be getting past the patrol car up ahead.

Why did it look so much further away than it had just a few moments before? He shook his head and wiped his eyes hard with the bottom of his palms. Damn, the booze was beginning to make him feel nauseous. Why the hell had he had to have that drink?

The pain started again, this time growing more intense. He had to stop and waited for the rush to pass. It didn't. In fact, it seemed worse. His stomach contracted. Even his kidneys ached. He had to bend over just to catch his breath. This was ridiculous. He would be spotted in a second carrying on like this. He looked to the side where there was a cluster of bushes and decided to rest there for a moment.

In the distance, the sound of sirens signaled the approach of still more fire equipment. Two ambulances zoomed by. A fire chief's patrol car, shrieking and blaring, flew past. Nick squatted by the bushes, leaning further into the darkness as the vehicles and their headlights went past him. He spit up again and again. The ugly, rancid taste remained in his mouth. His stomach felt as though it were coming apart. He pressed his fingers against it, finding slight relief with the pressure and then suddenly there was an uncontrollable evacuation of heavy warm stool water. It trickled down the side of his legs, soaking through his pants and leaking into his shoes. He couldn't believe what was happening and then began to scream as what felt like a corkscrew began to rip up the inside of his intestines. He fell over, semi-conscious.

A few minutes later his head started to clear and the realization came over him. Then the panic. CHOLERA! Fucking, fucking son of a bitch! He had the fucking cholera! How the hell could it be happening to him? Why weren't there any signals before? Why now? He recalled some of the things Dr. Bronstein had said at the meeting earlier in the afternoon. The fact that there was an incubation period. That was one of the reasons people were quarantined in the first place. So they could be helped if they got sick. Help. That's what he had to do. He had to get some help.

He waited for the flow of the bowel liquid to stop but it just seemed to go on endlessly. He might die, he realized, he could die right here and now. All those ambulances rushing by. They could save him. They'd have to! If only he could flag one down!

He struggled with great difficulty to get to his feet. The pain fought him all the way. His stomach was pushing everything up now and the spitting turned into foul smelling vomit.

There was the sound of another siren. Thank God, he thought. It was coming down the main highway, around the corner and toward the hotel. In a matter of seconds it would be close enough so he could get it to stop. He'd get them to turn around. Once they saw his condition they'd forget about all the people in the fire and concentrate on getting him to the hospital. They had to. His life was at stake.

He took a few steps forward, each one bringing on more and more agony, more and more nausea. It was all he could do to keep his head up. The headlights appeared a quarter of a mile away. The siren got louder. His plan was to get out in the middle of the road and wave his hands till they saw him and stopped, but the pain became so intense, that he doubled up again. The vehicle was getting closer and closer. If he was ever going to do it, he had to do it now. Now was the time to move.

Using the little strength he had left, he emerged slowly from the bushes. He forced his legs to carry him out into the center of the road but when he looked up, it wasn't an ambulance after all. It was another huge red fire truck, charging directly toward him. He tried to move back but he couldn't. Christ, he thought and raised his hands in a vain effort to push it away.

It came as a complete surprise to the excited driver. He and the two firemen beside him had devoted most of their attention to the great blaze in the distance. It hadn't occurred to them that someone might be staggering out on the road. The sight of Nick Martin falling into their path was unreal. There wasn't even time for a reflexive turn of the wheel.

The truck smacked his body with such force it splintered his skeleton; joints separated on impact. His spine and neck snapped and his arms waved and twisted as if they belonged to someone else. The crash sent him sprawling more than a hundred feet. His skull splattered and crunched as it bounced over the road. Blood poured out of every orifice, even from behind his bulging eyes. Contorted, his body finally settled in the bushes as the fire truck came to a halt more than a hundred feet beyond.

In the good book, it was called retribution.

epilogue

The nurse kept the door open behind her.

"You can go in now," she said, smiling more warmly than usual.

"Thank you," Bruce said. He walked past her and into Fern's room.

The bed had been tilted up, and although she still had an IV attached to her arm, she had regained some of her color. Because she knew Bruce was coming, she had even put on some makeup and fixed up her hair.

"Hi," he said.

"Hi."

He took her free hand and bent down to kiss her on the cheek. She squeezed his fingers tightly.

"On the road to recovery." He reached back and pulled the chair closer to the bed.

"That's what they tell me. But I still feel so weak."

"You'll bounce out of here before you know it."

They looked at each other for a long moment. Then Fern's lower lip began to quiver.

"Hey . . . c'mon."

"I can't stop thinking about Charlotte," she said. He nodded. "Her mother called me this morning and wanted me to tell her everything we had done every minute up to the point of my getting sick. It was eerie."

"It must be very difficult for her, losing a daughter in the prime of her life. It sort of makes you realize how tentative life really is . . . how you have to take advantage of all the good things it has to offer and live every minute to the fullest." He bent down and kissed her once again.

"What are you going to do now?"

"I'll probably hang around a few days more. There's a lot of paperwork to be done and I promised Ellen Golden and Sid I'd help out wherever I could. Besides, I thought I'd wait until you were ready to be discharged. We've got a lot of catching up to do."

"I'm going to have to feel a lot better than this."

"You will."

"I didn't even get the chance to show off my new hairdo."

"Sure you did. The people in the emergency room were talking about it all night!"

She laughed. The sound of it brought them both a sense of renewal. Her eyes regained their light. He took her hand again and they remained there like that for an hour, talking with increased energy, rushing to know each other. Words became increasingly inadequate. More could be said with a smile, with a movement of the eyes. They were impatient. Their need to be drawn together had grown not only from a shared tragic experience, but because they both believed that in their union there indeed existed a true beginning.

They believed in the words "Once upon a time. . . ."

They gathered in solemn union on the lawn in front of the old farmhouse. Most of them had been with the hotel for years, but even some of the more recent staff people were present. Behind them, the rubble still smoked. Two volunteer fire truck companies had stationed some men and equipment nearby to wet down the charred remains and keep the sparks from setting fire to the grass.

Some of the staff members sat on the lawn; some stood by talking quietly in small groups. When the screen door opened and Magda, Sandi and Ellen emerged, everyone stood up and turned in their direction. Ellen stood at the top of the wooden stairs. Magda put her arm around Sandi's shoulder and they moved to her right. The group was very quiet. In the distance car horns beeped. The Sunday morning sky was spotted here and there with cottonlike cumulus clouds. There was only a slight breeze, but some strands of Ellen's hair lifted and caressed her cheek.

"Thank you so much for coming here," she said. "I know most of you have had little sleep." She paused. Everyone's eyes were still on her. It seemed as though she was trying to smile. "I've been sitting inside for the past hour looking over papers, gazing at some albums. This place has a very rich history, as all of you know." She looked over at the old-timers. "Some of you even know more about that than I. At any rate, the Congress had always been something special, even when it consisted of only this farmhouse."

She took a deep breath. No one made a sound; not an expression was changed. All waited on her every syllable.

"I've been told so many stories about the way many of you

acted; your heroism, your unselfish efforts to reduce the loss of life and the amount of injury. Many people owe their lives to you.

"We have all lost some very dear and beloved friends," she went on. Some people looked down and others nodded slightly. Sandi thought about Grant Kaplan and the fact that he had never been found. And about Mr. Halloran. If he hadn't pulled her away from the office, if she hadn't led him down through the Teen Room . . . Tears started streaming down her cheeks. Magda sensed her thoughts and tightened her embrace.

"Nothing we do now can ever compensate for that loss and our thoughts and sympathies go out to the families.

"I know many of you are wondering what will happen now. We have given it great thought. It would be easy to walk away at this point and I'd be less than honest if I didn't tell you the temptation was great. But my daughter and I have come to a conclusion." She turned and reached out for Sandi. They clasped hands and Ellen pulled her to her side. "The Congress was my husband's life, and it was the dream of his parents." She straightened up. "It is our intention to rebuild this place from the bottom up, to use the insurance money to create what will become the New Congress, an innovative modern resort that we hope to make the showcase of the Catskills. It will combine all of the best of the past with the best the future has to offer."

She was interrupted by an outburst of applause.

"Most important, I want every one of you to know there will always be a place for you here if and when you want it. The New Congress may be ultra modern in facilities and design, but above all, it will still value the old-fashioned concepts of loyalty, personal attention and service and staff whom we look to as fulltime partners. You have been and will always continue to be a loved and valued part of our family." She steadied herself. "We will keep you posted as we progress, so until we meet again, God bless you all. Stay well."

She kissed Sandi and there was a great cheer. Then the group broke up, heading away from the farmhouse. Ellen, Magda and Sandi stood watching silently for a moment. Then Ellen and Magda turned to go inside.

"I'll be in in a minute," Sandi said.

They left her alone with her thoughts. She pressed the side of her face against the porch column. She remembered standing out here like this many times before, crying over one little thing or another. How long ago it all seemed!

Thank God the farmhouse didn't burn, she thought. Thank

God we can start over again. Suddenly, as if in a revelation, it all became clear to her.

The hotel was as important to her as it had been to her grandmother and grandfather, her father and her mother.

The resort and all that it represented was in her blood, too. In this union between her and all that her family had built rested what was truly essential and important. It was part of her heritage. She was part of its tradition. The insight made her feel like a different person. She suddenly understood what responsibility was all about.

It was as though her father had reached back across time and spoken to her.

She heard his words unmistakably.

She would cherish and carry them with her forever.